A Taste of Darkness and Life

Jason Bustard

Midnight Tide

Contents

Praise for The Seeker's Kitchen

"When I opened *A Taste of Darkness and Life* I fell right into Amandine's story, her life, and her adventures. With enough intrigue to keep me falling into each page until the last, Bustard's newest is a thrill from begin to end."

- AE Stueve, author of *First Born*

"An excellent expansion and maturation of the world and stakes...it's the rare sequel that recognizes the assignment and gets the job done. Highly recommended."

-A. Parise, author of *The Fork*

This book is dedicated to my mom, who encouraged my love of reading and endured my early attempts at writing with grace and kindness. She introduced me to fantasy with an illustrated edition of The Hobbit at an impressionable age, and I have never looked back. Through all the ups and downs of my personal and professional life, she has remained a constant source of encouragement and unconditional love. Thanks, mom!

Cat and Pig

"One of my favorite cheeses to cook with is mist cheese. It derives its name from the unusual and specific nature of its creation. Originating in Zulath lands, in the mountain ranges separating the plains and steppes from Western Olgothia, mist cheese starts with a combination of milk – Part highland cattle, part goat's milk. The cheese curds are cooked and pressed until almost completely free of whey, in the manner of hard, aged cheeses, but after being formed into wheels, it is left in a wood-slat shed for two nights so that the clouds and mists in the high elevations add moisture back. Then, the cheese is salted and wrapped (or waxed) and aged for a shorter amount of time. The end result is a semi-soft, mild sweet cheese, with only a hint of goat tang, that, when heated, melts into the most delicious topping for nearly any baked dish. Worth the silver, when you can find it, as only the finest cheese makers in the lowlands have discovered ways to replicate the conditions required to craft it."

- Seeker's Kitchen, Chapter 3, Essential Ingredients

"HIGH!"

"Low!"

"Sweep!"

Amandine turned at the final command and swung the end of the staff she was holding so that it slapped against the back of Dena's left leg. Dena frowned, holding her own staff in a neutral stance.

"What is that?" she asked.

"A sweep!" Amandine said, panting for breath.

"I'm still standing."

"You're heavy!"

Dena raised an eyebrow. "Well yes, but I don't think that's the problem."

Amandine frowned and planted her staff. She narrowed her bright green eyes and tried to not let her frustration show. Sweat dripped from every part of her tan skin. The tight chest wrap of rough, dark cloth she wore was nearly soaked through, and the short-legged pants she trained in with Dena were dusty and beginning to wear in places.

Dena was dressed similarly, but with additional wraps around her forearms and wrists. A sheen of perspiration covered her own brow. Her hair was tied back with a leather cord to keep it out of her face. She was at least four hands taller than Amandine, taller even than Chef, and he wasn't a small man. The muscles of her abdomen looked like someone had carved them from stone. Her pale, slightly freckled skin made her appear like a statue of Kayla with the body of Berindor. It was simply not fair that she could look so good while training this hard. Amandine felt like egg whites that had been whipped too fast, with edges and puffs sticking out all over the place.

With a sigh, she ran a hand through her short, dark brown hair. A local woman in the hamlet kept it trimmed for her, despite Dena and Sunflower's protests that she would look better with longer hair. She liked it short, and having someone with skill keeping it cut and styled meant that it actually looked nice for once in her life. That is, when it wasn't plastered to her scalp with sweat.

"Any road..." Dena said, as she noted Amandine's crestfallen expression. "If you have the right leverage, it doesn't matter the size of your opponent. The length of the staff works in your favor. Let's try it once more. Guard up!"

Amandine reluctantly raised her staff into the guard position as she'd been taught. Counting off the steps, Dena walked through the exercise again. Their staves clacked as they met, blocking and striking. At the end of the pattern, Amandine's staff struck Dena's leg again, and this time the larger woman stumbled a bit, lifting her foot and stepping back to avoid being tripped.

"Better!" Dena said with a broad grin. "You need to work on your arm and shoulder strength, but there is nothing wrong with your form, Amandine."

"I'm no good at this," Amandine said, dejected.

"Well, I don't think you'll ever be a soldier, but learning to defend yourself is not a waste. Your talents obviously lie elsewhere. But this is still good for you. And at least a little fun, right?"

Amandine smiled, mostly for Dena's benefit, and nodded.

"Come on then, let's clean up and have something to eat." Dena collected Amandine's staff and stacked it near others next to the rain barrel.

The barrel rested against the side of the cottage that Dena and Chef shared. They weren't married, but mostly behaved like they were. Amandine had grown, to her surprise, to like living here with them. It was a different feeling than anything she had ever experienced. It was warm, and not just because of the well maintained hearth.

Amandine took the lid off the barrel. It was only half full. The Shiv was approaching, and the weather was already becoming erratic. When First Winter arrived and passed, the seasons would swing so sharply that crops would be impossible to grow. Violent storms and blistering sun during the Scorch would bake the world dry and scrub it like a pot-brush, until finally the Second Winter, the Shiv Winter, would blanket the world once more before True Spring could return. The rains were late, a bad sign.

She used a long-handled dipper to pour water over her head. It was slightly briny. Chef had added a mixture of salt and wormwort to prevent moss and insects from taking over. They all used it to bathe. It wasn't as nice as the servant's bathhouse at Manor L'Eau, but it was close and clean and convenient, if a bit cold. Now that she was earning more money, Amandine would sometimes treat herself to the fancy bathhouse run by Madam Raven outside of Stoneman.

Dena took her turn at the barrel as Amandine shook herself off to start drying. "I hate this too," Amandine said, picking at her chest wrap.

With a shrug, Dena swished some of the water in her mouth and spit it out to the side. It wasn't very good to drink, with the salt and powdered herbs mixed in, but it was refreshing.

"You don't have to wear it at work, but if you'll take some advice from a woman with experience, you'd be wise to. For women who fight, like me, it keeps your breasts from dragging, bouncing or getting bruised. Could you imagine wearing chainmail without one? I sure can't. And nearly every woman I know who has a physical job wears one. Like Heather. She and I sometimes shop together for the fabric."

Heather Mince was the Matron of the stockyard and butchery in the nearby town of Stoneman, a small but important trade port along the Wolfshenta river. She was also half-tusker, with large upward pointing tusks, leathery skin and heavily muscled arms that made Dena's look like twigs. Amandine had trouble imagining the fearsome-looking woman doing anything so... mundane as shopping for chest-wraps.

"If you say so, sah." Amandine took another ladle to better rinse her hair.

"Don't you 'sah' me, you little duckling." Dena punched her lightly in the arm. "Save that nonsense for Serand."

Serand was Chef's actual name. Although she had permission to use it when not training in the culinary arts, Amandine had trouble thinking of him that way. She had been nearly a year in his employ before she had learned he went by anything other than his professional title.

And the truth was, she appreciated Dena. She and Serand had legally adopted her, but she didn't try to mother Amandine. Dena was more like a big sister. At least, she was how Amandine imagined a big sister would be. She had never known her actual family.

Amandine's life before coming to the Gold Hills had been spent in an orphanage run by the Night Sisters, a religious order dedicated to Ravenex in the city of Artemis. The Sisters had taught her about human biology. She understood her cycles and where babies came from and all of that. However, their primary purpose, and the focus of her education, had been to deal with people who had recently died. They had prepared the bodies' remains while the deceased's souls traveled on to the next life. Dena's lessons, by comparison, were practical and came from a different perspective than anything that had been taught to her by the Sisters.

Amandine smiled at Dena, genuinely this time, and handed the ladle back to her. She sniffed the air. "I think Chef is making twice-baked egg hash."

"How can you tell?"

"It's not just wood smoke. I can smell the onions. Their fragrance changes if you bake them until crispy."

Dena shook her head. "The two of you," she said fondly. "Your hearts are never far from the kitchen. If you're right, then I want some, so let's hurry it up."

They quickly finished washing and donned loose, buttonless vests over their wraps before going inside. Chef liked to act 'scandalized' if they came in 'half-dressed,' which always made Dena roll her eyes, but they did it to humor him nonetheless.

Chef leaned over an iron skillet, turning long strips of bacon as they fried. He was a tall man, but seemed shorter than he was because of his perpetually slouched shoulders. His skin was rough and darker than Amandine's, and his hair was nearly black, salted with bits of gray. His shockingly blue eyes darted like a spearbill's and missed very little going on around him. Chef was already dressed for work at Manor L'Eau, with his cuffs rolled up to keep them out of the breakfast he was cooking so that he would arrive at work clean. Dena quickly pecked him on the cheek and then retreated to the back bedroom to change. She wasn't on guard duty in Stoneman today, but would likely find something useful to do. There was always firewood to split or repairs to make to the cottage. Dena never stopped moving.

"Hand me the cracked glint pepper, Apprentice," Chef said as he turned the last piece of meat. Amandine was already halfway to the spice rack before he had spoken. He always used the pepper on bacon right as it finished.

She handed him the tin, and he opened it, sprinkled a liberal pinch across the meat and then took the pan off the fire and lidded the stove. Chef's kitchen belied the simple cottage it lived in. The hearth was dwarven-fitted granite, built by Stoneman's engineer Boomer McKragen, and had three hooks for kettles and pots. His stove was an expensive full iron standing type, with hinged ash box doors, handled fire-lids, and a flue that ran to the ceiling and out the roof. The work area next to it was raised to a perfect height so that Chef didn't have to slouch, any more than he did naturally, to cut, chop, clean and prepare his ingredients. The oven built into the bottom was also iron and heated by pyrestone, like the furnace at Manor L'Eau that provided heat to the giant house. The coldbox next to it acted like a miniature root cellar, kept cool by some sort of crystalline construct built into its top. The countertops were half sanded, beeswax sealed wood and half smooth stone—so finely ground that the surface shone like glass. To Amandine it was like staring at a masterwork of art crammed into a chipped and splintered frame. Chef's personal kitchen was probably worth half of the Gold Hills hamlet put together. The oven alone was worth more than his cottage.

Amandine sniffed. "I think you overcooked the root vegetables."

"Bah," Chef said, dismissively. "Ye undercook 'em! They have ta soften up and soak in the spices with the eggs. Don't be confusin' how you treat 'em in bakes like ye do with stews! Totally different, fingerling."

Chef's cat, Spice, emerged from under the table at the sound of his name. Upon realizing Chef hadn't actually called him, he trotted over and rubbed against Amandine's leg instead. The rangy, orange-furred creature seemed scrawny until you picked him up. Like his human, Spice was wiry and tough and an even better mouser than Grendel, Manor L'Eau's tubby kitchen cat.

Amandine scratched his ears and Spice sauntered to the door and pawed at it. Chef left a window cracked so that Spice could come and go as he pleased, but he seemed to like making humans do what he wanted. With a smile for the cat, Amandine obliged him and opened the door.

Chef eyed her sideways as she shut it again. "Ye spoil the little shite. I make him use the window while I'm cookin'."

"Yes, well, I'm not cooking at the moment, and I like him," Amandine admitted. "I make him use the window when I am practicing too, so I'm not spoiling him."

There had been a time, not too long ago, when Amandine would have quailed at contradicting anything Chef said, even something as silly as when to let the cat out. Working as his apprentice had altered their relationship somewhat. She did everything he asked, to the smallest detail, when they were cooking. Outside of her training, she no longer walked on eggshells around him.

Amandine watched as Chef checked the oven and cleaned up his station. She knew his routines almost by heart at this point, but she never knew when he would do something that she hadn't seen before, or reveal some technique or method for cooking which bolstered her growing knowledge of the art, and so she watched carefully.

Dena emerged from the bedroom, dressed in the clothes she wore for chores: sturdy pants, a dockworker's shirt that revealed her wrap, hair tied in a bright cloth, and her favorite fingerless gloves fashioned from grimalk-hide.

Chef put his hands on his hips and frowned at the gloves. "Not sitting for Breakfast, Dena?"

"It's Ironday," Dena said. "I was just going to have some of that on bread. It smells delightful, by the way. You two usually eat on the way to the manor anyway."

"Now, lover, I know ye don't keep track of these things as such, but today marks a year since Amandine became my Apprentice and joined this croft. Kivel will be running breakfast at the manor this morning, so don't be in a rush to go get all sweaty again!"

Amandine gasped. "It's really been a year?" She hadn't been keeping track either, but apparently Chef had. A warm feeling filled her chest.

Dena looked equally surprised and then laughed and broke into a huge smile. "Oh, gods! That's *right*. Is that why the fancy breakfast this morning, Serand?"

Chef nodded as he slid on a thick blacksmith's mitt to reach inside the oven and remove the stoneware dish that held the bake. The room instantly filled with the smell of spices, cheese, and baked eggs.

Amandine's mouth began to water. The bake was crusted in brown, baked cheese and crispy onions. The bits of egg she saw peeking through were light green, whipped frelkin eggs. Her favorite. The lizard-like, winged animals were often raised alongside chickens for their eggs, which had dark green yolks that were extremely thick and creamy. A familiar, savory scent rose from the dish.

"You added bogwort!" Amandine said. "I never thought to use it in a breakfast dish!"

"Aye, we have so much now, it'd be a shame to jus' let it wither." Chef set the baking dish on the stove to rest.

"Is that *mist cheese*?" Dena asked in awe as she took a seat at the small square table they shared. "I thought Jacinda stopped selling that in preparation for the shiv?"

"I had some tucked in the hold fer a special occasion," Chef explained. "Go get dressed before it cools too much, fingerling. We'll wait fer ya."

Amandine practically ran into the bedroom and closed the door to change. She took off her sweaty wrap, but put a fresh one on. Dena probably had a point, and Amandine had certainly endured things far worse than wearing something a little uncomfortable. She pulled her Apprentice clothing off a small rack of personal belongings and put it on as fast as she could. It was a tan set, pants and shirt, with long sleeves and pockets sewn into the arms and the sides. A flap at the collar could be unbuttoned and folded down when the heat of the kitchen became too much, and the cuffs were wide and could be rolled up to keep them clean. She took care to make sure it was adjusted properly, but did not waste any time preening. Special day or no, she and Chef would be wanted at the manor by teatime.

A small mirror stood on the table that held a bowl for washing, alongside Dena's comb and brush. Amandine had no use for them; her short hair mostly fixed itself if she simply ran her hands through it. The mirror had been one of Chef's first gifts to Dena. Amandine couldn't imagine how much it had cost him, but she did pause to use it to examine the scar behind her left eye. It had faded over the last year, thanks to Telvor's medicines, but the thin, puckered half-circle still marked where she had been struck by the skellix. She traced it with a finger and frowned. The smell of baked eggs and crisped onions wafted in through the crack in the door. Amandine pushed away those dark memories and turned from her reflection.

When she rentered the cottage's main room, she found Chef had transferred the bake dish to the table, set upon a slate so it wouldn't singe the wood. Plates and forks had been laid out for all of them, and mugs steamed with hot, spicy tea.

Amandine pulled up her chair as Chef cut squares out of the bake and served a portion to each of them. He gave Amandine a corner, which was always extra crispy. She sometimes had to fight Dena for them, but today, Dena said nothing as Chef served them. With a quick silent prayer to Delinkhal for the food, Amandine dug in.

It was divine. She was becoming better with eggs in general, especially with pan-fried eggs. They weren't quite as good as Sunflower's yet. But Chef's eggs, from bakes like this to his famous dessert egg puffs, were on another mountain, taller and broader than the small hill Amandine was just now reaching the summit of. The medley of cheese and aromatics combined with the egg and root vegetables. The spicy bacon on the side. The way the eggs *stood up* like a cake. It was very nearly magical and she *would* learn how to do it.

A contented silence descended as they ate. Even Dena, who loved to chatter endlessly, counterpoint to Chef's taciturn nature, remained completely absorbed in her meal. Spice jumped up into the open window and sniffed at the air. Chef laid down a small tea plate with a piece of un-spiced bacon and a lump of baked egg and cheese without the vegetables. The cat meowed hungrily and leapt down to join them.

Amandine cleared her plate, and then, without shame, cut herself a second helping. Dena followed suit shortly after.

"This is why I keep you around, Serand," Dena said with conviction as she closed her eyes and took a bite. "Aunt Mari doesn't understand, but then, she refuses to come to dinner."

"Her loss," Amandine said between bites. Dena came from an enormous family where she landed somewhere in the middle of eight siblings. Her mother's sister, who had no children of her own, had helped raise all of them and done much of the cooking.

After Dena's mother had passed, Aunt Mari took the reins as the family matriarch, and she roundly disapproved of Dena's and Chef's unconventional relationship.

"Yer Aunt Mari might lack fer inspiration, but yer grams is a fine cook. Especially her duck," Chef said.

Amandine would normally have been shocked to hear Chef praise any cook outside of his own kitchen, but she had tried the roasted duck once too. Dena's elderly grandmother could make common waterfowl taste like something destined for a lord's table, and nearly everyone knew it.

"It's not that Aunt Mari's food is *bad,*" Dena said, waving her fork. "It's just... I don't know. Boring? Utilitarian? She was mainly concerned with making sure there was enough to go around. Grams will tell her all the time to add salt and stop sparing the rindcuff. Aunt Mari just doesn't see cooking as anything but a chore. This," she speared a crispy chunk of egg and cheese, "this is art, Serand."

Chef grunted and didn't reply. He often received compliments on his food, but always seemed slightly annoyed by them.

Amandine knew more about Dena's family than Chef. Serand Brutshe was a legend in the culinary world of Serentia, and yet he resided near a small trading post in the Wolfshenta River valley. His manner of speaking and the country he claimed as home, Tren, spoke to a life spent on boats and amongst sailors. Indeed, he would sometimes share brief anecdotes about his time on both the rivers and oceans of Beregoth. But the rest? Amandine suspected from past conversations, and by the way that he interacted with members of the town, that he had once been a Seeker, or at least involved with the Seeker's Guild in some fashion. Seekers were like mercenaries, in that they often did work for coin, but really, deep down, they were explorers. Adventurers—those who sought out darkness in all its forms to bring light in its place. When she had tried to wheedle details of his time with the Guild, Serand had always found a way to change the subject.

There *was* one detail she wanted to know that he was not the sole keeper of. He seemed in a good mood, so Amandine picked up her courage, took a chance, and asked.

"So… how did you two meet? I mean…" Amandine asked, trailing off at the end. It had felt like a safe thing to ask, but the look Serand gave her made her wilt a little. Was it too personal?

"Jack's balls, Serand, stop glaring at her like that! It's not a huge secret!" Dena swatted him gently on the arm with the back of her hand. "We met during a shiv. Two shivs back, so almost ten years ago? I was still a recruit then and he had just arrived in Stoneman. I would stop and eat my lunch at his cart."

"Wait, a cart? Like the ones in the market that sell fried sausages and fish?"

"Yeah, only Serand was making pies. These cute little things about the width of your palm. Filled with meat, fish, sometimes sweet stuff too. He would stack up a makeshift charcoal oven made of river stones every morning and start baking before the sun rose. By the end of the High Bell, his stock would be sold out and he'd leave, so I made sure to be there early, every day that I could."

"Oh!" Amandine said as she recalled her first memory of Chef's food. "Like the meat savory you gave me when we first met! Are they the same?"

"Well, that one was baked in a proper oven—" Chef began.

"You be quiet! This is my story. Teach her how to make them later," Dena chided. "Anyway, yes, apparently he collects women by feeding them."

"Now see here," Chef began again.

"Uh uh!" Dena raised a finger. "Heather? Martinique? Yasmina? Hells, even Jacinda agreed that if she hadn't already been married to Bertrand she might have taken a shot at you. I practically had to beat them off with a club!"

"Yasmina is crazier than a bogling." Chef folded his arms defensively, his mouth twisting into a grimace. "She likes hurtin' people too much."

Amandine gaped slightly. She knew Yasmina. Miss Jacinda, the local cheese-maker and wife of the innkeeper of the Stomping Golem, Bertrand Kale, was one of the most important people in Stoneman. Her half-sisters, Yasmina and Gabriella, appeared to work for a somewhat seedy man named Mando Fame who ran the Dockman's Union. Many considered them to be little more than thugs. Had Chef really been *involved* with all of those women? Including Heather Mince? *Really?*

"Didn't stop her from trying to hook you," Dena said with a shrug. "In the end it just proves you have better taste than that."

Chef actually cracked a smile, a rarity for him.

"So," Dena said, returning to her thread. "I beat the lines every day that my duties would let me, just to get one of his pies. I thought he was just a talented street cook, but then someone passing through Stoneman recognized him. The youngest cook ever to earn the title of Chef and winner of the King's Bounty in Tren on account of his cuisine. Working a colorless lunch cart on the other side of the colorless world! The uproar it caused!"

"Dena," Chef said, trying to interrupt again.

"My sto-ry!" Dena said in a sing-song voice, cutting him off again. "I thought to myself, 'He must have done something wrong to be hiding out like this at the back-end of nowhere', and so I set about investigating where he had come from."

"She began stalkin' me."

"Investigating!"

Amandine wasn't sure whether to laugh or be appalled. She was certainly getting more than she bargained for from her silly question.

"I found out he had several former colleagues who lived in the town. Including Master Kale and Master Aran. That's also when the strumpets started diving at him like fisher birds."

"Honestly, Dena."

"Only one who was honest about it was Heather, and you couldn't get past the tusks."

"Not true."

"One of you is fibbing and I don't think it's her, Serand."

Chef sighed and looked up at the ceiling, seemingly resigned. Dena continued her story.

"It was a Shiv year, like I said, and supplies were running low, but Serand always had enough to make his pies. I started to dig and discovered him sneaking out of town to the old Kystrom 'stead. I thought he was stealing the flour, perhaps. So I followed him one night. I wanted to be promoted past guardsman trainee, and I figured if I caught a thief, especially one who was fleeing trouble in another country, Captain Stolm would see my value."

"What was he doing?" Amandine asked.

"Not stealing!" Chef said, eyes still on the ceiling.

"Obviously." Dena patted his arm. "No, he was actually trying to catch someone who *was* stealing food. His upfront payment from Master Kystrom was in flour. Enough product that he could continue his street business, with a promise of gold if he managed to catch the criminal. Turns out, it wasn't a human thief."

"Provac nest," Chef grunted.

"Which I fell into," Dena said with a nod.

Amandine winced. Provacs were mole-like fae rodents the size of badgers and had eerily human-like hands—one on each leg—that could manipulate things like latches and knobs. Their overly wide, toothy maws allowed them to eat nearly anything, including loose earth and stone, although they seemed to prefer plants. That said, she had seen at least two corpses during her time with the Sisters that were due to someone carelessly falling into one of their nests. Little more than gnawed bones had been left.

"They had all been sleeping and started to stir. There must have been thirty or forty of them. I thought I was dead for sure. The nest was easily twice the depth of this cottage and it was a cloudy night. My lantern lay broken on the ground and the oil was going to burn out at any moment. Then the creatures would eat me alive."

Transfixed, her food forgotten, Amandine gasped. "How did you get out?"

"A face appeared in the hole above. Serand. His cat, Spice, was there too, both of them looking down at me. I didn't dare yell and rouse the creatures more quickly, but he seemed to know I was asking for help."

Dena paused and sipped her tea.

"And then what happened?"

"You want to tell this part, Serand?" Dena asked with a smirk.

Chef continued to stare at the ceiling. "I dumped bread rolls on her head."

Dena winced. "Gods, you're bad at telling stories, but yes, that's the Serand-shortened version. He dumped bread rolls on my head. An entire sack full of them."

Amandine couldn't help it, she laughed. "Bread?"

"Bread."

"Bread."

Meow, Spice added.

"Why?" Amandine asked, still laughing.

"Well, I didn't know at the time either," Dena said. "I was confused, and furious, and scared, but then Serand, very calmly and precisely, started telling me to lay it all out in a circle around me, no spaces wider than a fist, in two rings, if I could manage it. So I did. I mean, what did I have to lose at that point? It was the first time I trusted Serand, hasn't been the last, and he's never let me down since."

"And the bread stopped the provacs?"

"The filling did. Serand had been hunting for the nest, and had a sack full of drug-filled bread rolls to eliminate the creatures. Provacs are clever, but when it comes to food, they will go for whatever is closest, even if it's a tiny morsel compared to the larger portion behind it. I had to dance about a bit to keep the rolls between me and critters as they awoke and went for the food. It wasn't perfect, a few found gaps and came for me, but I killed them. By the time my flame finally guttered out, the entire nest was dead or senseless from the herbs. Serand made his way down and we finished them off, then took proof that we had cleared the nest."

"Proof?"

"Like the head of the skellix we had to take to the Sheriff last year? I think you get the idea. It was grisly."

"So then you became friends?"

"We did, and it wasn't long after that we became more than friends, despite the other trollops' best efforts. Serand used his reward money to build this cottage, and the next year, Lord Estevan invited him to cook at Manor L'Eau. Two years after that, the Chef at the time there, Orren, passed away during the middle of an important dinner function and Serand took over. He's been their Chef ever since!"

Dena made a little flourish and a mock bow to Chef, who was still staring up at the ceiling.

"Gods, you had to take over a full dinner service midway?" Amandine asked. "That must have been dreadful."

"Worse for old Orren," Chef said, finally looking back down towards her. "I improved the menu ta boot. Orren's tastes were conventional and drab."

"All of that, and *that's* the part you take away?" Dena said with an amused smirk. "You two really were cast from the same colorless mold!"

Dena cleared their plates while Chef and Amandine finished their tea. She paused by Chef's chair to kiss him again before departing.

"We really make a pair like a cat and a pig don't we?" she said.

"Why is Chef a pig?" Amandine asked.

"No, kiddo, he's the cat. But pigs are really smart, you know. We'd probably ride them about like horses if they weren't so... delicious."

She drew out the last word while stroking Chef's cheek before she sauntered out the door. Chef cleared his throat and downed his tea.

Amandine wasn't an idiot. "Do you need me to go on ahead, Chef?" she asked. He and Dena got very little private time with her now living there, after all. Dena was never very coy about her affections, but Serand was more private by nature and she was sure that her presence interfered in their relationship, at least a little bit.

"Nah, she's just being a tease, Amandine," Chef replied. "I promised her some time alone the next time you go ta help Jacinda. Don't ye worry about us."

He stood and gathered his small satchel. Chef almost never took his tools from home to the manor's kitchen. Amandine gathered her satchel as well. Once, it had held all of her worldly belongings. Now it contained a couple of cloth bandanas for her hair, her notebook, and her own personal small knife set for doing fine work and trimming fish and meat. She looked up at the larger knife hanging on the peg next to where her satchel had rested. The *Olatharr* was a dagger made from a rare alloy of metals called water-steel. It had been designed for fighting, with a flowing, curved blade made for slicing an enemy and not vegetables. Once it had belonged to a Seeker, named Birch, who was now retired and worked for Heather at the stockyard. Amandine had ordered the handle replaced and re-wrapped so it could be held more like a butcher's knife or cleaver, but it wasn't great for everyday kitchen work. Still, it had saved her life once. She touched it for luck, but left it where it hung.

Chef eyed the knife with a thoughtful expression. "Ye had the handle changed, but ye never take it off its peg," he said as he checked his satchel's contents.

"Well, yes, but even with the cleaver's grip, it doesn't really belong in a kitchen."

"Then why keep it?"

Amandine shrugged. "I don't know. It feels wrong to get rid of it."

"I suppose you'll know when it be needed then, eh? Is yer cargo secure?"

"Yes, let's go cook!"

Trimming Fat

"It takes no actual magical ability to create wards that suppress and redirect anima. The most basic of wards are found throughout nature itself. Running water, especially in large quantities, is an effective barrier against many forms of earth or fire infused anima. Common shrubbery, grown into particular shapes and carefully cultivated, can act as an aegis against air and water infused anima. Simple substances such as salt, charcoal, crystal, smoke, and even basic geometric shapes made from clay can be employed to repel or dissipate specific forms and hybrids of anima."

– Thaumaturgical Primer, Volume 1, Chapter 5, Anima, Wards, and Elementals

DENA WAS CROUCHED up on the cottage's roof when they came outside. She waved at them and then went back to inspecting the curved tiles. A stack of fresh ones, delivered from the potter last tenday, were stacked on a palette near her ladder.

"If ye finish early, I wrapped a lunch in the coldbox," Chef called. "Master Lyle's been saying the late rains have kept the silverbelly runnin'. Might take yer lunch an' the rod an' have a swing at some if ye feel up to it!"

Dena replied by blowing him a kiss. She loved to hunt and fish, and Chef enjoyed cooking whatever she caught. Amandine was convinced they made a good match, despite Dena's joke at breakfast.

She helped gather Juniper, Chef's elderly dun-colored horse. He had his own rain shelter in a small enclosed pasture next to the cottage. The old horse nuzzled her as she opened the gate and led him over to his harness. Once Juniper was hooked up to the cart, Chef produced a raw root vegetable from his pocket, the semi-sweet blue kind that Stone Folk called "anklers". Amandine remembered seeing a jar of them in Chef's pantry at manor L'Eau. They weren't cheap to import from Anvilroot, but Chef spoiled him more and more these days. Juniper had nearly run himself out last year as Chef had galloped him around in a panic trying to rally help for the boglings of the Silver Fens.

The root quickly vanished and Juniper whickered softly at Chef, nuzzling his hand. His ears twitched and his front legs pranced a bit, still spry despite his age. The special treat always seemed to perk the old fellow up a bit.

"Aye, thanks fer yer help, as always, old friend," Chef murmured. He patted the horse's flank and climbed into the driver's position, taking the reins. Amandine climbed up next to him.

They sometimes discussed the day's menu as they rode to the manor, but today they rode in silence. As they passed through the hamlet, various residents waved or shouted a greeting. Chef waved back to some of them, but otherwise seemed distracted.

The hamlet called itself Gold Hills after the region it resided in, but it didn't exist on any map. There were many such small communities scattered about the plains and river valleys of Serentia, unnoticed except by the noble families that oversaw their produce. Even by the standards of such places, Gold Hills was small. Roughly two dozen cottages and half-houses surrounded a central market square and well. The only brick and mortar building was Master Hawthorne's bakery. The roads were packed dirt. Still, the hamlet's Hill Folk and human residents took pride in their tiny community. Flowerbeds adorned most homes, and ornate shingles with family names and professions hung above every door. The Hill Folk homes had smaller doors and lower windows but were the same size as the human abodes. The diminutive people often had large families, with twins and triplets being fairly common.

The sounds of morning activity filled the air. Neighbors greeted each other, goats bleated, chickens squawked, frelkin hissed. The odd dog sometimes added its voice and the ring of a hammer on metal echoed from somewhere out of sight.

When they passed Timald Gert, who everyone just called 'Old Gert', Chef pulled Juniper to a stop and waved for him to come over. Timald was an aging human man with pale, sun-reddened skin that was stained dark in patches from a childhood bout with swamp-scale. He was leathery and wrinkled and a huge white beard covered his face like an overgrown fern, tufts and spirals jutting out in every direction. A large, stiff hat with a wide brim sat perched atop his head and a pair of heavy leather gloves were tied to his belt alongside a can that would emit smoke. Amandine wasn't sure how it worked or what it was for, but she had watched Gert use it near his bee-boxes. Finally, there was a pair of goggles, incongruously shiny and new, around his neck. The success of his honey-farming scheme had allowed him to buy some new equipment.

"Timald," Chef said, by way of greeting.

"Serand," Old Gert replied.

Amandine could never tell if they were friends or hated each other. It might have been a little bit of both.

"Your bee farming has been goin' well, I hear," Chef said.

"Just hear? You've been orderin' my stock for them floppy hats fer cycles, Serand."

"Aye, aye, but I be speakin' 'bout the bees themselves. How do ye plan to keep 'em durin' the shiv? Wild bees often die off fer lack of flowers durin' the Scorch."

Old Gert narrowed his eyes, "I have a plan, but why do ye want to know?"

"I were talkin' to Telvor, and he might..."

"Ye can tell Telvor I'll have nothin' ta do with his strange plants and foreign cures!" Old Gert spat. "I ain't tellin' no one my plans, so give it up, ye old stump!"

"Ain't no one tryin' ta steal your business," Chef growled. "We're just tryin' ta help."

"Aye, like that Olgothian woman Kale married? Tried to bribe me into giving her part of my profits!"

"She tried to give you money to build more boxes and hire hands." Chef sighed. "Believe me when I say I have my moments with her too, but she was lookin' ta make ye money, ye fool, not steal it. It's called an investment."

"Bah! Olgothians never give, Serand, they take. You know that better than anyone! Or are ye going senile before me?"

"Miss Jacinda is not a thief!" Amandine said sharply. She sort of liked Old Gert, but she wasn't going to stand for anyone disparaging the woman running the soup kitchen.

"The grown folk are talkin', moppet!" Old Gert snapped back.

Amandine opened her mouth to speak again, but Chef gently put a hand on her arm, and she swallowed her retort.

"I'm sure you have a plan, sah," Chef said in a level voice. "But shivs are when we band together for the sake o' the entire crew. Ye should consider trustin' *somebody*. It would be a colorless shame if the bees died and yer amazin' discovery was tossed in the wake."

"I don't need yer concern, sah," Old Gert drawled. "Get along to feedin' yer floppy hats, now!"

"Luminous day to ya, Timald."

"Bah!"

Chef shook his head and got Juniper moving again. He muttered something under his breath that Amandine couldn't make out, but she was pretty sure it wasn't polite.

"Where does he get the nerve to say horrible things about Miss Jacinda like that!" Amandine groused.

The sideways look Chef gave her seemed to say he didn't entirely disagree with Old Gert, but also that he wasn't going to say so.

"Besides," Amandine continued. "She's only half Olgothian! Her mother was an elf from the Court of Breaking Dawn. Miss Jacinda is Serentian! And some Olgothians are lovely people! Like Madam Sheeria Stolm!"

"Aye, well, I don't know Sheriff Stolm's wife as well as I probably ought ta," Chef admitted. "But ye haven't known Jacinda as long as I have, Amandine. I wouldn't go so far as ta say she's a bad person, but she always has an angle."

"She's been absolutely wonderful to Gil and I."

"She likes you an' the baker boy," Chef said. "And ta be fair, yer both likable people. Still, use yer sense. Everyone knows her sisters work for that riff raff runnin' the Stoneman Docks, and if there is a green copper ta be made in a deal, Jacinda Kale will find it. Mark me."

Amandine folded her arms and stuck her lip out, but Chef was mostly immune to her pouting, and absolutely never stood for it during her training.

"Fish will nibble it if ye leave it stickin' out like that," he muttered.

With a sigh, Amandine ceased her frumping and sought out the pleasant mood Old Gert's behavior had stolen. "So what did you and Master Aran have that would help him?" she asked.

"A nectar rich, hot-weather flower from the Southern jungles. He says it's mainly a medicinal ingredient that relieves itchin', and also it needs ta live in his glass house until the roots take. But after that, the sprouts could be put in the soil outdoors fer a season an' keep their blooms. He thinks it might be somethin' the bees could feed from when the Low Summer and Fall wildflowers don't appear durin' the shiv."

"Oh! Huh," Amandine sat back and considered that. It was sometimes surprising how intelligent Chef was given his earthy ways and course language, but he spoke several languages, could read in at least three of them, and knew a fair bit about plants, animals, fae creatures, and elementals. There was a shelf in the cottage bedroom filled with books he had collected. Amandine was better at reading now, but she had been functionally illiterate when she had first arrived in Stoneman, and still took lessons to improve. "That's a really good idea," she said after a moment.

"Yup." Chef's voice held a sour note. "No use mournin' which way the wind is blowin'. We have shiv preparations ta make as well. The salts an' oils from Anvilroot should be arrivin' by delivery cart today."

"Hrm, pickles." Amandine tried not to sound too disappointed.

"I know they ain't yer favorite foods, fingerling, but knowin' how to make 'em is vital. We need ta have nearly a year's stock saved, plus some extra, an' still have meals ta serve, so you'll be busy."

Amandine nodded. Pickles were definitely *not* her favorite foods. The Sisters fed the orphans pickled vegetables and fish almost exclusively during shivs. The ghostly taste of vinegar and rock salt still haunted her tongue.

They continued to roll through the hamlet. Master Hawthorne, the baker, did a double take as they approached. He ran a hand through his flour-dusted red-brown hair and leapt off the stool he had been using to hang his shingle. His ruddy cheeks puffed as he jogged over to them, his gleaming white apron flapping about in the breeze. Gil Crouste, Hawthorne's human apprentice and her best friend, had told Amandine that he often changed it during the day so he could always meet customers looking fresh. The Hill Folk man was shorter than the wagon's wheel, but his voice was a rich baritone that seemed out of size for him.

"Serand? Amandine! Oh, good! I sent the boy ahead to tell you, but since you're still here…"

"Sent Gil to tell us what?" Amandine interjected.

"There won't be a delivery today," Hawthorne said, wringing his apron in his hands and looking up at Chef with a sorrowful face. "Do forgive me, and please help me smooth things over with Taster Nous. I don't want to lose our contract…"

"Easy, now," Chef said in a mollifying tone. "That old badger controls the coin, but I decide what enters my galley. Just explain to me why the bread won't be comin' an' I'll make sure he keeps his nose out of it."

"Thank you, sah!" Hawthorne said breathlessly. "Thank you!"

"Aye, aye." Chef waved him down. "Really, I'm sure it's nothin' worth abandoning the ship over. Spill it, man, what's got yer sails in a twist?"

Hawthorne took a deep breath. "Rot slimes. They found their way into the silos, Serand."

Chef hissed through his teeth and winced. Amandine gasped. Spearbills and other fae predators mostly kept the slimy pests in check, but even a few could ruin large amounts of food if left alone. What they didn't consume they left fouled in their wake, rendered completely inedible and poisonous.

"How many?" Chef asked.

"Three of five for sure," Hawthorne replied solemnly. "Butterfly and Greenroot are checking the fourth, but there are signs it may have also been entered. The fifth is secure."

"How did they get in?" Amandine asked. "The wards and wax seals should keep them away."

"We don't know yet, lass," Hawthorne said with a rumbling sigh. "But Lord Estevan is being notified. The hamlet council voted to stop all sales until we take stock, so I have no flour to spare today until we know if we'll have enough for the shiv."

"Ye all have a steady hand on the rudder," Chef said as he stared up at the towering silos on the other end of town. "Lord Estevan and Lady Gia are reasonable folk, for nobles. I don't think they will fault ya fer sparin' the supplies. As fer the bread, we still have a few loaves I can re-hull into somethin' edible fer our patrons. Ye might send to Stoneman for Master Iblid. He has them critters what can sniff out the rotters."

"Ah yes, Riverstone also recommended his services. A fine idea, we will send for him. Thank you, Serand!" Hawthorne reached up to clasp Chef's ankle on the runner. He didn't say anything more but Amandine thought she saw tears welling in his eyes before he released Serand and hurried away. She had *never* seen the baker in such a state. Except when scolding Gil, he always seemed to be on the cheerful side of sunrise.

"Gods," Amandine breathed as they trundled out of the hamlet onto the main road. "Four silos ruined? There won't be enough for the Shiv, will there?"

"Nope." Serand sucked at his teeth in a thoughtful manner. "Not nearly."

"What's to be done?" The silos represented a large portion of the stores that would not only feed the Gold Hills hamlet and Manor L'Eau, but many of the surrounding areas, including Stoneman.

"Lord Estevan will have to petition fer relief from a major hold. Anvilroot, Artemis, Greenest, maybe Theldin Town or Greyrock Fall. Emergency grain is kept in such places fer trouble like this, but the cost will be dear."

"How dear?"

"Well, whoever was supposed ta be watchin' those wards will be havin' a bad time of it, but at the end of that line the Magistrate is goin' ta hold Lord and Lady L'Eau to account fer the loss. They can probably afford it, but it's goin' ta be a deep cut, fingerling."

Amandine considered this silently as they rolled past barren fields filled with the dry, cut stumps of the wheat that had only recently been harvested and threshed. The magnitude of the loss settled on her like a large, heavy weight. People with money would find a way, by paying coin to those who had extra, as Chef had said, but what about all of the shanty-folk she saw every tenday at the soup kitchen? What about the hamlet workers who maintained the fields, coops and barns for those wealthy patrons? A lot of people stood to go hungry unless the grain was replaced. She couldn't imagine Lord Estevan and Lady Gia letting people starve; they were careful with their wealth, but didn't hoard it in the way some of their peers did. Lady Gia was a primary patron of the soup kitchen, in fact. Would the deep cuts Chef was talking about also affect her work there?

A horse approached them from the direction of the manor. Amandine squinted, but she was pretty sure she knew who it was. Sure enough, Gil Crouste, Master Hawthorne's apprentice, was riding their way on his chestnut horse, Crust. He was getting taller, like Amandine, but was still thick-limbed and rotund, with a cheerful round face and sandy blonde hair and freckles that crossed his nose like a paint splatter.

"Morn, Mister Crouste," Chef said as Gil passed them, then turned his horse to walk alongside them. Chef didn't slow the wagon; they had already had too many delays and would be late if they stopped again.

"Luminous day, Chef Brutsche," Gil said politely. He always seemed a bit nervous when talking to Chef, which Amandine understood completely. Still, Gil could be both the bravest person she knew and the biggest chicken at the same time.

"Master Hawthorne sent me..." Gil started.

"Aye, we know, boy," Chef drawled. "Yer Master told us as we were departin'. Who did ye talk ta at the manor?"

"Kivel."

"Not Nous?"

"Gods, no!"

"Good lad. As far as that old tusker knows, ye made yer delivery today and brought news of the silos and that's it."

Gil nodded. No one liked Henri Nous, the L'Eau Taster, but he held an important position at the manor, so everyone who wanted to be paid on time stepped lightly around him. Except Chef.

"If we bake anything today, I'll see if I can get you something," Gil said.

"Aye, but don't be sacrificin' yer own breakfast so the L'Eaus can have toast," Chef said. "I'll handle them."

"Right, ok. See you tomorrow at the soup kitchen, Amy!"

"See you then!" Amandine called to him as he turned his horse around and sped off back towards the hamlet.

They crossed over a low hill and Manor L'Eau came into sight. It was three stories tall, with expensive glass windows. The walls were wooden beam framed with plastered white bricks in between. A large walking garden with concentric hedge circles and full grown shade trees sat on the Sunrise side, while a gated area containing the wagon yard, coops, pig sty, and a large vegetable and herb garden covered the Sundown side. A small out building that the servants used as a latrine and bathhouse sat across from the windowless wall that abutted the wagon yard. The front walk was packed earth and gravel with huge carved wooden doors that bore the family crest, and today a banner flapped from the highest balcony with a blue and gold version of the same sigil, as well as the symbols for High Summer and the glyph that symbolized the coming shiv season. It was opulent compared to Chef and Dena's river-stone and mortar cottage, and a palace compared to the shanties and half-houses many people in Stoneman lived in. Even so, Amandine felt at home here. Especially in the kitchen and servants' areas.

Chef pulled the wagon into the yard and dropped the reins. Juniper stopped, content to nibble at some wheat grass near the verge. Chef would come back out and move him to a shaded picket with food troughs after they were sure they didn't need to go any other place for supplies.

Amandine skipped ahead of him and opened the back door to the kitchens. The familiar sights and smells of Manor L'Eau greeted her. Kivel, tall and round with a bulbous red nose, was at the fry slate making the cook's breakfast. The L'Eau family would have already been served. Sunflower, a diminutive Hill Folk woman with golden hair done up in braids, tended a pot of tea over the hearth while taking the rinds off of some soft-peel fruit. Jambors this morning, judging by the bright red, bumpy skins. The scullery, who had been hired to replace Amandine when she was promoted to Chef's Apprentice, was a Hill Folk youth with dark, curly hair named Bramble. He was one of Master Hawthorne's many nephews and even shorter than Sunflower, so he had to use a wooden box to reach the washtub. Still, Hill Folk were uncannily strong for their sizes and he dipped the large copper pan in the wash-water with only one hand as he scraped it with a brush.

The kitchen itself was not as fancy as Chef's, but was large and functional. Two long tables, one topped with a hardwood butcher block slab, made up the primary work areas. There were cupboards for dishes and pots, and hanging racks for pans, spoons and tongs. The cooking hearth and the red-brick high-oven sat on opposite sides of the kitchen from each other, while one wall was dedicated solely to the cooking stoves, fry slate and woodbox. The oddest thing was Chef's personal pantry. It was made of sanded cedar and had a door that was locked by an intricate mechanism that some called a "Dwarven Lock," even if the actual devices were made by Stone Folk. She and the cooks had taken a peek inside last year and Amandine knew it was filled with all manner of exotic meats, strange spices and rare herbs, all of which were kept fresh by a glowing fae crystal similar to the one that maintained the coldbox at the cottage. Chef had lifted the ban on her, and only her, entering his sanctum, but only when accompanied by him, and usually with some kind of lesson attached. It was otherwise kept locked tight at all times.

"Good morn, Chef!" the room chorused as Chef Brutsche entered behind Amandine. He grumbled something at them in his usual manner and scanned the room. Finding nothing to complain about, he strode to the door leading into the servant's hall and the house proper.

"I need ta' confer with the Taster an' our patrons," he said. "Amandine and I already ate. Ye all have a nosh then begin preparin' fer tea. I'll be returnin' shortly."

"Yes, Chef!" everyone replied, including Amandine.

Chef departed and Amandine hung her satchel and rolled up her sleeves. "Bramble, when you're done with that pan, please gather seven plates and cups for tea. When we arrange them, leave anything that might spoil or go cold off three. We'll reserve them because the L'Eau's may have visitors at teatime today. Kivel, I know I already ate, but that smells really good. I just want a small taste to see how you spiced it, not a full portion. Sunflower! You look lovely, I like the new braid style! Thank you for making tea already. Prepare the blend for another pot, but don't put it on yet. Same reason as for the plates."

Kivel smiled and slid a small plate with half a sausage and a fried egg to Amandine. He had already anticipated her request. She found a fork and ate while she considered what needed to be done. It sometimes felt a little strange to be giving orders in this kitchen. This time last year she had been doing Bramble's job and Sunflower and Kivel had been teaching her. Now she technically outranked everyone in the kitchen except Chef, even though Sunflower and Kivel had far more experience and were twice her age. So, when she led, she tried to be gracious, rather than stern and shouty like Chef, and the others seemed to appreciate that.

That experience also meant she didn't need to lead all that much. Kivel and Sunflower knew what to do and were good at their jobs. She instructed Bramble on his sometimes, since it had been hers not that long ago, but otherwise let the kitchen run as it needed to unless Chef had given her explicit orders for something.

"So what's the tizzy about, foal?" Sunflower asked as she packed a tea ball. "Who might be droppin' in for tea? Is it about the slimes that slipped into one of the silos?"

Amandine realized Gil's information might have been incomplete, so she explained to them what Master Hawthorne had said, and a collective gasp ran through the room.

"That's awful," Kivel said solemnly. "So much wasted grain."

"It's a disaster!" Sunflower moaned. "My brother and his family must be beside themselves. They worked hard to bring in that crop this summer!"

"Mine too!" Bramble chimed in a high pitched voice. "Da 'll prolly be a cryin' and ma 'll be flickin' 'is ears and tellin' 'im ta grow a spine even though she feels the same way! My brothers worked in three passes ev'ry day ta scythe the fields!"

"What'll they do, you think?" Kivel asked, looking at Sunflower.

"Well the hamlet folk 'll endure, nary a scrap of a thing to what they have seen before, but Stoneman? Manor L'Eau? The Fording Towns? Waterbeetle? Lots o' townies with no bread 'll be a snarl for certain."

"Chef said our patrons will have to petition for aid from places that store extra grain for emergency," Amandine said. "I don't know how much they will send, though."

"Too little most like, and at a price that would make an Olgothian Cartel Prime weep," Kivel grumbled.

"Which the Magistrate 'll make the L'Eaus pay for," Sunflower added. "Oh, this is bad."

"Surely there is enough other food stored to keep people fed?" Amandine asked. "Even townies save for shivs."

Kivel laughed and Sunflower shook her head.

"The smart ones do. You'd be shocked how many don't, especially those with means," Kivel said. "They just pay the markup during shivs and take the loss of coin. They'll still pay, but the prices will go so high that common townies will be unable to afford it. Not to mention those poor souls you help at the soup kitchen every tenday. There won't be a crust left for them, Amandine."

A loud meow made Amandine look down. Grendel, the fat, gray striped kitchen cat sat near her feet. He stared up at her with half-lidded eyes, his tail swishing in an annoyed fashion.

"Did I forget to greet you, Gren?" Amandine asked. She bent down and scratched his ears. He began to purr. As she touched him, her senses sharpened. The crackle and pop of the burning wood under the slate became more clear. The muffled noises of chickens and frelkin out in their yard seemed to penetrate through the walls. Small details filled her vision, like a new notch in Grendel's ear that had scabbed over.

"Oh, you've been fighting again haven't you!" Amandine gingerly touched the wound, causing Grendel to flick his ear in irritation. "You need to stay away from that feral tom! He'll just keep hurting you."

Grendel meowed again and Amandine sensed a sort of smug satisfaction from the cat. It was almost as if he were telling her that she should see what the other cat looked like.

Amandine sighed. "I'll clean that for you later. Maybe you finally ran him off this time."

The others turned back to their tasks while she talked to Grendel, although Sunflower eyed her sideways with a look of concern. Hill Folk in general didn't like cats. Feral ones sometimes attacked Hill Folk children, as tiny as they were, and many families kept a dog, snapjaw, or other protective animal to run the predators off if they lurked. Most of the Hill Folk who worked in the manor were fine with Grendel, if wary, but none of them really liked him, especially when he got into mischief.

As for her strange ability to see and hear better when touching Grendel, it was the remnants of a spell cast on her by Old Wizard Hemm last year before she and her friends had their adventure in the fens. It hadn't faded with time, and in some ways seemed stronger now. Even after she stood back up, the heightened senses she had gained from touching Grendel persisted, and wouldn't begin to fade until he exited the manor or she went home for the evening. She hadn't told anyone about the strange spell except her friend Fredderick, who had once been a student of Hemm's and was a novice magician himself.

Thinking of Fredderick soured her mood. Their friendship lately had been fraught. Amandine didn't want anything else to ruin her day further. She had enough to worry about, so she stopped thinking about Fredderick and instead dove into making up a tray of sundries for tea.

She sliced fruits and large stickle-berries, then arrayed them by color like a rainbow. Under that, she added a selection of trimmed greens and crisp vegetables to appear like trees, shrubs and grasses. Cut cured sausages and aromatic chewleaf made for the earth, and as a final flourish, she sliced and stretched a type of salted sea squid into a light blue river that flowed between it all.

"Oh! That's a pretty one!" Sunflower said as she stood on her toes to peek. "Better than the mountains ye did last time."

"I have never seen mountains, so I probably got them wrong," Amandine said as she adjusted her tray. "This is more familiar."

"Lady Gia will love that. Just don't forget the side plate with the derby for Lord Estevan."

Amandine nodded. Derby was a kind of nutty, chewy bread that the Lord enjoyed with tea. He was not fond of sweet things or salted meat, even though his children both clamored for them. With a side plate for him, everyone would be satisfied.

As teatime approached, Amandine began to worry. Not about the tea service—everything for that was set—but about Chef. He still hadn't returned, and an ominous feeling had begun to take hold of her. Nous finally arrived and stood stiffly in the doorway. Amandine rolled the tea cart to him.

"Four additional cups. Guests are arriving," he said.

Amandine noted his tone. The pale, lanky, mustached man *loved* to lord his position over the kitchen staff. He rarely missed an opportunity to speak down to them from his perch in the doorframe that separated their domain from his. His behavior was oddly subdued.

"Missed it by one, then," Amandine said. "Bramble, one more cup, quickly, please. Don't keep the Taster waiting!"

The small boy leapt up on a stool he had already positioned and lifted down another cup and saucer. Sunflower added the silver and arranged it on the cart.

"Thank you, Cook Amandine," Nous said as he departed with the service.

"Any o' ye think that were a bit wracked? What in Delinkhal's Green has gotten into the Taster?" Sunflower asked, incredulous.

"Yeah, weird," Amandine agreed. "He didn't say a single mean thing. And since when am I a cook?"

"Since now," Chef said as he entered the kitchen through the doorway Nous had vacated.

"Chef," Kivel said in a strained voice, "What in the hells is going on?"

Chef Brutsche silently untied his apron. He hung it on a peg by the door and then reached into a pocket and handed Amandine an ornate brass key.

The key to his special pantry.

"Kivel, I am sorry, lad. Ye have been released from service here."

Stunned silence. Grendel slunk away to hide under the washtub.

"And why are you giving me this?" Amandine asked in a voice barely above a whisper.

"Because I am leaving too. As of today, I no longer be the Chef of Manor L'Eau."

Complicated Things

- Ancient Elven Children's Hymn. Lyrics transliterated and rhymed by Lyra of Stolen Songs

"OH, GODS, AMY, that's wretched!" Gil exclaimed as he paused what he was doing with oats, flour and honey. He wiped his hands and shook his head. "Kivel and Chef Brutsche both released on the same day? I mean, if the L'Eau's needed to make cuts, I can sort of understand Kivel. He's really nice, but lazy as a snapjaw in the sun."

Amandine sighed and stirred a pot of rice soup. It was a soup kitchen day, and normally she loved helping Miss Jacinda feed the less fortunate in Stoneman, but after two full days of running the kitchen on her own, Amandine felt wrung out.

"I don't know how I made it through dinner, Gilly. Sunflower and I had to do everything and she had to go serve too. Taster Nous also released Hedgehog and Sundrop. Sunflower couldn't stop crying. Bramble tried to help, but that kitchen is not made for Hill Folk to use properly and he's still a child. Sunflower barely manages and she's had years of practice."

"And they did it because the Magistrate is going to make them pay for the lost grain? That doesn't seem fair," Gil said. "They didn't put the rot slimes in the silos."

"No, but after work, back at the croft, Serand explained that they were going to release half the staff, even Nanny. But Nanny is dedicated to Milintanth and had been donating almost all of her pay to the temple anyway, so she agreed to stay on as a devotion, for meals and board only, for the sake of the children.

"Nous managed to keep more than half his staff, but that put Serand in a position where he would have had to let everyone go but me. I didn't count. As his apprentice, I was paid from his salary, not by Nous. Serand offered to step down himself to keep Sunflower and Bramble on staff and make me a cook with my own salary. Even with my promotion, it saved the house more money that way, so Lord Estevan agreed. Kivel still got dropped though. Too many other staff had complained about him and Serand was the only thing keeping him there."

"You're using his name, Amy. Why?" Gil asked.

"It doesn't feel right to call him Chef if he's not..."

Amandine's fatigue combined with the retelling of the last evening and she felt tears in her eyes. With her free hand she tried to wipe them away, but they kept coming. She took a deep stuttering breath...

Arms enfolded her. Gil's chin came to rest on top of her head. She cried quietly into his shoulder and dropped the soup ladle.

After a moment, she managed to compose herself and pushed him away. "I'm a mess," she said, annoyed. "No one died, I'm still Serand's apprentice and have a home to go to and so many friends. It was just so *much*, all at once."

"I understand. I remember the first time I had to take over a daily bake when Master Hawthorne stayed home because his littlest had the green pox. I was a wreck all day. Kept dropping things, burned six loaves, I even shouted at a customer. I thought Master Hawthorne was going to kick me out after he heard, but he just patted me on the knee, sent me home early and told me: 'Only birds need to fly on the first try. Do better tomorrow.'"

Amandine smiled in spite of her melancholy. "And did you?"

"Yup. That was two years ago. I can run the bakery by myself any day he needs me to now."

"But you had been an apprentice. I only just started. And now I'm barely a Cook and I have to run a Lord's kitchen. It feels overwhelming."

"You aren't barely anything, Amy. You're the best cook I know, aside from Old Badger Brutsche, and if he trusts you can do it, then you just need to trust yourself!"

"Thanks, Gilly."

"No thanks required for the truth!"

Gil nodded emphatically and returned to his task.

"What are you making anyway?" Amandine asked.

"This thing a traveling merchant was selling last Low Summer, before all the excitement with the boglings. I have been trying to duplicate it for a while, but it needs honey and sugarsap and both are so expensive. But Old Gert has his boxes now, so I have been doing chores for him on Irondays in exchange for small pots of his extra."

"So it's a sweet?"

"No, that's the thing. You combine oats and crushed nuts and dried fruit with the honey and other binders then lightly bake it to make these, um, sticks of crunchy, chewy stuff that keep for a really long time. The merchant said he bought them from elves at the Court of Breaking Dawn. I think it might be a good thing to make for shivs."

"That sounds simple, so what are you stuck on?"

"You need a second binder besides honey. I haven't figured it out. They either come out rock hard, or fall apart."

Miss Jacinda entered the kitchen carrying an empty soup pot. "Is the next one ready, Cook Amandine?"

Amandine wilted a little bit at the title. "Yes, sah, it's ready."

She caught Amandine's mood and clucked her tongue. For all that she acted like a mother hen, Jacinda Kale was one of the most beautiful women Amandine had ever met. Flawless dark brown skin from her Olgothian father mixed with the soft brown eyes, silky black hair and slightly pointed ears of her elven mother. "Now, now," she scolded gently. "Get used to the title. You got quite the promotion and others are recognizing your skill. Chin up!"

"That's what I've been telling her!" Gil added.

Jacinda looked at his table. "Are you making *meela*?" she asked in surprise. "That's a very good idea. Portable, nutritious and lasts through shivs. But you are doing it wrong."

Gil's mouth hung open. "You know how to make this?"

"Of course I do! Any elven youngling old enough to understand simple instructions is taught how to make it. It's a staple. You need to add butter."

"But I've tried butter! It just falls apart!"

"Not by itself—add it to the sugarsap. Who taught you how to make this?"

"Uhh..."

"Oh, by dawn's light. Take some butter, melt it into the sap until they combine—not too hot! Then add the rest, mix it and press it firmly into a long flat loaf with squared sides. I think you can do the rest, yes?"

Gil nodded and Miss Jacinda grabbed the soup pot off the stove with a pair of mitts and hauled it out to the serving area.

Amandine smirked at Gil. "You've been trying for a year, and never thought to ask Miss Jacinda, the one non-scary elf we know, how to make an elven food?"

"Half-elf. And no I didn't," Gil mumbled.

"Oh, Gilly!" Amandine laughed. "Honestly!"

"Shut it, Cook Amandine, and fetch me a pot of butter!" Gil declared in the voice he used when imitating Chef Brutsche.

Amandine laughed harder, but helped him find the butter.

Towards the end of the service, as Amandine and Gil were cleaning the kitchen, Miss Jacinda pulled her aside.

"You're going to quit, yes? When?" she asked with her arms folded.

Amandine had been dreading this conversation. "Yes, sah, my new duties will take a lot more of my time, and the kitchen at the manor is not built for Hill Folk. Sunflower would struggle to work it alone. I can come for one more tenday—Lady Gia insists, as she's a patron—but after that... I'm sorry."

Jacinda smiled. "Don't be sorry, Amandine, I am happy for you. You'll be missed here, but Gil will keep coming to help and I may have someone willing to volunteer for your spot. That said, you are always welcome here, any tenday you have the time!"

She wrapped Amandine in a tight hug. Amandine returned it, fighting back tears again. She loved this place, almost as much as her new home and the kitchen at Manor L'Eau.

"I'll make time, I promise!" she said.

"I know you will. Do me one more favor, will you?"

"Anything!"

"Tell that old bat to dry up and die, will you? She was in here again, on your off day, criticizing every aspect of how I run the kitchen. She does it on purpose, in front of the folks I am trying to feed, but I can't be seen shouting at a godsworn in front of half the colorless town."

The 'old bat' was Sister Capucine Corbin, a godsworn of the Lady of Night—Ravenex—and one of Amandine's former caretakers and teachers at the orphanage.

Her adoption by Dena and Serand had not managed to rid her from Amandine's life. She had contested the loophole in the writ that had saved Amandine from being forced to return with her to Artemis. Not wanting to make enemies of her order, Magistrate Everdawn had offered a concession. Sister Corbin would be allowed to continue her education of Amandine until her majority, in exchange for her order's services to the town.

"I have lessons with her every other Starday," Amandine said. "I'll need to get her to move those to evenings, but I see her this tenday. If I can get her to stop harrowing you, I will, sah, but she doesn't listen to me more than anyone else."

"I don't think you'll stop her, I just want her to know, from me, how much I despise her."

Miss Jacinda said the words with a smile, and Amandine had to admit to herself that Serand had a point. There was a hard edge to Jacinda Kale. She hid it well, but it was wickedly sharp.

"I will do exactly that, then."

"Excellent. Will you two be back off to the hamlet soon?"

"I wanted to stop by the Golem for a bite and to say hello to Master Bertrand," Gil said.

"Just Berty?" Jacinda asked with a wry smirk.

Gil cleared his throat and blushed.

"I'll go with him and keep him out of trouble." Amandine grinned.

Jacinda nodded, and still smirking, patted Amandine on the shoulder and left the kitchen.

Amandine and Gil hurried to finish their tasks and made their way across town to the inn. Stoneman wasn't a very large place, it was barely a spot on a city like Artemis, but it held an important position along the Wolfshenta River, and it was built inside an old Mage War era fortification, so it was well defended. An ancient automaton still patrolled the outer wall, giving the town its name. It never harassed anyone unless they tried to impede its unending vigil, and so most folks left it alone. The inn Miss Jacinda and her husband owned was named after it: The Stomping Golem.

They crossed the square between Wizzlecog's emporium and Master Telvor Aran's glass-roofed apothecary. Amandine held out a hand to touch the spray from the clockwork fountain that sat between them. Brass monsters and animals danced, shooting water in arcs and mists in an ever changing pattern.

Wizzlecog would shut it off soon for the Shiv. Not because water was scarce—they were next to a major river. He used the slower business during the shiv seasons to clean the fountain, add new animals and make repairs. Amandine had only ever seen it open one other time and was hoping to catch the old Stone Folk man tinkering on it. She really wanted to know how it worked.

The Stomping Golem was a massive three story structure of sturdy material, but built in a way that made it seem somewhat haphazard, as floors and wings had been added here and there over the years. It was further expanded by the creamery that adjoined it, where Miss Jacinda plied her own trade. It catered to merchants and sailors, godsworn, nobles and sometimes even Seekers. Everyone found comfort and warm food there. It was the place that had taken Amandine off the streets, and she visited every chance she could.

The common room was quiet today. Only a quarter of the tables had guests. The ships wouldn't be back in for another tenday, and then this room would be full to bursting. Amandine liked the crowds, especially if they included musicians or storytellers.

Before they could take a seat at the end of the large bench table in the middle of the room, Tillandra, the inn's server and bartender, intercepted them.

"Gil! Amandine!" She said with almost a squeal in her voice. She gave Amandine a quick hug and then Gil. Amandine noted that she held him a bit longer, pressed herself against him a bit tighter. When they parted, Gil's face was flushed red, and he purposefully didn't look at Tilly while they sat down.

"Hi, Tilly, that's um, a nice scarf," he said.

"Thanks, Gil," she replied.

Tillandra was a pretty young woman, at her majority and maybe four years and a shiv older than Amandine. She was Master Aran's niece and shared his dark Zulathan hair, although hers was tight and curly. She also had the wan, beeswax colored skin those people were known for. Her eyes were bright gray, however, indicating someone non-Zulathan in her heritage.

She was obviously infatuated with Gil, a fact that had taken the big aurochs ages to figure out, and now that he had, he had no idea what to do with it. It amused Amandine to watch them.

"What would ye like?" Tilly asked.

"What's special today?" Gil asked.

Tilly began to recite the menu in her thick townie accent. It reminded Amandine of the way people spoke back in Artemis, with its jaunty cadence and clipped words, but she was barely listening. Instead she watched Gil. His eyes were firmly locked on Tilly's chest. It *was* rather large and pronounced, but his fascination bordered on the absurd.

Amandine glanced herself and noted that the top two buttons of Tilly's shirt had been removed. She wasn't wearing a wrap. It made her think about what Dena had said the other day.

"No wrap?" Amandine asked, interrupting the litany. "Seems a good way to get a burn."

Tillandra looked down at herself and then grinned at Amandine. "Yeh, I take a risk with a hot plate, but the sailors an' caravanners, some drop an extra coin for a wee peek, an' I don' mind that! Ceptin' the Dwarves o'course. They don' seem ta care a wit 'bout human bits and bobs. They just want their tankards full!"

"Then Gil should pay double with how hard he's staring. Tea, dried gojo, and cheese, please."

"Amandine!" Gil hissed, his blush deepening.

Tillandra laughed out loud. "Master Crouste can look all he likes... for free."

She gave Gil an absolutely saucy wink and sauntered off to get the food Amandine had ordered.

Gil folded his arms on the table and melted into them in embarrassment.

Amandine reached over and patted him in consolation. "Look at it this way, Gilly," she said. "Now you have explicit permission."

"Just stop, Amy," Gil moaned into his arms.

"Oh, come on. This time last year, she was being as weird and awkward about it as you. She really likes you. Just be... *you* and everything will be fine, I'm sure."

"Really?" Gil looked up at her with a frown. "What about you and Fredderick, then? Are you still avoiding him? He's been asking about you, you know."

Amandine's smile slipped. "Don't," she said flatly.

"He's sort of an idiot, but he really likes you, Amy. You should talk to him."

"If he likes me so much, then he wouldn't be courting Marlette L'Eau, would he?"

She expected Gil to take another stab, but he just wilted back into his arms, the wimp. "Romance is complicated," he muttered.

That, she totally agreed with. Amandine reached out and clasped his hand in hers. She could almost tangibly feel his frustration and confusion. He was longing for something and she didn't know how to help. He looked up at her and smiled and it felt warm. Gil was family. As close as any she was likely to have, all things considered.

"I was hopin' you two would make an appearance!" a deep voice boomed.

Amandine turned. Bertrand Kale stumped up to their table, a slight limp to his gait. He was a massive tower of a man, well into his years but still built like the walls of Stoneman. He grinned and ruffled Amandine's hair. She sighed and endured it. Bertrand would never stop treating her like a child, but she really didn't mind.

"Luminous day!" Gil said, brightening. "I'm sorry about the deliveries being short."

"Don' fret over that," Bertrand rumbled. "Shiv will be hard this year, but we'll endure." He smiled fondly at Amandine. "Cook Amandine! Yer just racing along, ain't yeh?"

"I hate that it was at Serand's expense." She ran her fingers through the hair Bertrand had ruffled to fix it. "He is keeping busy. Mended Juniper's saddle for proper riding, helped Dena with the new roof tiles, and reorganized his pantry. I think Dena likes having him around more, but he seems bored."

"Oh, don't you worry about that old goat. He'll find something soon. I actually offered him a job here when I found out. He turned me down, o'course. Last time I gave him a job, he nearly lost an arm."

He chortled at that, but when he saw Gil and Amandine's shocked expressions, he seemed to realize he might have said too much.

"Never mind that now, have the fruit and cheese on me today. And when yeh all get back to the hamlet, tell 'em the basement stores are clean and I'll not be troubled if they need to cancel orders."

Amandine nodded but did not press him for details. She was certain Bertrand had once been a Seeker, like Serand and others in town, but like both Serand and Master Aran, he was also very reserved about it. If she could figure it out, she was certain other people knew, so why did they all hide their pasts with the Guild?

They chatted a bit longer and then Bertrand excused himself to see to other customers as Tillandra arrived with their food. The grin Bertrand shot them made Amandine think he'd actually backed off to allow Tilly to continue flirting with Gil, so she sat back to watch. It was every bit as amusing as she hoped it would be.

"Breathe," Amandine said after Tilly left. Gil was deep red again and looked stricken. She took a slice of cheese and a slightly sticky wedge of dried gojo, pressed them together, and handed it to him.

He scowled at her but took the food and mumbled his thanks.

"She only lays it on so thick because of your reaction, you know," Amandine said as she took her own slices.

"Not fair," Gil muttered as he chewed, heedless of manners. "Colorless woman has my brain in knots."

"So not much different than usual."

"Hey now!" But before he could say a word more, the door opened and Wizard Hemm entered.

The few customers, mostly locals, quickly went silent. Barnabilius Hemm, Wizard of the High Robes, was a fixture in Stoneman, but made everyone wary, like an especially fearsome gargoyle. He lived in one of the town's defensive towers, which Amandine knew from first hand experience was heavily enchanted. The old mage was also known for walking about talking to himself like a madman, through the streets or atop the defensive walls near his tower, which no doubt fueled the townies' wariness.

Most were convinced that he really was quite mad, but Amandine knew better. Everything Wizard Hemm did had a purpose. He hadn't been seen in public for two seasons, though. His robes, bright green and thickly embroidered, looked dusty and a bit frayed. His wispy white hair was windblown and there was a stubble of beard on his normally clean-shaven face. Had he been traveling?

"Luminous day, Wizard Hemm!" Tilly called from the bar. "Can I get–"

"Bertrand!" Hemm said, speaking over her. "A word in private, please?"

Bertrand nodded solemnly and motioned for Hemm to join him in the kitchen. Bertrand did most of the cooking, so it was the one place they could hold a private conversation. Tilly came to stand by their end of the table.

"Where has that old crust been?" Gil whispered.

"He really frightens me," Tilly admitted. "Remember when he turned Lord Miller's son into a duck?"

Amandine remembered. The fool had deserved it, but people generally distrusted and feared mages. Many evils had been wrought by magic. Amandine had feared them once too, but she had begun to understand the whys of it and so she was not as terrified as she had once been. Hemm's sudden appearance and behavior worried her, though.

"What!?" Bertrand's voice bellowed from the kitchens. A moment later he strode out through the shutter-flap doors and limped directly to them.

"Tillandra, go fetch your uncle, lass. Then go and find Boomer, Heather, and my wife. Tell them we need to meet upstairs here. Be quick!"

Tilly hurried out the door to do as he'd asked. Gil stood up. "Anything we can do, Master Kale? What happened? Where did Wizard Hemm go?"

"Hemm departed out the back. Has other places to be, no doubt. As to what happened, I don't want to make a panic with so many ears about. We got early word on account of Hemm and his magic."

He learned over the table and lowered his voice to a bare whisper. "Gold Hills wasn't the only store to suffer a massive loss. Slimes have destroyed grain and root vegetables as far out as Tailknot and there was another skellix sighting. Further East in the Narrows."

Gil looked confused, but Amandine understood immediately. "We won't be getting aid from any of the nearby holds, even if the L'Eaus pay, will we?"

Bertrand nodded. "It would seem that way, but never judge a battlefield by the terrain alone. Something is happening, but if we start a panic, it will help no one. Just Hemm showing up like this will cause enough speculation, so only tell Dena, Serand, and Mister Green, although that bastard probably already knew. The rest will find out when word comes by normal means."

"Not even Master Hawthorne?" Gil asked.

"No one but those I listed, swear it!" Bertrand said. His voice was unusually sharp.

Gil nodded. Amandine did as well.

"Off with ya both then. Take the food. What a colorless mess this is."

Solutions

"Majority age in most human lands is sixteen years, accounting for an average of four shivs during the child's lifetime. Some regions will declare the adolescent an adult early, at fifteen, if they were born during a shiv, or the shiv would directly interfere with their sixteenth nameday (meaning five or even six shivs rather than four). In some less civilized areas, young men and women are considered adults only after they have achieved a certain task or labor. In the Southern Jungles of Serentia, for example, this is often the child's first successful kill during a hunt, or first dream-walk with the primitive gods of that verdant forest."

- Lecture Notes, First Starday, High Summer 1202

AMANDINE SHIFTED IN her seat. The "Lord's Suite" was a large room on the second level of the Golem, reserved for important dignitaries, traveling nobles of high rank, or others that might need a place to stay if Everdawn's enclave could not host them. She had never been inside. Everything was upholstered and padded. Even the simple chair she sat on had a cushion built *into* the seat rather than set on top. It was as if a room from a palace had been plucked away and squeezed into a corner of the inn.

Gil was next to her, cross legged on the floor. Serand and Dena sat on the edge of the massive oak-framed canopy bed. Bertrand stood by the door, speaking quietly to Boomer McKragen, the town's Dwarven engineer. Jacinda and Heather sat in two of the remaining chairs, although Heather's large size made the seat look like something built for a child that she had sat upon by accident. Telvor Aran was seated in the last chair. His hands rested on his simple woven pants and his eyes were shut as if he were sleeping while sitting up. The intricate tattoos that covered nearly his entire body made Amandine dizzy.

"Making everyone wait on his time, like usual I see," Miss Jacinda commented dryly.

"He'll be here," Serand said as he put an arm around Dena. "He has his own reasons fer things, like any mage, but I don' think he'd shirk this."

As if summoned, the door opened and Mister Green entered. He was an elf from the Court of Starlight, with long hair so pale it almost seemed white, and narrow, sharp features. He dressed himself in finely tailored clothes of a human fashion, complete with the large floppy hat that nobles were often associated with.

His eyes were the thing that made Amandine squirm, though. Others saw them as bright, emerald green, but that was a glamour that hid their true nature. A glamour that, for whatever reason, Amandine could see through. They were orbs of solid black, like polished stone, but the centers seemed to swirl darkly, absorbing the light. Voids of colorless night that still saw everything, even things that were hidden.

"Forgive my late arrival," he said in a flowing cadence. "I attempted to contact Barnabilius, but he seems to be out of range... or he is ignoring me. Both are equally likely. Miss Amandine, it is good to see you. I understand your new title will mean forgoing lessons during the day, so I will come to you in the evenings, if that is amenable."

Amandine nodded. Mister Green had been tutoring her alongside Lord Estevan and Lady Gia's daughters, Marlette and Fiona. He had been teaching her to read—something the Sisters had refused to do for odd religious reasons—among other topics. She enjoyed the lessons, even if her tutor still made her uncomfortable.

"Must the children be here?" Bertrand asked, not for the first time.

"The *children*," Dena said, imparting the word with a touch of scorn, "are close to majority. They also fought a skellix last year and lived. Serand and I agree, they get to stay."

Serand nodded. "I would have invited that rascal Fred as well, if'n I knew where ta dig 'im up."

Mister Green looked to the empty air to his right. "See, I told you."

The air seemed to ripple and Fredderick Stolm appeared next to the elf. His small, squash-faced dog, Dumpling, wiggled in his arms. He was dressed in fine linen clothes with sigils that marked him as the Sheriff's page and his straight dark hair was tied back in a tail. With a wince he waved at everyone in the room.

Amandine felt her neck growing hot. He was *not* handsome. Liars and scoundrels weren't allowed to be. What in the hells did he even see in Marlette? Was it money? Was it because she was older than Amandine and closer to his age? Amandine had never expected to find romance. Apprentice Bone Guardians didn't have time for such nonsense. Full Sisters in the Ravenex order rarely married. She had been so focused on her goals that the thought had never crossed her mind... until last year. So what if he had shirked her for Marlette? Why couldn't she let it go?

Fredderick stared at her, a stricken expression on his face. Amandine realized she had been staring back. With a sniff, she purposefully looked away.

"Is this everyone, then?" Bertrand asked.

"Aye. Peak ain't comin'. Uriel is too far away, and Rally... she passed two years ago. Illness."

Silence settled across the room. Then Telvor spoke; his thick Zulathan accent held a note of sadness. "Old Jack finally caught her. A gambler's debt must be paid." His eyes remained closed as he spoke.

"Aye," Chef said softly.

Amandine didn't know any of the people named, but had the impression that they were old acquaintances, perhaps former Seekers like Serand, Telvor and Bertrand.

"Well then, let's get to it," Jacinda said. "Tell us what Hemm said and we'll all compare notes with what we have heard."

Bertrand cleared his throat and relayed Hemm's message in its entirety. It painted a picture even more bleak than the short version he had given Amandine and Gil. Slime infestations, which had seemingly popped up out of nowhere, had ruined large stores across Serentia. A leviathan had died, a rare occurrence in itself, but the massive floating beast had crushed a warehouse outside of Irongate and destroyed stores there as well. And the skellix...

"It ate three herds?" Dena asked. "How big was the colorless thing?"

"And killed half a dozen Seekers. Good ones from the Hall in Irongate," Bertrand said. "Reports say it was as long as a wagon train."

"I'll bet the Antecedent feels foolish for ignoring our report last year." Jacinda sniffed.

"Don't feel too smug, love," Bertrand said. "If that monster had arrived here, I doubt anything would be left of this place. Good men and women died to bring it down."

Amandine was horrified. She still occasionally had nightmares about the one she had faced and it had hunted full grown horses and cattle. This thing they were talking about would have been five times the size, maybe more. She shivered.

Gil patted her leg in solidarity and she smiled at him. He knew. He had been there too.

"As I have said before, skellix should not be roaming outside the Conflux. Something is very wrong." Telvor said as he finally opened his charcoal colored eyes.

"But unless another shows up here, that isn't our biggest problem," Heather said in her rough, gravelly voice. "How do we make sure this place isn't abandoned when the Shiv drains all of the remainin' stores?"

Another silence settled across the room. "She ain't wrong," Serand pointed out. "Most places 're only two missed meals from a mutiny."

"If no one has extra to spare, then how do we stretch what we do have?" Jacinda asked.

"What I want to know," Fredderick interjected, "Is what business of ours is it? Shouldn't Magistrate Everdawn and the noble families be solving this problem?"

For a third time the room became silent. Everyone turned to look at Fredderick, more than a few scowls directed his way. Amandine winced. She had been thinking something similar, but Fredderick also needed to learn some caution with his mouth. That especially.

Telvor wasn't scowling. Instead he smiled and shut his eyes again. "Ah, the idealism of youth. Too long a stranger."

Around the room, scowls softened. Heather shook her head and let out an enormous sigh.

Serand spoke. "The nobles will be doin' what is in *their* best interests, lad. They're content to toss each other overboard in a pinch, Estevan and Gia L'Eau as recent proof. When the storms are high, they ain't about ta turn the ship ta rescue the cabin-rat."

A murmur of assent circled the room.

"It's up to common folk to see to each other," Bertrand added. "This group is only one such, in and about. The merchants and trade caravans and others, they will be havin' similar meetin's soon. No one with half a wit is going to wait for the nobles to come and save them."

Fredderick hunched his shoulders, looking wounded. His cousin and her wife weren't exactly noble, but they were close. It must be hard for him, Amandine thought, for all these people he respected to say such harsh things about his folk. About *her*.

Amandine grinned smugly in spite of herself. The reasonable part of her knew that it was petty to be jealous of Marlette, but the rest of her didn't care. She noticed Gil watching her with a frown and so she tucked away the grin, but held onto that feeling of vindication.

"That brings us back to my question," Jacinda said. "What do we do to extend what's left to keep people fed, especially the less fortunate that do not have private stores for the Shiv?"

"Aye, that," Serand said. "and a larger question of what is causin' the flood o' slimes and skellix and a colorless levi fallin' from the sky. If we can get ta the root o' that, maybe there be a way ta halt the spread. Ain't no guarantee that the smaller private stores won't be next. The big ones is just fatter bait fer the vermin."

There was some muttering at that and concerned glances. Hemm's report proved the silos in the Gold Hills were not an isolated incident, and if private stores were also lost, it would be a catastrophe. Amandine frowned and thought.

"What kills or eats rot slimes besides spearbills?" she asked.

"Provacs and lurks," Serand said immediately. "But they would both be tradin' one leak fer another."

"There are magics that ward and deter them, but the most basic of those have proven to be unreliable," Mister Green said. "Anything more... rigorous would have impacts on the land we would not desire."

"That's all well," Jacinda said, sounding impatient, "You lot continue your investigation, but those of us that haven't professionally hunted monsters should solve the more practical problem. Thoughts, Heather? Dena?"

"Cull herds," Heather said. "Won't be enough feed for them now anyway. Save breeding stock and make sausage and jerky out of as much of the meat as possible."

"That will be a hard sell to some of the nobles who own those herds," Dena said. "The practical-minded ones will agree, but those that enjoy an upper hand in the Southern and Eastern markets will not want to give up so much stock. They'd starve their hamlets first."

"Not to mention such a wide-scale plan is outside our authority," Mister Green added. "Despite our talents, the amount of leverage we possess is limited."

"So we need something simple then. A solution that we can share with everyone without involving the nobles?" Amandine asked.

Heads nodded.

Boomer grunted. It was the first sound he had made the entire time and Amandine had nearly forgotten he was there. His green-tinted goggles were pushed up on his head, revealing odd, double irised eyes. When he spoke, twin rows of sharp teeth, like a shark's, were visible.

"Anvilroot," he said.

"Eh?" Heather asked, looking confused.

"Ah," Telvor said, opening his eyes again. "Yes. Hemm's report made no mention of the Kingdoms Beneath."

"Tha' one gets it," Boomer said with a nod. "Always fergetin' 'bout those Beneath. We can na' help ye if ye never ask. Against the Promise in Stone. But if ye were ta ask nice like..."

"Are you suggesting *we* petition the Seven Hammers clan directly for aid?" Jacinda asked.

"Nah, ye ain't got the stone fer treatin' with tha elders. Some floppy hat from Irongate is likely ta be doin' tha already. But we has our common folk too. Pebbles 'mongst boulders. We cou' go ask some o' them."

"And what sort of aid do you think the 'pebbles' of Anvilroot could provide?" Mister Green asked.

"A way ta deal with slimes fer a start. If'n ya won't learn ta eat 'em, then we has ways ta kill 'em."

"And how is that?" Serand asked.

"No idea!" Boomer yanked his massive, braided beard in a self-satisfied way. "But one o' my buds is a farmer. Good stone, tha' one. That *gyre* can sort ya if any can."

"You have a friend who's a farmer? Underground?" Amandine asked.

Boomer began to chortle in an odd guttural way. It almost sounded like he was choking.

"A 'bud' is a dwarven child," Serand said. "He be talkin' bout family."

"Aye, ye can always count on family in a cave-in," Boomer said. "If only ta eat 'em if yer starvin'."

He began to chortle again. Serand grinned, but Amandine noticed that Dena and Jacinda seemed a bit uncomfortable. Heather too, and very little bothered her. She had always thought of Dwarves as large Stone Folk with extra hair and strange eyes, but there was obviously something here she was missing.

"It's not a terrible idea," Bertrand said. "But it would have to be Serand. He's the only one who speaks their language and spent any time there."

"I speak it badly, sah," Serand said, waving a hand. "Human tongues are the wrong shape fer it."

"Sa true!" Boomer said between choking laughter. "Ye sound like a drunk leaf-lover, but ye get tallies fer effort!"

Mister Green frowned down at Boomer at the use of the dwarven epithet for an elf, an unusual display of emotion from him, but quickly recovered his composure.

"I agree with Master Kale," he said. "You are best qualified to treat with non-humans and are recently unemployed."

"Aye, but I have a 'pprentice ta train, shiv seasons ta prepare fer and..." He looked at Dena, who shook her head.

"I'm fine, Serand. This is important."

"Sunflower and I will manage, sah," Amandine added with more confidence in her voice than she actually felt.

Serand sucked at his teeth. "Right, fine. I'll leave in three tenday when the barges come back up river."

A wave of agreement and well wishes passed around the room.

"In the meantime," Jacinda said. "We'll try and sort things here as best we can and make a list of supplies you might request or negotiate for that would help us."

Mister Green cocked his head, then turned suddenly and yanked open the door. Tilly, who had apparently been leaning against it, nearly fell into the room.

"Hello, Tillandra," Telvor said placidly without turning to look. "Is your curiosity satisfied?"

"I was just... I didn'..." Tilly began, but she shrank under the withering stares. "I'm sorry, sahs, I didn' mean harm..."

"How much did yeh hear, lass?" Bertrand rumbled.

"No need," Telvor said as he turned to look at his niece.

She shrank back further. More from shame than fear, Amandine felt. Tilly was a brave person who was more than capable of holding her own in a fight, but her relationship with Telvor, who was both her mentor and her guardian, was sometimes strained.

"I was going to tell her everything later, Bertrand. She is merely impatient and impetuous. Sins we have all been guilty of," Telvor said.

"Aye, she was like to hear some version o' events when the boats come from Anvilroot next tenday," Serand added. "Least this way she gets it straight an' not some half-baked account from the gob of a drunken sailor."

Bertrand seemed somewhat mollified but still said: "And who is watching the commons while we confer?"

Tilly squeaked and hurried out of the room, her footsteps racing down the hall.

"Oh, Berty," Jacinda said in exasperation. "You are such a grumpus sometimes." She stood and hurried out the door to follow Tilly.

"No faultin' a man fer lookin' after his business!" Bertrand grumbled. But Amandine thought he looked somewhat abashed. Everyone liked Tilly, and she almost never shirked her duties.

"She will be circumspect," Telvor assured the room. "I believe there is little more to discuss yet? I will also return to my business."

Anvilroot. Amandine had wanted to see it her entire life, it felt like, and now Serand was going there. It wasn't likely to be a fun trip, she knew, but a pang of envy filled her, which triggered an equal amount of shame. Serand had lived there. He spoke their language. This was too important for her to be in the way, and besides, she had a real job now. She couldn't leave Sunflower and Bramble alone with Taster Nous. Still...

Everyone rose and passed out goodbyes. Heather released her after a bone-crushing hug, and Amandine spied Fredderick standing by the door. He opened his mouth as if to say something and then looked away. Dumpling whimpered and hid behind his legs.

Amandine grimaced and simply walked past them and into the hall. She had to return to the manor and relieve Sunflower for the dinner service. There just wasn't time for such things; boys, and romance, and... things! She had two tendays to learn how to at least fake what Serand did in the kitchen before he departed, and there were already enough distractions.

So why did she feel so guilty?

Local Sources

"The economy of Serentia is primarily founded on agriculture and timber. The regional Magistrates main purpose is to see that all of the landed nobles under their purview produce adequate amounts of food and material, not only for the feeding and stability of the nation itself, but for trade with the rest of the world. Olgothia, bereft of most of its arable land since the Great Mage War, is the primary consumer of this surplus, but Serentian beef, pork, and vegetable produce are traded the entire length of Beregoth. The second largest clients are the Dwarves. Their desire for meat grown in the sunlit world, as well as wheat and barley for beer, has provided Serentian merchants with a ready made source of trade for rare earths, metals and gemstones, which have become a booming secondary market in the last century."

- Lecture Notes, Third Fireday, Low Summer 1202

AMANDINE WOKE UP to a familiar ceiling.

The patched and cracked plaster of the warm cellar made her think for a moment that the past year of her life had just been a dream. Grendel lay on her chest, his head tucked between his paws. The air flowing from the massive pyrestone furnace suffused Amandine with warmth like an extra blanket.

The illusion didn't last. Her sleepy haze faded and she remembered setting up her old cot down here after finishing in the kitchen. It had been well after dark and she had told Sunflower to come in later today since she had worked so much without Amandine yesterday.

She rubbed her face and instantly regretted it. Her hands still stank like vinegar and made her eyes burn. Amandine sat up and Grendel tumbled into her lap. He continued to snooze for a moment and then opened one accusing eye as if to ask why she would do such a callous thing.

With one hand absently rubbing Grendel's belly, Amandine stretched the other above her head, and hoped Dena wasn't worrying about her too much. She had warned her and Serand that she might sleep here overnight after preparing the first batch of pickles. The task had kept her up past when most sane people had long since found their beds.

She turned and put her feet down. Grendel playfully attacked her hand and then rolled out of her lap and dashed up the stairs into the kitchen.

"I'm coming, I'm coming," Amandine muttered as she yawned. She pulled her apron off a wall peg next to the cot and put it on as she climbed the stairs.

The old iron cauldron still sat over the hearth. A row of large glass jars sealed with cloth and wax sat on the butcher block. An array of strainers, utensils, and knives still lay about. She took a moment to clean and replace the sharps and then moved some things for Bramble. He would be there before Sunflower and could help with the cleanup of the pickles.

She inspected her jars. It was a kind of red root vegetable called rikol—cut into quarters and brined. She hoped they came out right. Chef's written instructions had been easy enough to follow. She had even tasted the brine to try and judge if the ratio of salt to vinegar had been correct, but it was her first attempt at making these and only time would tell. Tonight she would do a large batch of shredded cabbages in a similar way.

A throat cleared behind her. Amandine turned to find Taster Nous, dressed and pressed, standing in his favorite doorway.

"Good morning, Taster," Amandine said while stifling another yawn.

"Gods, you look dreadful," Nous said with a sniff. "Did you sleep in your clothes?"

"Would you rather I slept naked, sah?" Amandine turned to scrub her hands in a bowl of cold water. She splashed some on her face for good measure.

"Of all the inappropriate, insolent..."

Amandine just shrugged. "Sorry, sah, that was crass. What do you need?"

Nous' mustache quivered but he ceased his grumbling. "I came to confirm breakfast."

"So early, sah? It's Godhome."

"The Lord and Lady are shortening their devotions this morning. Lord Miller is expected and we must show proper hospitality."

"Guests for breakfast? Why wasn't I told?"

"That's not your concern."

"It is if you wish me to have enough plates prepared."

Nous opened his mouth to retort, but Amandine interrupted what she was sure would be something stupid and hostile.

"That's not meant as disrespect, sah, that's just truth."

The Taster seemed to swallow what he was about to say and instead muttered: "I wasn't informed until late last night."

"I was here. Making pickles for the Shiv." Amandine gestured to the jars. "You could have mentioned it."

"Just do it!" he snarled. "It's not your place to question our patron's wishes!"

"I am not questioning Lord Estevan's or Lady Gia's wishes, sah," Amandine said with a polite bow. *Just your competence*, she thought to herself.

Nous blew out his moustaches, turned on his heel and left.

"Hateful man," Amandine whispered at the door frame. Still, her mind was in motion, planning an early Godhome breakfast for at least six people. There was still plenty of low summer fruit that hadn't been slated for preservation. Bacon would be fine for Lady Gia and the girls, but Lord Estevan would want oats and Lord Miller liked fresh meat. She didn't have time to pluck and prepare a chicken. Maybe there was a shank in the smokehouse? But that would take bells to cook...

Amandine pondered the problem while she put oats on to boil and collected eggs. As she came back into the kitchen from the cold cellar, she was shocked to see Serand standing next to the pickles on the block. For a bare moment she thought that perhaps he was there to help her, but then she saw that he was dressed in the plain, undyed shirt and pants he wore for chores. A straw hat rested on his back, tied to him by a leather cord around his neck.

"These look adequate," he said as he spied her entering the kitchen. "Cabbage next?"

"Yes, sah," she said as she put her flat of eggs on a table. "I am preparing an early breakfast for company. Lord Miller. Why are you here?"

"Am I not allowed ta check on my 'prentice?" Serand huffed. "An' Dena wanted me ta bring ye that."

He pointed to a cloth bundle on the block. A silvery tail fin poked out of one side.

"Dena caught some silverbelly. Had me haul part of the catch out ta ya in case ye had a nee–"

"This is perfect!" Amandine said as an idea rushed into her head. "Lord Miller wants fresh, so bacon is out, but I can poach that, maybe with greensprig and garlic. No! Rindcuff, less aromatic. Quick, I need that filleted and fetch some 'sprig from the herb garden! I'll whip the eggs and..."

Amandine suddenly grew cold as she realized who she had been ordering around the kitchen. She turned, expecting Chef to shout at her and call her a fool, but instead *Serand* broke into a rare smile and then threw back his head and laughed.

She stood there, stunned. Serand wiped one eye with a finger and then put his hands on his hips, still grinning.

"And here I was afeared ye was gonna drown, bein' thrown in the deep water. Instead ye just pop up with a shark in yer mouth and ask how ye should cook it."

"Sorry, sah."

"Sorry? Fer what? It's yer colorless kitchen now, not mine! Gods. Just over four days and yer already thinkin' like a Chef, even with no help."

"I'm not a Chef, sah."

"Not yet. But ye will be someday or I'll eat this colorless hat! You get what's needful together and I'll fetch herbs and cut a fish. But I need to be gone afore Nous finds me here and makes trouble fer ye."

Amandine nodded, and feeling better than she had in days, began putting together breakfast. Serand brought in the herbs and skillfully fileted and boned the silverbelly in less than half the time it would have taken her.

"Rindcuff is a good choice, but if'n ye really want to impress that fat provac, Miller, go into the locked pantry and get some *pomar*. It's the orange-brown powder in the blue painted tin on the fourth shelf, left side. Finish with a pinch on the fish and another pinch in the whipped eggs before ye cook 'em."

"What is it?"

"Olgothian spice. Only found in sandcrab burrows after spawnin' season. It adds a layer that compliments fish and poultry as it's not so fierce as blackspice or cinderbloom."

"That must be incredibly expensive—are you sure?"

"Hells, they paid fer it, fingerling, not me. Use it. And if he don't like it, then there's somethin' wrong with his tongue!"

Serand placed the fillets on a plate, and with another grin and a wave of his hand, slipped back out the door.

Amandine began cooking. Bramble arrived and she set him to cleaning and putting pickles into storage. By the time Sunflower walked in, the entire kitchen smelled like fish, herbs and bacon.

"Delinkhal as my witness, that is the best smelling... what is that?" she asked.

"Eggs!" Amandine said as she slipped small plates over for her and Bramble. "Try some, then help me garnish. Nous will be here for the tea any moment and I'll go serve this time."

Sunflower took a bite of the slightly orange-tinted whipped eggs and her eyes grew wide. "I...what did you put in this?"

She showed Sunflower the blue tin and told her what it was. The small woman wrinkled her nose.

"I'm glad I tasted it 'fore you tol' me!" she said. "It's one of them odd things from Chef's pantry then, yah?"

Amandine nodded. "I can't take credit, though. Serand told me to use it."

"Sweet green, if you make eggs like this now, what'll I do?" Sunflower said with a wink.

"Cut cabbage," Amandine replied with a wink of her own. "I do *not* want to sleep here again tonight."

Nous arrived and gathered the tea service and Amandine exchanged her apron for a clean one and pushed out a cart with food ready to serve. He raised an eyebrow at the plates of poached silverbelly, but made no comment.

Manor L'Eau's dining room was windowless, positioned off the parlors and between the kitchen and the entry hall. Every wall was painted a light blue color, and a hanging glowstone chandelier provided light. The table was long and set with chairs for twenty people, but only the six at the far end were occupied.

Lady Gia sat at the head of the table today. She was a slim woman with pale skin and hair the color of light tea with cream. Her usual welcoming smile was muted somewhat as she watched the two men to her flanks.

Lord Estevan, square-faced and dark haired with wings of gray on the sides, sat opposite Lord Gerant Miller. Miller was a broad man with heavy jowls that sometimes wobbled when he spoke. He wore simpler clothes than other nobles of his rank and station. It made him look more like a merchant than a noble, with his thinning blonde hair and beady eyes. Despite that, Amandine found him to be rather jolly and easy going, but today he had a dead serious look on his face, one arm rested on the table as he gestured with the other.

The pale-haired woman to his side, Miller's wife, Tammera, could not look more disinterested if she tried. She almost never accompanied her husband on social visits and was considered something of a mouse and a shut-in.

Marlette and Fiona, the L'Eau children, sat next to their father, prim and attentive. Fiona's blonde curls bobbed slightly as she fidgeted. Sitting still was difficult for the effervescent girl. Her older sister, by comparison, with her dark hair and sharp features, had perfectly adopted her father's stolid facial expression and seemed to be staring down Lord Miller as if he were addressing her.

"You know I don't like this arrangement, Estevan," he was saying. "Your hamlet and farms provide nearly all of my raw. I'll be starved for profit this Shiv, and this will pinch me as much as you!"

"Then provide more reasonable terms, Gerry," Lord Estevan replied. "A lease instead of a purchase. Rights to the grazing for your horses, and access to three more feeder streams to collect grindstone and shellfish. It's not a bad deal."

"For you!" Miller said, pointing a finger down at the table. "I stand to lose thousands in shiv contracts due to forfeiture penalties! Extra horse feed and some clams aren't going to match that. The land is valuable, though. Fertile. It could save my house."

Nous began refilling tea and signaled for Amandine to be ready to serve. Lady Gia made a hand gesture to thank Nous when he refilled her cup and he nodded to her. Gia L'Eau did not speak and couldn't hear. She conversed with her hands, using a modified form of the gesture-based language called *livette* that elves from the Court of Breaking Dawn had invented to speak silently when hunting.

She waved to get the attention of the two men and then made several flowing gestures. Amandine understood one or two of them, but not the rest. Marlette spoke, however, translating them for the sake of Lord Miller and his wife.

"Why not a compromise, sah? If we sell you all of the land, we would have nothing to replant on to recoup our losses. But there is a stretch between the streams with trees. The soil is too rocky to plant. You could harvest the lumber, and also use the waterways for shiv gathering and transportation of the wood."

Lord Estevan seemed to consider this for a moment and then nodded. "I could agree to that. It splits my land in a strange way, but after you have claimed what you want of it, and we have made our loss back, I would be willing to repurchase it at an additional profit to you."

"Hmm, yes. Most lumber of that type is imported from the North. It might be... gods, what smells so good?"

Nous made the signal to serve, and Amandine rolled the cart forward, lifted the lid and served plates, Lord Miller and his wife first, as was appropriate with intimate guests.

They both made appreciative noises over the fish. Lady Gia gestured her thanks for the colorful fruit arrangement, and Lord Estevan also nodded to her as she set out his simple bowl of oats and a fresh spoon.

Marlette refused to look at her, but Amandine resisted the urge to drop the plate on her fingers and moved on to Fiona, who she had given an extra strip of bacon.

"For Grendel?" Fiona whispered in her ear.

Amandine just smiled and winked. If she got caught feeding the cat, there would be trouble, but Fiona loved the tubby rascal as much as Amandine and so they both spoiled him.

After taking her place by the corner of the table near Lady Gia, Amandine cleared her throat. "Breakfast, lords and ladies, is poached silverbelly, ala Brutsche, whipped eggs with Olgath spices, cut fruit, oats and estate raised bacon. The fish was caught locally from the feeder streams into the Wolfshenta. If anything else is required, I stand ready."

At the mention of where the fish were caught, Lady Gia smiled at her and made the gestures for 'Clever' and 'Girl' beneath the table with one hand.

"Wait a moment, aren't you the orphan that Gia convinced Estevan to take on as a garbage scull? What's going on here? Where's that Trenash bastard?" Lord Miller asked, wrinkling his brow.

"There have been some staff changes due to the emergent problems we face," Estevan said.

"Oh gods!" Lady Miller exclaimed. "Stop grousing and taste it, Gerant!"

Everyone seemed surprised that she had spoken, especially Lord Miller. He blinked and picked up his fork. "Certainly, love, let's see..."

He took a bite and Amandine tried to control her face as Miller's eyes widened in disbelief. He took another bite, as if to confirm the first.

"This is incredibly delicious!" Tammera exclaimed. "I know you like that other fellow's food, Gerant, but this is just as good."

"It is, indeed, very well prepared. I apologize if my outburst seemed rude... and, uh, you say this was caught in Estevan's streams?" Lord Miller asked. He speared another bite on his fork and closed his eyes as he savored it.

Lord Estevan looked to Amandine, seeking an answer to the question.

"Yes, sah," she replied, barely keeping her nerves in check. "I know the one who caught it personally. I can present her if it pleases you."

"Oh, no need for that, Cook Amandine. Thank you, that will be all," Lord Estevan said, dismissing her.

Amandine quickly walked away. She saw Marlette glaring at her as she passed, but pretended not to notice. Sugar on top.

She finally allowed herself to breathe once she returned to the kitchen, and flapped her arms to release all of her nerves.

"Oh no," Sunflower said, misinterpreting the gesture. She stepped down off the boxes she had stacked to cut cabbage on the block. "Was something amiss with breakfast, foal?"

"No!" Amandine cried happily. "It was perfect. I felt..."

"Like a real cook?" Sunflower finished.

"Yes!"

"Foal, ye have been one practically since ya walked in that co'orless door. But congratulations for finally noticin'."

"Thank you, Sunflower!"

Amandine picked her up in a massive hug, which one normally didn't do with Hill Folk, but Amandine didn't care.

Sunflower made a surprised sound, but was laughing when Amandine set her back down.

"Now if'n ya let me help ya pick out a nice dress to match yer eyes..."

"Nope!" Amandine said, still smiling.

"I had to try!" Sunflower shrugged. She went back to the block and continued shredding cabbage.

Demon Eyes

"The Bolath people have suffered greatly since the Great Mage War. Their independence from Olgothia after the mass rebellion of the subject nations was marked by a series of weak leaders who made poor alliances and squandered what little wealth remained to the country. Then the Mage War occurred and Bolathvia sided with a faction of The High Robes against the Circle of Magi and the Conclave. It was a strike by this faction that created the Sea of Glass and scorched the earth of Olgothia over three hundred years ago. The retaliatory strike by the Circle and Conclave led to the event called the Tearing, or the Calamity. The entirety of Bolath lands were rendered unlivable, its people scattered, and the only reason the blight on that territory did not spread to the rest of the world was the creation of the Conflux, which holds the wild energies swirling at the heart of that fallen nation in check."

- Lecture Notes, Third Starday, Low Summer 1202

STONEMAN WAS BUSY on Starday. Merchants packed the market circle in anticipation of the barges down from Anvilroot, laden with the produce from the Dwarven nations and looking to return with things grown and harvested in the sunlit world.

Amandine walked among the stalls and carts, examining which fruits and vegetables were still in season. She was worried to see so little being offered. Word of the grain shortage was beginning to spread and people who normally wouldn't were buying extra and storing it in their homes. Unless it was properly pickled, dried, or candied, the produce would not keep for the entire Shiv. Much of it would probably end up thrown out, and Amandine lamented the waste of it.

She had been forced to leave Sunflower by herself again. Sister Corbin was expecting her at the mandated lessons today, and she had not yet spoken to her about moving them into the evenings.

There were many other things Amandine would rather be doing, but the order of the Magistrate had been clear: Amandine must attend these sessions every other tenday, or the writ she had circumvented would be enforced.

A hawker of knives called out as she passed and Amandine allowed herself to be distracted. She pulled several large cook's knives from their sheathes and checked the grain of the steel. The number of pins in the handle. The weight and balance.

"Adequate," she muttered as she inspected the edge of one blade. She tested its sharpness with a thumb.

"A popular choice!" the merchant said with a wide grin. He was a Bolath man with skin nearly the same shade as Amandine's and dark brown hair and eyes. He seemed enthusiastic at her custom, despite her age. Amandine had found many merchants tried to cheat her or ignore her or treat her like she was going to steal something. "Although I think you will find it more than 'adequate.' That is good Anvilroot steel, *doja.*"

The word meant 'daughter' in the old Bolath language. The rest was Olgothian, of course, the same as everyone spoke. That empire had once ruled the entire land, but every nation had words that held over from their former tongues. In this case it wasn't meant to be condescending. All adult Bolath people referred to those under a certain age by *doja* or *keja.*

Amandine shrugged. "Mayhaps it is," she said. "But if so, it's cheap stock. Good Anvilroot steel has a blue tint and rings when you strike it."

She tapped the wide blade against a metal bar that hung nearby for sharpening. It gave a short metallic clink, but did not resonate. "Still," she said, "It has a fine ground edge and sturdy pins. How much do you want for it?"

The merchant eyed her shrewdly. "You are well informed for one so young."

"I am Chef Serand Brutsche's apprentice and a cook at Manor L'Eau."

"Oh yes, apprentice of a world famous Chef *and* a cook in a lord's kitchen. Quite the list! Oh my!"

He *was* condescending her now. Amandine tried not to roll her eyes. Of course he didn't believe her. Some days she could barely believe it herself.

"I will pay you five silver for this perfectly *adequate* knife," she said firmly, looking into his smirking face with a level expression of her own.

"That blade costs a gold mark."

"It would if it were actually 'good' Anvilroot stock. Five."

"Eight."

"Six and five."

"Seven and six."

Amandine continued to stare and slowly shook her head. She began to resheathe the blade.

"Fine! Yes! Six and five," the merchant blurted.

"Knock on wood to make it good," Amandine said.

"Oh, so now we are an Olgothian merchant as well? Just pay for the knife, you are blocking other customers."

She wasn't, but Amandine only shrugged and pulled out a gold mark and placed it on the table. She had the price in smaller coins, but she was making a point.

The merchant stared at the coin a moment, actually weighed it, as if *she* were trying to cheat *him*, and then made her change for the knife.

Amandine nodded, tucked away her money, put the knife in her satchel, and turned to leave.

"Colorless demon eyes," he hissed, probably to himself, but Amandine still heard him clearly.

"What did you say? What did you call me?"

The man jumped and, for a wonder, actually looked frightened. "Go! You cannot curse me, I abided our bargain. Go! Shoo!"

Curse him? She wanted a better explanation, but the merchant was making some sort of strange cross-fingered gesture with one hand while actively trying to shoo her away with the other.

Perplexed, Amandine shrugged again and walked away, eliciting a sigh of relief from the merchant. What did he mean by 'demon eyes?' Serand would know. Or Mister Green. She would try and remember to ask one of them.

It was time to stop procrastinating and go see Sister Corbin. Amandine spared a few more glances for the stalls and carts and began making her way towards the Temple of Akradath, on the other side of the market circle.

A girl's laughter snapped her attention away from thoughts of what to serve at dinner. Ahead of her, at a cart selling bead necklaces from Zulathia, was Marlette L'Eau. She wore a long blue-and-silver dress. Her dark hair draped loose about her shoulders. Small earrings with green gemstones glinted between the silky black strands.

Behind her stood Fredderick.

He was not in his page's uniform, and instead sported a matching set done in smoky grays and charcoal black. His hair was tied back in a neat ponytail, and a single silver ear-stud caught the afternoon sunlight. That was new.

Amandine caught herself admiring him. He always looked better in darker colors. With a sigh, she shook her head. He didn't deserve her attention. She had other places to be.

Marlette turned then, holding a necklace she was trying to show to Fredderick. She noticed Amandine and her smile quirked up on one side. With a small flourish, she turned her eyes back to Fredderick and put the necklace over his head.

Fredderick had seen her distraction and turned in Amandine's direction. Amandine quickly looked elsewhere, ducked into the crowd and picked up her steps. She wasn't going to be seen running away, especially from colorless Marlette L'Eau, but she wasn't going to hang about like some lost kid goat either.

She ducked between two stalls and sidled through to the outer circle and the most direct path to the temple. Of all the days to randomly run into—

"Can we talk?"

Amandine stopped and spun around. Fredderick stood right behind her, still wearing that stupid bead necklace.

"Did you just ditch Marlette to chase after me?" Amandine asked. "She is going to be very cross with you."

"I left an illusion of myself behind. I am getting better at that sort of warping. She won't know the difference."

Amandine glanced through the gap in the stalls. Sure enough, a replica of Fredderick still stood behind Marlette. It even nodded occasionally as she displayed necklaces to it.

"So, then, you told her?" Amandine asked.

"That I can do magic? No, she and the other L'Eau's still don't know that. I think maybe Lady Gia has figured it out, but I don't go around flaunting my ability too much, Amandine, and you know why."

"That's not what I am talking about."

"Then what are you talking about? You have been avoiding me for over a cycle! I tried to come by the cottage in Gold Hills and got run off by Chef Brutsche. You turn and walk the other way every time I see you!"

Amandine really couldn't believe how dense Fredderick was sometimes. He wasn't a stupid person. He was brave, and had always been kind to her. More than kind, actually. That she had to spell it out for him annoyed her to her very core. She liked him, even still. Really, *really* liked him. Why was he so blind to her feelings?

"Have you told her that you kissed me?"

Fredderick turned slightly red and hunched his shoulders. Amandine hated when he acted pouty like this.

"No."

"Well she sure behaves like she knows. She looks at me like I stole her cake, Fredderick. You've heard about the changes at the Manor? My promotion?"

He nodded.

"I can't have her looking at me like a dark raincloud at every meal. Grab your courage and tell her, or I will!"

"Tell her what?" Fredderick asked with a scowl.

"I don't know? Something? That you were courting the Chef's apprentice before her, but—"

"We weren't courting," Fredderick interrupted. "We—"

"What in the hells was it then?" Amandine snapped back. "Just a game? Another stupid con like you are always trying to pull with the merchants? Was it... a jape?" Amandine felt tears welling up, but held them back. She was *not* going to cry. She wasn't!

Fredderick clamped his jaw shut. He looked away.

Amandine slapped him. She didn't hold back. Cycles of heavy pots and pans, hard kitchen work, and training with Dena flowed into that slap. Fredderick rocked sideways with the force of it and nearly lost his footing.

People shopping nearby turned to stare. A sympathetic coo of pain echoed here and there. One passing sailor shook his head and grinned at Fredderick while a young woman running a vegetable cart pumped a fist at Amandine. "Tha' was a good one! 'It 'im again!"

Fredderick rubbed his face in shock. Amandine ignored the catcallers.

"You should go rescue Dumpling. I am guessing you tied the illusion to the poor little fellow? Marlette will be surprised if she turns about and discovers the wrong dog attending her."

More catcalls. Fredderick didn't move. He just stood there with that stupid look on his face. Amandine was done with this. She turned and continued on to her lessons with Sister Corbin. Even that was preferable to watching him flounder.

Her hand stung, but her heart stung more.

Obligations

"Ravenex is the matron of the grave, the Lady of Night. She holds sway over Darkness, Vengeance and the inevitability of Death. Her followers seem to revel in the grim and macabre, but this is merely a byproduct of their unique perspective. They celebrate death, not for its own sake, but for the peaceful transition into the eternal that it represents. Rites for the dead are often performed by Dedicated to Ravenex and many a cemetery, crypt and morgue is staffed and maintained by those who revere her. As for her aspect as the goddess of Vengeance, Dedicated attached to military units often fight alongside their troops, as well as attending to the fallen, making Ravenex one of the most militant orders beside those of the god of War himself. Ravenex is darkness over light, vengeance over mercy, and the inevitable final sleep."

- Lecture Notes, Second Thirdday, Fall 1202

SISTER CAPUCINE CORBIN had taken up residence in a small outbuilding, little more than a shack, near the mausoleum behind the Temple of Akradath. Part of the compromise reached with Magistrate Everdawn had included taking on tasks for the town and the other godsworn that they didn't want. Sister Corbin was a Bone Guardian, a sect of the followers of Ravenex that possessed specialized skills—namely, seeing to dead people. In addition to caring for the mausoleum, which was reserved for godsworn and rich temple patrons, she now acted as Stoneman's undertaker. It had been shrewd of Magistrate Everdawn to enlist Corbin to help the town, but Amandine still wished she had simply returned to Artemis and left her alone.

The door stood slightly open, and a flickering light made shadows seem to leap through the gap. Amandine caught the smell of elf-mint before she reached the entrance. So it would be a cadaver today. Preparing herself, she stepped inside.

Sister Corbin, dressed in simple gray robes, leaned over the table in the middle of the single room. Her hair, with its white stripe that made her look like an especially mean badger, was tied back with a strip of black cloth. Weathered hands held rags steeped in mint-infused oils that she slowly rubbed into the skin of the dead body on the table. She chanted in a low voice while she worked and seemed oblivious to Amandine's arrival.

"Excellent, someone died," Amandine said.

"Don't be flippant," Sister Corbin said, breaking her chant.

"I am just glad to be helping him and not have to listen to more religious lectures."

"Don't. Be. Flippant."

Sister Corbin had stopped moving and glowered at her. Amandine grimaced. She *was* being flippant. Whoever this poor man had been, he deserved better than that. So Amandine shut her mouth and put her hands behind her back and waited while Sister Corbin resumed her work.

The corpse was a man with gray-white hair. No visible wounds. Slightly emaciated. A cloth draped over his waist and legs hid everything but his feet, which were bare and thickly calloused. They looked as if they had seen a lot of use, likely without shoes.

"Shanty folk?" Amandine asked.

"One of the beggars, yes. Found in his usual place. Died in his sleep."

Stoneman contained a surprisingly large number of destitute people for a town its size. All sorts passed through, on barges and wagon trains, and some found themselves stuck—unable to get hired for new work due to age or injury, and without the coin to buy passage. Some were addled by drink or herbs that muddled the mind. Still others had simply fallen on hard times and lost control of their circumstances. Amandine herself had drifted among these people for a time when she had arrived—a runaway who had spent all her meager funds on the passage to get here, but without the means to go on. Jacinda and Bertrand Kale had shown her kindness and gotten her off the streets, but they couldn't help everyone.

Amandine reached out and touched the pallid, ashen skin on the dead man's gnarled foot. "May those to whom you brought Joy in your life remember those moments, and you, in their hearts. For we all close the circle."

"For we all close the circle," Sister Corbin echoed.

Amandine could tell by her expression that she didn't approve of her choice of eulogies. It was a prayer of the cult of Kayla, a lesser goddess, the daughter of Milintanth and Akradath. It was still appropriate to the situation and *not* flippant, and so Sister Corbin couldn't say anything against it.

On the whole, Amandine preferred Kayla to Ravenex. She was the Daughter of Joy, and besides her aspects as the goddess of beauty and womanhood, she also represented strength of mind and joy in living. She didn't hate Ravenex precisely, but Amandine was done dedicating herself to the inevitability of death. There was too much else worth living for.

"You will do the eyes, student," Sister Corbin said as she withdrew and replaced the oiled rags in their bucket.

Amandine sighed. She hated doing the eyes. Sister Doom-and-Gloom was probably punishing her for using a Kayla prayer instead of one of the Five Dirges.

Reluctantly, Amandine stepped over to a small table with an array of wicked looking metal implements. She picked up a small spoon-shaped tool with sharp edges and a long handle.

Using practiced motions, Amandine began removing the dead man's eyes. She placed them in a jar on the table that had been reserved for that purpose. Once the second had been removed, Amandine used a rag to wipe away a small trickle of blood and then dropped the spoon into a bowl of vinegar.

Sister Corbin took the eyes to another table that supported a ritual brazier filled with red coals. It was the source of the light flickering ghoulishly off the walls. With a prayer intoned to Ravenex, she burned the eyes while Amandine used needle and thread to sew the empty sockets shut.

The dead body didn't bother her. Corpses bled very little and the chill, lifeless feel of them didn't unsettle her like it did other people. She felt a vague sense of sorrow for the nameless man, and when she touched him, there was a quiet that seemed to fill her mind. It was peaceful. Like watching snow fall through a window. Cold and silent.

"He has no kin, so he will be given to the earth as ash and bone. The pyrekeepers will come in three days. What are the preparations we must make?" Sister Corbin asked.

Amandine rattled off the correct list of oils to rub the body with and prayers to invoke. Sister Corbin seemed satisfied.

"Your talents are wasted with that man," she said. It was a common refrain. Amandine wasn't interested in arguing for her apprenticeship to Serand again. She had done that often enough.

"What are 'demon-eyes?'" she asked instead.

Sister Corbin's eyes narrowed. "Where did you hear that term?"

"A merchant in the market circle called me 'demon-eyes' today. I thought he was just mad that I had haggled a good price for a new knife, but he acted strange. Made a gesture with his hand like he was afraid of me."

With a frown, Sister Corbin made the hand gesture the merchant had used, her fingers twisted over each other. "Like this?"

"Yes! What does it mean?"

"Was this man Bolath?"

"Yes."

"It is a heretical vestige of a god that no longer exists. Superstition and nonsense. Put it out of your mind. It means nothing."

"It means something to him. I'd like to know what it is."

"I will not teach you heresy. The man who made this symbol is ignorant. Ignore him."

"Then how about teaching me something useful, like whatever it is you know about my parents."

Sister Corbin had tried to tempt Amandine into coming back to Artemis with her by hinting that she knew something about her parents—why she was an orphan.

"The cost of that information is known and you refuse to pay it. I will not."

Amandine glared at Capucine from across the table, but it was no use matching wills with the woman. She may as well be made of granite.

"I need to move our lessons to evening hours," Amandine said, changing the subject. "In addition to my continued training, I have been made a full Cook at Manor L'Eau and I am needed for meals."

"An unusual thing. One does not normally take on the full responsibility of a job they are still being apprenticed for."

"The loss of the grain in Gold Hills forced the L'Eau's to make staff changes."

"I see. I refuse."

Amandine blinked. "But why?"

"Evening hours are sacred. I reserve them for my devotions. The L'Eau's misfortune is not relevant to our arrangement. You will continue to come at the prescribed times or default on the Magistrate's compromise."

"Why must you be so inflexible?"

"Why must you run from your sworn obligations?"

Amandine seethed. The Sisters had made a practice of swearing children in their care to apprenticeship as Bone Guardians, sometimes far earlier than such things were normally done and often without the young apprentices fully understanding the vows they were taking. Amandine had taken them, and three years later, after a fire at the orphanage, she had fled to be rid of them.

"I have obligations that I am trying to honor here."

"The ones you made to Ravenex supersede anything you have promised to the L'Eau's."

"I hate you. So does Miss Jacinda, by the way. She asked me to let you know."

"I do not care what that fae-spawn thinks of me. I care about your opinion more, but it will not sway me, Amandine. We have wasted enough time. Next lesson."

"We're not done discussing this!"

"We are. Next lesson."

With effort, Amandine shoved aside her anger and indignation. At Sister Corbin. At Fredderick. At Magistrate Everdawn for putting her in this awkward position as an apprentice to two different people.

"Fine," Amandine said. "Next lesson."

Elementals and Onions

"Elementals are a varied and unusual sort of creature. Not really alive but something more than the energies that cause them to manifest, they fill a role in fae ecology similar to that of plants, fungi, or insects in other life cycles. Hybrid elemental forms function both as prey and scavengers, while more aggressive amalgamations, such as lurks, actually predate living material and incorporate it into their structures. The vast majority are not dangerous to people and larger animals, but the few that are can be a grave threat if not handled carefully."

- On The Nature of Elementals, Foreword, Excerpt

"HAVE YOU BEEN reading the book I gave you?" Mister Green asked. He was seated on a stool near the high oven. One hand held an open book, the other was... doing something that made a nearby teacup float. A silver spoon slowly stirred the contents within.

"Yes, *soeje*," Amandine said as she chopped onions for yet another batch of pickles. She eyed the floating cup warily. "I'm really sorry it's taking me so long. Some of the words are hard, but it's interesting."

"I'm glad you like it," the elf replied. The spoon stopped stirring and floated itself over to the washtub. He took the cup physically in hand and inhaled the steam. "I wrote it, so my opinion is biased."

"I think Serand wants to read it too. He keeps peeking over my shoulder when I have it open."

"Master Brutsche is also welcome to borrow it, but I think he probably knows almost everything in that particular tome. He is rather well educated in the nature of elementals."

"What a curious thing," the other person in the kitchen said. "Why would a chef know anything about elementals?"

Fiona L'Eau sat on another stool with her elbows on the block and her chin in her hands, watching Amandine work as she spoke. She was still dressed in riding clothes from earlier in the day, despite the late hour. Her lessons with Mister Green had been before lunch, but she had declared that she wanted 'extra marks' when she took her seat on the stool by the block, and hadn't moved since. The golden curls ringing her face made her seem somewhat owlish as she followed the knife's motions. Amandine tried not to be distracted by the attention, but Fiona seemed absolutely hypnotized by the simple chore.

"Oh, well, I don't know his full history, and I shall not spread rumors about former colleagues. He has wandered quite a path, though. Much stranger than any common cook I have ever known." Mister Green snapped his book shut. He sipped his tea and made a contented noise. "This is quite good, Amandine."

"Thanks. I got the recipe from Wizard Hemm's, erm, assistant. I like it too."

"Fascinating." Mister Green eyed his cup with renewed interest. "The real question is, what have you two learned about elementals?"

"Um, that they are fragments of the forces that collide to make this world, and they are imbued with, um..." Amandine struggled to remember all of the strange words in the book.

"Anima!" Fiona answered for her. "It's what makes them act alive!"

"Some might argue that they *are* alive," Mister Green said with a nod. "Not in the way a human, or fae, or even a cat is. Perhaps something more akin to a plant. But even then, they have a certain sense of purpose that is more readily apparent than what we can observe in an onion. All living things contain anima, but the qualities of that energy vary from creature to creature."

Amandine grinned at the mention of a cat. She glanced down at Grendel, who was hiding under the washtub. He sometimes behaved strangely around Mister Green. Today he was in one of his moods. Amandine mouthed the words "scaredy cat" at him. Grendel laid back his ears and hissed quietly in response, but did not come out of his shelter.

"Can you name at least three types of elementals?" Mister Green prompted.

"Oh, wisps are one. I have seen those in the fens. They are aspects of light and sometimes fire," Amandine replied.

"Correct, and?"

Amandine stopped cutting onions a moment and thought. "Lurks are another. Darkness and earth."

"Also correct. One more?"

She really hadn't paid as much attention to the bestiary portion of the book. It was full of complicated words and things in elvish subscript. She knew about the other two because of her own experiences and from listening to Serand. "I'm not sure."

"Miss Fiona?"

"Zephs, quasits, flinders, nocts, klyberts, auqirs, fire slimes, rot slimes, ice slime—" Fiona began reciting, but Amandine interrupted her.

"Wait, rot slimes are elementals?"

Mister Green shifted his tone to the one he used when lecturing: "A hybrid form, yes. The anima infuses a type of slime mold that is itself infused by water and earth. It is thought that this is why they will, quite often, seem to simply appear out of nowhere. The progenitor mold is sometimes difficult to spot when it is dormant. That is why we use beeswax and wards to guard food stores. The wax is very good at killing fungi, and the wards deter the anima from bonding."

"So both would have had to fail for the slimes to get into the silos," Amandine said.

"An astute observation. Yes, both would have had to be lacking in some way for a full infestation to occur."

"Oh," Fiona said. She had stopped watching Amandine and looked at Mister Green with a stricken expression. "That's really unlikely. Are you saying that someone did this on purpose? That they did this to my family to hurt us?"

Amandine set her knife down. "I think it's going to hurt everyone, sah. The word from the barges yesterday is that it's not just the L'Eau silos that were ruined."

"I... I didn't know." Fiona looked ashamed.

"It is natural to seek something or someone to blame for a misfortune such as this." Mister Green reached over to pat Fiona on the shoulder. "There is undoubtedly a reason for it all, but that truth remains to be discovered."

"Would you like more tea?" Amandine asked as Mister Green drained his cup.

"No, thank you. It has grown late and I must return to my meditations. I am pleased with your progress, both of you. Safe night, students."

"Safe night, *soeje*," Amandine and Fiona said together.

Mister Green smiled and rose to his feet. As he left the kitchen, Grendel slunk out from under the washtub and crept to the door, then crouched by the frame as if to pounce upon the elf should he enter again.

Amandine shook her head at Grendel's behavior and resumed cutting onions. Fiona continued to watch, but looked pensive. She was only a little bit younger than Amandine, perhaps a year and a shiv, and was fond of asking her inane questions. In fact, she was almost impossible to quiet once she started talking, but tonight she was strangely silent.

"Do you think you earned your extra marks?" Amandine asked, just to break the silence.

"What? Oh. No, I just said that because I wanted to stay and watch you, and I didn't want *soeje* to send me away."

"Watch me?" Amandine said with a small laugh. "This can't be all that interesting. It's... onions."

"Don't laugh!" Fiona said sharply. Then, more quietly: "Please, don't laugh."

"I wasn't making fun," Amandine said quickly. "I swear it, but... why?"

Fiona lay her head on her arms and scrunched up her face. "Maybe you *should* laugh. It's foolish."

"I swear to Kayla that I will not take your Joy," Amandine said solemnly.

Fiona smiled at that, but turned her head away. "It's just... most of the staff, the nice ones anyway, all left. And my big sister is courting that page from House Stolm, and mother and father are so busy, and..."

"You're lonely?" Amandine asked gently.

"Yes! And booooooooored." She drew the sound of the word into almost a wail. "Even Grendel doesn't come to see me as much as he used to."

Grendel stood up from his ambush spot at the sound of his name and dashed across the kitchen and under the butcher block. He must have been rubbing on Fiona's legs. She looked down at the floor and smiled. Amandine heard the cat purring.

"I understand being lonely, I think," Amandine said. "Even when you're surrounded by people, you can still feel lonely sometimes. As for being bored..."

Amandine rolled an onion across the wood and bounced it off Fiona's arm. She stopped paying attention to Grendel and looked down at the vegetable in surprise.

"Want to learn how to properly cut an onion?"

She had meant it as a sort of jape. After all, who in their right mind, besides her and Serand of course, would think that the method for cutting an onion was at all interesting? Amandine was amazed then, when Fiona's face lit up like the sun. Her dour mood seemed to evaporate like steam off the side of a kettle.

"Do you mean it? Can I use a knife?"

Amandine laughed. "Well, yes. You can't cut anything otherwise."

Fiona leapt off the chair and began rolling the sleeves of her riding shirt. "Show me!"

She did. For several minutes, Amandine explained the different kinds of cuts: diced against chopped, slivers against crowns. Then she demonstrated how to peel an onion and handed one to Fiona.

"Oh, that's pungent! I mean, I could smell them from where I was sitting but..." Fiona said as she struggled with the papery outer layers.

"Rolling it gently on the wood sometimes loosens the thinner top layers," Amandine said. "Like so."

Fiona did it and the layer separated, allowing her to finish peeling. "That's lumi," she said in awe.

"We're going to do slivers and crowns for the pickles, so follow my lead, and go slowly." She handed Fiona the knife she had purchased the other day. It was good enough quality that Fiona would have no trouble, but was smaller and not quite as keen as the large knife she was using—the one that lived in the Manor's kitchen.

"Fingertips tucked in. Yes, that's right," Amandine moved Fiona's hands into the correct position. "If you slip, you might skin yourself, but you won't lose a finger."

Fiona pressed her lips together and looked a bit uncertain, but as Amandine began to slice, so did she.

Amandine could sense Fiona's determination, her obsession with being perfect, and equally felt her frustration when the slices came out uneven anyhow. She could understand that. Good knife skills took practice.

"Oh, my eyes." Fiona blinked back tears from the fumes.

"That's why these kinds of vegetables are called aromatics. It's worth it once you cook them. Wait! Don't—"

Too late. Fiona tried to rub the tears out of one eye and gasped. "Oh gods, ow! Ow, ow!"

She flapped her arms as tears completely unrelated to the onion fell down her face. Amandine quickly wetted a clean dishcloth and pressed it to Fiona's eye.

"It will pass," she said.

Fiona looked completely crestfallen.

"Hey, you know," Amandine added, "when I first did this, I did the exact same thing, only I got both eyes and had to dunk my head in the washtub."

Fiona laughed through the tears. "Thank you, Amandine."

"Do you want to stop?"

"No!"

Squinting her afflicted eye shut, Fiona draped the dishcloth over her shoulder and resumed slivering the onion. She kept at it until the entire batch was done, in fact. Amandine would have some explaining to do about the uneven cuts if Serand surprised her with another inspection, but on the whole, it had come out well. It had been nice to have someone to do it with.

Fiona grinned like a fool as she washed her hands and then wiped them on her riding pants. "Pants really are amazing," she said. "You can get them all dirty and no one cares a bit. I wish I had started taking riding lessons earlier!"

Amandine nodded. "I agree, pants are best."

"Dresses are nice too, though, especially the ones with pockets." Fiona stared off into her own thoughts for a moment. "I'm exhausted. I should go to my rooms."

"It *is* rather late. Will your parents scold you?"

"Maid Sundrop was always the one to see me at night. Sometimes mother, but always Sundrop. I miss her."

Amandine nodded again. She hadn't known Sundrop all that well. The older Hill Folk woman had sometimes also acted as Lady Gia's interpreter.

"I'm glad you are one of the ones that stayed," Fiona said.

She smiled at Amandine and the warmth of the compliment radiated off her like daylight. Amandine smiled back.

"I will hang this here," Amandine said as she took the smaller knife and dropped it into the pegboard for the cutlery. "Any time you want to come and help, it's yours."

Amandine hadn't thought it was possible for Fiona to glow any more brightly than she had before. She nearly tackled her with an enormous hug.

"I'm glad you're my friend, Amandine!" Fiona said with her chin on Amandine's shoulder.

Friends. Were they? Amandine wasn't sure. They both loved Grendel, and spending time together had been fun, but there had always been a distance. Could she really be friends with the daughter of the people who paid her? She decided it was worth a try. Gil would always be her friend, but more was better, right?

"Me too," Amandine replied.

Turnovers

"Apples are a crop attributed to humans and the Arrival, and are grown in several varieties in every nation. Even fae, who normally crave those plants cultivated for centuries in their own gardens, such as jambors and gojos, show an appreciation for apples. They are incredibly versatile as an ingredient, and hardy enough to weather harsh shivs. While most people are content to snack on them raw, or bake them into sweets, they can be used as an accent, added flavor, or even the main ingredient in a wide variety of other dishes. I personally enjoy adding them to salads, or reducing them to a sauce and employing them in glazes, marinades and soups."

- Seeker's Kitchen, Chapter 3, Essential Ingredients

"AMANDINE, SHOULDN'T YOU be walking already?" Dena asked as she reentered the cottage. She still wore her exercise clothing and was drying her hair with a sheet of heavy cloth.

"I am learning how to make turnovers!" Amandine flipped a lump of floury dough in a bowl.

"Is that wise? Flour is rationed and—"

"Had a bag startin' ta clump," Serand said as he sliced apples. "And we have half a basket of fruit here that was goin' ta turn and was no good fer preserves. Ye don't like turnovers?"

Dena grinned. Amandine knew they were one of her favorites. Serand was teasing her. "Absolutely hate 'em," Dena said.

"More for me!" Amandine declared.

"You wish, duckling."

"Right, that's enough. Don't beat it up too much, Apprentice. Fetch the sugarsap and the jar of cinnamon. We'll be makin' the filling next."

"You're still going to be late, aren't you?" Dena asked as she entered the bedroom and swung the door mostly closed.

"Lord Estevan and Lady Gia are visiting Lady Ophelia's estate today," Amandine said. "Marlette went with them. Sunflower said she would make breakfast for Fiona and the staff. I will go there after lunch and continue with the pickles."

"Still at it, eh?" Dena called from the bedroom.

"Neverending." Amandine sighed.

Spice emerged from under the table where he had been napping and wove around Amandine's shins. She reached down to scratch his ears.

"Eyes ahead," Serand grumbled. "Apples first, pickles later. Spice, go bother a mouse, would ye?"

"Yes, Chef," Amandine said quickly. It felt good to call him that again. She got to so rarely now, it seemed. It had been over a tenday since Fiona had helped her with the onions, and she had been coming every evening since, sometimes even sneaking out of bed, to continue assisting with the chore. Amandine didn't understand her fascination, but it had made things less lonely in the kitchen. Even fun, at times.

"Right, grate the cinnamon extra fine. It goes in directly, 'stead of as an infusion. Next we are goin' ta add a pinch o' salt to the apples and stir in the 'sap. That'll make 'em creamy-like and keep 'em from burning when they bake."

"And the sugarsap will brown in the oven and change flavors," Amandine added.

"Exactly right. Aye, that be an adequate grate, but hold the stick like so. Ye'll get more down to the nub. Save the ends fer tea."

Amandine adjusted her grip and continued to rub the cinnamon bark against the fine-toothed steel grater that Chef used for making powders. She could also grind it with a mortar and pestle, but this tool seemed to do the job faster and more evenly and left her less tired at the end.

Spice, bored with what the humans were doing, meowed once in a dissatisfied way and leapt up and out the open window.

"I didn' ask yer opinion!" Chef called after him. "Some critters have no sense of taste," he muttered to himself.

Amandine laughed. "Maybe I'll make him one with fish paste using the leftover."

Chef made a face and shook his head. He always complained when Amandine spoiled his cat, but he never tried to stop her either.

As Amandine reached the nub of the first cinnamon stick, her thoughts strayed to the unusual encounter with the merchant in the market circle.

"Can I ask you something, Chef?"

"'Course," Chef said with a grunt. "Jus' do half of the next stick, otherwise too much cinnamon."

Amandine nodded. "A few days ago, in the market, a Bolath merchant said something strange to me."

"Did ye out haggle them on somethin'? I get them ta say all sort of strange things when they reckon I came out ahead of the current."

"Well, yes," Amandine admitted.

"Well done." Chef chortled.

"But then he called me 'demon eyes'," Amandine continued. "What does that mean?"

Chef paused at slicing apples and sucked at his teeth. "Well, now, that is somethin' I ain't heard in a tok 'r three."

"So you know what it means? I asked Sister Corbin and she said it was some old superstition. He acted afraid of me."

"She said that, did she?" Chef's tone was thoughtful. "That woman has a thick hull to be callin' anyone out for superstitious nonsense."

"So she's wrong?"

"Not really."

"Then what do *you* know about it?"

"Let's start with facts: do ye know what a demon is?"

Amandine thought. "I mean, are they real? I have heard stories. The Sisters said they were creatures of shadow that would imitate people."

"That's... actually not far off." Chef resumed slicing. "They be partly elemental in nature."

"Like the slimes!"

"Aye, like they say in that book Green wrote. They ain't mindless, though. Wicked, smart, and dangerous."

"You've seen one?"

"Only once. Nearly killed Bertrand. Hope never to encounter one again."

"What happened?"

"The thing was preyin' on folk by makin' itself look like people they knew."

"Preying on them?" Amandine asked in a whisper.

Chef put down his knife and turned. "Yes, fingerling. Eating them. We were tryin' ta figure out what were doin' it. Thing tricked ol' Bertrand and he was in a bad state when we found him."

"Is this when you were still both Seekers?"

Chef grimaced. "We're off course. The words that merchant used are no compliment, but ye got that part. The thing here is yer eyes."

"What about my eyes?"

"Demons are shadow infused. They be great mimics. But there's a tell. Their eyes 're always lighter than the rest of 'em. Imitatin' someone pale as Dena, their eyes would seem washed out. Like paint on a chair left too long in the sun. Hard ta miss that. Looks unnatural."

"Oh! So you can tell them by their eyes?"

"Yup. Easier ta spot in Bolath camps or Zulath lands. Everyone with a bloodline there has dark eyes. Brown or black. Nearly impossible fer a demon to pull off, especially against lighter skin tones. But Olgath tribe, they can sometimes have gold, or blue eyes. So most encounters with 'em tend ta be in Olgath lands where they can blend in easier. Or at least places Olgothians frequent, like the trade towns in Tren. Or border cities like the Maw."

"But my eyes are green, Chef."

"And that's why it's a load of shite. Dark skin an' light eyes. That's all that carp fish at the market saw. Capucine had a good notion fer once, even if she don't know all the facts."

Amandine tapped the end of her cinnamon stick and placed the unused half back in its jar. "So he wanted to insult me? But he acted really afraid, Chef. More afraid than angry."

"If you've ever lived in a place a demon has decided to hunt, ye'd have an eye to yer keel too, I'd wager. Doesn't make what he said kind or right..."

Chef turned and leaned in close to Amandine. He gestured to his face with a finger. "Guess how many times that curse has been spit at this old shipwreck?"

Amandine looked into his vividly blue eyes. His skin was nearly as dark as that of the Bolath merchant she had bought the knife from.

"Where are you from?" Amandine asked. "Is it really Tren?"

Chef stood back up and shrugged. "It's the earliest place I remember," he said. "And you? Ye really born in Artemis, ye think?"

Amandine shook her head. "I don't know."

"Exactly."

"What?"

"Exactly, so why fret it? Thoughts like that will tie ye in knots. All my friends as a boy had red hair, eyes like yers, an' more freckles than Apprentice Crouste. You and I ain't from any one place, fingerling."

"That seems sad."

"Is it? Hells, with yer eyes an' skin an' hair, ye could have parents that were Bolath, Trenash, Olgathian—all three? Maybe some Zulath in there fer good measure? When yer someone like us, Amandine, ye ain't from nowhere. Yer from everywhere!"

Amandine thought about that. She grinned. "Yes, I like that notion. Now I just have to go see everywhere."

"That's the thinkin'," Chef said as he flourished his knife. "Ye can travel nearly anywhere an' most folk wouldn't look twice. Now give me that cinnamon, let's get this all rigged up proper!"

She handed him the plate of powdered cinnamon and watched closely as Chef combined the ingredients for the filling. Her mind wandered a bit as they worked, though. She really did want to go everywhere—she always had. Chef's words made her feel like it was a birthright. But she had so much to do and learn here still. When would she leave? It would take at least as long as two more years, counting the colorless Shiv, so that she was at majority and could tell Sister Corbin where to go with herself.

Dena emerged from the room some time later as Amandine was checking the oven. Five large turnovers sat on a tray, awaiting their turn.

"Those smell great, can I have one?"

"Only if ye take two," Chef said. "Give one ta Guard Primrose for me. She did me a favor. I owe her a treat."

"See?" Dena said in a low voice to Amandine. "Collects them!"

Amandine laughed as she pulled the tray from the oven and set it out to cool. Chef rolled his eyes and muttered under his breath as he cleaned his board. His gaze turned to Amandine as she set up the second batch in the oven and then began preparing more apples for a third.

Dena carefully wrapped two of the steaming turnovers in a cloth. She was dressed in the leathers she wore under her chainmail, which stayed in the guard's armory in town. Her uniform's gloves were thick enough that she didn't even flinch as she grabbed the hot food.

"Have fun, you two," Dena said. She pecked Chef's cheek and reached the front door's handle.

Someone knocked.

"Oh!" Dena withdrew her hand in surprise, and then reached out and opened the door as the knock came again. "Oh, hello! I haven't seen *you* in a while."

Amandine leaned slightly to peek out the door while she continued to stir her bowl of apples. Her lips pressed into a line. She stopped moving her spoon. Fredderick waved at her from the doorway, Dumpling at his feet.

"Uh, hello, Amandine," he said. "Do you have, uh, a moment? I stopped by the manor first, but—"

"She's taking lessons, ye—" Chef began, but Dena quickly pressed a hand over his mouth, which elicited a glare from Serand.

Amandine rolled her eyes at all of them. "Chef is right, I'm busy, sah," she said as she turned her attention back to her bowl of apples.

"Oh, just go say hello at least," Dena prodded. "It's a long walk from Stoneman, after all."

"Dena..."

"But he looks so sad, Amandine!"

"I'm fine, really," Fredderick said.

"See, he says he's fine." Amandine stirred her apples more vigorously.

"Not him, the little dog!" Dena said with a plaintive coo in her voice. "Look!"

Amandine looked. Dumpling had lain down under Fredderick's feet and was gazing up at her with enormous, watery eyes.

"Fine!" Amandine plunked the bowl down on the counter and walked to the doorway. She opened her mouth to speak, but stopped short as a gentle hand touched her shoulder. Dena guided Amandine out the door and shut it behind her. Amandine turned and glared at the planks for a moment and then faced Fredderick. He was wearing his page's clothing. Had he shirked his duties to come bother her?

"Well then?" she asked.

Fredderick had his hands in his pockets. "I... I wanted to apologize."

Amandine knelt down and scratched Dumpling on the head. He whined and licked her hand.

"For what?" Amandine asked.

"The thing you are mad at me about."

Amandine rolled her eyes. "The thing? Do you honestly not understand why I'm mad?"

"I mean, I have some theories—"

Amandine sighed. "If you don't know what I'm angry about, then I'm still mad at you, Fredderick Stolm." She reached under Dumpling's chin and scratched. He rolled over for a belly rub.

"Well then, are you upset that I've been courting Marlette?"

"It annoys me, sure. She's a rotten apple, but it's not my business who you choose to court, so no."

"It was my father's idea. He thinks that—"

"I just said that's not really it."

"Then what? Is it because I kissed you?"

Amandine stood up. "No, I actually liked that. A lot."

"Then what is it, Amandine?" He sounded a bit frantic.

Amandine took his face in her hands. He looked confused and sad. She wished she could understand what he was really feeling. If it was an act, it was convincing, though. Softly, gently, she pulled him closer and kissed him.

It was a short kiss. Just a peck on the cheek, but Fredderick turned red like a rikol root. Amandine smiled at him.

"Does this mean that... I'm forgiven?" Fredderick asked.

"That?" Amandine said with a small laugh. "Oh, that was just a joke, Fredderick! Do you get it now?"

He blinked and Amandine watched as his cheeks began to darken. With an embarrassed cough, he turned his head aside. Dumpling whined pitifully.

Amandine walked back inside and slammed the door behind her.

Dena sat at the table, with her gloves off, eating a hot apple turnover. Chef was filling the last batch that Amandine had abandoned.

"So," Dena asked as she licked her fingers. "How did it go?"

Amandine smoothed her apron and went to check the oven.

"I suppose we'll see," she said. "He really is a box of rocks sometimes."

Cheesecake

"The Hill Folk have a saying: 'No rest for the small folk.' It's often uttered, sometimes in jest, when hard work is in the offing. The truth behind the ancient turn of phrase is dark indeed, however, and it is with that in mind I bring before you my recent discoveries. The songs of the Hill Folk belong to us, and our songs belong to them. Listen now, as I recite their past, not to shame any member of this venerable body, but to ensure that the same mistakes are never again repeated."

- Speech given by Lyra of Stolen Songs before the High Robes Conclave, partial transcript, Low Summer, 1192

"TWO SHANKS, PLEASE, and the half rack," Amandine said.

Heather Mince, the stockyard matron and butcher in Stoneman, nodded and scratched some glyphs on a slate. She was dressed in a stained, rough-spun apron and a set of leather clothing that made her seem even larger than usual, if that was possible. Her black, braided hair was tied back under a large, colorful cloth that had a blue and white pattern like ripples on a pond.

"You gettin' used to being in charge of the kitchen?" she rumbled in a voice that held deep bass notes.

"Not at all, sah," Amandine sighed. "I still have to ask Serand for advice all the time. There is so much to keep track of. I can't imagine how he remembers it all without writing it down."

"Yeah, that man has a mind like a steel trap," Heather said. "He can tell ye what was said in conversations he overheard years ago, word fer word. Has an eye fer detail. I reckon that's what makes him so good at what he does."

"Really? Some days, I can barely remember how I got my clothes on. Or which way the sun is."

Heather grinned at her. Her large upward pointing canines made it seem fearsome, but the creases at the corners of her eyes betrayed amusement.

"Then yer not alone. Give me a few to cut and wrap this."

"Thanks, sah. I'll be right back then."

Amandine stepped out of the butcher's shop that sat adjacent to the corrals and pens where Heather housed the animals under her care. The Stockyard was where merchants passing through, or selling their animals, could keep them and feed them while they conducted business. Auctions were sometimes held for livestock here as well, but today that podium and the pen next to it sat empty.

Many of the pens were empty, in fact. Some farmers had decided to cull their herds, given the grain shortage, just as Heather had predicted. Not enough of them though. She passed a large fenced area where sheep were being housed and spotted Birch, Heather's assistant, carrying a bag of feed for them.

Watching a Hill Folk person carry something twice their size and weight always amazed Amandine a little, even though she had witnessed such feats of strength plenty of times since arriving here. Mister Green had said it was to do with superior muscle and bone density, but it was still something to see.

"Hallo, Amandine," Birch said as he dropped the bag by the fence. "Stocking the kitchen?"

"Trying to, sah. The prices have gone up and my budget is so tight. It will be a godsworn miracle if I can keep this up through the shiv seasons."

"Aye, we'll all be eatin' root soup if no help comes. But, it wouldn't be the first time."

He shrugged and tore the bag open to pour into the feed trough. Amandine still had errands to run, but she watched Birch work a moment longer. The dark-haired man had been a Seeker once – and not a very nice one either. He had tried to stab her over a perceived insult. She still had a small scar on her arm from that encounter. He'd used to behave awkwardly when she would visit Heather for meats, avoiding her gaze and busying himself with tasks so that they wouldn't have to talk. She didn't hold her injuries against him. Her arm had been hurt because he had tussled with Chef. The skellix had given her the other. Amandine had gone into that colorless swamp for her own reasons, and encountering Birch with the boglings had been entirely happenstance.

Those events had changed him. The skellix had eaten his cousin, Thornberry, and the boglings had cruelly used him as bait to try and ambush the monster for their own purposes. Between losing his cousin and nearly being eaten himself, the entire experience had badly traumatized him, to the point that he could barely speak for cycles afterwards. Heather had managed to give him purpose again, working with the animals in the Stockyard. Now, he was sunny and helpful, if a bit reclusive. Amandine could still sense a hurt in him though. He had just buried it so deep, she wondered if he even knew it was there any more.

"Do you miss it, sah?" she asked.

"Miss what, lass?"

"Being a Seeker?"

He paused. His back was to her, but it wasn't difficult to tell she had upset him. Amandine regretted the question. Those wounds were probably still too raw for him to talk about. It surprised her when he answered.

"Yes. Yes, I do."

Birch turned around. His face was solemn, but he didn't seem angry. "It's just not the same as when I were doin' it with Thornberry. She and I were a team; we had each other's backs. I couldn' go back to it. All of that colorless nonsense wouldn't mean a bean without her to keep me on task."

"I didn't mean to pry, I just—"

"Stop. I ain't mad, kid. Yer just thinkin' the same thing every young sap does close to their majority. Wouldn' it be grand to run off and have an adventure? Hell's, you already killed a skellix to boot, so I get it."

Amandine looked at her feet. Was she that transparent? The notion of being a Seeker did sound exciting, but the encounter with the skellix had given her a dose of reality. "That was sort of an accident," she mumbled.

"You'd be surprised, I think, to know how much of 'heroics' is jus' accidents where you managed not to die." Birch shook his head. "The real heroes are the folk that have to deal with the mess you leave behind. I'd be dead or walking the streets like a colorless madman if it weren't fer Matron Mince. She's the landlord's pick, if'n ya ask me."

Amandine recognized the reference. It was from a romantic storybook that Dena had a copy of on the bookshelf in the cottage. *The Landlord and the Singer.*

"I've read that book! The landlord picked the most humble woman to marry, right? The one who sang so beautifully." Amandine grinned. "It was rather spicy, if you ask me."

Birch blushed suddenly. "Err, that were crass of me, nevermind ya heard that," he muttered.

"I promise I won't tell, but you should probably tell her, yeah? I mean, the landlord in that silly story chose for love, not gold or power. I think that's sweet."

Amandine had hoped to pry a story out of him about his days as a Seeker, but this sudden, unusually romantic turn in their conversation was a hundred ways more interesting.

The poor man turned even redder. "Gods, no. I mean, she would probably laugh her arse off. I practically fit in her apron pocket."

"But the smith near the North Gate, Holmes, married that Hill Folk woman from Waterbeetle. And he's not short for a human or anything. Besides, you can lift at least eighty stone, right? I'd put even money on you winning in an arm wrestling match."

"Bah, yer just teasing, kid. Get on, now!" Birch folded his arms. The way his muscles bulged was impressive for his size. Amandine had only been joking with him a little. She was happy he was talking to her. He didn't talk to anyone really, aside from Heather. Amandine had wondered for ages if he didn't speak to her because she had been wounded after saving him, or if he just lumped her into the rest. Her hand began to drift up to her scar involuntarily, but Amandine caught herself.

"I meant it, but I'll stop pestering," Amandine said as she stuck her hand in a pocket instead. "Still, if you do ask her, and she says yes, I'll bake you both a cake. By Kayla's heart, I promise it."

Birch's grin finally returned. "I might hold you to that!" he called as she walked away.

Amandine made her way to the market circle and went down a mental list of things to purchase for the Manor's stores. As she passed a merchant with his wares laid out on a folding table, something familiar about him made her pause.

"Welcome, welcome, ripple!" The red-haired man said with a wide grin. "Mandagoran powder? Excellent in soups! All the spices you could wish for from the sea and the stone!"

Amandine put her hands on her hips. "How about bogwort?" she asked.

The face the merchant made confirmed it. This was the same Trenash spicer she had sold half a bogwort to last year. It had *not* been a good deal for her.

"Oh, that's something rare. I haven't heard anyone mention that since—"

"Since last year, when you bought a half from me, paid ten crowns less than it was worth and then acted like you had been swindled?"

"Well now, I wouldn't say—"

"That you cheated me? Yes, yes you did. But you know what? The spices you sold me *were* quite good, and I have a need for more. So perhaps you can make it up to me?"

"I am not giving you anything for free, kid." The spicer narrowed his eyes.

"I wouldn't dream of asking you to." Amandine matched his stare.

Minutes later, Amandine was back on her original task, but her satchel clinked with several new tins of high end Trenash and Olgath spices. Including more *pomar*. She had gotten a *very* good price on all of it.

The shopping went quickly enough. The spicer had wanted to unload goods before crossing back over the Wastes for the season, so he had been inclined to haggle. The local growers and grocers, however, were sticking hard to their high prices and small stocks.

Amandine considered the depressingly small basket of vegetables she had managed to procure. Even simple things like turnips were already selling for three times their normal prices. How was she going to serve meals that would please her patrons when even common foods were becoming difficult to get? At the best of times, the manor's garden only provided some of what they needed. With the Shiv coming, most of what remained was being made into pickles, so the market was Amandine's only option.

She began making her way back to the Stockyard. Halfway there, as she was passing the barracks, a gruff voice called out to her:

"Oi, kid goat!"

Boomer McKragen unfolded himself from where he had been crouched next to some water barrels. He glanced up at the sun and then waved at Amandine to come to him.

Amandine had only very rarely spoken to Boomer. He mostly went about his business of maintaining the town's aqueduct, drainage, and walls with quiet efficiency. She stepped under the eaves where he was loitering and shifted her basket.

"What is it, Master McKragen?"

"Ye live in the same warren as ol' Brute, ri'?" he asked in his odd guttural accent.

"Yes?"

"And tha' tall female, Dena. Ya, that's 'er name. The stone what run the town guard. She's his mate. She lives there too, ya?"

"Um, yes, she's his, err, mate, but she doesn't run the guards, sah, that's Captain Rivaldo Stolm and Sergeant Xia."

Boomer chuckled. Amandine would never get used to dwarven laughter. It sounded like he was choking on something.

"Yer a smooth slab, kid goat. Anyone with eyes can see who is really in charge o' this box o' wumpuses. Stolm is more interested in how shiny his armor is, and Xia is fierce like a grim, but tha' hunter is his ta course. They bark orders and show their teeth, but the tall stone, Dena, is the biggest grackle 'ere."

"If you say so, sah," Amandine said. She wasn't quite sure what to make of his opinions. She didn't know enough about the rest of the Stoneman Guards to have one herself.

"If? I just did, ya? Ye humans have a lo' o' extra words fer simple things."

"Ok, well why do you want to know then?"

"I came 'ere lookin' for tha' tall stone. I got a letter from my bud, Herric. Wanted to pass it along ta ol' Brute, seein' as he'll be headin' up to meet that *gyre* when the barges float up from Irongate in a tenday and five. It's full of useful words."

"Oh, so you want me to pass along the letter? I can do that for you. I should see him tonight."

"Grand." Boomer opened a wide pocket on his tool vest and pulled out a slip of gray-ish paper. It was folded neatly, and when Amandine unfolded it, she realized it was written entirely in Dwarven runes. Very, very small ones. She squinted and tried to make some out. She could read a few now, but these were so packed and scribbled together she couldn't make heads or tails of it.

"He teachin' ya proper rune smithin'?" Boomer asked.

"Mister Green taught me to read some, but this is beyond me."

"No doubt 'cause ye have that leaf-lover teachin' ya runes. Only proper way ta learn 'em is in front of the Obelisk. Feelin' em with yer fingers. The shapes have truer meanin' then."

"I'm sure Serand can read it, he knows a lot of languages."

"Aye, that ol' stone knows 'em. Give 'im tha' from me, and when he sees my bud, give tha' *gyre* this."

Boomer pulled out another letter, written on normal colored paper, but this one was wax sealed. Amandine nodded and tucked both into her basket.

"I can do that."

Boomer lifted his goggles and squinted at her with his strange, double-irised eyes. He grinned, showing two large rows of pointed teeth. "Ye humans grow like jump moss. Yer at least three and seven kliks taller than last tenday."

Without further explanation, either to why that mattered or what a 'klik' was, Boomer replaced his goggles and walked into the sun with a disgruntled hiss. Amandine watched him go. She really wished she understood more about Dwarven society. They were just so... *strange* compared to other people, even fae like Mister Green.

Amandine made her way back to the butcher shop. She burned with curiosity about what was in the letter from Boomer's child. What would a farmer underground grow? Mushrooms maybe? Or perhaps those blue carrots that Juniper liked so much. When she stepped inside the shop, Amandine found Heather behind the counter, staring out a side window. Her arms were folded and she was smiling at something.

"Luminous day, sah," Amandine said to get her attention.

Heather jumped as if she had been goosed. It was the strangest reaction Amandine had ever seen from her.

"Forgive me, Amandine. Didn't hear ya' come inside. I have your meat, just wait here." Heather shot one more glance out the window and then went through a curtain into the back.

Amandine leaned over the counter to look out the side window. It was a view of the main stockyard where several cattle were corralled. Birch was in the yard, hauling large bales of hay from a shed for the animals. He had his shirt off. The definition of his muscles, especially in his torso, was incredible. He lifted the bales, three times his size, as if they weighed nothing, which made his body compress and flex in the most *fascinating* ways.

Footsteps approached and Amandine quickly pulled back so she wouldn't be caught peeping. Heather entered and placed a large sailcloth-wrapped bundle on the counter.

"One and six," she said.

"So much?"

"I don't like doin' it, girl. But feed has tripled in price. I am givin' you the same discount I give Serand."

Amandine nodded. She wasn't going to haggle with a friend, and she didn't think Heather would cheat or lie to her. Prices were high, and would likely get higher.

"Say, Heather?" Amandine asked as she counted out silver. "What kind of cake do you like?"

"Cake?" Heather asked. "I, err..."

She looked genuinely confused by the question. The face she made was so out of place on her that Amandine almost laughed.

"Yes, cake."

Heather scratched one of her tusks and considered the question. "Never had much occasion to eat it, but now that you mention it, Serand once made a beautiful strawberry cake. Had the candied berries on top, and underneath was some sort of sweet cheese with a crumble bottom. The cream on top was stiff somehow and shaped like waves on water. Never had anything like it since."

"That sounds fancy, what was the occasion?"

"Shiv's End feast," Heather said. "Why?"

"Just curious!" Amandine's voice lilted slightly as she sang the words with a smile. "Thank you for the cuts!"

Heather nodded, still looking confused as Amandine left the shop. Just outside the door, Amandine peeked back over her shoulder before it shut. Heather was gazing out the window again.

Cats

"Many traditions set Olgothian nobility apart from their peers in other nations, but there is one in particular that is remarked upon far more often than its importance would suggest. Sitting stools. The tiny, padded, three-legged stools are nearly impossible to sit upon comfortably. The ability to endure an audience by sitting in one of the five allowed positions is considered a sign of great refinement among the elites. To outsiders, the ludicrously small chairs and ridiculous-seeming sitting positions are a point of mockery. Although intended to belittle and offend, many in the upper layers of Olgothian society take a kind of pride in the commentary. Yllien of the Severed Reeds even offered a bounty to anyone, of any caste, who could tell her a stool-based jape she had not yet heard."

- My Journey In The Wastes - Thoughts and Reflections, Chapter Seven

"OH, WHAT ARE these called?"

Amandine paused her knife work to look over her shoulder.

"Radishes, Fiona. You've had them before."

"But these look like little turnips."

Fiona stepped up to the block and picked up a radish. It was red on top, white on the bottom, with dark green leaves and a long, stringy, slightly dirty tap root. These particular vegetables had come directly from the Manor's garden and were some of the last. The small tilled patch near the coops would remain fallow until after the Shiv.

"Well to be fair, they are usually cut up in a salad or stew, or mixed into some other dish as a seasoning. I suppose you might have not seen one whole before, but that is definitely a radish."

Amandine resumed her slicing. She removed the tops, then the tap root. With a damp cloth, she wiped the rest clean and then sliced it into quarters before putting the pieces in a nearby jar. The leafy greens she also washed and set aside. Radish and rikol tops were edible, and nothing would be wasted going into a shiv. Fiona sniffed the radish she was holding, shrugged and took a bite out of it.

"Oh," she said, making a face as she chewed. "That's sharp!"

"I would have warned you," Amandine said with a laugh. "But I kind of wanted to see your face."

Fiona pinched off the tap root with her fingernails and took another bite. "Actually, I sort of like it," she said with her mouth full.

Amandine laughed again. "Fine, but don't eat too much. There was barely enough in the garden for a jar as it is."

"Is this all we are making tonight?"

"No, there is more rikol as well." Amandine liked that Fiona had taken partial ownership of the chore. The nightly pickle-making process really had become a joint venture between the two of them. Fiona usually wore her riding clothes when she came to help, as they included the only pair of pants she owned, but tonight she was still in the light blue dress she had worn to dinner. She pushed the sleeves up to her elbows.

"Excellent," Fiona said as she fetched her knife off the peg board. "I'll start cleaning them after I sharpen!"

"Not too many strokes. You just sharpened it the other day, and if you hone the blade too fine, it's more liable to chip."

"Yes, Chef!"

"Ugh, don't call me that."

"Why?"

"Because I am not one," Amandine said, putting her knife down. "Becoming a Chef means you have invented new recipes *and* been acclaimed by one of the three Guilds. Like the one that puts on Tren's famous contest every year. I am barely managing as a cook, Fiona."

Fiona shrugged again as she started sharpening her knife. "Well, I'm not a Guild-Master, but I think your cooking is lumi, Amandine."

"Lots of people's cooking is lumi."

"Yours is better."

"Why?"

"Because it's yours, of course."

Amandine sighed and picked her knife back up. She wished Fiona wouldn't tease her, but arguing with someone who was trying to praise you was stupid. The comment made her begin to see why Serand sometimes acted like a grumpus when people lauded his work. Amandine wasn't doing it for the salutations. She did it because she loved it. Really, really loved it. Even these disgusting pickles.

"Oh gods, look!" Fiona exclaimed as she dug through the woven sack of rikol roots. "This one has legs!"

Amandine glanced up. The red root Fiona was standing on the table was a double. It happened sometimes with carrots too, where the root would divide and grow two taps that connected to one top. This one looked like a pair of short, chubby legs. It made her smile.

"Yeah, it does."

"And see, it even has a big tush!" Fiona spun the root around. The split made it look like the rikol had enormous butt cheeks.

Amandine snorted as she tried to control a laugh. Fiona grinned and made the root dance while affecting a parody of a deep masculine voice.

"Mister Rikol van Big Butt, at your service! I would bow, but I might knock something over!"

Laughter spilled out of Amandine. "Oh gods, stop it."

Fiona just grinned wider and went on: "I once met the Emperor of Olgothia, but I broke every stool in the palace and they had to roll in a wheelbarrow!"

Tears welled up in Amandine's eyes, she was laughing so hard. The silly voice made the joke just so perfect, even as juvenile as it was. The tiny seats Olgath nobility used were the subject of many off-color jokes in Serentia, but the image of a giant fat-bottomed rikol root squashing one made Amandine laugh anyway.

"When my pants are tailored, they use the pattern for a horse warmer! Sometimes my laundry gets mixed up with the tack!"

Amandine was completely lost to giggles now. She had to set down her knife again, and held her sides as she laughed. Fiona started laughing too. Grendel hopped up on a stool and looked back and forth between them as if they had both gone mad.

Fiona picked up her knife. "I almost feel bad chopping up Ser van Big Butt now," she said between giggles. "Buuuuttt, I suppose that would be wasteful."

A new fit of laughter overtook Amandine as Fiona drew out the word. She leaned forward onto the block to try and catch her breath, but that made the tears from her laughter drip onto the radishes.

"What is going on in here!"

Amandine looked up. Marlette stood in Nous' favorite door frame. Her eyes went from Amandine, to Fiona, to the knife she was menacing the rikol root with. Fiona bit her lip and hid the blade behind her back.

"Are you playing with a *knife*?" Marlette asked, incredulous.

"Leave her alone, Marlette," Amandine said with a chuckle as she finally controlled her laughter.

"And who are *you*, to tell *me* what to do in *my* house, Cook Amandine?"

Amandine stiffened and clamped her jaw to avoid snapping back. She took lessons with the L'Eau girls, but Marlette had made it very clear, even early on, that she did not consider Amandine to be anywhere near her equal. More than one choice retort came to mind, but yelling at the Lord and Lady's eldest daughter would probably only get her dismissed. She didn't have Chef's seniority in this profession to use as leverage.

Marlette turned back to her sister. "Honestly. I was trying to read in the parlor and I could hear your racket through the walls. I thought a crazy person had invaded the kitchen."

"One just has," Fiona said sharply as she stared down her older sibling.

Marlette just frowned. "Your barbed tongue is proof you have been spending far too much time in the company of those beneath your station. Put that down and go find some other amusement, or I..."

"Or you'll what? Ignore me some more? Tell father? Cry into your beau's shoulder about how *mean* your little sister is?"

"I will tell the Taster that you have been feeding the cat again."

"You wouldn't!"

"Test me."

Amandine winced. Grendel was not popular with the Taster. He had already tried to dispose of the cat at least once, and like Kivel, part of the reason Grendel had stayed on as the Manor's mouser had been Serand's insistence. He was too mischievous for his own good, and Taster Nous looked for any reason to get rid of him, despite the love Fiona had for the cat. Grendel was on especially thin ice now that Serand no longer held any sway in the household. For his part, Grendel looked supremely unimpressed with the threat just leveled against him and responded with an enormous yawn.

Fiona folded. She slapped the knife on the table, which made Marlette jump a little, and stormed out of the kitchen, fighting back tears.

"That was cruel," Amandine said. Lord's daughter or not, some things just had to be called out.

"Don't think I am ignoring your part in any of this. A child should not be running our kitchen."

"I'm not a child."

"Are you at majority yet? No? Then you're a child. Just because you've been entrusted with a job and finally grew breasts doesn't make you a woman, Amandine."

"So bullying and threatening people does?" Amandine shot back. "Are you competing with Nous for the 'Most Hateful Person' award?"

Marlette smiled at her and smoothed her dress as she looked Amandine up and down. It was black silk and probably cost more than Amandine made in a year, even with her promotion. Marlette had her mother's figure, but her father's stature. It pained Amandine to admit, but the elder L'Eau daughter was not unattractive.

"It bothers you doesn't it?" she asked.

"What bothers me?"

"That Fredderick dumped you to court me?"

"That's not true."

"What isn't?"

"He..." Amandine struggled to find the words. Had he dumped her? He had said they weren't courting, even though he had kissed her. What *was* she to him?

Marlette's face took on a smug expression. "You still like him, don't you? Men like him will sometimes dally below their station for a lark, but he is in an *actual* courtship now. You'd be better served chasing after that grubby baker boy."

"Gil is not grubby! Your family eats well because of his hard work and mine! Fredderick may not want to court me, but he does appreciate my food! You don't own him! He could change his mind!"

"As if you had any chance whatsoever with a Stolm. Further proof that you are a fool, Amandine."

Amandine shrugged and made the *livette* hand gestures for "sour apples". She didn't know enough of the language to hold complete conversations, but had learned a few words by watching Marlette and her mother speak.

Marlette, in return, made a series of shapes with her fingers that included sharp, snapping wrist motions.

"I have never seen those gestures," Amandine said. "I have no idea what you said."

"That's because my mother doesn't often use language that vulgar. Have fun figuring it out."

She spun and left the kitchen the same way she had come in. Amandine tried not to grind her teeth. Her hands gripped the block as she stared down to hide her anger.

"Sow! Raven! Colorless, stinking..." Amandine growled.

"Milintanth's Mercy," a voice said behind her. "If it's not the cookware, it's the butcher block?"

Amandine blushed and turned to face Nanny, who was coming in through the garden door behind her.

The old woman glanced at where Marlette had retreated and then looked back to Amandine. How much had she heard?

"I just encountered Fiona crying in the garden. She ran away and wouldn't tell me what was wrong. Do you know, child?"

Even though being called a child made Amandine bristle after her argument with Marlette, she didn't blame Nanny. Ursula De'lum had been Lady Gia's childhood caretaker as well. She spoke to everyone in the house, aside from Nous, as if they were a child, and everyone accepted it. Nanny was Nanny.

"Marlette threatened to tell Nous that she's been feeding Grendel again," Amandine explained.

"Oh, now that's unfortunate." Nanny shook her head. "I wish they could find their joy in each other again, but Marlette has something to prove to everyone, only she hasn't quite figured out what that is yet."

"If you say so, sah."

"I do! You do as well, I think. What did that table ever do to you?"

"It... wasn't directed at the table, sah."

Nanny nodded. "That doesn't refute my point one bit, I think."

Amandine scowled, but Nanny just smiled placidly as she almost always did, and she couldn't find it in her to be mad at the old woman.

"Sorry, sah. I hope I didn't offend."

Nanny simply nodded and turned back to the garden door. "I'm not offended, but the table might be. I'll go find Fiona, so don't you fret over her."

With a soft tsking sound, Nanny exited back into the garden and quietly shut the door behind her. Grendel leapt off his stool and dashed out behind her before it closed.

Amandine sighed and looked back to her radishes. She finished the jar and then did the rikol as well. It was late when she was finally done, lacking Fiona's help, but she still had letters to deliver to Serand, so sleeping at the manor was out of the question.

Mister Rikol van Big Butt was spared the knife, however. She placed him on a shelf that sat in front of the door frame leading to the house, so anyone who entered the kitchen would be faced with his lumpy red posterior. With a nod of satisfaction, she turned down the lamps, locked the pantry, and began to make her way home.

The road past the wagon gate was lit along the edges with chunks of glowstone. It was an ore that would glow at night if left out in the sun during the day. The light they emitted was a dull silvery-yellow, and the road was heavily rutted, and so Amandine also lit a small oil lamp that she used when forced to travel after dark. She looked up at the clear sky and followed the stars for a bit as she walked. In the distance, high in the air, a pod of leviathans drifted. They glowed an eerie blue color against the night sky. It was considered good luck to see them after dark, especially on starless nights when the complete absence of light could be highly disorienting.

"Thank you," Amandine whispered. It was foolish. They couldn't hear her. She wasn't even sure if levis *could* hear. But after tonight, she felt like a good omen deserved a thank you.

There was a rustle in the hedgerow. Amandine moved to the middle of the road and turned her beam to the bushes. A field mouse dashed out into the light, stopped short at the sight of Amandine, and reversed course. Just then, Grendel exploded from the same bush, landed where the mouse had been, looked left and right, swatting the ground with his paws, and finally turned just as the mouse disappeared back into the foliage.

Amandine put a hand to her chest to catch her breath and slow her racing heart. Grendel sat on his haunches. He started cleaning a paw and glared up at Amandine.

"I'm sorry, Grendel. I spoiled that didn't I?"

She reached down and scratched his head. The sounds of the night came alive in her ears: small movements in the bushes, a bird calling in the dark, the wind passing by leaves and rattling the shutters on the manor down the hill from her.

The small oil lamp became a ball of fiery light and the glowstones lining the road glimmered like torches. The previously starless sky bloomed with light from hundreds, maybe thousands, of stars in all sorts of colors. Previously so faint that they had been hidden from view, they now bathed the world below in a dusk-like aura. Amandine could see almost to the horizon where the silhouettes of trees stood watch over one of the many creek beds running through the hills. Grendel began to purr.

"It's no wonder you like being out at night. This is beautiful, Gren."

Grendel wove around her shins and when she started walking again, he began to follow her. Amandine turned down the oil lamp; it was practically blinding her now. She stopped occasionally to listen or admire the view. It really *was* very pretty. People feared the night. She had feared it. But Mister Green had once told her the greatest weapon against fear was knowledge. She knew what lay out in the darkness now, and although there were valid reasons to remain wary, the idea of being outside at night no longer terrified her. So long as she had Grendel around, in any case.

At the halfway point, where Grendel usually departed and returned to the manor, he continued along with her. "Are you coming to visit Serand?" she asked. "He has a cat living with him too, you know. Maybe you'll be friends."

Grendel's tail twitched and he shook his head as if to ward off a fly. He moved ahead a little bit as if he was leading the way now. "Oh? So you've been there before?"

Meow.

"Hey, I wasn't doubting you!"

The hamlet was quiet and dark. Many houses had turned in for the night, with only one or two sleepless souls leaving their candles still flickering in windows. Amandine was surprised to find a light still burning inside Serand and Dena's cottage when she arrived. She opened the door and found Serand sitting at the table across from someone she hadn't seen for at least two tendays.

"Kivel!" Amandine said.

The rotund man smiled weakly and waved at her, a steaming mug of tea in his other hand. He opened his mouth to speak but was cut off by a yowl and a loud hiss.

Spice launched himself out from under the table and dashed to where Amandine was standing. He and Grendel faced each other, backs arched, hissing and spitting. A low threatening growl emanated from both cats. Amandine stepped back, unsure if she should try to intervene, but then, just before she was sure blood was about to spill, both of them abruptly sat down facing each other and began cleaning their paws as if nothing had happened.

"Well then, now that introductions have been made." Serand frowned at the cats. "Kivel jus' stopped by fer a visit. Dena be on night watch an' won't be back 'til mornin'. Good thing too, with all the colorless racket."

Spice shook his head and looked back at Serand, slowly blinking his eyes.

"Go on then." Serand waved his hands. Spice stood and trotted outside. Grendel followed him, and Amandine shut the door behind them.

"Hello, Amandine," Kivel said. "Chef tells me you and Sunflower have been holding the line at the Manor."

"Barely, sah," Amandine replied. She frowned. There was a soft slur to Kivel's speech. He slouched a bit in his chair, which wasn't unusual for him, but he also looked disheveled. His dark hair was a tangled mess, and his nose was even redder than usual. Was he drunk? Her eyes turned to Serand. He seemed sober. Although she had seen him drink on occasion, she had never seen him out of sorts with it.

"Pull up a chair, Apprentice," Serand said. "I know yer probably seekin' yer blankets, so we won't burn too much more oil."

She took a seat in the third chair. "Boomer gave me letters to hand to you, Serand." she said. "He was trying to get Dena to take them, but he couldn't find her, probably because she was off watch during the day." She dug into her satchel and pulled the folded papers out. "Here. He said the open one was from his bud."

"Did 'e now?" Serand took the letters and carefully unfolded the strange gray one. His lips moved as he silently read the letter to himself.

"We sure Boomer is a *he*?" Kivel chuckled over his mug.

"What?" Amandine asked.

"He's drunk and bein' crass, fingerling, pay no mind," Serand said absently as he continued to read.

"They're both," Kivel whispered to her conspiratorially.

Serand sighed. "They be neither. Dwarves use whatever male or female words humans around them use based on their own headings. It's jus' ta make us comfortable, see? Among their own, they are all the same. No men, no women, just *Ur'Mord*."

"*Ur'Mord*?"

Serand lowered the letter. "That's who they are. 'Dwarf' just be a label humans slapped on 'em 'cause they resemble something our folk once knew from long, long ago. Same with elves, giants, and lots o' other things in this world. The *Ur'Mord* have been around longer than the giants, even. Ain't Mister Green teaching ye any o' this?"

"Well, yes, but on history days we are still covering Olgothia and Serentia."

Serand raised the paper again and resumed reading. "Yah, that be a long menu, an' not all of it savory."

Amandine nodded. She had about a thousand questions now, but also wanted to know what the letter said, so she resisted the urge to interrupt again.

"I saw a dorf once withou' the beard," Kivel said as his head bobbed. "Was bein' punished for something. Skin was all pebbly. Like a lizard."

"They ain't lizards, drink yer tea, sah," Serand said in a long-suffering tone.

"And their little ones grow right off their bodies! In these huge blisters. They can walk as soon as they pop out too!"

Serand kept reading and Amandine looked back and forth between them. She couldn't help herself. "And that's true?" she asked Serand.

He lowered the letter again. "Aye, it's the only colorless thing he's gotten right s'far. Now, can I finish readin' this colorless letter?"

Amandine pondered that as Serand continued reading. Kivel grew quiet and began to nod off in his seat. He still hadn't had any of his tea. Spice jumped into the cottage through the open window, followed shortly after by Grendel. Amandine put an arm down and wiggled her fingers. Both cats ran up and rubbed their heads against her hand. Spice swatted at Grendel once when he tried to push the smaller orange cat away. Grendel reacted by rolling onto his back. Amandine leaned down to rub his belly, and Spice, content that he had made his point, walked away to lie down on the hearth.

"Well, that's an ominous wind," Serand said as he finally put down the letter.

"Why is that?" Amandine asked.

"Well if I am understandin' the meaning right, Boomer's *Ur'nyre* is goin' ta limit exports to everyone, on account of their own troubles. Didn't go into detail, but they seem willin' to try an' help anyway."

"*Ur'nyre?*"

"A *gyre* is an individual. They use the word like we use 'he', 'she', or 'they'. *Nyre*, is a family. Immediate kin. Parents, children, maybe grandchildren. Past that, there is *Ur'nyre*. That's the clan. The whole crew. Some 'r as small as a few hundred souls. Some tens o' thousands. Boomer's is the Seven Hammers. They're the biggest one, fingerling, so that ain't good news fer trade on the rivers. Boomer's bud, Herric, isn't part of their inner circle or nothin', but they've heard enough rumors ta warrant a warning ta us."

"But his... bud, is still willing to help?"

"If'n they can, yeah, seems so. What's the other letter 'bout?"

"It's for Boomer's child. Herric? The one you're to meet."

"I can do that. I need ta get this carp-fish back to 'is own bed."

Amandine looked at Kivel. He had fallen asleep with his head on his arms, his tea now cold.

"Is he well?"

"I brought him on to my crew as a way ta help 'im out, the poor sod. Bein' let go is makin' him slip back in ta old habits. There's a bite in the cold box fer ya. I'll make sure he gets tucked in and I'll hide 'is bottles."

Serand hauled Kivel onto his feet. The large man woke up a bit. Enough that he wouldn't have to be carried, but he was obviously done for the night.

"Be back shortly," Serand said.

Amandine noticed that Grendel had curled up next to Spice on the hearth-stones.

"I have an overnight guest, I think," Amandine said.

"Maybe longer," Serand said as he guided Kivel to the door. "Cat 'll only follow ye home if they intend to stay a while. Oi, come on ya anchor! Use yer own feet!"

"Good to... Amandin..." Kivel mumbled before Serand shut the door behind them.

The cold box contained slices of lamb roast and a jam tart. Amandine ate the tart, shared the meat with the cats, and then dressed for bed. Her folding cot near the hearth was twice the size of the old one in the warm cellar. She had two squashy pillows stuffed with duck feathers, and a heavy wool blanket. As she curled up into them, she thought about Serand and his trip to Anvilroot. He would be leaving in roughly one more tenday, as soon as the barges came back upriver from Irongate. She wished she was going with him. A new place, with strange people. Blue carrots and smoked meats and who knew what else. Whole new tastes to discover and things to see... and here she was making pickles.

Amandine looked up at the pegs by the door, where her *Olatharr,* a rare Olgothian war knife made from water-steel, hung next to her satchel. She sighed and then closed her eyes.

Patterns and Paths

"Zulathia's martial arts are notable in that they focus heavily on the idea of horse-mounted combat. Masters in their disciplines favor weapons that can reach an opponent on horseback (spears, staves, polearms), disable a rider or their mount (nets, hooks, caltrops), or that can be effectively used while in a saddle (short bows, swalee swords, lances, and flails). Hand to hand styles vary by region, but focus heavily on mobility and speed, rather than powerful strikes. High and jumping kicks, grappling, and counterstrikes are all part of nearly every variation, again playing to the theme of a foot soldier who might be facing cavalry."

- Hevin Crell - Insights into the Myth of a Man Who Defeated an Army, excerpt

"IT'S THIS WAY, Amandine, come on!" Gil said.

Amandine sighed as Gil dragged her through the wall-side alleys on the North end of Stoneman. "Gilly, I am supposed to be here to buy ingredients for dinner, then I have to go to Sister Corbin. I don't have a lot of time today."

"But this is totally lumi! It won't take long!"

"Then why not just tell me what it is?"

Gil looked over his shoulder and made a face. It was the 'because it's probably dumb, but I want to show off' face. He made the same face when he wanted to display some new pastry he'd "invented." Or that time he'd found a nest of kunger beetles and thought they were baby dragons.

Amandine sighed again. "Are we almost there?"

"Almost!"

They turned the corner behind a large smithy that stank of burning charcoal and hot oil. Gil ducked low against the plank fence of the adjoining yard and put a finger to his lips to indicate they should be silent. The yard was attached to a townie house. Single story. The sort a well-to-do craftsman might own, albeit the location left much to be desired. It was surrounded on every side by the smithy, a tannery, and a soap maker. Amandine held her nose and made a face of her own.

"Who would live here?" she whispered as they moved to a gap in the planks. "And why should we care?"

"Telvor Aran! Look!" Gil motioned for her to peek through the gap.

Peering at the inside of the yard was like looking into another world. A riot of plants in various colors filled the space. A clear pond speckled with green fen moss took up one corner, and fruit trees, some still bearing the withered remnants of late summer sweetrinds and gojos, filled the opposite. Paths of smooth river stones wove through the lush garden, and in the center there was a raised wooden platform, like a stage. The planks had been sanded smooth and fitted tight. On top of that stood Master Aran...and Tilly.

Telvor was dressed as he always was, in his plain loose shirt and woven pants, but around his arms were tied scarves. Two black scarves on his left arm, and one green scarf on his right. Tillandra had only one green scarf on her right arm and no black. She was clothed in a manner similar to how Amandine dressed when training with Dena, but her wrap was dyed a beautiful shade of light red, like a sunrise, and printed with a bright blue pattern that resembled flower petals. It made Amandine wish she had one so pretty.

The pair stood facing each other silently in the middle of the platform, eyes closed. Their hands were folded before them as if praying. Then Telvor exhaled, and stepped one foot back. He raised his hands, palms up as though each were balancing a tea tray. His eyes opened.

"Begin."

Tilly exploded into motion so fast it made Amandine gasp in surprise. Her arms swung and stabbed, her body twisting with each strike. She even went up on one foot and *kicked* Telvor in the *head*. Or she would have, but Master Aran was moving just as fast, his open palms deflecting her blows as they moved in a whirling pattern too fast to see. He ducked the kick to his head as though he could see behind himself and then dipped and swung a leg low.

With a soft grunt, Tilly jumped over the sweep and grabbed Master Aran from behind, her arms restraining his shoulders and head. He shifted his weight and she tumbled across his back, but instead of falling flat, Tilly turned and somehow came up on her feet on the other side of him. She resumed her attack and Telvor continued to block her every attempt, though he rarely countered. Finally, one of her fists made it through the pattern, but stopped short of striking her uncle, hovering a finger width from his nose.

"Good," Telvor said simply. He dropped his hands to his sides and then clapped them once in front of himself. Tilly stepped back and did the same.

"Staves."

Telvor held a hand out to one side and black motes converged from the air to form a hexagonal, rune-covered staff. Amandine gasped again. She remembered it. When Telvor had entered the fens to help Serand find her and the others, he had been carrying it. She'd had no idea it was magic.

Tilly trotted over to the edge of the platform and picked up a staff lying on the planks. It was similar to Telvor's, without the runes, and had holes drilled in the ends. As she walked back to the middle, she spun it in a quick pattern with one arm and it whistled in the air.

"It's like the 'Journal of Hevin Crell'," Gil whispered. "That story about the Zulath warrior that defeated an army with only his staff! It's amazing, right?"

Amandine nodded. She had read that book too, after Gil had loaned it to her. Twice, in fact. Dena had liked it also.

Telvor and Tillandra took stances very similar to what Amandine had been taught and then began moving through a staff pattern. The beginning was almost identical to what Dena had been teaching Amandine, but they did it at three times the speed. It continued into an even more complex dance that she had trouble following. Whenever their staves struck, a chime-like sound accompanied the clacking of wood, and Tilly's staff made whistling noises that hummed musically through the air.

"I never knew it could be so beautiful," Amandine said softly.

"She's lumi, for sure."

"I was talking about the fighting, Gilly."

"Oh."

The pattern ended and they stepped apart. Telvor's staff vanished in a swirl of dark motes, like spots you might see if you stared at a candle too long. "Your focus is lacking, Tillandra. But I understand your distraction. Please, go ahead. I know you want to."

Tilly bounced on her toes, turned and looked straight at the gap Amandine and Gil were peeking through. "What'd ya think, Gil? I've gotten better righ'?"

Gil straightened and peered over the fence. "Uh. Hi, Tilly," he said. His face had turned bright red. "That, uh... was really good. Really, really good! Did you know I was here the whole time?"

"Yup! And last tenday. And the one 'fore that. Hi, Amandine!" Tilly waved enthusiastically at the gap.

Amandine stood up and waved back sheepishly. She leaned towards Gil a bit and whispered, "Did you really drag me out here so that you wouldn't feel weird about peeping on Tilly?"

Gil's shade of red deepened.

Telvor eyed them both with a raised eyebrow, but said nothing and turned around to step off the platform towards the house. Tilly ran to the fence, still holding her staff. "I'm glad ya liked it! I usually mess up the las' part. I 'spose I sort o' still did, it should 'ave been a *sebi* and not a *haki*."

"Oh, right! Totally seeby," Gil said.

"We have no idea what you are talking about," Amandine added as she punched Gil in the arm.

"Oh! Well, all o' the traditional staff motions 'ave names," Tilly explained. "An' the dance is a way ta practice 'em all in sequence. There's 'bout fifty o' them."

"I practice that first part with Dena sometimes," Amandine said. "But at a turtle's speed. And I stink at it."

"I cou' show ya some time!" Tilly bobbed excitedly. "Tha'd be fun!"

"I like the way the staff sounds," Gil said.

"It's called a song-staff." Tilly held it up higher for him to see.

Amandine noted that he was totally *not* looking at the weapon. "I like that wrap. It's beautiful. Mine are so plain."

"Thanks!" Tilly said. She pulled it up gently at the top to show the full pattern. Gil coughed softly. "I have to buy them extra long, and double wrap them, or I fall out of them when I train with Uncle Aran."

She spun to show how it was tied in the back around her neck. Amandine nodded. Gil made a faint choking sound.

Amandine eyed Gil sideways and grinned. "Stays in place even when you jump?"

"Yup! See?"

Tilly demonstrated and Gil turned a slightly different shade. Amandine was enjoying this.

"That kick you did was amazing. I wish I was that flexible."

"Ya cou' be, wi' daily stretchin'. I find it a relaxin' way ta start my mornin'," Tilly said. She casually brought a leg nearly straight up and hugged it, balancing on one foot.

Amandine caught Gil's elbow under the fence to keep him from tipping over as he stared.

"Ya feelin' ok, Gil?" Tilly asked as she put her leg back down. The question was genuine, but Tilly was smirking at him.

"He's feeling great, I'm sure," Amandine said.

"Amy!" Gil protested.

"I could show you both another pattern?" Tilly offered.

"I, err," Gil stammered.

"Gilly would love that." Amandine poked at him and grinned. "But I am already late for my errands and need to return to the manor. Have fun, you two!"

"Lumi! I'll go open the gate!" Tilly trotted over to the back fence.

"Amy I—" Gil began.

"Stop being a wimp, Gilly," Amandine said. "Let me know how it goes. But I wouldn't let Master Aran catch you kissing her. I think he's on to you two."

Gil's red shifted to white. Amandine put a hand on his shoulder and nodded solemnly. "Good luck."

"Gil! O'er here!" Tilly called.

Amandine turned and walked away. "Be right there!" Gil called back. She smiled. At least he had stopped stammering.

She hurried to the market to complete the shopping needed for the next two days. Speed was important because she still had to take lessons with Sister Corbin today, and if she finished early, she could return directly to the manor without delay. Sunflower was being incredibly gracious about her absences every tenday, but it wasn't fair to keep making her do so much during those days by herself.

By the next bell she was hurrying to the temple, a full basket under one arm and a salted ham over her shoulder. Sister Corbin did not abide tardiness, and Amandine didn't want any more lectures than were required. She arrived, out of breath, at Sister Corbin's shack, relieved to find it free of dead bodies.

Sister Corbin stood from where she had been kneeling next to her personal shrine and glanced at a nearby sand-glass without turning around.

"Three fingers late," she said.

"I ran as fast as I could!"

"Your failure to track your time and manage it properly is not my concern. My time with you is valuable." Sister Corbin turned to glare at Amandine. She wore her hair down today, something she rarely did. It somehow made her seem older. The strands of white from her stripe seemed to diffuse into the surrounding hair like melting snow. "As penance, you will recite the first three verses of the Dusk Epistle, flawlessly, and then sweep the work area. Afterwards, we will resume the lesson at the temple. Meet me in the Chamber of the Holy Mother."

Amandine was at a loss for words as Sister Corbin brushed by her and strode towards the main temple yard. That she wasn't staying to listen to her "flawless" recitation of the Epistle was not the oddest thing about the entire exchange. She wanted to continue their lesson in the wing of the temple dedicated to Akradath's wife, Milintanth? Milintanth and Ravenex were ideological opposites and their clergy often reflected the divide.

Puzzled over what could possibly be going on, Amandine erred on the side of caution, and after finding a clean place to stow the food she had bought, carefully recited the three verses, out loud, in case Sister Corbin was lurking. Then she took a straw broom and swept out the workshop, wiped down the resting table, and ordered the shelves. Once she was satisfied her teacher would find nothing to criticize, she made her way across the grounds to the large stone stairs leading to the temple.

The inside of the temple was grand, in every sense of the word. Polished marble walls and carved columns held up an arched ceiling that featured keystones as large as wagons. Parts of the temple were still being constructed. Light peeked through on a side wing where a transverse had not been completely walled yet, but it was still awe inspiring. It was the biggest building in Stoneman by a yarn, nearly the size of the temple of Ravenex in Artemis. The cost to build it must have been extravagant, and while no one would say it aloud, many wondered at how needful it was when there were so many other things requiring improvement in the small town.

Still, the central gallery with its rows of wooden benches and raised dais felt familiar to Amandine. The statues of Akradath and Milintanth that stood upon it were also in an unfinished state, with a large drop cloth over the latter. Hammers and chisels rang out even as a trio of acolytes sang devotional hymns in an alcove. Only a handful of worshipers were using the benches, but on Godhome, this room would seat half the town, easily, with standing room to spare for latecomers.

The other gods, who did not have temples in Stoneman, were represented at the Shrine of the Revered, on the opposite side of the yard. Amandine visited when she felt the need, but had only attended Godhome services in the main temple a handful of times.

One of the wings off of the main gallery, known as The Chamber of the Holy Mother, was dedicated to Milintanth specifically. All temples of the Holy Couple had such a space, fashioned to whichever one of them was not ascendant at that particular location. This one was richly appointed and easily twice the size of the Shrine of the Revered. A smaller dais, with the sunrise symbol of Milintanth and inlaid in bronze, extended from the back wall. It held a simple altar for devotions, draped in white cloth. There were benches for worshippers also, but a portion of the room was curtained off so that the Healers who practiced medicine here could have privacy with their patients.

Amandine walked past the curtained area, to a small nook near the back, where Sister Corbin was deep in conversation with a silver-haired woman wearing white robes emblazoned with the rising sun in gold thread.

"Ah yes, this is her, Mother," Sister Corbin said as Amandine approached. "Amandine, this is Mother Greymist Jarl, the Bright Light of this Temple. Express proper devotions, please."

With a start, Amandine bowed deeply and touched her lips, then her heart. The Bright Light was the highest ranking servant of Milintanth in each major temple.

Her spouse would be The Seeker of Truth, Akradath's high servant. This wasn't just a high priestess, she was *the* high priestess for the entire region. The nearest major temple aside from this one was nearly a cycle of travel away in Artemis.

Mother Jarl smiled at Amandine as she stood, and it was warm and welcoming.

"It is wonderful to meet you. Having both a Bone Guardian and her apprentice in Stoneman has been a great comfort to those who have lost loved ones recently. We have been too long without. Your work here is appreciated."

Amandine just nodded. She didn't dare say that she was only doing it because she was required to. Greymist's voice had a soft, musical quality to it. She sounded and looked younger than she seemed, as well. Amandine noticed that she was not white-haired from age. The strands were pale silver, much like Mister Green's. She did not have any other elven features, however. Her round, cheerful face and solid build were undoubtedly human.

"Oh, you are Kalebite!" Amandine said. "I'm sorry, that was rude, but your hair is like my *soeje's*. He's also from there."

"Manners, child," Corbin snapped.

"Now, now, Sister, being educated in geography is not a sin," Greymist gently chided. "Your teacher is *Soeje* Arentilinanthian, is it not?"

"Yes, sah. We just call him Mister Green, sah."

"I see."

"May we proceed, Mother?" Sister Corbin prompted.

With a wry glance for Sister Corbin and a wink for Amandine, Greymist nodded. "Indeed. It has come to my attention that, as a Devoted, you are approaching a critical time in your training. You will reach majority soon, yes?"

"A year after the Shiv, sah." She resented the timing. The shortened years did not count as full years when determining age towards majority, and so she would be saddled with Corbin for the difference, until her next actual nameday. That could be half a year or more, depending on how long the shiv seasons lasted. The thought made Amandine's gut clench, but there was no help for it.

"I see. At that time you will be asked to complete your obligations and be accepted into the ranks of your clergy. Now is the period that we begin preparing you for such responsibility. Normally, your Sworn Sister would see to all such matters, but..."

Sister Corbin grimaced as Mother Jarl looked to her. "I must return to Artemis," she said. "A courier read to me a letter from the Night Matron. I am required there, and it can not wait another year and a shiv to see to. I may try to return during the Scorch, assuming any merchant caravans will brave the heat, but barring that, I will not return until after Second Winter. While I am away, Mother Jarl will be seeing to your continued education on what it means to be part of the sisterhood."

"The Matron *wrote you a letter*?" Amandine asked in surprise.

"A hint as to the urgency of the missive, you no doubt understand. I burned it appropriately after it was read to me." As a rule, the Night Sisters eschewed the written word in most of its forms. The fact that a letter had been sent, especially to a member of the clergy not high enough in the ranks to even read it, was *highly* unusual. Just as strange was Sister Corbin's desire to return during the Scorch. Very few traveled during the short, intensely hot stretch between the two Winters. Wildfires were common. Animals and people alike would succumb to the heat without adequate water and protection.

A different thought entirely supplanted the strangeness of it, however. Sister Corbin was *leaving*? A swell of hope filled Amandine, but she tried not to let it show on her face. "What does this training involve?" she asked instead.

"History and tradition," Mother Jarl said. "The Sisterhood is made up of clergy from those who serve each of the Three in the Trinity of Time: Milintanth, Ravenex and Delinkhal. You will learn not only what your responsibilities to your own order are, but how you should interact with your Sisters in the others."

"Lessons and mysteries specific to Ravenex will be reserved for when I return," Sister Corbin added. "But for everything else, Mother Jarl's tutelage will be sufficient."

"I... look forward to your instruction, sah."

Mother Jarl smiled and raised an eyebrow as she studied Amandine intently. Amandine blushed. Did she perhaps know more about how Amandine actually felt than she was letting on?

"Then I will leave you to it, Mother," Corbin said. "I must prepare for my travels."

She made proper devotions to Mother Jarl and then turned and left. Greymist watched her go with a thoughtful expression, but didn't speak. Amandine began to fidget. Finally, when Capucine was out of sight, she turned to Amandine.

"Walk with me a bit?"

Amandine nodded. Greymist led her out of the Chamber and through an arched doorway that opened into a small walking garden.

"Tell me truth. You do not like her, do you?"

The direct question surprised Amandine. "No," she replied.

"My last student didn't like me either."

"Truth? You seem really nice."

"Whether I am kind or not isn't the issue," Greymist said. "What matters is whether the student wishes to learn."

Amandine frowned and looked at the ground.

"Do you wish to learn, child?"

She stopped walking and turned to face Amandine. There was no judgment in her eyes. She seemed completely calm. It was merely a question.

"I didn't ask for this," Amandine said.

"We don't often ask to walk the paths laid before us. What matters most, I think, is what you decide to make of the journey."

Amandine's hands curled into fists. "And what if we wish to build our own path, sah, that was not laid down for us?"

She looked up into Mother Jarl's face, expecting to see disappointment, but she was smiling. It was radiant.

"My last student said nearly the same thing. I think we will get along just fine, Apprentice Amandine."

She started walking again, and after a moment, Amandine followed her. "Who was your last student, sah?"

"My youngest daughter, Silversky."

"And did she find her own path?"

"She did."

"Where did her path lead her, then?"

"She died. Fighting the skellix that recently ravaged the Heartlands."

Amandine swallowed. "I... I'm sorry, sah."

"I mourn her, but her sacrifice helped prevent the deaths of hundreds, maybe even thousands. For that, I can only be proud of her. Anything less would tarnish her memory."

She looked over her shoulder at Amandine as they turned a corner in the garden path. "You have seen one, I hear. A skellix."

Amandine nodded. "I have, but how did—"

"I am aware of the kind of people that have settled in Stoneman. Among the fishermen and sailors, herdsmen and merchants, there are those who have suffered true hardship. Who have faced evil and survived. You possess uncommon strength of character and a brave heart for someone so young, Amandine."

"I don't feel very brave."

"Bravery is less about what you feel, and more how you act in the face of those feelings. You would do well as a Sister of Ravenex. It takes courage to walk in darkness."

"It takes ignorance not to bring a lamp."

Amandine regretted the words as soon as they exited her mouth. It was an incredibly rude thing to say about godsworn, even if Greymist's order was ideologically opposed to Sister Corbin's.

Greymist Jarl laughed. It was not a small laugh, either. She threw back her head with it. The echoes reverberated in the quiet garden.

"Sweet Milintanth's Mercy," she said. "No *wonder* they chased you halfway across Serentia!"

Amandine tried not to start fidgeting again as the high priestess looked her up and down.

"We will keep things short today, so that you may return to your other duties. I am very interested to see what sort of path you carve for yourself, Amandine."

Ledgers

"The three elder Sisters of the Trinity of Time have a troubled relationship. Milintanth and Ravenex, the twins, are quite literally night and day to each other. Their younger Sister, Delinkhal, is often overlooked by them amidst their disputes, but is an elder goddess in her own right. When she has had enough of the two of them, she will interject herself forcefully into their disagreements. While they can barely abide one another, Milintanth and Ravenex both dote on their younger sibling. When she puts herself between them, it often leads to a truce, if only temporarily."

- Sisters Apart: Milintanth, Delinkhal, and Ravenex, excerpt

IT WAS WELL past luncheon before Amandine found herself back on her way to Manor L'Eau. The sun beat down and made her sweat. The ham and the basket were heavy. She stopped several times to switch shoulders. Part of her wished she had tracked down Gil in order to have him ride her back on Crust, but if he was still with Tillandra, then she wasn't going to make herself a wedge.

The rest of the lesson with Mother Jarl had covered etiquette between orders. There were a lot of rules to follow—of hospitality, of seniority, of decorum. Some didn't make much sense, like the one that said if a Sister higher in rank asked you to pour water at a meal, you could politely tell her no if she was in your own order, but must not reject the request if you were Ravenex being asked by Milintanth, or Milintanth being asked by Ravenex. Delinkhal Sisters were not allowed to reject any request for food or drink, no matter the speaker or rank. It felt to Amandine as if, in order to preserve peace, an agreement of mutual annoyances had been settled upon, just so that everyone could be equally nettled with each other.

When she finally entered the manor's wagon yard, Amandine found Sunflower sitting on an overturned crate next to the kitchen door.

"Hello, foal," Sunflower sighed. She sounded tired.

"I'm really sorry." Amandine unslung her heavy basket. "Sister Corbin—"

"I'm leaving," Sunflower said.

Amandine lost her thought. Her complaints about Sister Corbin died on her lips. Sunflower didn't just look tired, she looked miserable.

"What happened?" Amandine reached out and put a hand on Sunflower's shoulder.

"Nous released me." Manor L'Eau had meant so much to her. Grief, like that of loss for a loved one, seemed to pour out of her, but there was also a sense of relief.

"Why would he do that! I can't do it all by myself! Besides, you have been here for years!"

"If'n ya hadn't noticed, Amandine, that mean old tusker don' give much sunshine to Hill Folk. Only one still on staff now, aside of young Bramble, is Maid Lily, and she's stuck to his arse like a leech. As for the rest, you'll have help...of a sort. I weren't jus' let go, I were replaced."

"By who?"

"Someone with longer legs who can reach the cupboards."

"Sun, that's awful! I know the kitchen was not built to accommodate Hill Folk, but you've *always* managed. Was that really his colorless excuse?"

Sunflower just shrugged and looked down at the dirt.

The door to the kitchen opened.

"You the cook?"

The voice belonged to a swarthy woman with dark brown hair tucked up into a headscarf. Her apron stretched across her like a tarp covering a mound of potatoes. Narrow, beady eyes peered past her long nose and focused on Amandine. She didn't even spare a glance for Sunflower.

"Yup, you must be," she said when Amandine didn't answer. "Uppity lookin' Bolath girl with green eyes and a chip on her shoulder. Well, you best dust it off and get that colorless food inside. We have meals to prepare and a shiv to stock for. Hop to!"

She turned and vanished from the doorway. Sunflower shook her head and slid off the crate onto her feet.

"Without even givin' 'er name," she said with disgust. "Nous might have found a match in tha' one!"

"Who is she?" Amandine asked softly.

"Helga Orm, some kitchen matron from Tailknot. Nous 'parently sent for her a while ago. It's a hike from that far South. Watch her, foal, she has a mean streak that makes Nous look like a floof."

"What will you do?"

"Don' fret 'bout me. Hedgehog has a cousin what offered me a job as a shiv gleaner. I had turned it down 'cause the coin was better here, even hard as it was after Chef left. Hedgy is a good man. I'm sure he will help me out."

Amandine knelt down and hugged Sunflower and began to sniffle.

"Oh, don' cry. Don' cry. We live in the same village, I will surely come and call. Hedgehog too, even if I have to drag him by 'is co'orless ears!"

"I'd like that."

"Chin up, foal!"

"What is taking so long, Cook! Get that ham in here and bone it!"

Sunflower released Amandine, nodded, and after wiping her own eyes, walked to the wagon gate with her head held high. Amandine followed her example and entered the kitchen.

She hauled the basket to a table and set it down and then began unwrapping the ham as she watched the other woman.

A pot bubbled on the wood stove behind her as she chopped greenstalk with heavy-handed strokes. Her expression made Amandine think the vegetables had wronged her somehow and she was taking her revenge. She didn't look up as Amandine passed her to get a boning knife.

"I'm Amandine, sah."

"I know."

"And you are?"

"Busy. But if you have a need, address me as Matron Orm."

She still hadn't looked up and had switched from abusing greenstalk to hammering at a rikol root.

"Very well, Matron Orm. Once I have boned the ham, how would you like me to portion it?"

"Ya won't be."

Amandine paused as she began slicing. "What?"

"I said ya won't be. Bone it and leave it on the block."

"I've done it before, I know how to..."

"No."

Matron Orm looked up from her task at last and gestured with her knife at Amandine. The blade made Amandine flinch. Serand would say that you never pointed a knife at anyone or anything you didn't intend to cut. If pointing was required, every cook had ten or fewer fingers that could handle the task. A memory of Birch menacing her with the *Olatharr*, blocking her escape from the kitchen, came unbidden to her mind and she took a step back and looked towards the door.

"Let's get this straight right off the start," Matron Orm said. "You have been a cook, wha? Three tendays, at most? I have been in a kitchen for thirty years.

I used to feed three hundred mouths a day, miners and porters, and how many "assistants" do ya think I had?"

She didn't wait for Amandine to answer. "None. There was a simple lad who took a blow to the head as a kid. He washed my pots and hauled the garbage, but the kitchen was mine. Unless you want the same job, child, you do only what I tell you to do, when I tell you to do it, and otherwise stay off my side of the trail. Lumi?"

Amandine nodded.

"Ya mute? I want to hear you say it!"

"L... lumi," Amandine said. "I won't, um, be on your side, Matron."

Orm held the knife out a moment longer, then shook her head and resumed her thrashing of the rikol root. Amandine wasn't quite sure what she was making. Soup perhaps? She didn't really care to ask. With unsteady hands, she began to de-bone the ham again. It shocked Amandine how much the knife had upset her just now. Chef Brutsche had often made threats, but they were usually ridiculous and only just words.

"When you're done with that, take out the leavings."

"We have a scull, sah. Where is Bramble?"

"The Taster needed hands to move furniture. Don't argue, just do it."

"Yes, sah."

Amandine finished boning the ham and then took the pail with vegetable ends and scraps out to the pigs. Why had Taster Nous hired that woman? It didn't seem like she knew a thing about serving a lord's table. She chopped vegetables like an angry tusker. Was she going to take over the pickles, though? That thought cheered her up a little, but that would also mean no evening visits with Fiona.

When she returned to the kitchen, Matron Orm had put the lid on the pot and was portioning the ham into thick steaks with the cleaver.

"What spices are in the soup?" Amandine asked, sniffing curiously. It wasn't exactly unpleasant, but...

"Pepper, sage, and korel seed."

"Isn't that what you use to hide bad flavors from ingredients that have turned?"

"And what would ya know about it, eh?"

"I grew up in an orphanage, sah. I volunteer at a soup kitchen."

"Then ya understand the need."

"At a lord's table? It's just not—"

"Not what?" Matron Orm said sharply, cutting her off. The cleaver hit the block with a thud that shook the entire surface. "Folk don't hire me when they want braised duck! They hire me when they need every acorn, every sausage, every grain of colorless rice to stretch. Yer aware of the holes in the L'Eau purse, yes? Still planning on feeding them dried sundries and elf-grown fruit during the Shiv?"

"But spoiled food? Surely not. Even the soup kitchen doesn't—"

"Then there is goin' to be a lot of starved folk come Shiv's End!"

Amandine just stood in shock, aghast at the callousness of it. "But the Shiv would be over then."

"You *are* new, ain't ya? When do you think a shiv is worst, child? At the beginning when stores are high, or at the end when all is depleted and the new crops haven't come in yet? Mark me, folks will give a hand away for a pot of soup like this by the time the Second Winter ends. And this one is goin' to start so badly, they might give up a foot too!"

Matron Orm folded her arms and glared. Amandine hated to admit it, but she wasn't wrong. It made sense. But still...

"Sorry, sah. I meant no disrespect."

The large woman nodded. "Better manners than I was led to believe, even if stupid things seem to exit yer mouth at the regular. I have a list that needs approval from the Lord. Not the Taster, mind, I was told to expense Estevan directly. Take it to his study and then hurry back here. We have work to do!"

She pointed to a sheet of rough paper that had been drawn up like a ledger near the oven. Amandine took it and scanned the contents. It was a list of ingredients for making a variety of stews, soups, and for preserving meat and vegetables. Much of the list had already been approved by the Taster before Serand had left, but there were numerous changes.

Amandine looked to Matron Orm, but she had already gone back to dissecting the ham and completely disregarded her. Restraining a sigh, Amandine took the servant's hall to the stairs. She usually only went to the upper levels of the manor for lessons with Mister Green, and had never seen the inside of Lord Estevan's study. The halls seemed even quieter than usual, with the reduction in staff.

When Amandine approached the door to the study, anxiety twisted her stomach. Had her and Sunflower's work not been good enough? Would Lord Estevan be upset with her? He was difficult to read, sometimes. Aloof and detached. Never cruel, but not exactly friendly either. She knocked twice to announce herself.

"Come."

For how well ordered the rest of the manor was, Lord Estevan's space looked like a pack of cats had fought in it. An odd assortment of books stuffed the shelves and the small settee was piled high with clothes, both folded and unfolded. Stacks of paper, rolled scrolls and empty bottles covered the tables, some of which had tumbled to the floor. The writing desk was similarly arrayed. Lord Estevan had cleared an area large enough to write, as he was doing now, but it seemed as if at any moment, a random arm movement could create a landslide of books and paper.

Amandine glanced up at a slate on one wall that was covered in numbers. The neat chalk handwriting above each column identified it as a hastily drawn ledger, similar to the one Miss Jacinda used at the soup kitchen to track supplies and funds. She frowned. If it was correct, then the L'Eau's were doing worse than she assumed. The debt number was much, *much* higher than the income number. She'd had no idea things were this bad.

"Pardon me, sah," Amandine said. "I have an expense request from Matron Orm, the new cook. It's mostly things the Taster already approved for Chef Brutsche, but she's made changes."

He didn't glance up from what he was writing. "Put it there," he said, without giving any indication of where "there" was.

The request swayed in Amandine's hand as she waffled about which stack of papers she was supposed to deposit it onto. Her delay finally made Estevan look up. "There," he said, pointing to a short stack next to his elbow.

He seemed exhausted. She didn't know him all that well, but Amandine recognized the look of someone who was wrung out and ready to give up. "I'm sorry, sah," she said as she placed the paper on the pile.

"For what?" he asked as he went back to writing.

"That all of this has happened to you and Lady Gia and the girls. It doesn't seem fair."

He looked up at her with an incredulous expression. It softened after a moment. "Unusual to hear kind words about high born people from the lips of the common folk. It's so rare that part of me at first thought you might be making a jape. That said, you never stuck me as the type to give false sympathy. So... thank you, Amandine. For what it's worth, you have always done a good job here. Chef Brutsche's and Gia's faith in you was not misplaced."

Amandine opened her mouth to reply, but Estevan had already returned to his letter, and so she decided to let it lie. She hated that Sunflower had been let go. She had done a good job also, but that had been Nous, not Lord Estevan. Bringing it up would likely only cause more trouble. She bowed politely and left the study.

Before she reached the stairs, a familiar face poked out of a nearby room.

"Oh! It's you!" Fiona said. She stepped out into the hallway. "What are you doing up here?"

"Running an errand for Matron Orm."

"Oh, that new cook from Tailknot? She's sort of scary."

"That's one way of putting it." Amandine recalled the knife and shuddered.

"I'm sorry they let Sunflower go. I really liked her breakfasts. But I am glad it wasn't you. When I heard the Taster had replaced a cook..."

"Nope, still here," Amandine said with a weak smile. "Although I don't think the new Matron is going to let me do much cooking."

"But why?"

"Because I am a child."

"Horse shite."

Amandine blinked. She had never once heard Fiona say anything so crass. Her expression must have betrayed her amusement, because Fiona blushed and quickly continued.

"It's a perfectly appropriate thing to say about such an unjust opinion. Your cooking is very good. She has no idea what she is talking about!"

"Don't tell her, but I sort of agree," Amandine said in a whisper.

Fiona giggled. "I had to hide Mister Rikol van Big Butt. I was afraid that Matron Orm would add him to a soup. The Taster commented on it too. Did you put it in front of his door to the kitchens?"

Amandine nodded and grinned.

"That was really funny!" Fiona said with a laugh. "I dressed him in some old doll clothes and I have been hiding him in Marlette's room. In her wardrobe, behind her mirror, and elsewhere. She keeps tossing him out and I find a new place for him. She'll get an eyeful the next time she opens her sock drawers."

"Oh gods, I can just see her face!" Amandine couldn't help it, she laughed in spite of Orm. The idea of Marlette being ambushed by the root's lumpy bottom as she got dressed nearly brought tears to her eyes. "Grendel followed me home a couple of nights ago," Amandine added. "He seems to have made friends with Serand's cat, Spice."

"Oh! Oh, that's good news. I was beginning to worry over where he had gotten to."

"I didn't take him," Amandine said. "He really came on his own and refuses to leave."

Fiona shook her head. "No, it's alright. If he's with you and Chef, I know he'll be cared for. I'm just glad he's safe!" Her expression grew dark. "You know, I'll bet it was her!"

"Who? What?" Amandine asked, confused by her sudden shift in temper.

"My *sister*." Fiona imbued the word with unusual venom. "I heard her complaining to father about how a child shouldn't be running the kitchen. That we needed someone experienced to prepare for the Shiv. I can't *believe* her!"

Amandine frowned. "Well, maybe, but Matron Orm has dealt with hard shivs before, so—"

"Don't you dare defend her!" Fiona snapped. "Marlette's always been awful to you, Amandine, and it's not right!"

"Yes, well." Amandine's mouth twisted into a grimace. "She's probably still sore that Fredderick had been courting me before her."

"Wait, what?" Fiona's look of complete surprise caught Amandine off guard.

"Marlette didn't mention that?"

"She doesn't exactly talk to me a lot lately. I had no idea that... that you..."

"It's... complicated," Amandine said, in an attempt to change the subject. "He's handsome and I like him, but he's such an idiot! Maybe Marlette *should* have him."

Fiona nodded, but was chewing her lip like she did when mulling over a hard question from Mister Green. "Is he really that awful?"

"He's not cruel, he's just dense as derby dough. I don't know what to do about him."

"Oh."

"Yeah."

"Do you think it would be ok"—Fiona asked—"if I came to visit Grendel? When I am out riding?"

Amandine's smile grew. "I think he'd really like that."

Farewells

"Shiv preparations vary slightly from region to region. Some areas at higher elevation prepare for dense snowfall and a longer freeze. People in lower, warmer climes often contend with flooding, or temperatures so high that it's unsafe to be out in the sun. All of them, though, prepare food for long storage. Starvation is the biggest threat shivs pose, and so it is where most communities focus their efforts. Because shivs can vary in length, wise communities often store more than what is strictly needed, as the end of a shiv tends to be more lean than the beginning of one."

- Lecture Notes, First Starday, Low Summer 1202

MORNING SUNLIGHT PEEKED through the cottage's curtained windows. Amandine blinked and sat up in bed. Grendel lay beside her on Dena's pillow, curled into a ball. When she shifted, he stretched his front paws and rolled onto his side, but continued to snooze.

Serand and Dena had taken a room at the Golem last night, and Amandine had been allowed the bed. The wool stuffed mattress held heat like an oven, and she was loath to remove herself from it, but she needed to start her day.

"Let's go, lazy butt." She poked Grendel. He opened one eye and just stared at her, but didn't move. "Unless you want to hunt for breakfast, you had better be in the kitchen before I leave."

She rose, washed her hands and face in a bowl on a night stand, and dressed for the day. She really should go outside and exercise, but without Dena to prod her, Amandine didn't feel like it. Instead, she used the extra time to practice making fried eggs. The egg crate in the cold box was only half full. She would need to visit the hamlet market circle before Godhome to buy more. As much as Serand cooked with them, he didn't raise his own chickens. He and Dena weren't home often enough during the day to properly care for them. Perhaps that might change now... no. Amandine didn't want to think about that. His forced departure from Manor L'Eau still made her want to cry.

Serand. Amandine considered his journey as she started the woodfire for the stove and heated a pan. The barge heading up river to Anvilroot would be here today. It might be cycles before he was back again, hopefully before the Shiv started in force and further stores were lost to slimes. He had taken Spice with him. The old cat had hopped up in the cart last evening and sat on Dena's lap, refusing to move. Maybe she would return with him, but Amandine had a feeling Spice was going wherever Serand went, and that was that.

Soon, the kitchen filled with the smell of cooking eggs and frying sausages, and Grendel, predictably, stuck his head out of the bedroom with ears forward as if on the hunt.

"Don't worry, I made some for you too," Amandine said as she turned the links in the pan.

Meow.

"Yes, and some eggs."

Grendel jumped onto Serand's empty chair and watched her work. Amandine used a spatula to carefully turn the eggs and dusted the cooked side with a mixture of salt and greensprig. She examined her work and nodded in approval. They would be good this time, she hadn't overcooked the yolks. She wondered what Sunflower would say when she mastered her recipe for fried eggs. The thought of going back to the manor's kitchen with Matron Orm instead of Sunflower made her feel tired. She tried to stop thinking about it.

Amandine was sitting down with her breakfast, and had set a small plate on the floor with nibbles for Grendel, when the door opened and Dena walked in. She was clothed as she had been last evening, with a traveling cloak wrapped around her "best" light gray dress and soft calfskin boots. She didn't wear those very often. Only on special occasions.

"I didn't expect you back so early," Amandine said. "There is some extra if you're hungry."

"Oh gods, am I!" Dena hung her cloak and fetched a plate to serve herself.

"Did Spice come back with you?"

"Of course not. That old furball and Serand are practically brothers."

"Did his ship leave already?"

"No, it won't be loaded and departing until well after high bell. But I didn't want to be a lurk. Long goodbyes make Serand frumpy. I said my goodbyes last night. Multiple times. And again this morning."

Amandine turned red and stuffed an egg in her mouth. Dena really had no decorum when it came to discussing private matters. She was pretty sure by the amused expression on her face that she had purposefully said it just to make Amandine blush.

Dena let the subject drop as she sat across from Amandine. "How are things going at the manor? Made inroads with the new cook yet?"

With a heavy sigh, Amandine set her fork down. "No. It's been four days but feels like four tendays. She's bossy, and rude, and—"

"So, like Serand."

"No! That's just it. I mean, Serand can be those things when he's Chef, but..." Amandine paused and thought about the differences in the two people. They did have some similarity on the surface. "He's a better cook, for one. Yarns better. It's not that Matron Orm is terrible, but she's like your Aunt Mari. She cooks to feed, not to delight. It's very plain... and stingy."

"Sounds like she'll be good to keep their stores intact through the shiv."

"Maybe, but more than that, she doesn't trust me. I barely get to cook anything anymore. I just help Bramble all day and fetch things. It's like... like..."

"Like you've gone back in time a year," Dena finished for her.

Amandine nodded and frowned at her plate. "Yes. Exactly. At least I don't have to make pickles anymore."

She had lost her appetite. Amandine pushed the uneaten half of her sausage around. Grendel's head tracked it from where he was sitting on the floor. Dena was quiet for a moment, watching Amandine as she ate her eggs.

"This is good," she said, pointing at the plate with her fork.

"Thanks."

"Serand gave up his position so that you could challenge yourself and continue to grow," Dena said. "That's not a guess—he told it to me straight the day he stepped down."

"He left to help me?"

"Sure. He had some doubts, but more than that, he sees your potential, Amandine. He wants you to succeed. It seems to me that if your position is now causing you to backslide, it might not be the place for you anymore."

Amandine looked up. "Are you saying I should quit my position at Manor L'Eau?"

"What is keeping you there? Serand is gone. Kivel and Sunflower have left. And most importantly, you aren't being challenged anymore. That was the entire colorless point, Amandine!"

Amandine nearly mentioned Fiona, but stopped herself. Her friendship with the younger L'Eau girl was nice, but was it really a reason to stay on at a place where she was miserable? If she left, though, it would really upset her. She hated that thought.

"I don't know," Amandine answered truthfully. She had no idea what the right choice was.

"Did you ever ask Serand if you could accompany him?"

"No."

"Why not?"

"It... I... I don't know."

"You *are* his apprentice, Amandine."

"Yes, but I was handed this big responsibility and—"

"That has been taken from you. By no fault of your own! So ask yourself, truthfully, what is the best place for you, right now?"

Amandine folded her arms and considered. Grendel meowed at her and rubbed against her shins under the table. Her eyes drifted to where the *Olatharr* and her satchel hung on their pegs.

"Would you be alright here alone?" Amandine asked.

Dena grinned. "I think it's sweet that you ask. But honestly, kiddo, I will be perfectly lumi. I might spend more time staying in Stoneman at the barracks with the recruits. Sergeant Xia *hates* babysitting the greenhorns. I'll keep up the croft though, don't you worry!"

Her mind racing, Amandine stood. "Then I need to hurry!" Grendel jumped up on her chair and meowed at her. "Sure, Gren, go ahead," Amandine muttered as she made a list of things she would need in her head. Grendel snatched the half sausage off her plate and ran under the cot with his prize.

"You still have five bells. It will take you some time to walk there. Juniper is staying with Bertrand and Jacinda while Serand is away," Dena said as she cleared the plates.

"I'll need my extra clothes, wraps, undergarments. My knives. Maybe I should bring some spices?"

"Slow down!" Dena laughed. "Just give me a moment."

She pulled a chair to the middle of the room and stood on it to reach a set of planks built across the rafters. Spare blankets, tools and other seasonal things were stored there. She pulled down a backpack. It was well-crafted from stitched leather, shiny with infused oils to make it water resistant. It had thick shoulder straps and multiple pockets sewn onto the outside around the center bag, which was stuffed full of something.

"I made this up shortly after Serand decided to take on this errand for the town. I wasn't sure if you would need it, and I felt like giving it to you would force you to make a decision rather than you making one for yourself. But since you've decided..." She stepped off the chair and handed it to Amandine. "Here."

Amandine gaped as she opened the center pouch and found it filled with everything for a journey. Folded clothes, tins of basic spices, a roll of oilcloth, a flint block and steel striker, a metal wedge for splitting firewood and a small hammer. There were also two books: one was a copy of the treatise that Mister Green had written on elementals, the other was a lexicon—the book Amandine used to practice her runes and letters.

"Where did you get the clothes?" Amandine asked.

"I bought three new sets for you. Things better suited to traveling than your kitchen clothes. Sturdy. Wraps and underclothes too. It's all there, kiddo."

Amandine dropped the backpack and threw her arms around Dena. "Oh, gods, I don't know what to say!" She felt a swell of emotion as she hugged the taller woman. Strong arms hugged her back. The embrace was filled with warmth, and love, but also fear. Dena was worried, even though she didn't show it.

"I'll be fine," Amandine said. "Please don't worry. I'll watch out for Serand too!"

Dena laughed, her fear melting away. "I don't doubt it! He may act like a grumpy wumpus when he sees you, but I think he'll be really pleased that you are going, Amandine."

"He won't be mad?"

"Not at all. The thing about Serand is he is full of wise advice, but won't ever tell you what to do if it's not his business. I think maybe he was waiting for you to bring it up, but when you didn't..."

Amandine nodded. "I think I understand that. That's another reason he's better than Matron Orm."

"Then change boots and hurry up and go catch him!"

She let Dena go and ran to the bedroom to swap her shoes for the heavier boots she owned. When she came back out, Dena was standing by the door with her coat and the backpack. She helped Amandine into both of them, and hugged her once more, kissing the top of her head.

"I'll miss you," Amandine sniffled.

"I'll miss you too."

"I don't know what Mother Jarl will do if I leave. I am supposed to be training with her while Sister Corbin is away."

Dena let her go and rubbed her chin thoughtfully. "Well, I can't say I am well acquainted with the godsworn in Stoneman. I would skip devotions on God-home to go fishing, to be honest. But she has a reputation for fairness. Speaking for myself, I don't give a hoot what colorless compromise Everdawn chose to make. You are legally our ward, and legally Serand's apprentice, and the Ravenex biddies can go scratch."

"Maybe I should still tell her," Amandine said. "It feels wrong to sneak off."

"That's between you and the gods, kiddo."

Amandine nodded and reached for her satchel, but found Grendel beneath it. He lifted his front paws, grabbed the bottom of the bag and meowed at her.

"I think someone wants to go with you," Dena said with a laugh.

Amandine took the satchel off the peg and opened it so Grendel could climb inside. He tried to squeeze into the pouch, but only fit after she moved her notebook and knives to her backpack.

"You get any wider and you're walking!" Amandine said as she lowered the flap. Grendel stuck his head out and sniffed the air in anticipation.

Dena lifted the *Olatharr* off its peg and handed it to Amandine. She took it and held the sheathed knife across her hands for a moment. Yes, this is what it was meant for, and she would need all the luck she could get. Amandine slung the strap over her shoulder so that it hung opposite her satchel.

With a deep breath, Amandine opened the door and walked out. Then she ran. People in the hamlet called out to her as she passed them, but she gave them little more than a wave. As she passed the bakery, Gil shouted to her.

"Oh gods! Are you going to Anvilroot too? Dena said you might!"

"Yes!"

"Bring me back a gift!"

Amandine laughed and waved as she rounded the corner. She hadn't felt this good in *ages*. Not since she had nailed that surprise breakfast for Lord Miller. Her legs moved as if they could run forever.

As she crested the hill before the Manor, though, she began to have some misgivings. Fiona really would be sad that she was leaving. And Grendel was going with her. She thought about not stopping, but at the last moment hauled up her courage and turned through the wagon gate. It was near eighth bell. Fiona would be at lessons with Mister Green.

She opened the door to the kitchen and Matron Orm stood up from where she was checking something in the oven. "There ya is! It's half a bell 'til breakfast! I need ya to set out plates."

"Do it yourself, sah," Amandine said as she passed through without stopping and entered the servant's hall.

"You little scab! The Taster will be hearin' 'bout this!" Orm's voice shouted from behind her.

Halfway to the stairs, Amandine ran across maid Lily. She and Bramble were the only Hill Folk left on staff, but Nous seemed to like Lily, possibly because of her perpetual sour attitude.

"Maid Lily, please tell the Taster—"

"Tell me what?" an oily voice said from a side closet. Taster Nous emerged, holding a box filled with Autumn dishware.

"Oh! Excellent. Taster, it is my pleasure to tell you, you get your wish. I am leaving the staff. Immediately."

Taster Nous genuinely looked surprised at the pronouncement, but quickly recovered his composure. "I see. Don't expect any pay this tenday on account of your short notice."

Amandine waved a hand. "Lumi. I am going to go speak to Fiona."

"No, you will see yourself to the door, urchin."

"Wrong." Amandine rounded on him. "I am still a ward of this House and a student of Mister Green's. And since I am no longer in your employ, I don't have to do a colorless thing you say. Luminous day, you dusty kobold."

Nous' face purpled and he began to sputter with indignation. Lily looked at Amandine as if she had sprouted horns, her mouth agape. Amandine just smiled at them both and hurried to the stairs.

She found Fiona right where she expected to, in the upstairs library. Strangely, Marlette was not there. Which was just as well, as far as she was concerned. Fiona was standing across a table from Mister Green. A silver disk lay on the tabletop. Both of them had their eyes closed.

"A moment, Amandine," Mister Green said softly. "Fiona. Are you holding the thought like I instructed?"

"Yes, *soeje*."

Amandine was used to Mister Green seeming to know when she came in, even when not looking, but had no idea what was going on, so she stood just inside the door and kept quiet.

Suddenly the silver disk popped up as if someone had jostled the table. Fiona jumped as it clattered back to the surface.

"Colorless night!" she swore.

"As I thought." Mister Green opened his eyes.

"Does this mean...?" Fiona's voice trembled.

"Indeed. You, Fiona L'Eau, have the potential to learn magic. It will take a great deal of work and study. You are of the subset of humans who can be taught, but do not manifest the ability innately. Therefore—"

"I CAN DO MAGIC!" Fiona shrieked.

She ran over and grabbed Amandine by the shoulders and shook her. "Did you see! Did you SEE! I moved the plate!"

"I... that's..." Amandine wasn't sure what to say. Fiona just hugged her and then ran to embrace Mister Green. He accepted it with a long suffering expression. His dark swirling eyes seemed to be distracted, however.

"Yes, yes, child. It's not common at all, you understand. That I would find two in the same house, even more so."

"When do I start lessons?" Fiona asked excitedly.

"Immediately, assuming I receive the proper permissions from your noble parents. I do not foresee them preventing you, Fiona. Having a mage in the family, despite popular sentiment against practitioners, will be seen as a great boon to them, I have no doubt."

Fiona stepped back and collapsed onto the stool she normally sat on when taking lessons. "I... I'm a mage."

"You are what my people call a *baikai*. An untrained neophyte. This is a wonderful thing, but will come with its own perils. I will endeavor to make sure, at the very least, that you will never be a threat to yourself and others."

His words seemed to have a sobering effect on Fiona. She had been educated, as had Amandine, on exactly how dangerous magic could be when used improperly. Even a trained mage could be a disaster if they acted selfishly or without caution.

Mister Green finally turned his gaze to Amandine. He seemed to note her appearance, especially the knife. "Ah, so you have decided to follow him after all."

Fiona looked at Amandine as if coming out of a daze. Her eyes latched onto Amandine's backpack. "Wait... you're leaving?"

Grendel stuck his head out of the satchel and glared up at Mister Green. He hissed.

Mister Green bared his teeth back at the cat. Grendel retreated inside the satchel. Mister Green grinned in a slightly feral, unnerving way. "I will go to the Lord's study and speak to him, Fiona," he said, looking away from the bag.

He walked past Amandine and patted her on the shoulder before closing the door behind him. Fiona didn't rise from her seat, but glanced up at Amandine with a stricken expression.

"I... I have to, Fiona," Amandine said. "I'm his apprentice, and there is nothing left for me to learn here. Matron Orm won't teach me. She won't even let me fry eggs."

Fiona nodded. Tears welled up in her eyes.

"Please, don't cry!"

Still sniffling, Fiona crossed the room to stand in front of Amandine. Grendel poked his head out of the satchel again and looked back and forth between them.

"Maybe Grendel should stay here with you—" Amandine began.

Fiona shook her head and reached out to scratch Grendel's ears. "No. He followed you, Amandine. If I am really going to be an apprentice mage, I won't have time to care for him, and Nous hates him. He is safer, and happier, with you."

Grendel began to purr. Fiona smiled. She had stopped crying.

"I sort of knew you would leave when that woman took over. Her soup is terrible, by the way. I have been sneaking into the kitchen to make my own food after she leaves for the day."

Amandine smiled back. "Really? Then, here, take this." She fished in the satchel under Grendel and pulled out the key to Chef's pantry. "This opens the locked pantry. All of the contents belong to your family anyway, and Orm wouldn't know what to do with any of it. She might just throw it away out of ignorance. Some of it is really valuable to the right buyer. If you don't want to cook with it, sell it to help your family."

Fiona took the key and looked at it for a moment. "Thank you, Amandine."

"Like I said, it's your family's—"

"That's not it."

She leaned in and kissed Amandine on the cheek. "Travel safe. Learn amazing recipes. And when you return home, I want to hear all about it!"

Silver Mountain

"Although it is common for the wealthy to have their children tested for magical talent at a young age, the limited number of magicians compared to the total population means that many people go through life without ever knowing their own potential. The disparity in testing is also why many high ranking mages are former members of the nobility, or from wealthy families. Rarely, a youth will manifest the ability to create magic spontaneously, although this is more common in fae, and those humans that share bloodlines with such. Most, even if they possess the talent, must be trained to unlock and harness it, and even then, the level to which they might employ magic is ultimately limited by their natural connection to it. Some may never be able to do more than create small balls of light, or levitate objects."

- Lecture Notes, Third Fireday, High Winter 1202

AMANDINE ENTERED STONEMAN a bell before High. The barges were in, so the streets were full to bursting with merchants, caravanners, sailors and more. Town guardsmen stood at the open gates, inspecting incoming cargo and taking portage fees. They kept an eye on foot traffic as well, but one of the guards, a Hill Folk woman named Primrose, was a friend of Dena's, and she waved Amandine through with a wide grin.

"Goin' on a hike, little duck?" she asked as Amandine passed. Her fiery red hair was cut shorter even than Amandine's, and stuck up on her head like a layer of fuzz. Her freckles were so dense, they wrapped her nose like a brown stripe. Despite her cheerful appearance, the maul over her shoulder probably weighed as much as Amandine, and Primrose could swing it one-handed.

"I am going to Anvilroot with Serand!"

"Oh my, that's excitin'! I hate boats myself. Came here from Waterbeetle as a lass and won't even get on the ferry to visit my mum unless I'm drunk."

The guard on the other side of the gate saw Amandine and called out from across a line of carts he was inspecting.

"She need that bag checked, Under Sergeant?"

"Nah, yeh green potato! This 'ere is U-sarge Dena's daughter! We're jus' jaw-in'!"

The other guard, who seemed to be new, made a hasty salute and went back to his business.

"Gods, I wish you wouldn't introduce me like that." Amandine cringed as the novice guard peered curiously at them.

"Why not? Is truth! She an' that salty man o' hers 'dopted ya, yah?"

"Yeah."

"It makes her quail too," Primrose confided in a lower voice with a smirk. "I'm not only tormentin' you, flower."

"I see, well, my ship leaves soon, so..."

"Yah, get 'long now! Have a safe trip!"

Amandine pressed through the busy streets as quickly as she could without jostling anyone. She was used to slipping through crowds, but the large pack on her shoulders made it incredibly difficult.

Her feet slowed as she passed the Temple of Akradath. The huge wooden doors at the top of the polished stone steps were slightly open and soft singing emanated from within. It wasn't Godhome, but there were prayers led on Third and Fifth, as well as on Stardays. Amandine knew she should inform the Sisterhood what she was doing, but worried that Mother Jarl would try to prevent her from going with Serand. Still...

She cautiously made her way up the steps and peeked through the open doors. A small group of acolytes was singing in one of the alcoves, a high-pitched rendition of a devotional to Milintanth. An older man in white robes who was lighting candles near the door spotted her.

"You! You are Mother Jarl's new student, yes? The Brutsche girl?"

Amandine started at being suddenly addressed with Chef's name. It was, legally speaking, hers now as well, but no one ever addressed her by it. "Oh, um... I suppose I am, sah. And yes, I am Mother Jarl's student," she paused awkwardly and tugged at her backpack straps. "Is she in? I need to speak to her."

"No, lass. The High Priestess left nearly two bells ago. Said she had business with an old acquaintance. I expect she will be back by High Bell."

Too long. Amandine would miss her boat for sure if she waited. "I'll return later, then. Thank you, sah."

The man nodded and smiled as she ducked back out of the doorway. That settled that. An attempt had been made to tell her, but Amandine didn't want to be delayed further. Mother Jarl seemed a far more understanding person than Sister Corbin, and they couldn't fault her for going where her Apprentice Master went. Right?

With a bit of a spring in her step, Amandine continued into the town. The added width of the backpack thwarted her plan to cut through the market by sliding between stalls. With a silent curse, she moved against traffic to make her way around the outer ring towards the Southwest gate and the path down to the docks.

"Oh! Amandine? Is that you?"

She winced. Of all the times...

Fredderick stood behind her. Or at least someone who had his voice. The middle-aged man in the black coat and pants was taller and wore a trimmed beard. The hair and eyes were the same, though.

"Another illusion?" She kept her voice down but people in the crowded street around them still looked at her when she said it.

With a grimace, Fredderick nodded towards a side alley between a pair of townie houses.

"I don't have time for this, Fredderick."

"Please?"

Even with the more mature face, his soft brown eyes made Amandine relent. Just a little.

"You get twelve ten counts, then I am walking away," she said as they ducked into the empty space away from the crowds.

He shoved his hands in his pockets and averted his gaze as he spoke. "Look, I've been thinking about what you said. I mean, it didn't make any sense at first, but I can be pretty stupid."

"Agreed."

His lips twisted into a halfway smile. He didn't look bad with a beard. Was this supposed to be an older version of himself? If so, then he would certainly age well.

"Also, I don't want to make excuses, but my life has been sort of strange lately and—"

"Eight ten counts left."

"Amandine, I am really sorry I hurt your feelings. I like you a lot, and I hate that you can't even talk to me anymore. Can we start over somehow?"

"Start what over, Fredderick?"

"Us. I mean—"

"No."

"But... why?" It was odd to see a grown version of Fredderick pouting. It occurred to Amandine why Marlette had not been at lessons.

"Because of this." Amandine gestured to all of him. "You ditched Marlette again to hound me, didn't you?"

"Not really, she's being fitted for a new dress."

"But Dumpling is still covering for you, isn't he? Sitting outside the tailor with an illusion tied to him?"

"Err..."

"Exactly the problem, Fredderick. Everything and everyone is a game to you. I won't stand for it. Your time is up."

She turned to leave, but Fredderick caught her arm.

"Amandine, please wait! You're not a joke!"

"You're right—I'm not." Amandine shook her arm free and kept walking. She paused after a few steps and rounded on him.

"You really should tell the L'Eaus you are a magician," she said. "Fiona passed some kind of test today and Mister Green is going to train her. It's likely that Marlette is the same."

"She... was it a silver disk?"

"Yes."

"And she made it float?"

"It bounced."

"And Marlette did this too?"

"I'm not sure, but Mister Green said there were two in the house, so you do the tallies. You can't keep playing your childish games and hiding who you are. I have to go. I mean to be on the same barge as Serand after High Bell. Goodbye, Fredderick."

"Wait, what? You're going with him to Anvilroot?"

Amandine did not turn around again. She just waved at him over her head and walked faster to make up for the time she had lost.

The gate leading to the docks was packed. Amandine waited with a group of sailors, fidgeting as she listened to the bells ring High. "What is taking so long? We haven't moved at all!"

One of the sailors shrugged. "I can't see it all from here, but it looks like some Halifax barker is arguin' fees with the Union Master."

"Colorless night! I'm going to miss my colorless boat because some carp-brained caravan shill doesn't want to pay loading fees?"

Several of the sailors chuckled at her language, but Amandine was furious. First Fredderick, then this. If she missed the barge's departure...

"To the Pit with that!" Amandine stepped out of the queue and stormed to the front. She ignored the amused muttering from the sailors. There was no way she was going to let this idiocy prevent her from meeting Serand.

At the front of the line, a wagon blocked the gateway. It was being towed by a pair of prongs, who had taken the delay as a chance to lie down. A Hill Folk man stood on the driver's bench and shouted at a human blocking his way.

Amandine recognized the human. Mando Fame was unmistakable, with his dark Olgathian skin and lurid red flame tattoos across his bald head. His folded arms and open shirt revealed a well muscled physique. He seemed completely nonplussed by the smaller man's tirade.

"What you are doing is extortion! You should be paying *me* for bringing trade to this backwater! Taxes have already been paid and my caravan's writ covers portage fees!"

"Portage fees are for roads, sah. You are welcome to turn your wagon about and use those instead. If you want to load onto a ship, you pay the dock fees."

"The Halifax owns the colorless ship!"

"Alas, they do not own the docks. Three in one hundred of the value. Paid upfront. No letters of credit."

"You let that wool merchant offer a letter!"

"He wasn't arguing about the fees."

Amandine scanned the area. The guards didn't seem inclined to intervene. Their job was to keep order, but interference in trade disputes always led to headaches. She wasn't looking for them, though. Sure enough, she found Yasmina, one of Mando's 'assistants,' lurking nearby in the shadows of the massive gate doors. She was a thin, dark-haired woman who shared a passing resemblance to Jacinda Kale, her half-sister. With her pale skin, fancy Zulath-style robes and perpetual scowl, however, the similarities were fleeting.

Mando and Yasmina caused Amandine to have second thoughts. Telling off the wagon driver she could probably manage, but Mando frightened her. Some folks likened him to a criminal, although nothing he did seemed to go against any laws. She approached the nearest guard instead.

"Excuse me, sah. Is there some way foot traffic could get through? There are lots of folk trying to get to their boats."

He looked down at her and shook his head. "Can't. Until fee disputes are resolved, traffic stops. Some folk a while back were using such arguments to smuggle things through without tariff under cloaks and in baskets. So Everdawn has ordered all to stop to prevent such foolery."

"Please, sah! I am going to miss my passage!"

"I really can't, even if you're Dena's kid."

How many colorless people had Primrose told? Grumbling to herself, Amandine approached the wagon. The driver was well into another verse of his diatribe.

"Excuse me! Please, sah, a moment!"

The Hill Folk man ignored her and continued his rant.

"Augh! Will you shut your colorless mouth!"

Amandine hadn't realized she had shouted so loud, but suddenly everyone was looking at her. Mando, the driver, the guards, Yasmina and all of the people in the queue behind her.

"Oi, who is this, then?" the driver asked.

Amandine resisted the urge to cringe at the sudden attention. "Just someone who is going to miss her boat because of your tantrum, sah! Please move and settle the matter with the Union without holding up the queue!"

A chorus of shouts supporting her rose up from the annoyed drivers and sailors in the line behind her. Amandine felt herself swell a little at the encouragement.

"A tantrum? Is it a tantrum to demand fair treatment when these thugs continue to squeeze silver from every merchant who passes through here?"

"Please move!"

"Or you'll what?" the driver said with a sneer. "Whine at me some more? I ain't movin' until I'm allowed to unload my cargo onto my own colorless ship!"

Amandine opened her mouth but didn't know what to say. She had no authority here. As rude as it was, the driver wasn't breaking any rules, he was just being a troll. What was she going to do?

People suddenly surrounded Amandine and she nearly jumped. The sailors she had been waiting in line with had moved up with her next to the cart. The one at the front was a burly human man with nearly white hair and a green sash around his waist. Amandine remembered from some story of Serand's that the sashes denoted rank among a crew. Green would make this one a third mate? Deck leader? She couldn't remember, but he did have an air of someone used to giving orders.

"The kid asked ya ta move so that she don't miss her berth," he growled at the driver.

The Hill Folk man's eyes widened. "Do you see this? Crass intimidation! Guards!"

The guard Amandine had spoken with merely rolled his eyes. "You could just move, wagonmaster."

"I will not stand for such brutish treatment! Call the magistrate! I will—"

He launched into a screed of all of the things he would do, but Amandine had stopped listening to him because the Green Sash leaned over towards the guard and spoke in a lower voice.

"Can we take care of this goon?"

"Oh! Please, no fighting!" Amandine pleaded.

Green Sash just grinned, but the guard nodded. "So long as the resolution is peaceful, we won't intervene."

"Hear that, swabs?" Green Sash called out. "Heave-to the load! Six left, six right! On three and three again! Panie, the prongs if'n ya please!"

With a collective callback of "Aye!", the sailors launched into motion. One of the women, Panie, Amandine assumed, began to unhook the prongs from their bar.

"You there! Don't touch my animals!" the driver shouted.

"Wouldn't dream of it!" she said cheerfully as she quickly undid the harness ties. Amandine noted that she never once touched the animals in the process.

The six largest sailors, two of whom looked to be part tusker, like Heather, surrounded the cart and crouched, grabbing runners and wheels.

"Once, twice, three!" Green Sash called.

"Unhand my wagoo… oh!" the driver said as his entire wagon, with him and its cargo, was lifted from the ground, shifted slightly to the side, and then set back down again.

"Once, twice, three!"

The sailors lifted and shifted again, heedless to the driver's protests.

"Once, twice, three!"

The wagon was moved again and finally cleared the road.

"Cargo set, stand down and fall in!" Green Sash barked. The sailors left the wagon and formed up around him again. He turned to the guard. "Crew of the 'Swirling Leaf,' back from shore leave, no cargo ta declare. May we pass, inspector?"

The guard waved them through. "Safe travels, sahs."

A cheer went up from the line.

Amandine saw Mando and Yasmina approach the wagon. Mando glanced at her, then nodded and grinned as if in recognition.

"Come along, lass," Green Sash said, ushering Amandine through the gate with his crew. Several of the sailors laughed and some passed coins back and forth to each other.

Green Sash pressed a gold crown into Amandine's hand as his crew walked on ahead of them towards where the ships were moored. "If yer smugglin' anything in that pack, I don't wanna know, but Jack's luck to ya."

"What is this for?" Amandine asked, holding up the coin.

"When ye stormed off to set that halfling's britches on fire, a wager was made on whether ye would have the stones to do it. I won three crown bettin' on ya, so a third is yours lest Jack turn his dice against me. Ye could hoist a mainsail from yer backbone, kid! Where are ye headed?"

"Well, I'm not a smuggler," Amandine said. Grendel poked his head out of the satchel and meowed. "Unless you count him. I am going to travel with my Apprentice Master to Anvilroot, but I am not sure which barge he's on. His name is Serand Brutsche."

"Well, dwarven upriver traffic will be at the end of the fifth pier. Ye can ask the dockmen there if they know which berth your master be on. Safe travels, sah."

"And to you, sah! Thank you!"

Amandine ran to the end of the fifth pier, slowing only when she found the first dwarven barge. They were long, wide ships with deep holds and flat decks. There was a rope and pulley attached to a cart that could be rolled from ship to ship to move heavier items, but the vast majority of cargo was lifted up the gangplanks by hand. Loaders swarmed the area, pushing trolleys, hauling crates and rolling barrels to their respective ships. Amandine wove through the chaos, trying not to jostle anyone with a load, and looked about for someone not too busy to ask about Serand.

As she passed the platform for a large, blue painted barge, she actually found him. He stood next to the gangplank speaking to a woman with white hair, dressed in silver robes.

With a soft curse, Amandine ducked behind some barrels. What was Mother Jarl doing at the docks? And talking to Serand, no less! She reached into her satchel and stroked Grendel. Her hearing sharpened and she began to pick up on their conversation.

"...never said that, sah," Serand said.

"Silversky looked up to you and Rally, Serand. I don't blame you for her fate, but I also hope that you have considered past experiences as you once again become a mentor to an exceptional child."

"Aye, I consider it daily, Grey. Ya don't need ta preach ta me what a colorless mess my life used ta be. The girl is safe, an' cared for. She'll be workin' a kitchen an' not some salt-blasted ruin."

"She'd be better off with one of the Orders."

"Oh? Because Ravenex has done such a grand job of seein' ta her education? More like keepin' her in a cave like a mushroom. Left in the dark an' fed shite."

They were talking about her, Amandine realized. Serand was being awfully rude to Mother Jarl. He seemed off put by godsworn in general, but the way he spoke to her, it felt as if they had a personal history of some kind.

Mother Jarl's voice was smooth, but Amandine thought she detected a hint of annoyance. "And allowing a breaker to teach her is a better option? Honestly, Serand, is that how little you respect us?"

"The elf is just teachin' her letters. History. Nature. Things you lot might have thought ta do if not fer the Night Sisters' ignorant ways."

"We had no idea they had her. The Light Academy or the Sisters of Dawn would have also welcomed her. My own order especially."

"Well, ya didn't, more's the shame. She's my ward now, an' Dena's, an' we don't need yer meddlin' in it."

A frustrated sigh emanated from Mother Jarl. "We're not 'meddling'. She has obligations."

"That were forced upon her 'fore she could understand what she were agreein' ta!"

"On that count we will simply have to disagree, sah."

"Bah. Don't be actin' like a jellyfish stung ya when she walks away from yer 'obligations' after comin' of age. Ye all made yer own bed with that, an' I had nothin' ta do with it. Green offered ta take her on too, but she chose *this* course she's on, an' she's not jus' gonna roll over fer yer wishes."

"We don't disagree that Ravenex did a bad job of it. But I still think she has a pious soul. Not everyone needs to be a godless cynic, Serand."

"Better a cynic than a fool."

"Belief in the gods is not foolishness. Do you consider me a fool, Serand Brutsche?"

There was a long pause. Amandine held her breath. Finally, Serand spoke.

"No, sah. That's one thing ya definitely ain't. My apologies if ya took that personal."

"Accepted. Although, if you want to make it up to me, my husband and I really did enjoy those candied gojos."

Amandine shook her head. Dena was right, he really *did* collect them.

"Give him my best," Serand said.

"I will," Greymist replied. Her footsteps began to move towards Amandine's hiding spot. She yanked her hand out of the satchel and scrambled on all fours to get around the other side of the barrels so that she wouldn't be discovered.

After a moment, she peeked over the tops. Mother Jarl was halfway down the dock. Sailors and porters alike stepped aside for her. Some bowed, while others made the sunrise symbol of Milintanth with their hands. It was respectfully done, but still reminded Amandine of how a swarm of minnows parted when a bigger fish swam through them.

"She's gone, Amandine. Ye can stand up, fingerling."

Amandine realized her maneuver to avoid the godsworn had left her right where Serand could see her. She stood, embarrassed, and looked at her feet.

"I didn't mean to be a snoop. I'm sorry, sah."

Spice came out from behind the gangplank and wove around Serand's shins. He squatted down to stroke the cat and sucked at his teeth while he studied

Amandine for a moment. When Grendel popped his head out of her satchel again, he snorted as if in amusement.

"How much did ya hear?"

"Enough to know you don't get along with Mother Jarl."

"Ah, well, we had a disagreement just now, but I consider her one of my oldest friends, Amandine. She's been askin' after ya since I found ya in Bertrand's kitchen, but kept her distance out o' respect for Sister Corbin. What little that crone deserves. Ain't no bad blood between us."

Amandine looked up. She tried not to fidget. "Sah, I... well, I quit my position at Manor L'Eau today. I want to come with you."

"Aye, I guessed that much from how yer outfitted. Dena decided to give it to ya after all then?"

"Only after I decided to leave, sah."

Serand nodded. One corner of his mouth twitched up. It wasn't quite a smile, but he didn't seem upset. If anything, he looked thoughtful. He cocked his head over one shoulder and shouted:

"Permission to come aboard with a new crewmate!"

A blonde-bearded dwarven face peered over the railing. A blindfold of woven cloth was tied around their eyes, but they still looked directly at Serand.

"An' who is ya bringin' aboard, galley-mate?"

"My apprentice, sah! Gonna teach her how ta make a proper *mak'lel!*"

"Oh, aye, tha' 'll be foon ta watch! Yer name, lass?"

"Amandine," she shouted back up.

"Permission granted. Welcome aboard the 'Silver Mountain,' Amandine!"

The Message of Mak'lel

"The Ur'Mord *are physiologically unique among the creatures of Beregoth. They are mono-gender, a trait not found outside of a few very small amphibians and some types of snail. While technically omnivorous, they have a distinct preference for meat, but have also been known to consume stone and earth, especially as juveniles. It is the belief of some that this mineral ingestion in their formative years is what makes their bones so incredibly dense. Their internal organs are tightly packed, and they have the musculature of predators: hard and lean. All of this makes them quite adept at living in the harsh environments of the Deeps, but it has one side effect. Try as they might, dwarves can't swim. They sink like stones. An apt metaphor perhaps, but this also means* mord *sailors are amongst the most fearless, skillful, and some would say crazy, members of their race."*

- Among The Mord, Chapter 4, excerpt

THE WIND BLEW across the barge's flat deck as Amandine stood by Serand at the rails overlooking the river. In the distance, on the far bank, smoke rose from chimneys in the town of Waterbeetle, a mostly Hill Folk settlement that worked the Southwest pastures and the Kindlebrick woods. Serand sometimes went there to buy foraged mushrooms.

"I've never been on a boat this large," Amandine admitted.

"Then we'll get to see if yer gut can handle it. I have some herbs fer water illness if'n it doesn't."

"Wait, but you used to work on boats, why would you have those?"

"Bein' a sailor don't magically change the way yer body grew. I gained a tolerance, but my water-farin' days are past, an' ridin' a boat now sometimes brings it back."

A dwarf wearing a red sash, the first mate, called out something in their growling, guttural language. The other dwarves began to move about the deck, checking line and hoisting a sail.

"We're 'bout ta get underway," Chef said. "Should be smooth as glass until we start into the upstream current. We can stay up here for a bit if ya want, then we should get below to the galley."

Amandine nodded. "What will we be cooking for the crew?"

"Eh, you'll see."

Spice dashed by them on the deck and leapt up on a lidded water barrel. Grendel followed close behind, but when he tried to follow, his legs couldn't quite launch him as high and he ended up hanging from the edge. Spice swatted at his head, causing him to flop back to the deck. With what Amandine decided was a somewhat frumpy expression, Grendel sat on his haunches and glared up at the orange cat.

A passing sailor eyed the cats, said something in dwarvish, or *Mord-seq*, and made a waving hand gesture with the flat of their palm before moving on.

"Why do they do that?" Amandine asked.

Serand looked at the cats and then back out over the water. "*Ur'Mord* like cats. They see 'em as fellow predators, and deservin' of respect. Havin' one on a ship is seen as good fortune. Two, even more so. It was wise ta bring yer tubby friend along."

"I don't think he would have let me leave without him."

He nodded, "Figured. That critter has always been drawn to ya."

The barge creaked and groaned as sailors with long poles braced and guided the large vessel into the open water, away from the dock. Once it was far enough from the pilings that the poles could no longer reach, the dwarves holding them split up onto opposite sides of the deck and drove them into the water. They walked in loops, pushing the boat upstream through the shallows. When a sailor reached the keel, they would haul up their pole from the water, jog up to the bow, and start over again. The ship crawled against the current, but gradually made progress upriver. Ever so slowly, the docks began to shrink behind them. The bustle and noise of Stoneman began to fade, replaced by the sounds of creaking wood, rushing water, and rustling leaves along the riverbank. Amandine felt a swell of excitement.

"When I first left Artemis, Anvilroot was my goal, but I got held up in Stoneman when my coin ran out," she said. "I'm finally going to get to see it."

"What made ye set yer sights on the Dwarven Kingdoms?"

"When thinking of all the places I could go and all the places I could see, Anvilroot felt the furthest removed from where I was. An entire city, an entire nation, under the mountains? Strange bearded people, new foods to try. I guess it just felt like the place to go."

Serand chuckled.

"What's so funny?"

"Nothin', ye just remind me of another star-eyed lad, lookin' ta see whatever place was furthest from where he sat. If you'll take a bit o' advice?"

"What's that?"

"Temper yer expectations. There will be sights an' sounds an' smells an' tastes ta be sure, but ye may be surprised how many do not agree with ya. That's the fate o' those that seek horizons, fingerling. Not everythin' ye stumble across is sugarsap."

"I... sort of knew that already," Amandine said thoughtfully. "Being stranded in Stoneman wasn't what I wanted, but I found something good all the same."

"That's the thinkin'," Serand said with a grin.

They watched the river pass by in silence until the docks disappeared behind them around a shallow bend. The Blue Fens, where Amandine had nearly been killed by the skellix, passed by on the starboard side. Everything was definitely not sugarsap.

"Let's get below," Serand said. "Time ta earn our keep."

"Will they push us with the poles all the way there?"

"When the shallows allow," Serand said as they made their way to the hatch and ladder that led below deck. "There are some places where just the wind will push us, and a few where they will throw out ropes an' have the barge towed by prongs or horses through rougher waters. But the poles get the job done, mostly. The fancier ones have golems ta do the pushin' an' the crew be smaller on such ships. Don't have ta stop at night either."

"Golems? Like the Stoneman?" Amandine asked as she followed him down the ladder.

"Nah. Smaller, made partly of clay and wood. Lighter. Somethin' as massive as the Stoneman would sink a boat, fingerling."

"That's still amazing."

"Aye, it's a sight, ta be sure."

They made their way through the aft cabins in a walkway just barely tall enough for Serand. He actually ducked a little to avoid bouncing his head off the doorframes. At the very back of the boat, in a narrow space against the rear bulkhead, was the galley.

Amandine had never seen a kitchen in a ship before. There was a stove, but it appeared to use charcoal and the firebox was covered in sheets of steel. There was no oven. Three lidded barrels sat lashed to the floor in one corner and a small pantry hung over the tiny work area. A strange black slate was nailed to one wall and a set of knives were somehow stuck to it.

With a cautious hand, Amandine reached out and pulled on the handle of one of the knives as Serand checked the barrels. It felt stuck fast, but with a little pressure, the blade seemed to peel off the slate. She felt an attraction between the metal and the stone, as if the knife were being drawn to it.

"How does it do that?" she asked.

"Lodestone infused iron. Useful thing on a boat. Always wanted a sheet fer my kitchen, but the *Ur'Mord* rarely sell it ta outsiders."

"It's fantastic!" Amandine exclaimed as she pulled a paring knife off the slate and released it, allowing it to be sucked back onto the black surface.

"Right, play with the lodestone later, Apprentice. Time ta cook!"

"Yes, Chef!"

Amandine reluctantly abandoned the slate and hung her satchel from a peg. She started to take off her *Olatharr* too, but Chef stopped her.

"Keep it on ya. Never be without a blade when travelin'. Have it near when ye sleep, when ye bathe, when ye eat."

Amandine nodded. "Oh, alright. You think we might be in danger here, though?"

"From the crew? Nah, not a wit. It's just a good habit ta have when out an' about. Dwarves will never fault a soul fer bein' armed an' dangerous seemin'. They prefer it, in fact."

Chef reached behind a barrel and produced a pair of long-handled tongs.

"What are those for?"

"For later. Go and fill this pot from the water barrel in the hold."

He handed Amandine a small soup pot. She left the galley and made her way back down the narrow hall into the cargo hold. It was full of wool bales that still smelled faintly of sheep. There was also a pen at the back with five nervous looking cattle, destined for dwarvish smokehouses, no doubt. A bored looking dwarf with a dark brown beard leaned on a stool near the cattle with a long prod in their hand. When one strayed too near the edge of the pen, they gently nudged it away with the stick.

"Excuse me, sah. I need water for cooking?"

The dwarf pointed to a pair of large barrels on a rack attached to the bulkhead, across from the cattle.

"Thank you, sah."

Amandine walked up to one, but before she could turn the tap, the boat suddenly listed to one side. Ropes creaked, and the cattle lowed and stumbled. Amandine lost her feet and fell flat on her rump. The dwarf merely adjusted their seat slightly and rode the motion without effect. They chortled in their odd, choking way.

"What was that?" Amandine asked in alarm.

The dwarf shrugged. "Wake from a 'nother skiff. Whirlpool. River dirge. Happens."

Amandine regained her feet. The boat still rocked slightly, making her head spin. She steadied herself on a bale of wool and tried to find her balance. The dwarf watched her impassively, occasionally prodding the cattle away from the edges of the pen.

"Why do you keep poking them?" Amandine asked while she let her knees stop wobbling.

"Cows 'r stupid as dung. Stick their heads thra tha slats. Ship rocks, ye then haf cows wit broken necks."

"Couldn't you just make the slats close together?"

"Sure, but thas a hold fer oil barrels. We just stuck the beef there fer this trip. Usually don' ship meat, but some o' yer farmers are thinnin' their stock. Good chance fer extra coin."

"That makes sense," Amandine said as she resumed her task. She reached for a tap, but the dwarf suddenly hissed.

"Nay tha' one!"

"Why?"

"Thas beer, ya daft bud." They pointed to the rune burned into the side of the massive barrel.

"That's a lot of beer." The beer barrel was three times the size of the one next to it.

"Might las' the trip," the dwarf said, rubbing their nose in a thoughtful way.

Amandine shook her head and filled her pot from the other tap. This one was clearly marked with the rune for water. She really needed to practice her runes more often.

"Thanks again, sah."

"Yah."

She wobbled her way back to galley. Chef had laid out vegetables and was boning a fish.

"There ya are. Get a charcoal pit burnin', slow poke."

Amandine set the pot on the stove and filled the fire box with charcoal. Using the flint from her backpack and some kindling, she soon had a smoky fire going. Chef stopped for a moment to slide open a small hatch that helped vent most of it out the aft of the ship. The galley still filled with smoke however and made Amandine sneeze.

"We'll only light a fire ta cook twice a tenday," Chef said. "Fire on a movin' ship is dangerous. Here, ya need these."

Chef pulled an iron hoop and rod from a cabinet and showed Amandine how they slid over the pot and then attached to the wall. He then gave her a thick pair of mitts.

"So how will meals work if we only light a fire twice?" Amandine asked.

"The soup is fer us. The crew won't be eatin' it."

"They won't?"

"Nah. *Ur'Mord* are mostly carnivores, fingerling. Predators. They can eat a vegetable in a pinch, an' they do farm a variety of mushrooms. But they mainly eat meat. Often raw."

"So what are we going to make for them?"

"Take a peek in that barrel there. The left one."

Amandine walked over and lifted the lid. The barrel was filled with something glossy, like the inside of her treasured seashell. Then she saw it move.

With a shriek, Amandine slammed the lid back on.

Chef folded his arms and sucked at his teeth. "Now that ain't quite the reaction I was expectin'. Ye got a problem with shrimp?"

"It was... white, and shiny... like..."

Chef's expression softened. "Ah. I didn't know that was still hauntin' yah, Amandine, I'm sorry. I promise it's not a skellix in there. Here, allow me."

He walked over and took the tongs off the top of another barrel and opened the lid. Amandine tried not to flinch. She knew it was stupid. Of course it was. A skellix could never fit in something so small, but the way it had writhed...

With a quick snap, Chef snagged a small white crustacean from the barrel and held it up for her to see. It had oversized claws, four of them, and multiple spindly legs. The carapace was glossy white. Long antenna flicked from its head.

"They're still alive?" Amandine asked as the tension began to fade from her shoulders.

"Aye. Best way ta keep 'em fresh."

"And they eat them raw?"

"Yup."

"Gross."

"Aye, well, aside from some smoked meats, the cooked fare we enjoy unsettles them just as much. Part o' being a good cook is knowin' yer ingredients. Part o' bein' a great one is knowin' what yer table likes and given' 'em somethin' special."

He dropped the shrimp back into the barrel and replaced the lid.

"What do we do with them? Just put them in a bowl?"

"Ye can, but that's a quick an' dirty presentation. Like choppin' plain lettuce into a bowl and callin' it a salad. Ye can't argue it ain't, but it's not a very good one, aye?"

Amandine nodded.

"We are payin' our fare by servin' the special meals. We'll be makin' a dish called *mak'lel*. It's a traditional thing. Somethin' ta raise the spirits an' bring some luck at the start of a voyage. But first, we will make fish soup for us. So chop some colorless vegetables!"

"Yes, Chef!"

She peeled a knife off the lodestone slate and took over the small workspace. Chef changed positions with her to tend the fire box and prepare the broth. Amandine chopped carrots and potatoes, greenstalk and armor-leaf. By the time it was done, her fear had vanished. She even went back to the barrel and forced herself to look inside. A good cook knew her ingredients. The wiggling mass of live shrimp was still unnerving, but just like with Mister Green's eyes, knowing what a thing was gave a measure of control over it. She picked up the tongs and flipped one on its back. It was softer on the bottom, like a tiny crayfish, but its oversized claws gripped the tongs firmly and she had to shake them hard to dislodge it.

Chef added her vegetables to the stewed fish and lidded the pot. The lid even had small hooks to keep it in place if the ship moved. Everything in the kitchen was either tied down or wrapped up. Amandine wondered if she would have to tie herself to something to keep from rolling out of bed.

"Adequate. I'll add some extra spice after it bubbles a bit. Ye ready ta make the strangest dish ye've ever?"

"Chef, I cleaned a skellix for a tribe of boglings last year."

"I know!"

"Oh my..."

Chef chuckled to himself. "Wait here."

He returned a moment later with a bucket and the largest piker fish Amandine had ever seen. It was nearly as long as she was tall, with dozens of spike-like teeth protruding from its lower jaw. The mottled brown scales still glistened as if it had just been pulled from the water.

"By the gods, where did you get that monster?"

"Bought it from the monger, Strawberry, this mornin'. Had it in a rain barrel ta keep it from dryin' out. I told him I'd buy the next piker what ended up in his nets, by weight, no questions asked, an' he had a good one fer me!"

"But aren't they terrible to eat?"

"Bah, yer still thinkin' like a human, fingerling. Piker meat is bland, sure. Too bony fer a proper fillet by far. Most fishermen toss 'em back. But to an *Ur'Mord*, a giant predator fish like this'n is a prize. Shows hunter dominance. A sign of strength. It ain't about the flavor, it's about the message!"

"The message..." Amandine repeated. She wasn't sure she understood, so she waited patiently for Chef to get to the point.

"Aye, the message! Humans do it too. Just think ta when ye really wanted ta impress someone with a meal. It's not just about the food, aye? It be also the presentation, the flourish, the side dish an' even the colorless plate. The *message*."

The idea that something like the plate a dish was served on could change the meal had never fully occurred to Amandine. She nodded as understanding settled in. It was like the bunny porridge Bertrand liked to serve her. He *could* place all of the bacon and fruit on their own plate, but put together as a cute rabbit, it altered the feeling entirely.

"Ok, so what's next?"

"Next, ye hold it, I clean it. No space to lay it out in here. Jus' keep its tail in the colorless bucket fer me."

Amandine held the fish over the bucket as Chef cleaned it and scooped the guts out. Then he pulled a needle and thread from his pocket and sewed the belly back up. By the time he was done, Amandine's arms were beginning to wobble.

"Hold steady there," Chef said as he inspected his work. "Got to make sure it's tight!"

"How are we... going to cook something... this large?" Amandine asked as she strained to keep the fish up.

"We ain't," Chef answered. "Adequate. Now we switch. I hold, an' ye get the tongs."

"Wait... you don't mean?"

Chef nodded and took the fish from her and walked it to the barrel. He pried the mouth open and then put his hands in the gills. "Aye. Get ta stuffin'!"

With a deep breath, Amandine lifted the lid to the shrimp barrel. She took the tongs and grabbed one of the wiggling shrimp.

"Good," Chef said. "Try ta get the most lively ones!"

"Yes, Chef..."

Amandine swallowed and stuffed the shrimp into the piker's mouth. She had to tap it down with the tongs twice before it stayed inside.

"Gentle, now! Don' want to crush 'em! They need to still be wigglin'!"

"Err, yes, Chef..."

She put in another, and another. Shrimp after shrimp, she stuffed the piker until its belly began to bulge and she could see the awful, writhing things nearly to the gills inside the hollowed-out fish.

"Aye, that'll do. Little bastards are startin' ta pinch my fingers. Close the mouth and pin it! Then do the gills the same, as I pull my hands out, quick-like!"

Amandine found roasting pins and used them, like Chef instructed, to close up the openings at the head of the fish.

"Right, now I will get this ta where the crew eats. Long room near the prow. I want ye ta go up on deck and yell '*roktul mak'lel*'. Three times. No more, no less."

He made her repeat the words several times until she had the pronunciation to his satisfaction. Amandine tried not to look at the way the belly of the fish moved while she practiced.

"Oh, by the way, can ye swim, lass?"

"Um, yes, sah. Why?"

"I may have boasted that if the cap'n didn't like this dish, they could throw us off the boat."

Amandine gulped and nodded slowly.

Chef nodded back and left ahead of her. With a deep breath, Amandine entered the hold and climbed above to the main deck by the same ladder she had come down.

"*Roktul mak'lel! Roktul mak'lel! Roktul mak'lel!*"

The first mate repeated the call, and dwarven voices across the boat called back. One especially burly *mord* tossed an anchor over the side. The sailors with the poles guided the boat until the anchor chain was taut and made sure it held before pulling them from the water.

The crew formed a line by the ladder. There appeared to be a sort of pecking order as some of the sailors bared teeth and shoved others aside to take places in the middle or near the front. A short scuffle actually broke out, and the winner stood, helped their opponent up, and then took the loser's former place in the line. The Captain, a grizzled-looking dwarf with white stripes in their beard, was at the front, of course, followed by their first mate. The old dwarf looked at Amandine and then nodded down to the hatch she was standing over.

"Oh...uh, right. Follow me, sahs."

Amandine went down first, followed by the queue of *Ur'Mord*. The former rowdiness had ceased. Every member of the line was dead silent. Only the soft shuffling of booted feet and the creak of the hull could be heard. Having them all behind her, moving so quietly, made Amandine feel like she was being stalked. It occurred to her suddenly, that this might actually be the case.

She was relieved when she made it to the dining table. The entry to the room had no door. A long pair of benches, bolted to the deck, flanked a table with a dark gray cloth draped over it. Chef was in the room, facing a corner, seeming to ignore the dwarves as they filed in and took seats silently. The Captain and the first mate sat in the middle, directly across from each other.

After the last dwarf had sat, Chef turned. He held the fish across his arms.

"*Mak'lel!*" he shouted into the silence.

"*Mak'lel!*" the table roared back at him.

He continued with a few more guttural words in their language while he hooked the fish by its pinned gills with a pair of fingers and used his free hand to loosen the mouth pins. Serand produced a small flask from out of his apron pocket. He pulled the cork with his teeth, tipped the contents into the fish's mouth, and then rocked it back and forth. A fizzing sound came from it as he did.

Then, to Amandine's surprise, he leapt up onto the table, walked to the middle and unceremoniously dropped the fish between the Captain and first mate. He took a meat cleaver that had been tied to his belt and handed it down to the first mate.

Chef looked at Amandine. "Give the cap'n yer *Olatharr*," he whispered.

Amandine gave him a confused look in response, but unsheathed her large knife and handed it to the Captain, handle first.

Their eyes widened at the sight of the blade. The old dwarf took it, almost reverently, and held it up to the light. Appreciative murmurs filled the room. They said something in their language. Chef nodded, then stepped off the table.

In unison, the Captain and First Mate raised their blades and swung down, chopping off the head and the tail of the fish. They each grabbed the part they had cut off and tore into it with their sharp teeth. White shrimp, glistening with the mixture of liquor and spices Chef had soaked them in, poured out of either end and scuttled across the table. The rest of the crew produced steel forks with two tines, like small fishing spears, and stabbed at the running shrimp. The successful hunters popped their prey into their mouths whole and growled as they chewed.

Amandine covered her mouth with a hand, but remained silent next to Chef.

"*Mak'lel!*" the first mate roared.

"*Mak'lel!*" the table roared back.

"Right. Time for us to go have soup and leave 'em to it, fingerling. Don't fret over yer knife. It'll be returned to ya," Chef muttered quietly to her.

"To be completely honest, the colorless knife was the last thing I was thinking about, Chef," Amandine replied.

They slipped out and away from the feasting dwarves. Entering the galley again, with the smell of fish and vegetable stew permeating the air, helped settle Amandine's stomach. Chef showed her how a pair of wooden seats folded down from the wall, and then set up bowls of stew for them both with crusty bread rolls.

Amandine ate quietly, trying to process what she had just been a part of. Chef eyed her over his bowl.

"Well, what's on yer mind, Apprentice?"

"You were right, Chef," Amandine said softly. "That was truly the most bizarre meal I have ever prepared."

Vermin

"Water-steel. It has an almost mystical reputation in Olgothian lands. Outside the Wastes, weapons and tools crafted from the complex alloy are considered some of the sharpest, most durable implements one could hope for. The secret to its creation is held tightly by Iron Sand Against Hot Winds, an Olgothian trade cartel. They control many of the foundries and mines along the Eastern Rim, all the way to the Crystal Pit adjacent to The Maw. This monopoly on the alloy has made them wealthier than any other mineral they peddle, and the smiths that know the recipe are so loyal to the Trade Prince that none has ever divulged it."

- The Metallurgy of the Six Tribes, Chapter 4, Olgothian Steel

"WAKE UP!"

Amandine opened an eye and glared blearily up at Chef, who stood over her cot with his hands on his hips. The lack of light through the small portal in their cabin told her that it was still before dawn.

"You're a troll," Amandine muttered. Her usual filters were completely absent in her sleepy state, and even though her brain registered that she had just called Chef a name, the rest of her didn't give a colorless bean.

"Been called worse," Chef agreed. "Roll onto the deck, Apprentice, an' put some pants on! Captain wants ta see us!"

That finally roused something in Amandine that pushed the fog away. "What? Is something the matter?"

Chef shrugged. "Hard ta say with *Ur'Mord* oft times. Better not ta keep that *gyre* waitin', aye?"

Amandine groaned, but rolled her legs out of the cot and sat up. Their cots filled most of the space, with a small spot for a washstand and pegs for their things.

The way the bed was angled on the cords and hinges that fixed it to the wall had helped her not to roll out of it as she had feared she might. Even the occasional larger rocking motions had, at most, forced her to turn over and put her back to the wall.

"I'll clear the deck so ye can dress in private. Jus' don't dally, aye?"

Amandine nodded. Chef walked out the door and pulled it shut. Or tried to. The door bounced off something and swung open again. With a grumpy mutter, Chef stepped back in far enough to grab the rope handle and swung the door shut hard. It closed with a bang.

A yawn cracked Amandine's jaw. Grendel emerged from under her cot and rubbed against her bare legs. She was still in her underclothes and a loose shirt that she wore as a nightdress. Given their tight living accommodations, it was nice Serand gave her as much privacy as he did. He had an *extremely* proper attitude about women, despite his salty demeanor. She had tried to wear her work clothes to bed, and he had flatly told her that he would wait in the hold until she had changed and taken to her blankets before he came in to sleep himself. The old crust would probably die of indignation if she tried to change in front of him. How exactly *had* Dena gotten past that wall of propriety?

She stood and scratched her rump and her neck. The rough wool blankets were warm, but itchy. Grendel meowed at her.

"Hang on, Gren," Amandine said through another yawn. She removed her shirt and paused for a moment to stretch. Her scar throbbed slightly. It sometimes did that when she was tired. Amandine rubbed it absently and fished a wrap out of her backpack, tied it on, and then pulled on pants. Someone coughed. Amandine paused with her hands on the drawstrings. Grendel was staring at the door, his tail swishing. It must have been Chef, she reasoned. The inside walls below deck were made of thinner planks to save weight. She hurried to finish dressing and opened the door. No one was in the hall.

"Chef?"

"In the hold, fingerling."

She walked into the hold and found Serand stroking Spice. The orange cat stood on a wool bale and pressed his head into Serand's palm eagerly. She didn't often see either of them showing much affection to each other, despite their obvious kinship. The sight warmed her somehow.

"I'm ready," she said.

"Aye. Spice, keep a lookout, friend."

Meow.

"Is there trouble, you think?" Amandine asked.

"Like I said, no tellin', but more eyes don't hurt, lass."

He led the way through the hold to the cabins on the same side of the ship that held the dining room. The Captain's cabin was the largest living chamber on the ship, but was still small. Serand had to duck to get in the door and remained bent over once inside. The room was appointed much like the one Amandine and Serand slept in. A cot folded down from the wall and pegs held cloaks and other articles. A large brass-bound chest sat in a corner, but unlike the other cabins, the middle of the room was dominated by a wide, carved oak desk covered in gray parchment scrawled with runes. A pair of heavy, hide-bound books sat to one side and an inkwell with a bone pen rested inside a carved out section that kept it from tipping when the boat rocked.

The Captain sat on a stool behind the desk, dressed in heavy woolen shirt sleeves rolled up at the wrists to reveal astonishingly hairy arms; hair so thick it almost seemed like fur. The Captain's gray-striped beard was tucked into the belt-strap of their pants to keep it out of the ink.

"Captain Cragllin, sah," Serand said politely.

"Aye, come," the dwarf grumbled as the quill continued to scratch a path across the parchment.

Amandine stood by Serand and waited quietly, as he did. She noticed that her *Olatharr* was lying on the Captain's desk next to the inkwell.

"Bah, that's done," the old dwarf said finally. They thrust the pen back into the well next to its twin and folded their hands on the desk. Beady, double-irised, yellow-green eyes shifted back and forth between them.

"I have to be frank. You two surprise the fur off me," they said in a low growl.

"Sah?" Serand asked.

"When you said you could make a *mak'lel*, I thought it was a jape. I actually lost a wager last night. A large one. But cut my beard, it was the best sand-blasted one I've had since I was a bud on my first hunt!"

"I'm pleased ye liked it, sah," Chef said.

Amandine was struck by how properly the Captain spoke. They had nearly no accent, unlike every other dwarf she had ever met.

"So, you won't have to swim to shore, as amusing as that might have been to see," the Captain continued. "Your meals will be welcome on this voyage. Can you also make *sek* and *balit*?"

"Easily, sah, if'n ye have the right stores."

"We do."

"Is that all, cap'n'?"

"Nay. I also want to discuss this."

Cragllin's wide fingers stroked the *Olatharr*'s blade. "This is finely made. One of the finest I've seen."

"Aye."

"And you realize it's a slaver's blade?"

Amandine's eyes widened, but Chef merely nodded. "Aye, I do."

"Neither of you seem to be Olgath, so I must ask, for the sake of halting rumor. Where did you get such a thing?"

"It's nay mine, sah, it's my 'pprentice's"

The Captain turned their gaze to Amandine. "This true?"

"Yes, sah," Amandine replied, trying not to fidget.

"What's the blade's provenance?"

Amandine looked to Serand, confused.

"It's a way of askin' where ye got it an' how," Serand explained.

Steeling herself, Amandine answered the Captain directly. "It was given to me by a Seeker, sah. A Hill Folk man named Birch. Where he got it, I can't say. I... didn't know it was a slaver's tool, sah."

"But you knew Olgothians keep slaves?"

"Yes."

"And that this is *Olgothian* water-steel, yes?"

"Um, yes, sah." Amandine was beginning to see where they were going with their questions and it made her deeply uncomfortable.

Serand spoke. "She grew up in an orphanage, sah. She's only been in my care fer a year. There's much she ain't learned yet."

The Captain's eyes never left Amandine. "And how then has an orphan, working as a cook's apprentice, been given such a fine weapon?"

Amandine's heart sank. They would never believe her. She looked up at Serand, but he only jerked his head towards the Captain for her to get on with it.

"I... I used it to kill a skellix, sah."

The Captain's eyes narrowed and they made choking, laughing noises, but stopped when they saw that neither Amandine nor Serand were laughing along. "That's really your tale?"

"Every word truth," Serand said. "She gave ya the blooded weapon of a hunter fer yer *mak'lel*, an' ya have the stones ta question her integrity?"

Amandine was surprised at how fierce Serand suddenly sounded. Cragllin folded his arms defensively and glared at him. "No disrespect was intended, galley-mate," they said, adding stress to Serand's title on board the ship. "But it is a highly suspect story."

"If ye have a doubt, send missive ta Sheriff Kimber Stolm ta confirm who collected the bounty on the beast," Serand snapped. "There were also half a dozen witnesses, all reputable members of Stoneman. Why would we concoct such a lie? If'n ye still want ta spew bile, we'll collect our things and our cats and go fer a swim now, by yer leave!"

Cragllin and Serand locked gazes and Amandine held her breath. If they really had to swim, she worried for Grendel. But after a moment, the old dwarf seemed to relent.

"Bah! Ain't no business of mine what fool story you have for the blade. You obviously aren't slavers. A cook that speaks our tongue and knows our customs? With a skellix-killin' apprentice in tow? I'd wager my beard you weren't always slinging pans and gutting fish. I will not ask you anything further. You are both still welcome on my boat."

Serand relaxed his shoulders and nodded. "And we'll be glad ta keep servin' yer meals, sah. You run a tight crew. Solid stone."

"They're a bunch of rowdy *gyre*, but solid, as you say. Dismissed. This is yours, I think."

The Captain slid Amandine's knife across the desk. She took it by the handle and tucked it into the crook of her arm, blade out, as she'd been taught. Its sheath was still in their cabin. Cragllin eyed her stance and nodded.

They turned and left the Captain's quarters. Inside the hold, Amandine noticed three dwarven sailors near one of the bales. They shifted their feet and glanced nervously about. Spice was up on the bale with his back arched, hissing at them. Grendel stood at their feet, and his bristling fur made his already prodigious girth seem to double as he also menaced the dwarves. One of the three sailors held a coil of rope.

"Stand down ye pair o' furry bastards," Chef barked.

Spice instantly quit his spitting and leapt down to follow them. Grendel also stopped what he was doing and sat on his haunches to begin cleaning a paw.

"Back to work, you useless pebbles!" Cragllin boomed from their quarters through the still open door. The three dwarves looked at each other and the one with the rope shrugged as they shuffled off back to whatever duties they had been assigned.

"What were they doing?" Amandine whispered as she followed Chef to the galley.

"Probably were meant ta tie us up in the hold and dump us overboard if'n the captain said so," he replied with a shrug. "Ye did well, by the way. When dealin' with *Ur'Mord*, truth an' strength will almost always lead ta a better outcome than a limp spine an' snivelin'."

Amandine ran her free hand through her hair, and exhaled. "It certainly has been an interesting trip so far."

"Just gettin' started. We'll be along with these fer near a cycle. Might be a stop or two ta take on water and food, but mostly we'll be crawlin' upriver, so tuck in, fingerling."

As they passed by their cabin, Amandine ducked inside to get the sheath for her *Olatharr*. She pulled it off the peg and draped it over her shoulder. Something moved out of the corner of her eye. When Amandine turned, it disappeared under Serand's cot.

Very cautiously, Amandine ducked low and peered under the bed. Nothing was there.

"What?" she muttered to herself. To be sure, she checked under her bed as well, but only found spare boots. As she stood, something brushed her foot.

With a startled yelp, Amandine leapt up and drew the dagger. She scanned the floor, holding the blade in front of her with two hands. Again, nothing was there.

On tiptoes, Amandine left the cabin and hurried to the galley.

"Chef, I think I saw something in our cabin. It ran under the bed, but I couldn't find it!"

He glanced at Amandine from where he was cutting a ham. Then he looked down at Spice by his feet. "Well, go see. That's yer job, matey."

Meow.

"Ye don't have ta eat it if yer not hungry, just make sure the room is clear, ye daft furball!"

Spice trotted out of the galley past Amandine.

"Does he really understand what you're saying to him?" she asked.

"Does that chunk o' butter listen when ye speak?" he replied.

Grendel was by the shrimp barrel batting an escapee about with his paws. The shrimp managed to clamp one of its four claws onto a toe and Grendel hissed as he flicked the offending crustacean into the wall.

"Sometimes I wonder if he's bright enough to even understand other cats," Amandine muttered.

Chef shook his head and resumed his task. "Don't ye worry 'bout it. If there is vermin on this ship, Spice 'll find 'em."

"Why don't you go help?" Amandine scolded Grendel.

The large cat glanced away from his toy shrimp and gave her a sulky look before slinking out of the galley as well.

"What shall I do, Chef?"

"No fire today. Cold soup for breakfast. Smoked meat and cheese fer lunch. I'll show yah how to make *balit*."

"What's that?"

"Raw eggs soaked in spices. Easy ta make as oats in milk. Common fare fer breaking fast among dwarves."

Amandine rolled her sleeves and began gathering ingredients per Chef's instructions. The meal was, as he had said, incredibly easy to make. They stirred a mixture of hot spices into cold water and beer, and then the eggs merely sat in them, shell and all, while Amandine held it in her lap to keep it from tipping as the boat moved. She hadn't needed the water-sickness herbs, as it turned out. Serand however, took a moment to stuff a sprig in his mouth to chew while he worked.

She watched him, but her mind wandered back to the conversation with the Captain. Would other people judge her the way he had because of the dagger? It was the first time any quality other than its rarity had been brought up. That people might mistake her for a slaver deeply bothered Amandine, but then, this particular weapon had been Birch's and used to slay a dangerous beast. It was sort of redeemed in that way, wasn't it? If only it were good for something other than killing...

"Those should be ready now. Get 'em to the long table."

Amandine fetched a ladle, and carrying the pot with two hands, made her way out of the galley. As she rounded the corner, something clipped her elbow. Spicy beer sloshed out of the pot and soaked a sleeve of her outfit.

"Hells!" she cursed as she quickly righted the pot. She settled it on a wool bale and shook the damp arm fruitlessly. "I'm going to have to scrub this or I'll smell like beer all day."

"Worse things ta smell like," a dwarven voice said.

She glanced over the bale and saw the same dwarf that had been tending the cattle. They scrubbed the floor with a long-bristled brush. A bucket of water sat next to them.

"I suppose," Amandine admitted.

"That *balit*?" they asked.

"Yes."

"Grand. I'll go tell tha crew."

Amandine nodded and felt a bit of relief. She'd thought she would have to make the call again, but apparently that was a special occasion sort of thing. Shifting her load carefully as the boat gently rocked, she made her way to the dining area. Bowls had already been laid out. Amandine put three eggs and a few ladles of spicy beer-water in each. The first of the crew began to filter in as she finished.

The procession was much louder and rowdier than last night's. Good natured chatter passed around as the dwarves settled in front of bowls. There was no specific order to it this time either. The captain sat at the end of the table across from the one who had dragged the anchor.

"It's about the message," Amandine muttered to herself. "Enjoy, sahs," she called as she left the room.

A few of the crew called back in both Olgothian and *Mord-seq*. They seemed perfectly friendly now, even though she and Chef had been in danger of being tossed overboard not even two bells earlier.

"Breakfast is served," Amandine announced as she returned to the galley.

"Good. We'll do prep today mostly. Make life easier fer us durin' the next tenday. Peel some gojo fer a sauce and then strip herbs," Chef said as he wrapped strips of ham in cheesecloth.

"Yes, Chef."

A strangled yelping sound came from outside the door to the galley, followed by cats yowling.

"Eh? They caught somethin'!" Chef peeked over his shoulder at the door.

Streaks of fur and paws tore through the doorway past Chef and Amandine. Chef turned and yanked a large knife off the lodestone. Amandine spun and raised the empty pot over her head, ready to throw it.

Spice and Grendel had cornered their quarry near the barrels. The quivering creature looked up at Amandine with large, liquid eyes and a pushed-in snout.

"Dumpling?" Amandine asked in disbelief.

"Oh, hells," Chef swore.

He turned, swinging an arm in a large hook. It seemed to collide with something in the air like an invisible pillar. With a twist, Chef flexed his arm into his ribs and then with a flourish he reversed the grip of the knife in his other hand and held it across the gap between his bicep and forearm. It looked ridiculous, but then Amandine's brain caught up with what was happening.

"Fredderick?"

The air rippled and Fredderick's head appeared in the gap, followed by the rest of him. His fingers pried ineffectually at Chef's arm. The sharp side of the knife was pressed up under his nose.

"Heyro Amnandin," he said as he tried to lift his nose away from the blade. Chef merely adjusted his feet and squeezed him tighter.

"Apprentice, shut the door," Chef said.

Amandine dropped the pot and quickly moved past them to pull the door shut, then rounded on Fredderick.

"What in the *hells* are you doing here?" she demanded.

Fredderick just winced.

"Answer the question, Fred," Chef growled.

"Ok, ok, bu mah noesh?"

"Serand, please?" Amandine asked.

With a grunt, Chef carefully drew the knife away, but continued to hold Fredderick's head under his arm.

"It's stupid, I know, but you were going to be gone for so long," Fredderick said as he struggled vainly against Chef's headlock. "You didn't even let me say goodbye!"

"I'm pretty sure that's exactly what I did, you carp-fish!" Amandine said. Something suddenly occurred to her that made her blood run cold, but her face burned as if it was on fire. The bump in the hallway, the creature under the bed... the cough that had definitely come from *inside* the room.

"You were in our cabin this morning!" Amandine said.

"I was hiding from the dwarves! They seem to be able to see me, even when—"

"You saw me *naked*!" Amandine hissed.

"Err... *half* naked," Fredderick corrected in a small voice.

"Cut him, Serand."

Chef's eyes widened at the statement, but then his brow furrowed and a low growl escaped his lips. Fredderick thrashed uselessly. With a flex, Chef pulled up on his neck and Fredderick made a soft choking sound. He kept the knife close, but didn't make a move to use it.

"Oi, stop wiggling, ya carp fish! Yer in a heap o' trouble an' not just with me an' my 'prentice! Snoopin' about, stowin' away on a *mord* vessel? Gods! Have ye no colorless sense?" Chef snarled at Fredderick as he tried to escape.

"Clap his ears, Chef! Wring his chicken-neck!" Amandine snarled.

Chef yanked up hard to hold Fredderick in place, and shifted his balance. He seemed to consider his options, but made no further move to harm Fredderick. The look on his face spoke volumes, however.

"Well now, fingerling, I weren't *actually* gonna hurt the lad. Although in light o' his behavior it be *mighty* temptin'."

Fredderick's face began to purple.

"You told me you never point a knife at anything you aren't willing to cut!" Amandine said coldly. She pulled her *Olatharr* out of its sheath. "You had it to his nose, right? He doesn't need an entire nose, does he?"

Chef looked alarmed, but Amandine didn't care. She was *furious*. She'd never been so angry at anyone in her life. Not Sister Corbin, not Nous, not Lady Everdawn, or Marlette or even that horrible Orm woman. She felt humiliated and embarrassed. If he had wanted a peek so badly, he could have just *asked* her.

The last thought pulled her up short. She was so mad at Fredderick, and had been annoyed by his behavior for so long, that the idea surprised her. If he had asked, would she have done it? Maybe. Before Marlette, perhaps. He wasn't bad looking, or cruel, he was just... an idiot, and careless with words. Maybe she was too. Some of her fire faded. Her knife was only a few fingers from his face, but her grip on the handle slipped a little.

"Amandine. Put the blade away, please," Chef said in a calm voice.

She took a deep breath, and then another. Slowly, she stepped away, but kept the knife pointed at him. Her face still burned, but not all of that was from anger.

If he had done all this just to get her attention, maybe she was wrong about Marlette. Maybe he was done with her? Why on earth would he—

"Serand, I think he stopped breathing."

Chef cursed and let up on Fredderick's windpipe. With a gasp, the young man's face began to return to a more natural color.

"Right. I changed my mind," Amandine said with a calm she barely felt. "I don't want to cut off his nose anymore."

"Tha... nk you." Fredderick coughed.

"I could cut something else off instead!"

She stepped forward again and mimed sawing the knife.

"Amandine..." Fredderick whined.

"You know Olgothians have them removed when they die right? Have them put in a little jar to be buried next to their heads. I know a quick method. Two slices—you'll barely feel a thing."

Fredderick went as white as snow. Chef raised an eyebrow at her. He could tell that she wasn't raging anymore, that she was only messing with Fredderick now. Mostly, anyway. But he also kept his silence and continued to glare at Fredderick while tapping the flat of his knife against his shoulder.

"What do you think, Fredderick? Would Marlette be terribly disappointed?" She bared her teeth at him.

"If I may, Apprentice?"

"Yes, Chef?"

"Ya may not have ta remove any o' his bits."

"Oh, why?"

"'Cause *Ur'Mord* don' take kindly ta stowaways."

"What do they do to them, Chef?"

"Eat 'em, o' course."

Fredderick fainted. Serand let him fall to the floor. His body hit the planks with a hollow *thud*, like a drum.

Amandine grinned. "Thanks. I feel better now."

"Ye weren't really gonna cut him, were ya, fingerling?"

"Nope. It's all about the message."

Chef threw back his head and laughed. It was a raucous sound, like a gull's cry.

Amandine slid the *Olatharr* back into its sheath with a soft *click*.

Stacks and Stowaways

"A good Chef normally wouldn't admit this, but I love stacks. Simple to make, with variations more numerous than stars. They can be tailored to any taste and can even be eaten one-handed while working. Truly, for a simple meal on the go, they can't be beat. I enjoy mine with thin-cut cured meat, greenwax cheese—sliced thin—chartreuse, mustard, and—if in season—leafy greens. I will detail some of my favored variations in the following pages, as well as other, easy-to-make meals for those who don't have the luxury of a kitchen, time, or complex ingredients."

- Seeker's Kitchen, Chapter 10, Simple Fare for Busy Seekers

"THIS IS YOUR own fault, you know." Amandine said as she knelt by the pen the cattle were kept in. She stared at the empty manacles fastened to the slats by a short chain. A curious cow stood over her, on the other side of the fence, looking down at the empty space as well.

"Come on, Fredderick, I know you're there. Drop the spell. I brought food."

The air rippled. Fredderick appeared with his left ankle in the manacle. His wrists were cuffed by another set and tied to the post. Dumpling, locked in a chicken crate, sat in his lap.

Amandine put a strip of cured ham and a peeled carrot into the cage for Dumpling. She pulled a bread roll out of her pocket for Fredderick.

"Bread and water again?" he asked.

"You're lucky it's even offered," Amandine replied. "Serand may have been japing about them eating you, but Captain Cragllin was still ready to toss you into the river."

"Sure, lucky me."

"These are from my rations, I'll have you know. The Captain definitely wouldn't give you anything meant for his crew. Do you want the bread or not?"

Fredderick sighed and opened his mouth. Amandine held the roll so he could take a bite. The cow mooed and ducked closer. It licked the side of Fredderick's face with a huge pebbly tongue all the way up the side of his head, making his hair stand up like a wave. He took on a long suffering expression.

"See, at least one lady on this boat still likes you," Amandine said, offering him another bite.

The cow licked him again.

"Oi, stop that! Shoo!" Fredderick grumbled.

Amandine laughed. The dwarf who looked after the cows, and now Fredderick, laughed also.

"Right, hilarious," Fredderick said.

"Oh, stop it. Like I said, you had this coming. Your poor choices were bound to catch up with you, Fredderick, and this is not as bad as it could have been."

"Were you really going to cut me?"

Amandine gave him a level look and tore off a chunk of bread before holding it out. She didn't answer.

"Well, if it matters at all, the peek was totally worth it," Fredderick said, opening his mouth again for the bread.

With a glare, Amandine stabbed the bread into his mouth so far he choked on it a bit and sputtered bread crumbs.

"Why are you so cruel?" he gasped.

"Why are you such a scab?"

"It was meant as a compliment, Amandine! Look at how much trouble it got me into!"

"You're in this particular trouble for being a stowaway, not for being a lecher. It's me you're in trouble with for that — among other things."

"How can I forget?"

Amandine rolled her eyes. "When we first met, Fredderick, I thought we could be friends. I really liked you, even with all of your mischief. You're like a naughty cat. But you take advantage of my trust, you hurt my feelings, and then you try to pass it off as a jape. I won't put up with it!"

"I still want to be your friend, Amandine. I like you too."

"You have a really strange way of showing it! I thought we had something, you and I, but then you start courting my patron's daughter? Won't even acknowledge that you and I kissed, even though Marlette *obviously* knows all about that. If you really like me so much, then prove it, you colorless fool! Because right now, I'm not even sure you deserve to be my friend!"

She stuffed the heel of bread into his mouth and stood up. "I need to return to work. I'll be back with a water flask and some sliced gojo in two bells."

As she turned, Fredderick managed to finish chewing and swallow the soft bread before he spoke again.

"I have been terrible, Amandine. I'm sorry. Thank you for the food."

She looked over her shoulder at him. "You're welcome, Fredderick. I'm sorry too."

That you have oats for brains, she thought to herself.

Amandine made her way through the hold back to the galley. As she did, she pondered what Fredderick had said. He had been chained up by the cows for almost two tendays now. The dwarves only let him up to use the privy, at spearpoint. She hadn't undersold how much trouble he was in with them. It had taken all of Serand's persuasive ability just to keep them from executing him. Would he take *nothing* seriously?

Grendel was lounging on a bale and rolled on his side as she passed. Amandine paused to rub his belly. "And how is my other naughty cat doing?"

Meow.

Her hearing sharpened. The cattle's stamping became louder. Their dwarf watcher snored softly.

"We really screwed up big this time, didn't we Dumpy?" Fredderick muttered. "Think she'll ever forgive us?"

Amandine sighed. It was tiring being mad at Fredderick. She barely thought about other people that upset her, like Nous or Matron Orm, so why couldn't she let Fredderick go?

She knew the answer, as much as it annoyed her to admit it. Fredderick was different. Other people mistreated her purely out of spite or because they wanted to be in charge. She had no doubt someone like Nous would step over her body if she lay dying in the street, and then complain about the mess. Fredderick wasn't like that. When she had really needed help, really needed a friend, he had been there for her. She could maybe forgive him if he sincerely apologized, but he had made a dent in her trust. You couldn't put an egg back in its shell.

Grendel rolled over and hopped down off the crates. She entered the galley and found Chef finishing a batch of *sek*. It was another simple dwarven staple dish: strips of smoked meat brined in vinegar and then flavored with small pepper fruits so spicy that just the fumes made Amandine's eyes burn. Chef had the vent open, even though there was no fire lit today.

"I think I smell those in my dreams now," Amandine commented.

"Aye, can't say I missed 'em."

"Meal break in one bell?"

"Ayup."

"I'll make stacks for us."

"That'll be fine. Say, the First Mate came ta see me while ye was feedin' the stowaways. We're due to stop in three days fer supplies at a river town called Myron's Bend. Cap'n wants ta put Fred and his dog ashore there. It's a long hike fer him back ta Stoneman, but it's like ta be the best offer he'll get, given the situation."

"I'm sure he'll be glad not to be tied up any longer."

Chef eyed her sideways. "Ye sure yer not worried about him?"

"Me? I'm fine."

"I don't usually pry, fingerling, ye know that. But I had the reckoning that ye two were a *bit* more than pals."

"He's courting Marlette L'Eau."

"Is he though? Truly courtin' her? I don't see that fellow sneakin' onto a dwarf-filled ship ta say farewell to that spoiled shite."

Amandine blinked in surprise. Had Serand just insulted Marlette? She had never heard him speak ill of any employer, former or otherwise. "Well, she's likely a magician, the same as him, so they probably have more in common than you think. Including being spoiled."

"Really? How do ya know she can do magic?"

She told Chef about what she had seen Mister Green doing with Fiona. "He said there were two in the house, as rare as that is. So maybe they can go be a happy magic couple together."

"Huh. He said that, did he?" Chef sounded thoughtful. "As fer Fiona, good fer her. She's a bright little light, that one. Won't have to dwell in her sister's shadow so much now."

"Anyway, I really don't want to talk about Fredderick anymore. What do you want on your stack, sah?"

"Just ham, cheese, and mustard. The good stuff from my jar, nay that over-vinegared mess the *Ur'Mord* have in the stores."

Amandine nodded. She used a barrel lid as a workspace and sliced a roll for Serand's meal. She counted out the slices of meat and cheese and then dug the small jar of mustard out of Chef's satchel. Finally, salt for the meat and pepper for the cheese. Her stack wouldn't have a roll—she had given it to Fredderick.

She had just put the top of the roll on Serand's stack and was admiring her work when suddenly the world turned sideways.

An enormous crashing sound accompanied that of splintering wood and shouting dwarves. *Sek* went flying across the room and the perfect stack Amandine had just created flew apart and into the wall. The cattle began to panic and thrashed about in their makeshift pen. The ship righted itself with a huge splash that sent water up through the vent-hole in the galley.

"Colorless night!" Amandine clung to the shrimp barrel to keep from falling. "Did we hit something?"

"No, Amandine." Serand steadied himself against the workspace counter. He cocked his head towards the ceiling, as if listening.

Amandine heard the dwarves above shouting as well, thanks to Grendel's enchantment, but she didn't understand a word of *Mord-seq*. The voices sounded angry, though.

"Somethin' hit *us*," Serand said softly.

"What did?"

"River pirates, Amandine. We're bein' boarded."

Blood Right

SERAND PICKED UP the large knife he had been using off the floor and stuck it to the slate. He went to his coat and slipped it on, then reached inside it and produced a pair of hatchets. They had wide, curved blades that drew up to hooks at the top. They were not tools meant for chopping firewood. Amandine had only seen them taken out from his chest under the bed a handful of times, for cleaning, sharpening, or to spar with Dena.

He kept an ear pointed up the entire time as he moved, listening to the commotion above. The boat rocked again.

"Ayup, we can't hide out fer this one, Amandine," Serand said softly. "Put yer hand to your hilt and follow me, quiet-like. We're goin' ta get Fred and then get off the ship if it's a rout. Ain't nothin' on this boat worth dyin' over."

"And abandon Captain Cragllin?"

"Not if there is a way fer us ta help. Dwarves 're stout folk. They're fightin' back, but a real battle ain't nothin' the same as that foolish book you an' Dena like so much. 'Nough talkin'. Follow."

Amandine followed Serand out of the galley, her heart hammering in her chest. A cat's yowl made Amandine look up. Spice and Grendel were at the cargo port, looking down at them through the slats. Serand also glanced up.

"Get clear, you two," he said in a low voice. "Swim to shore! We're comin'!"

"Chef, I don't think Grendel can swim," Amandine said.

"All cats swim, most just don' like ta. Now keep yer ears open, we have to move."

As they crept through the cargo, she listened to the mayhem above. Metal clashed, and dwarves swore and screamed. There were other voices too, some speaking Olgothian.

"Hold them! Get the food stores! Get the silver! Gred! Give 'em another shake!"

"Amandine! Hold something!" Serand snapped.

The boat rocked again and Amandine grabbed onto a rope that was being used to secure the wool bales. Serand dropped to his belly and gripped a support beam. Some loose barrels rolled around the bales and something crashed into the far wall. Amandine's feet slid and she tumbled to the deck, but managed to keep ahold of the rope. The floor leveled with an enormous splash.

"Quick now!" Serand jumped to his feet.

Amandine hauled herself back up and dashed across the hold behind Serand. The scene at the cattle pen was pure chaos. The fencing had been smashed through. One of the animals was dead, lying on its side. Its limbs had been broken and its neck was at a bad angle. The others were piled against the wall, trying to regain their footing. They lowed and grunted as they struggled, adding to the din.

"Fredderick!" Amandine called as panic gripped her.

"Don' shout!" Serand hissed. "We don' want the pirates to know we are here. Use yer eyes and ears!"

She nodded and searched frantically through the wreckage. The post Fredderick had been shackled to was snapped off at the deck. The chicken cage Dumpling had been in lay open and empty. She swore she could hear a dog barking somewhere above.

"I don't see Fredderick," Amandine said quietly, "but I think I hear Dumpling."

"Aye, if he's smart, he's already swimmin'. Let's go."

Serand moved to the ladder on the port side of the hold and peered up at the hatch. Sunlight shone down through it, making a lattice of shadow across his face.

"I think they are mostly starboard. I go up first, then you. If we need ta jump, swim downstream ta port."

"I understand." She tried to sound confident, but the hand holding the hilt of her *Olatharr* wouldn't stop shaking.

"We'll be fine, fingerling. Focus, move with purpose!"

Serand stuck his hatchets into his belt and climbed the ladder. He pushed the hatch open, peeked out, ducked back down, and then clambered the rest of the way onto the deck. Once he was clear, Amandine followed.

It was bedlam. The dwarven sailors had formed a ring around two fallen comrades, facing outward with their backs to the injured. They used barge poles to hold the attackers at bay.

Six large forms loomed over the huddle. They had dark, hairy skin, enormous muscles and huge protruding teeth below animal-like snouts. Amandine had never seen an actual tusker before, but she knew enough about them to realize that's what they were. They were massive, even bigger than she had imagined. Another dozen people, humans and Hill Folk, were rummaging through barrels and breaking into the aftcastle deck house.

Amandine and Chef were on the opposite end of the boat from the beleaguered dwarves, near the aftcastle. Several pirates nearby watched the scrum of dwarves fighting the tuskers. The sounds of shouting and doors crashing reverberated through the structure. Serand waved a hand back at Amandine and tried to duck down behind some barrels strapped to the deck, but one of the humans was pointing at them. He had a waterproofed cloak and better made clothes than the others and seemed to be the leader. He clutched a large harpoon-like weapon in one meaty fist that he jabbed in their direction.

"Hey! There's more of 'em!"

A human woman wielding a hook-like weapon broke away from the group of pirates and rushed Serand. He caught her blow in the curve of one of his hatchets and pulled her off balance. He swung at her with the other one, but turned the blade and struck her with the flat side. She fell senseless to the deck, but was immediately replaced by a Hill Folk pirate armed with a long, curved sword.

"Amandine, back to a wall, blade out!"

Amandine drew her dagger in a shaky hand and put her back to the aftcastle. Serand had incapacitated the Hill Folk attacker but was now trying to hold off two more.

"How do I help?" Amandine cried.

"Stay back, stay down! We're..." Serand paused to deflect an attack and swing back, causing the man he was fighting to leap away. "Gonna jump!" he finished.

"Tilt 'em!" the leader called. He drove his harpoon into the deck. The other pirates grabbed rigging or rails, and the six tuskers harrying the dwarves dropped to all fours like animals.

There were loud sloshing and splashing sounds as waves coming from the starboard side of the ship slapped against the hull. The water below the railing began to churn and foam. Amandine gasped as a massive form rose from the river. It was so large that even standing in the riverbed, it was still taller than the tuskers on the deck. Its entire body was covered in slick orange-brown fur, matted and tangled, that seemed to repel the water and hid whatever eyes it had. Long, floppy ears draped down the sides of its head. Its snout was squashed against its face with giant nostrils that opened and closed as the water retreated down its oily fur. The thing's mouth opened wide enough to swallow a human whole and was filled with huge grinding teeth in the back and giant incisors up front like a rabbit. It made no sound other than a low grunting rumble and then swung its long shaggy arms up out of the water. Giant hands with four meaty fingers each rocked the barge like a toy boat in a washtub.

The dwarves tumbled, but grabbed a hold of each other in a chain that ended at one of them holding the mast: the big *gyre* that would pull the anchor. Serand's eyes widened and he dropped to the deck, embedding a hatchet into the wood. Amandine began to slip. She tried to duplicate Serand's move by stabbing the wall of the aftcastle with her *Olatharr*. The tip stuck into the wood, but it wasn't enough. It pulled free and she tumbled backwards. The boat righted and she slid to a stop against the railing. A plume of water washed onto the deck, soaking her.

"You ok?" Serand called as he regained his feet.

"Owwwwww," Amandine said as she coughed up water.

"Good enough!"

The pirate leader yanked his spear out of the deck. "Good work, Gred!" he yelled over his shoulder at the beast. "Down ye go! Hold her steady!"

The giant hairy beast slipped down into the water again with a grumbling, bubbling noise. The dwarves tried to reform their defensive position but the tuskers were already in the middle of them, tossing the smaller people about like ragdolls.

"It's no good," Serand yelled. "Swim, fingerling! I'll catch up!"

Spice leapt on the back of a pirate armed with a pair of daggers and raked his head and neck with his claws. The man yelped and tried to swat at the cat, but as he was distracted, Serand drove the back of his hatchet into the man's gut, doubling him over, then lifted a knee, knocking him backwards, out cold. Spice jumped off the unconscious man and ran for cover.

"Go!" Serand yelled again.

One of the tuskers had moved away from the scrum with the dwarves. He slunk low behind the rigging. Amandine could see him from her position, but the sail blocked Serand's view.

"Serand!" she yelled. "Under the mast!"

He turned just as the tusker ambushed him. Its huge hands grabbed Serand's arms, first one, then the other as he tried to swing his hatchets. The human pirate he'd been fighting took advantage and swung his blade. Serand twisted, but the tip still caught him across the leg. He cried out in pain.

Amandine scrambled to get her dagger, which had slid under a tarp. She grasped the handle and pulled it free, and turned to help Serand. She wasn't going to run away! She couldn't!

Serand kicked the human pirate in the gut as he grappled with the tusker, but was obviously overmatched. They fell to the deck in a tangle just as the pirate leader called for the beast again.

With a groan, the creature rose and tipped the barge once more. Pirates and dwarves hastened to grab whatever they could. Amandine dropped as Serand had done and drove the Olatharr into the deck. Water splashed over her like a tidal wave. When the boat settled, Amandine tried to regain her feet, slipping on the wet planks.

He was gone. Serand and the tusker he had been wrestling were nowhere to be seen.

"No! Serand!"

Amandine hurried to the railing and looked over the side. The water below was still churning from the boat crashing back down. She searched the waves and whorls. Serand could swim, right? He was a sailor, of course he could. He couldn't drown.

"Serand! *Serand*!"

"Help!"

Amandine looked towards the prow and saw a dwarven sailor hanging onto a rope. Their feet were already in the water and their thick fingers were slipping.

"Help!" they shouted again.

Amandine looked to the churning water where Serand had fallen. She hesitated a moment longer, praying that he would pop up. When the dwarf called again, she turned from the railing with tears in her eyes, and ran for the rope they were dangling from.

"I have you, hold on!" She pulled and heaved, but the rope was wet, and dwarves were not light. Slowly the rope came up, but she was quickly tiring. Behind her, the remaining sailors had organized a defense again somehow, but many more were battered and bruised. They weren't going to hold much longer.

"You can jus' let that go now, girl."

Something sharp poked into Amandine's back and she sucked in a breath at the pinprick of pain. A female pirate stood behind and to her left. The tip of her long, thin sword pierced Amandine's jacket, just under her ribs.

"I won't fight you, sah," she pleaded, "But let me pull them up!"

"So the hairy little troll can cause trouble for us? No. Drop it. Or I'll just end you and solve two problems."

So this was it. Amandine had idly wondered, during her time as an Apprentice Bone Guardian, what her own death would be like. Peaceful, in bed as an old woman? A stupid accident falling down stairs or having been kicked by a horse? Decimated by some affliction? All wrong. She was going to die, soaked to the bone, holding a dwarf on the end of a wet rope.

"Then do it, you colorless hag."

The pirate's mouth drew down into a line. She began to push her blade.

A dog barked.

The pirate turned and looked down. Dumpling sat at her feet, barking angrily up at her.

'What?" the pirate said in confusion.

Fredderick appeared on her blind side. "There's a spot on your coat," he said.

She whipped towards him. He brought a hand up and pressed it into her sternum. A clap like thunder shook the deck's planks. The woman *flew* away from Fredderick, like a leaf caught in a gale, and screamed as she pinwheeled out over the river and crashed into the water.

For a moment, everything on deck halted. The dwarves looked at Fredderick, the tuskers looked at Fredderick, the remaining pirates that weren't carrying bags of loot, looked at Fredderick.

"What are you shites waiting for?" The pirate leader bellowed. "*Kill him!*"

Fredderick turned to face the tuskers as they charged. He swiped a hand low as if sweeping something away. The water on the deck *moved*, as if alive, and then froze into a crystalline sheet of ice. The tuskers tumbled and slid past Amandine and Fredderick. Two of them fell over the railing and into the river.

Amandine slipped on a patch of ice that had drifted too close to them. The weight of the dwarf on the rope drew her across the deck, but she managed to brace her feet on the railing before tumbling over the edge herself. She heard the hapless sailor cry out below, but it still felt like they had a grip on the rope, so Amandine strained her arms and held on. Something tugged at the back of her shirt; she looked down to find Dumpling, his tiny teeth latched onto her hem, valiantly trying to pull her backwards.

Behind her, Fredderick held his ground as half a dozen pirates cautiously wended around the icy patch to try and surround him. He drew in a deep breath and stretched his arms wide.

When he clapped his hands together another thunderclap broke through the noise. The air seemed to ripple with the force of it. The entire ship rattled as if it were a giant drum. Amandine could almost see the path it carved as the shockwave tore across the planks, scattering pirates like matchsticks. It ripped a hole in the sail and blew barrels across the deck. The water past the railing roiled away from the boat as if a giant, invisible hand had slapped the surface.

The huge hairy beast rose out of the water with a howl, its massive hands clamped over its floppy ears. It turned towards shore to escape the echo of Fredderick's spell and sloshed away as fast as its half-submerged state would allow.

With shrieks of fright, the two remaining tuskers scrambled away on all fours like beasts. "Mahgee! Mahgeeee!" one of them wailed as they dove into the river.

The pirate Captain looked stunned. "What in the hells?"

Fredderick extended a hand down by his side and a small ball of fire appeared in his palm.

"He's a mage! Get clear, ye bastards, get clear!"

The cowardly pirate leader leapt off the side of the ship. The pirates that were still conscious did the same. A pair of dwarves hurried to Amandine and helped her haul up the soggy, but still breathing sailor she had been anchoring. She collapsed to the deck, exhausted, as Captain Cragllin began barking orders to the survivors. Fredderick came and stood by her.

"Want a hand?" he asked.

Amandine nodded wearily. She wasn't going to think about Serand right now—that could be dealt with later. With a bone-deep sigh, she extended a hand.

Fredderick grabbed her with the hand still holding the ball of fire. Amandine felt a moment of panic, but then, the fire didn't burn. A warm tingling extended through her body and a scent like over-boiled water and burnt toast hit her nose.

She wasn't cold anymore. When she looked down at herself, her clothes were dry, all the way to her toes.

"Mister Green's drying spell. Small fires. Useful." Fredderick grinned. Dumpling barked as if in agreement.

"He might be sore that you stole it," Amandine said.

Fredderick just shrugged.

"Bind 'em! Every scree-blasted one of 'em. Someone grab the first mate a blade. We'll make this quick!"

At the words, Amandine turned from Fredderick. The dwarves were tying up the unconscious and wounded humans and Hill Folk. She could see their colleagues, who had abandoned them to their fate, swimming or paddling away on small rafts. The dwarves clearly intended to execute the remaining pirates.

"Please, sahs, no!" she shouted.

"Stowaways might get mercy, human, but pirates can feel steel!" Captain Cragllin growled.

Fredderick grimaced, but Amandine persisted. "No, please! There's been enough killing!"

The Captain rounded on her, "Nay! I lost six crew. Some were friends, some were *nyre*. Blood demands blood!"

"Piracy is an offense punishable by death, Amandine." Fredderick placed a hand on her shoulder. "It's not pretty, but it's his right as Captain."

"Oh, so the stowaway speaks in my defense, eh? You can shut yer hole, or you can join 'em!"

Captain Craglin seemed to bristle as he addressed Fredderick. His ire was intimidating. Amandine had never seen a dwarf angry. Boomer, at home in Stoneman, had always been polite and mild, if a bit gruff. The Captain was more than a little frightening.

"But Captain, sah! He saved your colorless life!" Amandine pleaded. The dwarves all stopped and turned to look at her, except for the two that were busy binding the prisoners. "As for the pirates, will killing them in revenge make your *nyre* less dead?"

The dwarves muttered amongst themselves and Captain Cragllin folded their arms and glared up at Amandine, then Fredderick. "Right. The galley-mate's apprentice has made a valid point of honor. You, stowaway, are hereby welcome on my ship, until our next stop. No repayment expected and your crimes are excused."

At the pronouncement, many of the dwarves nodded in agreement and muttered back and forth in *Mord-seq*.

"But the pirates, by every law both humans and *Ur'Mord* have agreed upon, have forfeited their lives by attacking my ship. With a bloody wumpus, no less!"

"That was a wumpus?" Amandine asked. "I thought they were just made up..."

The Captain rolled their eyes.

"Look, that's not important." Amandine tried to keep her tired mind on track. She thought frantically. "If it's laws that dwa— I mean *Ur'Mord* have agreed upon with humans, then shouldn't a human magistrate have a say? Perhaps at the next stop?"

There was a mixture of muttering at that, and Amandine took hope, as at least some of the chatter was positive.

Another idea struck her. "And... what if there is a bounty on these cutthroats? They damaged your ship and stole your cargo, sah. Collecting on their bounty might get you back some of your coin."

Captain Cragllin eyed her skeptically. "Your Apprentice Master fought like a demon before he went over the side. And his apprentice not only claims to have killed a skellix, but knows how bounties work. I said it before, but you two are passing strange, even for humans. No pair of cooks the like I've seen before."

"He... he was also my adoptive father," Amandine said. Something broke inside her at the words. Tears she had been delaying began to fall, despite her efforts to hold them in.

The Captain closed their eyes and took a deep breath. "So that's the way of it."

Amandine nodded. She sniffed, trying not to completely break down. Fredderick put an arm around her. She let him. He had earned it... and she needed it.

"We have both lost *nyre* today, then. You have my sympathy. This also means you have a blood right. I won't lie, it pains me, but our stores have been pillaged. If these scoundrels do have a bounty, it would be unwise not to claim it. Never let it be said that Cragllin O'Nillon ignored the law for revenge!"

The Captain turned to his crew. "Tie them good. We'll collect their blood money for the *nyre* of the fallen, and if human justice is quick, we'll stay to see them hang too!"

The head nodding was unanimous this time. The other dwarves quickly went about securing their prisoners and checking what was left of the cargo.

A dwarf tugged at Amandine's sleeve. It was the one she had rescued. They said something in *Mord-seq* and placed two hands to their chest.

"That *gyre* don't speak much o' tha Olgath tongue," the first mate said. "But that's a thank ya. Says the warren of their *nyre* is yer haven, from this day forward."

Amandine nodded. She didn't trust her voice. Instead she went back to the railing and looked out over the water. Could Chef swim with a hurt leg? Her eyes blurred as she scanned the banks, desperate for any sign that he was alive. The crew worked around her as she watched the river, but eventually, Amandine had to move so they could use the poles to push the boat out of the shallows and get back underway.

Fredderick led her to the aftcastle where they took refuge in a small room used for storing dry goods and rigging material. It had been thoroughly ransacked, but they still found a place to sit on a pile of unfolded sailcloth. There, out of sight of the crew, Amandine finally let herself cry. Fredderick held her, and didn't speak. Dumpling whined and curled up in her lap. She cried until there was nothing left—until she felt wrung out, like an old dishrag. And then, with an arm around Dumpling and leaning on Fredderick's shoulder, she drifted off to sleep.

First Kisses

"Apprenticeship is fundamental to magical training. Even more so than those learning a craft, those learning magic must be shown by an experienced elder how to use their talent, and how to not use it, for their own safety and that of others. The ability to alter reality to one's will is not something to take lightly, and failures carry larger consequences than a burnt loaf or shoddy seam. That said, mages are discouraged from having more than two apprentices at any one time, especially amongst the Highrobes order. This has led to the formation of schools where initiates with low potential might be instructed in a group. Only three such schools exist: one in Olgothia and two in Tren, and none have an enrollment of more than a dozen students at any given time. Despite the low expectations placed on those remanded to these places, a few have managed to make names for themselves after reaching majority. The famous Seeker, Orraphon of Blowing Embers, was a ward of the Ifron Academy in Olgothia, as an example."

- Lecture Notes, Fourth Ironday, High Winter 1202

WITH THE REDUCED crew, the remaining trip to Myron's Bend took two days longer than anticipated. Damage had been done to the boat's outer hull. Water had filled the bilge and caused the ship to drag in shallower sections of the river. The dwarves made repairs in transit, aided by Fredderick. He used Mister Green's drying spell to quicken the pitch seals put in place as a temporary measure. A different spell helped push the water out of the lower hold and saved the dwarves the trouble of bailing it out with buckets. The added effort seemed to please Captain Cragllin, and Fredderick was allowed to sit with the crew for meals.

Amandine continued to cook, but without Serand's guidance and with the ship's stores ransacked, those meals became a much simpler, drab affair, despite her best efforts. The pirate prisoners were kept in a storeroom and Amandine fed them broth from a batch made with the albino shrimp. She and Fredderick ate it too, along with some half-withered apples. Everything else that was human-edible had been taken by the raiders.

"Chef said that most places are two missed meals from a mutiny," Amandine said.

Fredderick and Amandine sat on the fold-out chairs in the galley. It was well after the dinner bell and the barge expected to arrive at the docks in the morning. Speaking the words caused Amandine a pang. Serand's loss still stung, like a fresh pot-lid burn. She turned over one of Serand's hatchets in her hands. A sailor had found it stuck in the deck.

"I don't know what you're getting at," Fredderick said as he tried to re-lace his boots. The cords had not been made for the wet, and the rough treatment had ruined the uselessly fancy things.

"I think I understand what he meant, is all," Amandine replied. "Despite everything those pirates took, the chest in the Captain's quarters with the sailors' payroll was untouched. None of the valuable dry goods were taken. Not the wool, or silk, or copper. They wanted food."

"Still don't get it. That's what brigands do, right?"

She sighed. "I don't think all of those people were hardened criminals, Fredderick. Some of them, sure. The leader with the tamed wumpus, certainly. The woman you threw into the river, perhaps? But a few of those in the storeroom are just farmers. Farmers, a weaver, an apprentice like us who was dropped because his master couldn't feed him. Don't you see? It's already happening. It's only been a little over a cycle since the stores were ruined and some people are already getting desperate enough to... to do that."

"To kill for food, you mean."

"Yes."

Fredderick stopped fiddling with his bootlaces and frowned at the wall. "You realize they are going to die for it, right? Your mercy is only delaying their executions, Amandine."

Amandine looked away from him. She knew. It hurt her just thinking about it. Even after what they had taken from her, she couldn't find it in her heart to want to see them die. But Fredderick wasn't wrong either. He was speaking truth, while she grasped for an illusion.

The backs of his fingers brushed her cheek. "I didn't mean to upset you. I'm sorry."

She took his hand and gently pushed it away. "I'm not mad at you, Fredderick."

His concern *seemed* genuine. It was hard to tell with Fredderick. Despite his frivolous behavior and irresponsible leisure activities, he had always shown a caring soul. The sincerity was comforting.

"What can I do? You're hurting and I feel like a waste of space."

What *could* he do? The things that would soothe her wounds were not under his control. Serand's loss had left a hole in her heart. Even so, the last few days on the barge with Fredderick had been nearly like the way things had been before. Before...

"Say, Fredderick?"

"Hmm?"

"Why *did* you kiss me then? That time."

It had been last Autumn, the ships had been out and they had visited the market circle together. He had bought her a new head scarf for work. Bright blue, like the open sky. The air had just started to turn chilly, and they had been sitting on the docks watching ducks and talking about their jobs. He had said something funny. He was good at making her laugh, but she couldn't even remember what they had been talking about. When she looked at him, a feeling pulled at her. The way the sun had profiled his face, that mischievous glint in his eyes. He leaned in and something warm inside made her lean in with him. Her eyes had been closed when it had happened, but Amandine remembered the feel of it, not just on her lips, but in her heart. None of his silly magic tricks could compare.

Fredderick exhaled and rubbed a hand against the layer of light-colored stubble that had started growing on his face. It was fuzzy, an early shadow of the beard his older illusion had worn.

"It... felt like the thing to do? We'd been having such a great day, and you looked so pretty with the sunset behind you. I just sort of did it."

"Oh..."

"Why? Was it the wrong thing to do? Did I have something in my teeth?"

Amandine shook her head and ignored his attempt at levity. "No. I said it before, I liked that kiss."

"Then why do you seem so forlorn about it?"

"I guess..." Amandine shifted in her seat. She felt like a fool. "I guess because I get the feeling that I liked it more than you did."

He grew quiet again and leaned back to look up at the ceiling. "Ah. It was your first then."

"Yes. You?"

"Gods, no," Fredderick admitted. "You are fourteen, right?"

"And three. I will be fifteen during the shiv."

"It's stupid that they don't count as full years towards majority, right?"

"Really stupid."

"But since shiv lengths can be variable, it keeps the accounting straight on ledgers. We're all a bit older than our ages suggest, so Farmer Dross is thirty-five and eight, rather than, 'well he could be anywhere from thirty-seven to thirty-nine and we have no colorless idea'."

Amandine sighed. "Yes, I get it. The Sisters explained all that."

"I'm not trying to lecture, believe me, I'm no Mister Green, and I understand how having a shiv just before majority can be frustrating, but I am seventeen and four, so I had my first run-in with romance a little bit before you, that's all. Not that it was anything I really want to remember..."

Amandine's eyes narrowed. "How many people *have* you kissed?"

It was Fredderick's turn to shift in his seat. "Just one... a girl in Irongate named Nareen. Lovely red hair and freckles. Trenash parents. She was, um, my tutor."

Her expression then must have been plain to him, because Fredderick cleared his throat and looked up at the ceiling again. "It wasn't like *that*. I was fifteen and she was the age I am now. All we did was kiss. A few times. But when my father got wind of it, he had her dismissed."

"Because she was your tutor?"

"Because she wasn't noble."

A melancholy expression overtook Fredderick's features. He spied her peering at him and smiled weakly.

"Do you miss her, then?"

"Not really. I... was just a passing fancy, it seems. I tried to pursue her, despite my father, but she made it very clear that I was not for her." A grin slowly returned to his face. "In hindsight, she was a terrible kisser."

Amandine swung her legs and poked his arm. "So our kiss was better?"

"Loads better."

Amandine smiled. "Good."

"I don't really like Marlette, you know."

"We don't have to talk about her."

A stubborn look settled over him. "But we need to. I need you to understand. Our courtship is an arrangement between my father and Lord and Lady L'Eau. I had no say."

"I don't understand. Why would you have no say in something like that? Mister Green says arranged marriages haven't been standard in Serentia for over a century."

The stubborn scowl shifted to a grimace. "Mister Green has never met Gregor Stolm. My father gets what he wants."

"He's on the other side of the colorless country! To the hells with him! If you don't like Marlette, you should tell her so. Leading her on is wrong."

"I tried that at first, but she's also someone who tends to get what she wants."

"I think if you had really tried, she would have gotten the message."

Fredderick rubbed the back of his head in an embarrassed way. "Or she might start rumors about me just to be petty. We've been, um, close enough that she could make me look bad."

"Then you've kissed her?"

"Yes. Only that, but it's enough for rumor."

"And yet?" She gave him an exasperated look and waved her hands as she shrugged. "Help me to understand why?" Amandine pleaded.

"Look, it's not like Marlette is hideous. She's really attractive, so it's not completely unpleasant, right? If I go against this arrangement, I'll be disowned, Amandine. I will have nothing left."

"So kissing a pretty girl you don't like is preferable to being poor?"

"That's not what I said!"

"It sure sounded like it!"

Amandine felt her temper rising again. She didn't want to fight with Fredderick anymore, but why did he have to be such a pig-head!

"Argh," Fredderick groaned, dragging his fingers through his hair. He also became silent, refusing to continue the argument.

"To be clear, I think you do have a choice," Amandine said, softening her tone. "Wizard Hemm and Mister Green have both offered it to you."

"It's not that simple." Fredderick put his head in his hands.

"It seems simple enough. How would apprenticing yourself to one of them be worse than an arranged relationship you don't want? A fully trained wizard could tell your floppy duck father to eat rocks and like it!"

"You know, you sure don't talk like someone who is fourteen and three. When I was fourteen, I was totally clueless."

"That really doesn't surprise me," Amandine said dryly.

Fredderick stared at her for a moment, then rose from his chair and quietly left the kitchen, his boots lying forgotten on the floor.

"Augh, Amandine, your colorless mouth," she said softly to herself. She rubbed her face with her hands and tried not to shriek in frustration. As aggravating as this all was, Fredderick had an actual problem he was struggling to solve. He had finally explained himself, more than before, in any case, and had been nothing but supportive and kind since the attack on the ship. Amandine felt like a complete troll.

With a sigh, she stood and gathered up his boots. Grendel emerged from behind the shrimp barrel and plowed into her ankles. Amandine stroked him. Spice had been missing since the battle too, and that also hurt.

"Come on, Gren, let's go apologize."

She found him on the top deck, staring out across the river towards the far bank, Dumpling at his feet. A swarm of wisps had congregated in the reeds and bobbed lazily through the brush and across the water. Insects and birds and frogs all went about their lives in the dark, despite the clouds blocking the stars. The crew had lit extra lanterns for her and Fredderick's sakes, and three dwarves were on watch, pacing the deck and muttering to each other in *Mord-seq*.

Amandine approached him quietly, trying to think of what to say. As she came up behind him, Fredderick turned his head slightly. "You know what? Sometimes I really hate you."

Amandine's eyes widened in shock. She silently handed Fredderick his boots.

Fredderick faced her as the boots came over his shoulder. He looked surprised and then his features twisted into a scowl.

"You should put them back on, you'll freeze your feet."

His expression softened. "Amandine, I—"

"I don't mind if you hate me." Amandine looked away. "What I said was unkind. I deserved that."

"What—hate you? Amandine—" he looked down. Dumpling whined. Fredderick turned his back to her and resumed looking out over the water.

"Goodnight, Fredderick."

He didn't answer. As she walked away, she heard him mutter. "...no different than last time..."

She climbed back below decks and went to her cabin. It was all hers now. Fredderick continued to sleep in the hold, despite the open bed. With the door secured, she collapsed into her blankets. Grendel hopped up and touched his nose to hers as she stared at Serand's empty bed.

He began to purr and she hugged him. "At least I still have you, right?"

Meow.

Myron's Bend

"Magisterial justice in Serentia is performed according to a set of policies agreed upon in council. These rules lay out the guidelines for how people accused of crimes may be held and questioned, as well as how they may defend themselves against accusations. There is a large amount of room for interpretation, however, and each regional Magistrate tends to put their own personal style upon how these rules are implemented. The primary enforcers of these rules are the regional Sheriffs. Depending on the size of the area being overseen, some Magistrates may keep as many as three or four in their employ, although most only hire a single Sheriff that oversees their mandates. The Sheriff, in turn, may retain a number of pages and deputies that help them with their assigned duties."

- Lecture Notes, First Starday, Low Winter 1202

MORNING CAME AND the Silver Mountain finally arrived at the docks. Fredderick had remained silent over breakfast. The memory of her disaster of a conversation with him had haunted Amandine all night. As she gathered her things into a satchel to take some shore leave, he entered the galley and stood in the doorway.

"Amandine?"

"Yes?" she answered without looking up as she continued to pack her bag.

"I really wasn't trying to spy on you. Dwarves can see in total darkness, you know? My illusions bend light, and so if the *mord* don't need it to see... that is, it doesn't seem to work on them very well at all. I was dodging them by hiding in the cargo, but that one that watched the cattle nearly found me out and... anyway, I'm sorry if it offended you. I was just trying not to get caught."

She paused. "Well, Fredderick, the thing is, you always get caught."

"Yeah, I'm pretty bad at being a sneak, even with magic."

"Then what in the Goddess' names are you doing here? You're trying to be a sneak around the wrong people. Elves and dwarves and former Seekers. Start smaller. Like hiding from Marlette. Oh, wait, you've already mastered that. Should be a useful skill once you're wed."

"I was trying to apologize."

Amandine shrugged. She didn't care anymore. He hated her, right? "If you want to do something for me..."

"Anything."

"Take that," Amandine pointed to Serand's backpack and satchel. "Get it to Dena, and tell her what happened."

"I— you're not going back to Stoneman?"

"No. Serand had a job to do, and I intend to see it through." Amandine patted her satchel. "I have the letters, and I know who I am looking for. There is no way I am going back there, to face Dena, to face everyone, without a solution to our problem. I at least need to make the effort."

Fredderick sighed. "Then... yes, I'll do it."

"Thanks."

"So where are you going now?"

"Into town. Captain Cragllin is escorting the prisoners to the local magistrate's offices, and I am not going to drink shrimp soup all the rest of the way to Anvilroot."

"I can come with you."

Amandine finally looked at him. His expression seemed hurt, which only annoyed her more. "No. I think I'd rather be alone for a while."

Fredderick nodded and stepped out of the way to let her pass. "Alright. Will you at least say goodbye before the barge leaves again? I'll probably be here a day or so to send letters."

She nodded. "Sure. Fine."

"Um, good luck."

She ignored him and climbed up on deck. A few sailors stood "watch," playing a game of stones on an overturned barrel. They waved to her as she made her way down the gangplank, and she waved back.

Myron's Bend was larger than Stoneman, but sprawled over the curving river-front as if someone had upended a jug full of warehouses, townie houses, and cottages against the shoreline. It stretched for half a yarn in either direction from the docks. Taller buildings peeked out here and there further inland, and smoke from chimneys and forges filled the air with a deeper haze than what she was used to. There was no outer wall, no gates. Perhaps its proximity to Greenest and Anvilroot afforded the town less need for a garrison?

As she thought the words, however, she spied a group of men and women dressed in mail with sigils marked on their shields and shoulders. They walked with the authority that she had come to associate with the Stoneman militia, and people rapidly made way for them. Myron's Bend was not *completely* without some sort of defense, it would seem.

She followed a trail from the docks up to a fence which served as a makeshift checkpoint between the docks and the town. There was a guard, but he seemed to be half asleep and barely took any notice as wagons and porters passed by without so much as a cursory inspection.

"Excuse me?" Amandine asked, waving at the distracted guard. "I'm new here, can you direct me to the market circle?"

"The what?" He blinked lethargically.

"Um, wherever it is that people buy food?"

"Oh, ya wan' to go to Grocer's Lane, kid. It runs by the temple of Delinkhal, that way. There'll be a sign."

"Thanks!"

He merely nodded and went back to staring at nothing, lost in his own thoughts. Amandine followed the guard's instructions and found the market he'd spoken of. It was surprisingly easy. Like Artemis, the town had added signs to every intersection, naming the streets and indicating who lived or worked on them. Stoneman had no such directions. You either knew where you were going or you didn't.

She was surprised to discover that Grocer's Lane was the longest road in the town, with triple the merchants she was used to back at home, but was unsurprised to find that, here too, some things were becoming hard to find.

"Three silvers for carrots?" Amandine asked in protest. "I understand that people are preparing for shiv, but—"

"I'm the last stall in town with any to sell," the merchant said irritably. "Since the black mold took the storage caves, there ain't any other choice. Either buy them or don't. I am not going to haggle."

Amandine bought them. She had no idea what 'black mold' was, but it would seem that Myron's Bend had similar, but different, troubles to Stoneman's. How far had the food spoilage and loss spread? Had the orchards near Artemis also been ruined? The elfin gardens? The berry bogs? A sinking feeling settled in as the next three stands she visited were the same. Food was either on the edge of spoilage, or so overpriced that she would empty her coin purse too rapidly unless she skipped buying several things. Amandine felt her stomach clench at the idea of subsisting off the shrimp broth any longer, but she would need some money once she actually got to Anvilroot, so she couldn't spend it all here.

As meager as the pickings were, Amandine found enough that if she were careful, she would not have to eat those horrible shrimp for a tenday at least. She bought a fried sausage from a cart as a treat and made her way back towards the center of the district. In the middle of Myron's Bend was a statue of the town's namesake and founder, a human, and the dwarf he had partnered with to build the docks. Amandine stopped to read the brass plaque bolted to the bottom of the huge base.

"In mem... ry of... Myron Tailor and Jirt MacGurren. A commi... err, community built on trust is stronger than one cast from fear." Amandine read out loud to herself. The quote was repeated in a series of Dwarven runes beneath the Olgothian script. It was a nice sentiment. Maybe that was why the town had opted to have no walls?

As if in imitation of the artwork, a group of dwarves, the crew from the Silver Mountain, passed through the square in the company of a human man. He was light haired and tall, wearing a deep blue cloak. What really caught Amandine's eye, however, was the long knife on his belt. The handle was carved with a raven. That marked him as the local Sheriff. She ate her last bite of sausage and discarded the stick it had been cooked on, then approached the group.

Captain Cragllin noticed her first. "Ah, Amandine. Will you tell this man we ain't lyin'!"

"And who is this, then?" the Sheriff asked.

"Our galley-mate. She was there when they attacked and lost her Apprentice Master in the scuffle."

"And I suppose she saw the wumpus too?" the man said with an amused grin.

"I did, sah," Amandine said. "It was taller than the boat, with matted fur and a mouth so wide you could fit a tusker inside it."

His mouth twisted into an annoyed grimace. "Sahs, with all respect, a wumpus hasn't been seen North of the Emerald in over a hundred years. Something tells me that *someone* would have noticed stripped trees and decimated fields if there was one really roaming about."

"But what if it was tamed, sah? It seemed like the pirate's leader was giving it commands." There was a murmur of agreement from the gathered dwarves.

"So now it's a tamed wumpus?" The Sheriff raised an eyebrow.

"Send a shipwright to inspect the Silver Mountain," Cragllin said. "The damage is proof!"

"Proof that a beast no one has seen in these parts for a century attacked your boat in the middle of the river? A beast, I might add, known to be reclusive, timid, and destructive only to trees and crops? You aren't aiding your case, Captain."

"Bah! You said yourself there were criminals among the folks we brought to you!"

"*A* criminal. The fellow with the scar is wanted for desertion and assault. He will be hanged and you've been paid his bounty. We have nothing on any of those others, and they maintain their innocence.

"So you'll take the word of a bunch of pirates over me and my crew because they ain't *Ur'Mord*, eh?"

"I did *not* say that, sah. But your word is *all* I have and your story is, frankly, quite unbelievable."

The dwarves muttered angrily at that. Amandine got the impression they did not care for their leader being called a liar, but the Sheriff was responsible for dispensing justice for a region when required, and so they didn't appear to have a lot of choice.

"Sheriff Rocher! It's been a long time, sah!"

Everyone turned as Fredderick approached the group. Sheriff Rocher squinted as he took in the young man's disheveled appearance.

"Are you— I know you. You're... Derrick?"

"Fredderick Stolm, sah. It's been a few years, but..."

"Oh yes, your father is the master of Stolm Depository in Irongate. I know your cousin well. We have worked together in the past. Last I saw you, you were almost two hands shorter!"

"Indeed, well, I wish to enter a statement on behalf of the Silver Mountain."

"You had best—" Captain Cragllin began, but Fredderick interrupted.

"Please, Captain, this is the only way I can properly thank you for both your generosity on this voyage and the valiant efforts of your crew in dealing with those that attacked your fair ship."

Cragllin eyed Fredderick suspiciously, but became silent.

The Sheriff looked thoughtful. "You were there, lad?"

"Yes, sah, I was traveling to Anvilroot with these fine people on official business for my cousin. I have been acting as her page for nearly two years now. We were beset by pirates, sah. Although some of them, I believe, may be locals who have turned to brigandry because of the shortages."

"That would explain *some* things," Sheriff Rocher conceded. "But the wumpus?"

"Strange but true. Like something out of a storybook, I know. It was being employed to hold the ship and shake her crew into the river."

"Gods, this is the last thing I need right now." Sheriff Rocher rubbed his jaw. "Fine, here is what I will do for you, Captain. I can't pay bounty on people with no bounty assigned, but I will have your dock fees waived while you seek repairs for your ship. If you wish to transfer cargos, I will also have portages waived. It's the best I can do, under the circumstances. Send one of your crew to collect the bounty you *are* owed and to sign statements. I will need to have a scouting group search the Millbreak woods for signs of these brigands."

"And if you find proof our story was not false?" Cragllin asked in a surly tone.

"Then I will make a written apology to you, and you will be paid a deputized fee for the prevention of banditry in the region. Same rates we offer Seekers who turn up malfeasance. If you have departed before then, both will be sent by courier to a holder of your choosing."

Cragliin nodded. "Aye, that is an offer I can accept. First Mate Highrock, you go with this floppy hat as my agent. Sign all the sandy papers he wants. I will go see to my ship."

"Aye, cap'n!"

The First Mate left with the Sheriff and Captain Cragllin turned to Fredderick. "That's twice you've helped me now. Three counting the patchwork to my ship. I don't like owing stowaways a debt."

"Then please consider it full repayment for my uninvited passage on your vessel, Captain."

The old dwarf nodded. "Done. Safe travels to you, lad."

"Thank you, and to you, Captain."

Cragllin turned to Amandine. "As for you. You are welcome to remain as our galley-mate, but we will be delayed. I know your destination was Anvilroot, but we need to wait for repairs or another barge. We could be here for a cycle or more."

"That long?" She had been counting on a remaining trip of no more than two tendays.

"Aye, perhaps longer. Despite the pitch, she's leaking like a cracked beer mug. I won't risk another soul on the river until I am sure she's watertight."

"Then... I feel I must depart your ship, sah. I will take an overland route the rest of the way. My business can't be delayed."

Cragllin nodded. "Your cabin is yours until you depart."

"Thank you, sah."

The pack of dwarves ambled off. Some of them waved to Amandine as they left. Fredderick folded his arms and watched them go.

"So you're going to walk the rest of the way to Anvilroot?"

"If I must. I don't ride well, and I don't have the money to hire a transport. Serand and I were paying our passage with work," she said.

"You have no money at all? What about the gold from the skellix bounty? I know my cousin only paid you the deputized rate, but that was still over a hundred crown."

"Most of that is safely hidden. In the Gold Hills. Or invested with Miss Jacinda. I only brought about three crowns, and was given a fourth because of a wager at the docks. I just spent half of that on food."

He winced at that. "Gods, I didn't realize it would be that bad here too."

"I think it's going to be that bad everywhere, Fredderick."

"Well... I know you have an offer from the Captain, but if you want, I have a room at the inn here. You can stay there until you leave, if you like."

Amandine made a face. "I don't want charity from you."

"Charity is what you do for strangers who have a need. Are we really strangers now, Amandine?" Fredderick's shoulders slumped as he spoke.

With a sigh, Amandine conceded the point. "I'll think about it. What's the name of the inn?"

"The Watery Crossroads. It's that way, past the counting house. Big green sign," Fredderick said rapidly. "I left Dumpling there to watch my things, so—"

"Yes, fine. I'll maybe come in for a bite later and we can talk. They have food?"

"It smelled like they did."

"Then I will stop by tonight."

"I look forward to it!"

Amandine tried to smile at him. He was making an effort, but she was heartsick, and exhausted, and now she had to plan an unexpected overland trip with next to no money. Fredderick seemed to notice her mood and his own smile faltered.

"We'll figure this out, Amandine."

She nodded and walked away. But figure out what, she wondered? How to navigate to Anvilroot, or how to navigate one another?

Either way, it seemed like a daunting task.

Lucky Salt

"Definition of a Crew: crews registered with a chapter will be no less than three individuals and no more than eight. At least one person must be registered as the Crew Lead, and may assign a second. The charter for a crew is tied to the Lead and is not transferable. If the Crew Lead is no longer able or willing, the designated second may renew the charter for the Crew under the same name with Guild approval. Otherwise, the Crew is disbanded and its name retired."

- Seeker Charter Contract, Appendix 4, definitions

THE WATERY CROSSROADS was a completely different experience from the Stomping Golem. It was only a single story, shaped like a horseshoe, with the common area in the middle. Long hallways with rooms for sleeping and... other things, made up the two sides of the horseshoe.

Amandine blushed as an attractive young man with tawny hair, and no shirt on, winked at her as he passed the table. He wasn't serving drinks or food. She buried her face in her mug of tea and tried to ignore him, but gave in and had a peek after he walked by. He was wearing incredibly tight trousers.

"You know, if you keep acting interested, they will keep making passes," Fredderick said with a grin.

"I'm not interested!" Amandine protested.

"The path of your gaze betrays you," Fredderick said, still grinning. "I mean, he's not bad looking at all. Neither was that woman with the red hair."

"Her wrap is so sheer you *can see through it*!" Amandine said in a low hiss. "I wasn't being a lech!"

"So you say."

"Fredderick!"

He waved a hand in a pacifying gesture. "I'm not trying to make fun. Well, maybe a little bit."

When Amandine glared at him again, he quickly continued. "I'm just surprised, is all. Surely Artemis had places like this?"

"I did not have much cause to frequent alehouses and whore dens while being an Apprentice Bone Guardian," Amandine said sourly.

"Harsh! I maintain this is still an inn. There is food and rooms for rent. The rest is just... entrepreneurship."

Amandine gulped her tea and wished her face would stop burning. Of all the places Fredderick could have taken rooms at! She tried to ignore the half-dressed men and women and watch the rest of the room instead.

It was a lively crowd, and varied. Dock workers rubbed shoulders with well-heeled merchants and even a few that might have been local nobles. There were humans and Hill Folk and a large number of dwarves. The servers, who wore proper clothing, thank the gods, were in constant motion, so business was good. They mostly focused on delivering ale and spirits. Very few people seemed to be eating. The interior was not as rough or dirty as she might have imagined, but the building definitely had a well-worn air to it, and was a far cry from Bertrand's immaculate common area.

A musician began strumming on a lurin as customers applauded and shouted out requests. That was another difference from the Golem: actors and musicians rarely passed through Stoneman. It was a small place, a shortcut between major holds primarily used by merchants. Performers tended to take the longer roads, which led to larger towns, and more of them. The chances to make coin were far better on those routes. As far as Amandine knew, the last group of performers to pass through had done so before the incident with the skellix: a drummer and storyteller who had only stayed a single night before moving on.

One table in particular stood out in the crowd. It was positioned near the bar. Five people sat around it having an animated conversation. The first was a short, round-faced human man with a circle of hair on the very top of his head. He wore gray robes and seemed rather dreary. Next to him was a Hill Folk woman with long hair that had somehow been colored yellow. Not blonde, *yellow*, like wildflower petals. By contrast to her neighbor, she was bright eyed and cheerful, with a wide, dimpled grin. She sat on a backpack to share the human-sized table with her fellows. The next one over was an elf. She was only the second elf, full blooded anyway, that Amandine had ever encountered aside from Mister Green. Her hair was light brown like acorn shells and her skin was freckled much like Gil's. Her blue eyes, however, had an unblinking... *wideness* to them that made her seem a bit crazed. A faint smile pulled at one corner of her mouth. The other man at the table was a bald, dark-skinned, surly-looking fellow with a squashed nose and patchy beard. He was dressed in lightweight armor, but had one arm in a sling.

The last, a human woman with silky raven black hair and pale skin, moved her hands to illustrate whatever she was describing to her comrades. A long, double-sided sword in a black leather sheath hung from her chair and she was dressed in leathers that reminded Amandine of what Birch had worn when he had still been–

"Say, Fredderick?" Amandine asked. "Do you think that lot are Seekers?"

He glanced over at the table and shrugged. "Could be. Or simple sellswords. Or even actors still in their roles."

"Do actors usually wander about armed?"

"Alright, so perhaps not actors. Why are you curious? Thinking of signing up with a guild chapter?"

Amandine sighed and put her chin in her hands. "No, I suppose not. I really like what I am learning and–"

Chef was gone. Who would teach her now? She let her hands fall, laid her head on the table, and watched the woman with the black hair tell her story. What *was* she going to do?

"Thinking about Chef Brutsche?"

"Yes."

"I'm sorry, Amandine."

She sat back up and shrugged. "I am not going to cry anymore. But I don't know what to do when I get back to Stoneman."

A server arrived at their table and put a bowl in front of each of them.

"At last!" Fredderick's tone was full of longing. "Something not shrimp flavored!"

Amandine was hungry too. It had been a long time since that sausage. She picked up a fork and stirred the thick stew, breathing it in.

A whiff of something sour, followed by something spicy, caught her nose, causing her to wrinkle it up. "I don't know," she said.

"Come on, it's my treat! Eat up!"

"Where did you get the money for this and your room, anyhow?"

Fredderick pointed to his ear. The silver earring he had worn was gone.

"You sold your jewelry?"

"Yeah. That, and then I found this fellow running a shell game. I put up my silver and walked away with more."

"So you cheated him."

"Only after he tried to cheat me. Eat!"

He followed his own instructions and scooped up a large bite of stew. Amandine followed suit.

"Oh gods," Fredderick said.

"I know," Amandine agreed.

"I think this is the worst thing I have eaten in my entire life."

"It's awful."

"Did you bring any shrimp soup from the boat?" Fredderick asked before swishing his mouth with tea.

Amandine studied her bowl. How could it be so terrible? Had the cook not even tasted it? It had all of the constituent elements: root vegetables, egg, green-stalk and some sort of fatty meat. Even unspiced it should be edible, but this was all wrong.

"No," Amandine said.

"Drat, because despite what I said, I'd rather have that right about now." Fredderick picked his teeth and grimaced.

"No, I mean I will not let this stand. I am going to talk to the cook," Amandine said, still staring at her bowl in consternation.

"Uh, you're what?"

"I am going to talk to the colorless cook! How dare they serve... whatever this is and call it food!"

Someone at a nearby table who had overheard her snickered loudly. Amandine ignored it and stood up with her bowl.

"Really, Amandine, you don't need—"

"And you, Fredderick Stolm, have absolutely no right to tell *me* what I *need*. You eat yours if you like, but I sure as hells won't."

She practically stormed up to the bar. Heads turned curiously as she passed, including the woman with the raven hair. Amandine planted the bowl on the counter with a crack, causing a server standing nearby to jump.

"I would like to speak with the cook," she said.

The server, a young man with shaved hair, blinked as if she had spoken in another language.

"Can you please go tell them?" Amandine stared the man down. "I won't eat this, and they need to make it right."

The server slowly nodded and slipped away, carefully watching Amandine as he did so.

"Carver is a shite cook, kid."

Amandine turned to find the dark-haired woman grinning at her. She pointed to the bowl. "Like eating a helping of dung, right?"

"Surely he doesn't make it like this all the time?"

"No, sometimes it's worse," the bearded man with the injured arm said. The rest of the table laughed, except for the fellow with the odd circle of hair.

"Alright, who is the colorless troll-arse that wants to get beat today?" a voice boomed behind Amandine.

She turned back to the bar and saw a scrawny man with a wispy, pointed goat-beard looking at her. His hands rested on his hips. The deep, resonant voice that emanated from him was completely at odds with how he looked.

"This one, Carver," the black-haired woman said. "Although if you want a wager, I think she could take you."

"If your tongue were as sharp as yer blade, Mel, you'd not be making such a jape. You lot still owe me a sizable tab!" he shot back. The wiry man eyed Amandine. He had a rodent-like look to him that she had come to associate with terrible people like Henri Nous. All he needed was a mustache. "Well, say your piece then, fool."

A fool, was she? Amandine curled her hands into fists and braced her feet. "Your stew isn't fit to be fed to pigs. You should be ashamed, charging money for it."

A round of amused murmurs circled Mel's table. She actually turned her chair and leaned forward to watch. Her grin grew even wider.

"You have a lot of nerve coming into my place and telling me anything of the sort!" Carver walked over, pulled a chunk of grisly meat from her bowl with his fingers and popped it in his mouth. "That's my secret blend of spices, and fine pork too! Nothin' wrong with it—now get lost, girl!"

"If your secret blend of spices includes pepper, sage and korrel seed, then the only secret is that you add half-rancid pork-ends that the butcher was probably going to use as fish bait."

Carver narrowed his eyes at Amandine. "Think you can do better, you little shite?" he growled. "It ain't meant to be fine dining. It's fuel to fire up bastards like this lot, so they can go get their limbs hacked off on a full stomach."

"I'll get my limbs hacked off on an empty stomach if the other option is your food, Carver," Mel said.

"Shut your trap, sword strumpet! If yer wits were as large as yer tits, you'd not be a Seeker. Sod off!"

Instead of being angry, Mel just laughed at Carver and put her hands on her chest in a *very* suggestive way while blowing kisses at the foul man. Amandine's fingers drifted up to brush her hair, covering her scar, as she cleared her throat and fought back a blush. She looked away from Mel and said: "I am pretty sure I could outdo your stew in my sleep, with the same ingredients."

Another round of murmurs, louder this time. Other tables were taking notice.

"That so? What's the action?" Carver asked.

Amandine blinked. "What?"

"Oh, she's precious, I like her!" Mel said.

"He's asking you what you'll wager on such a claim, kid," the bearded man added.

"Oh, um, the cost of my friend's room, our meals, and um..."

"Our tab," Mel said.

"But I don't—" Amandine began.

"Look at her, Mel, she ain't got that kind of coin," Carver said with a chuckle.

"I'll cover it," Mel said calmly. The Hill Folk woman stood on the backpack to whisper something in her ear. "Oh, and rounds for the table tonight until we pass out."

"You're full of shite," Carver said.

Mel reached into a pouch on her belt and produced a large green gem. It was multifaceted and the size of a crow's egg. She set it on the table. "I'm covering it. Are you in or out, you provac?"

Amandine was speechless. A gem like that was worth hundreds of crowns. Not even Lady Everdawn owned jewelry with stones that size. It was one of the most amazing things she had ever seen. The room around her had gone very quiet. Everyone was paying attention now, and even the musician had stopped his strumming.

"I can't cover that," Carver said, his eyes shifting.

"You don't have to. If you lose, you just pay what was said. If you win, you keep the difference."

Carver licked his lips, obviously weighing the odds. "Sod it. I'm in."

"One condition," the elf said, interrupting. Everyone turned to look at her. Her large, unblinking eyes locked onto Carver. "You cannot be the judge. The first person—human, fae, or *mord*—to walk through the door after she finishes will taste it. Their appraisal will stand."

"And what if I don't like that condition?" Carver sneered and raised an eyebrow.

The female elf just continued to stare at him in an unnerving way. It even made Amandine uncomfortable and she wasn't the one being stared at.

"Fine!" Carver relented. "Please just turn yer colorless bug eyes onto some other poor soul! Come on then, miss...?"

"Amandine, sah."

"Follow me, miss Armadillo," Carver said as he stormed back through the door into the kitchens.

"You *do* know how to cook?" Mel asked with a grin before Amandine could walk away.

"Yes, sah. I was a Chef's Apprentice."

"No, really," she said with a chuckle.

"No, really, I was. His... his name was Serand."

Mel seemed to notice the past tense and her smile slipped. "Well then you should trounce the pants off that fool. If he tries to alter the terms, ignore him. He's addicted to wagers like a dwarf to raw meat. It's the only reason he took this foolish bet."

"I want to watch!" the yellow haired woman announced. "I'll make sure Carver minds his manners!"

"Good idea, Blueknot," Mel said, her grin returning. She leaned back in her seat. In a louder voice, she called in the direction of the kitchen: "At worst, we all might get a decent meal out of this latrine for once!"

"I heard that!" Carver shouted from the back.

She gave Amandine a friendly wink and turned away as the fellow with the odd hair slid a small slate across the table for Mel to look at. Amandine turned and walked through the door into the kitchen, followed by the Hill Folk woman, Blueknot.

"There you are, Amatrine!" Carver said with a scowl.

"Amandine, sah."

"That's what I said!"

Amandine shook her head. The kitchen was atrocious. She had never seen one so filthy in her life. Cobwebs hung from the ceiling, and dirty bowls sat by a tub of water covered in a greasy sheen. Scraps and rags littered the floors. Amandine was certain she saw something move.

Carver pulled a grimy pot off a stack in the washtub and dropped it on a table in front of Amandine with a clatter.

"There you go. Meat's on the block. So let's see it then."

With a grimace, Amandine looked at the pot. It badly needed a scrub. She'd have to do that first. The meat was as she expected: grisly throwaway ends that most people wouldn't find palatable. She rolled up her sleeves.

"Water?" she asked.

Carver pointed to a pump near the door. They had an indoor pump? "What a novel thing," Amandine muttered as she used it to rinse and clean the pot. Blueknot leaned against a beam while she watched. A pair of circular blades with handles, weapons of some sort that Amandine hadn't noticed before, clattered against her hip.

"She's already up on ya, Carvy. She knows how to wash a pot," she said.

"You stay out of it!" Carver hissed at the tiny woman.

Out in the common room, the lurin player struck up a tune with a dramatic cadence. The strings melded with a hollow thumping beat as the player drummed on the wide base of the instrument between chords. Amandine grinned, put the pot on to boil, then got to work.

The vegetables were sad, wilted things, and some had begun to turn. Slicing quickly, Amandine trimmed all of the gray ends, soft spots and yellowed portions. She diced the vegetables extra fine. If a root was going bad, it was better to make the pieces smaller and cook them fully, than risk leaving uncooked centers. Next she went to the meat. The thinner tissue she left on the chunks—it would melt into the meat and add flavor—but all of the hard sinew and tough fat, she removed. As the water began to simmer, she tossed the fatty trimmings and gristle in and added salt.

A look at the spice selection proved it to be equally abysmal. She found the trio used for covering spoilage, but the only one helpful to her was the pepper. Many of the dried herbs were stale and unusable. She did find a small tin of jitti powder, though. It was used to make a spicy stew-like dish from Zulathia. The can was so covered in dust that she doubted Carver even knew what it was.

"I hope you like spicy stew," Amandine said to Blueknot.

"I'm impressed. Ye really do know how a kitchen works," Blueknot said. "As for spicy, I'll eat anything with a pepper in it. Ragall is the big baby when it comes to spice."

"Which one is he?"

"Bald, bearded fellow doing the tusker impression."

"What happened to his arm?"

"Had a run in with a troll. Real one. Gave Rag quite the thrashing. Bastard got away too, but we didn't pursue it. Wasn't the job."

"So you're Seekers?"

"Yup! Holbrook chapter. We're registered as Vibrant Dawn. Pleased to meet ya, by the way."

"And you, sah," Amandine said as she cubed meat. "So you named your, um, group?"

"Yeah, the name was Mel's cracked idea. She acts the rogue, but has a romantic heart under it all. And they're called 'crews,' you know, like on boats. We've been a crew for over two years now. Had some success too."

"You gonna talk or make stew?" Carver said.

"Girl talk, Carver, sod off." Blueknot turned back to Amandine. "So that fellow at your table. He your beau? He has nice hair."

Amandine felt her face running hot again. "Uh... no. We're, um, friends, but not—"

"Mel's right, you're adorable," Blueknot said with a laugh. "I didn't know a Bolath girl could blush that red."

"I'm not, he's not—" Amandine tried to find the words to defend herself, but everything she could think of sounded like an excuse. "I have to fry the meat, sah."

Blueknot laughed again, but let the subject drop as Amandine took the better chunks of meat and began to fry them in a small pan. It was too small, so she had to do it in batches, but by the end, every tiny chunk had a crispy brown edge. She used a spoon to fish the boiled tendon and fat out of the hot water and discarded it. Then she put the vegetables in, allowed them to boil for a bit, and added the meat.

"Do you have anything that could be a thickener? Milk, cream? Even some flour?"

"Same ingredients, girl," Carver sneered.

"Well, ok, but then it'll have to boil longer. You have three bells?"

Carver frowned. He looked conflicted, but Amandine could tell he didn't want to wait that long. "There's acorn powder. In the pantry."

Amandine nodded and went to find it. It was old, but hadn't rusted. The flavor would be more astringent than she wanted, but should thicken the base nicely. She cast about for something to take the edge off it. "May I have a mug of beer? Dark is better."

"I ain't serving a kid beer," Carver said, folding his arms.

"You'd sell your mother for a copper, Carver, don't be an arse," Blueknot said.

"I don't want to drink it, it's for the stew," Amandine said.

Carver blinked at that. "You want to put beer in stew?" he asked incredulously. "That sounds vile."

"Maybe," Amandine admitted. She had never tried making stew this particular way, but had seen it done, and the malt in a thick beer would definitely cut the acorn flavor.

The rat-like man grinned. "Well certainly then!" He went out to the taps and came back with a tall, foamy mug. The brown foam meant it was dark, possibly something dwarvish. Just what she needed. Amandine added everything to the pot and lowered the coals to let it simmer.

"Half a bell," she announced.

"So," Carver said. "What do you say we up the stakes a bit?"

"This wager is already more than I can afford without Mel's help, so no."

"That dagger has to be worth something. Olgath steel, right?"

Amandine touched the hilt of her dagger and eyed Carver warily.

"Mind manners, Carver," Blueknot said. She had one of her odd hand-blades off her belt and held it in a fist. She made a show of testing the edge with a thumb.

"Ain't none of your—" Carver began, but the look he received from the yellow-haired woman brought him up short.

It made Amandine wary as well. The jovial, happy person that had been teasing her about Fredderick was gone. The aura of menace Blueknot gave off was unsettling.

"Bah, fine," Carver said, folding. For all his bluster, Amandine was beginning to realize he was an enormous coward.

He retreated from the kitchen, leaving Amandine and Blueknot alone.

"So you really trained under a Chef, eh? Some fancy dining place in Irongate?" she asked.

"A lord's kitchen in the Gold Hills. Near Stoneman."

"Oh? I've been through there. Have a couple of distant cousins in Waterbeetle. Nice little garden, but sort of an odd place for a Chef."

"That's what I thought too, sah," Amandine agreed.

"And you said his name was Serand?"

"Yes, Serand Brutsche, sah."

Blueknot blinked. "Brutsche, you say?"

"Yes, why?"

"Oh, it's probably just a coincidence. But that's a fairly well known name among Seekers. The Serand Brutsche I have heard of ran with a crew called Lucky Salt. A crazy godsworn named Rallindra Evos was its leader, but the stories are that she and Brute shared the top spot as well as a bed. They were the ones that took out the Stone Giant lord, Lorogos. Gods, they are practically legends! Amongst guild folk anyway, I guess. I imagine not many outside the chapters knew of them."

"Yeah, maybe it is just a coincidence," Amandine said softly. 'Rally' had been her name. The woman everyone had been mourning after Wizard Hemm's news. Gods, why had Serand been hiding in Stoneman? Why were any of them, if they had been famous Seekers and heroes?

"You ok, kid?" Blueknot asked.

"Oh, yes, I'm fine, thanks. I just hope this stew comes out well and you don't lose that beautiful gem."

Blueknot laughed. "If my nose is any judge, we have nothing to worry about."

"What else can you tell me about Lucky Salt?" Amandine asked. "I'd like to hear some stories."

For the next half a bell, Blueknot told Amandine every tale she had of the famous Lucky Salt. They had explored mage war ruins, fought trolls and North March fae, killed a Giant Lord, rescued an Olgothian trade prince. There was even the story Serand had told her about the demon. It had been in Olgath's Maw. Something had changed after that, apparently. The crew had broken up. Rally and Serand had disappeared into the East, and rumors of their deaths were numerous.

Amandine knew they were both dead now. She wondered if Blueknot would be disappointed in the way it had happened. With a sigh, Amandine wiped her face and found tears in her eyes.

"Wait, are you cryin', kid? I didn't say somethin' to upset you, did I?"

"No, sah. I'm fine," Amandine said, offering a smile.

"Time's up!" Carver called.

Amandine found some mostly clean dish cloths and used them as mitts to carry the hot pot of stew out into the commons. She set it on the back counter of the bar upon a metal sheet next to the pot of Carver's stew.

When she took her seat at the table with Fredderick again, he was grinning.

"What's so funny?" she asked.

"When you went into the kitchen, this room lost its mind. I've never seen so many coins exchanged. Your wager with that rodent isn't the only one, Amandine."

She cringed a little. "I just wanted him to apologize for the terrible food."

"To hells with that, this is way more fun," Fredderick said with glee.

"How much did you wager?" Amandine frowned.

"A gentleman doesn't discuss such things."

"Honestly, Fredderick!"

The bell above the door chimed. The entire room erupted into cheers. The old, white-bearded human who had just walked in stood stunned as the entire room clapped for him. The red-haired woman with the see-through top led him by the hand, sat him on a stool by the bar and draped herself over him.

"Did my name-day come early?" he asked wheezily, brow furrowed. "Ah, hello, Umie. Yer a fine sight even if it ain't," he added with a grin for the red-haired woman.

"Better," Carver said. "Because yer about to win me a sack of gold."

The old man blinked. Amandine winced. The stew was really spicy—what if it was too hot for him? If he didn't agree it was good, then it was very likely she would have a pack of Seekers after her hide.

Carver placed a still-steaming bowl in front of the man and added a spoon. Amandine gripped the cloth of her pants. The old man looked about nervously. Everyone stared back at him expectantly. Finally with a sigh, he took the spoon, winced and scooped up a bite of stew.

"Oh, gods," he said, closing his eyes. "That has a *bite*. Beer please, if'n ya don't mind?"

Amandine shrank down in her chair and hid her face.

Carver poured a mug with a wide grin. "Awful shite, am I right, Jacob?"

The old man gulped some beer and wiped his chin. He coughed. "Actually, it's just spicy. It's like that stuff we'd get in Zulath lands when I was still caravanin'."

Carver's smile slipped. Amandine peeked between her fingers.

"Just needs ale to cut the spice. This is actually really good. Did you finally hire a cook, Carver?"

Most of the room erupted again into cheers and the old man jumped in his seat. The red-haired woman, Umie, planted a huge kiss on his cheek. He looked completely baffled.

"Pay up, you weasel!" Mel shouted with a laugh. "First round, right here, right now!"

Carver's eyes shot daggers at her, but as people came up to the bar to order a bowl of Amandine's stew, he seemed more than willing to take their money for it.

A well-dressed gentleman walked by their table, stopped briefly to drop a small stack of silver next to Fredderick's arm and then walked away with a sniff.

Fredderick split the stack neatly and dropped half of it, four silver, in front of Amandine. "Jack's tithe. You didn't think I would bet against you?"

She looked up at him with a raised eyebrow and a twist to her lips, but found that she didn't really care about the gambling, it was his money, after all. Her expression slipped into a grin, and then she laughed. "Oh gods, Fredderick. You're such a fool."

"Maybe, but even in the unlikely event I had lost, it would have been silver well spent. That was excellent."

Another person approached their table. It was the Seeker with the strange haircut from Mel's table. His gray robes swirled about him and he was a fair bit taller than he had looked sitting down. He placed two bowls on the table in front of them. Amandine's stew.

"Thank you, sah," Amandine said. "I didn't catch your name?"

He nodded silently and pointed to a small slate tied around his neck. On it was written the word "Tobe."

"Your name is Tobe?"

He nodded again.

"Thank you, Tobe, it was a pleasure to meet you all."

"Hah," he said with a smile. When he opened his mouth, Amandine was horrified to realize he had no teeth. Also, no tongue. Tobe grabbed his slate and rubbed it off with the heel of his hand then quickly scratched something else on it with chalk.

"A pleasure to meet a fellow godsworn," Amandine read. "But, sah, I'm not—"

Tobe nodded solemnly and made the hand symbol for Berindor, god of war and strength, fists pressed together at the knuckles. He pointed to himself. He made the hand symbol for Ravenex, cupped hands interlinked, followed by Kayla, crossed palms over the heart, and then pointed to her and cocked his head.

"No, no! I'm not godsworn. I was raised by the Night Sisters, but—"

He arched an eyebrow, made the symbol for Ravenex again and then just shrugged. With a wave, he ambled away.

"What was that all about?" Fredderick asked.

"I haven't any idea," Amandine admitted.

Summer Rain

"The Obsidian Highway is one of the oldest maintained roads in the world. Stretching from Greyrock Falls all the way to Irongate, the only road that can claim to be longer is the Western Wastes Trade Route (also known as The Shattered Road). Originally built in collaboration with the Seven Hammers clan, the Obsidian Highway is one of the most vital trade routes in Serentia, and all Magisterial regions it touches receive a stipend from Irongate specifically to see to its maintenance."

- Lecture Notes, Second Fireday, Fall 1202

THE SILVER MOUNTAIN rocked slightly on the waves as Amandine stared at the ceiling of her tiny cabin. She had said farewell to Fredderick last night, and rebuffed another suggestion that she stay at the Watery Crossroads. Despite his foolishness, she really did like him, but she wasn't going to be a clinging nettle on his relationship woes with Marlette. Keeping his father happy obviously brought him no joy, but what did he actually want? Amandine couldn't fix his problems, and lecturing him was wrong. Marlette seemed happy with the arrangement, at least, but Amandine struggled to find the grace to wish her joy in anything. So why was Fredderick chasing her, then? He was going to so much trouble, had gotten in so much trouble, and yet...

That night on the boat still weighed on her heart. Why had Fredderick said he hated her? Had it just been anger? He had never apologized for or explained the comment.

Amandine sighed. Lying here thinking about it was just going to make her morose. The dawn gloom was starting to brighten the small portal in the cabin. She had a long walk ahead of her and it was time to get to it. With a groan, she hauled herself out of the cot and gathered up her backpack and satchel.

"In the bag, Gren, we need to say our goodbyes to the crew."

Grendel looked up and yawned at her from where he had been snoozing on Serand's bed. He meowed, but didn't otherwise complain as she lifted him into her satchel and then slung her pack. He fit inside it better now. Grendel's time running about the ship with Spice had trimmed his bulk a bit.

Her farewells to the crew were short, but heartfelt. Some of them gave her gifts of dried fish for Grendel or asked to stroke him one last time for luck. The dwarf she had rescued during the attack, Norrel, actually embraced her. It was a sign of deepest friendship from one of the *Ur'Mord*, and Amandine felt oddly touched and honored at the gesture.

Captain Craglin emerged from their cabin below decks and saw her personally to the gangplank.

"I want you to know that I don't normally accept humans on my crew," they said. "But your Apprentice Master was the best galley-mate I have had in tens of years. You also did well with little to spare after the sand-blasted pirates. You fought to protect my crew, my *nyre*, even when you could have just bailed and swam for shore. If your future travels cross mine ever again, I'd be glad to call you a friend."

"Thank you, sah," Amandine said. "I'd like that. I'm sorry I can't stay."

Grendel popped his head out of her satchel and meowed. Captain Craglin grinned and made the hand waving motion at the cat. "Stand to!" he bellowed. The milling crew on the deck stood up straight and faced him. "Galley-mate Amandine is departing the Silver Mountain!"

"Aye!" the crew called back.

The Captain thumped his chest in a sort of dwarven salute and stepped aside to allow Amandine to walk down the ramp. "Safe travels, lass."

"And to you, Captain." she replied.

As she passed back through Myron's Bend, Amandine stopped to buy additional supplies for her trip, including a small hand-warmer and lantern. With Grendel, she might not need the light, but the thought of having it at night gave her courage. She had planned her remaining journey so that she would only have to sleep outside two nights in the next tenday, but even that was risky. She hoped she could find a campsite secluded enough to have a light on those nights.

She exited the North end of town and followed a narrow road to a ferry, where two copper saw her safely to the opposite bank. That placed her on the Obsidian Highway, a trade road that would pass through several more towns before finally ending at a fortress city known as Greyrock Fall, the gateway into the Great Deep and Anvilroot. If she was lucky, it would only take her two more tendays, the same as if the Silver Mountain had continued upriver. When traveling against the current, barges didn't move fast, but walking the road was more dangerous. At least, it *had* been more dangerous. Amandine wasn't sure if anyplace was truly safe now.

Grendel walked with her, or ran ahead, as she passed through the lowlands along the Wolfshenta River's banks. He disappeared for a while at one point, which made her worry, but then turned up again with a bird in his mouth, looking rather pleased with himself. She found some wild stickle berries growing by the roadside as well, and took a moment to carefully harvest as many as she could fit into an empty spice pouch. The leaves had begun to turn on some of the trees, signaling the end of High Summer. Amandine hoped that the weather would stay warm enough to camp outside, as she only had a small bedroll and her cloak, and nothing in the way of winter clothing. She *should* make her destination before the end of Low Autumn, but the trip back, assuming she had to walk again, might be difficult without such provisions.

That evening, the first of the two nights she had planned to camp outdoors, she managed to find a secluded hollow away from the river. The ground was slightly sunken, and scrub willows and blackroot trees created a mesh over her head that seemed adequate to hide the light from her lantern.

She ate a meal of raw carrots and smoked ham while watching the sun dip down behind the trees. Grendel had curled up in the satchel already, with his head tucked in.

"You have the right idea, I think," Amandine said softly to him. "It's going to be a long walk tomorrow if we're to make it to Ivybough like I planned."

Amandine set up her small bedroll, arranged her cloak, and followed Grendel's example. Then, a bell later, it began to rain. It wasn't a light shower either. The sky opened up as if all of the late-coming High Summer rains had decided to converge at once. Despite assurances of quality from the man she had purchased it from, the seams of her cheap lantern leaked and doused the flame. Grendel hissed and retreated as far back into the satchel as he could. Amandine pulled her bedroll and things out of the sunken area, which was rapidly filling with water, and tried to take shelter next to one of the larger trees. What was she supposed to do in this situation? She wasn't really experienced at sleeping outside. Even when she had been in the caravan coming from Artemis, there had been wagons to hide under when sporadic rain occurred.

"Colorless night!" she swore under her breath as she huddled in her cloak. Her bedroll was soaked. The water-sealed leather of her backpack was doing well, though, which made her wish she could crawl inside it. At least her food and spices and extra clothes would stay dry. Grendel meowed mournfully from inside the satchel.

"And what do you expect me to do, Gren? I can't control this!"

The temperature began to drop and Amandine fished out the hand warmer. It was a small clay pot with a brass inner lining. To use it, she needed a hot coal, but she hadn't made a fire, and so it was useless. With a sigh, she put it back.

Lightning flashed, followed shortly after by thunder that shook the ground. The rain began to fall even *harder*. Amandine shivered under her cloak, which was completely saturated now. There was nothing for it, though. She whispered a silent prayer to Kayla, and then, because it was night, she offered one to Ravenex as well. She imagined that she wasn't really on the best of terms with that particular goddess, but the night was her domain, and so if she was going to get any sort of divine aid, the Mistress of Shadows seemed a more likely source for it.

Grendel meowed again and Amandine reached into the bag to try and comfort him. Even with the enhanced vision the contact provided to her, she could barely see a thing against the backdrop of falling water. Unpleasant memories of being caught in the rain in the Blue Fens flooded into her. She had been blind, alone, wracked with worry for her friends, and until she had discovered the spell on Grendel, completely without recourse. Now even that boon was being denied to her.

Amandine felt miserable. She was so absorbed in her self-pity that she almost missed the sound of branches snapping in the brush nearby. Her hand moved to her knife handle as she sunk back against the tree, trying to not make a sound. She pushed her hand into Grendel's fur, hoping, praying, that he didn't yowl again. What was out there? It sounded like footsteps—the heavy crunching was too plodding and regular to be an animal—but that didn't mean it was a person, either. A creeping dread started to crawl up her spine.

Something began to resolve in her enhanced vision. It was a shape, outlined by water like a curtain, as if it repelled the raindrops to create a sort of moving waterfall. The mass of shifting water drew closer to her flooded campsite. Was it some kind of elemental? A fae creature she hadn't heard of? There was no visible face, or arms, or anything else she could make out. Amandine loosened the *Olatharr* in its sheath.

A low growl emanated from the thing. Amandine held her breath.

"I know, Dumpy, but I swear to the gods, I heard a cat over here. Maybe it was feral, but it was worth a look, right? Come on, help me out here, you mangy—"

"Fredderick?" Amandine said in utter surprise and relief.

The watery mass approached her voice and her vision resolved a human form under the sheet of cascading liquid. There were no colors. Without light, her magical vision was like a charcoal picture, fuzzy and lacking depth, but the shape of the hair was right, and a small round form with four stubby legs circled its feet.

"Amandine? Is that you? I can't see a colorless thing! Please, take my hand," Fredderick's voice said.

Was it a trick? Was she suffering from cold sickness and hallucinating? Fredderick should be on his way back downriver. Amandine hesitated, but Grendel had stuck his head out of the bag, despite the rain, and seemed completely at ease. She extended her hand and touched the arm of the amorphous thing.

Water rushed by her as if she were emerging from beneath the surface of a watershed pond. The rain stopped striking her. It was like an invisible tarp had been dropped overhead. She could see the outline of Fredderick's face now. It *was* him, she wasn't hallucinating, but what in the goddess's name was he doing here?

"One moment," he said, just before a small blue sphere of cold light bloomed in his hand. Colors returned to Amandine's vision, albeit everything had a distinct blue tint because of his magical light.

"Oh gods, it *is* you," he said, the relief evident in his voice. "It would just be my luck lately to fall into a lurk's trap or be seduced by a nixie."

"Something tells me you might actually like the latter," Amandine said.

"Yup, it's definitely you," Fredderick said with a nod.

He was completely dry, but Amandine was still shivering. She didn't let go of his arm, however, for fear of breaking whatever warping was keeping the water off of her. Grendel was spared by the spell's effects as well and emerged from the satchel with a chirruping sound. Dumpling wagged his entire bottom and sniffed at the cat in greeting.

"I have so many questions," Amandine said after failing to pick one to start with.

Fredderick touched the backpack where it sat next to the tree and transferred the blue glow to it. He put his free hand over Amandine's and crouched down next to her. His palm was warm, which only made Amandine feel even more chilly.

"Well, let me try and guess some of the more obvious ones. Why am I here instead of doing what I said I would and returning to Stoneman? That's pretty simple. I am, strictly speaking, incredibly bad at doing anything I *should* be doing, sometimes to my detriment. In this case, I decided that returning by myself, to bring bad news no less, was not something I wanted to do, even though you asked me too. So I'm sorry for that.

"Next. Yes it's magic. Something relatively new I picked up. You saw me use it on the boat perhaps? I can infuse water with a trickle of anima and make it do what I want. Freeze it, thaw it, move it, or in this case, make it not touch me. Blasted rain. No manners at all, right?"

"It's... amazing," Amandine agreed, her teeth chattering.

"Oh hells, where *are* my manners?" Fredderick said. He removed his warm hand and produced the small ball of wispy flame. Amandine knew what to expect this time as he touched her again and every drop of moisture on her body and in her clothing steamed off with that strange, burnt-toast smell.

The chill in her skin and bones lingered, but being dry immediately helped her feel better. "Thank you," she muttered.

"May I sit with you? You found a nice tree. I might be able to… yes."

Fredderick touched the tree and the invisible tarp extended to cover everything beneath its shrubby branches. He pulled his arm away from her, which caused Amandine to feel a moment of regret, even though it was no longer needed to maintain the spell. With a groan, he unslung Serand's large backpack and placed it next to her smaller, glowing one.

Amandine scooted over to make space for him and he collapsed against the tree with a relieved sigh. "That pack is really heavy, you know? I think there's an iron pan in there."

"There's three, nested together," Amandine said.

Fredderick rubbed the back of his neck. "You're not mad that I followed you?"

"Given the circumstances, no, I'm not." Amandine offered a weak smile. "I… I'm sorry I have been so snappy at you, Fredderick. I've been jealous and lying to myself about it. I still want to be your friend, no matter who you are courting. Losing Serand like that on top of everything else. It just—"

He reached between them and held her hand. He gave it a squeeze and she squeezed it back. She had no idea what he was feeling. With Fredderick, Amandine always felt at a loss, like she just couldn't understand what was in his heart at all. With a sigh, she leaned in and rested her head on his shoulder. "Why did you say you hated me? On the boat."

Fredderick looked over at her as she turned her head to gaze up at him. The corners of his eyes seemed sad, but he was still smiling. "I don't hate you, Amandine. I never have. Not even for a moment."

"But then why—"

"Please," Fredderick said, "Can you accept that answer for now? I… am not ready to say anything more. I'm sorry."

Amandine sighed and nodded. He didn't hate her. That was all she really wanted anyway. For now. "How long will your water spell last?" she asked instead.

"Now that I have anchored it to another living thing, it will continue until I make it stop by withdrawing the anima. It… tires me, but it will stay if you want to rest. The rain will not be a problem tonight."

Dumpling barked. Amandine looked over to the satchel. Grendel had climbed back inside. Dumpling looked up at Fredderick and barked again. With the hand that wasn't holding Amandine's, Fredderick made another ball of flame and dried the satchel too. Grendel meowed and shifted, making space in the bag and

Dumpling crawled in as well. The dog and cat lay down next to each other, half-covered by the open satchel, and closed their eyes.

"That's cute," Amandine said. She was beginning to feel sleepy. What had been looking to be a terrible, cold, fearful evening had turned into something magical instead. "How ever did you find me? We're a ways off the main road."

"I was on the road and, well, nature called," Fredderick said, sounding a bit embarrassed. "After I had dealt with that, I thought I heard a cat, and I knew you had Grendel with you, so..."

"So you might have completely passed me by if you hadn't had to relieve yourself?" Amandine said with a snicker.

"I suppose so."

Amandine offered a silent thank you to Kayla, and for good measure, to Ravenex as well. If that kind of coincidence wasn't divine intervention, she didn't know what was. She snuggled closer to Fredderick. "I am going to use you like a pillow," she announced sleepily. "Not sorry."

Fredderick released her hand and draped his arm around her instead. "It would be my pleasure. Sleep well."

Dreaming

"Ironically, the best time to harvest mushrooms is during the Fall season before a shiv. In my experience, mushrooms, for whatever reason, grow in abundance just before a shiv occurs. They are larger and more plentiful, especially those that grow near tree roots. This means it is also the best time to find rare caps like Lady's Slipper, Roan Blisters, and Lace Hats. As always with mushrooms, know how to identify them safely or source them from a reputable gleaner."

- Seeker's Kitchen, Chapter 3, Essential Ingredients

THE WOODS WERE dark. The ground squelched under Amandine's feet. The outlines of paddle-leaf and cattails filled her black and white vision.

"Hello?" Amandine called. She immediately knew it had been a mistake. The sounds of the night ceased, and even the murmur of the flowing river nearby seemed muted. A dragging, slithering sound filled her ears.

The ground began to tremble.

"No!" Amandine cried. "No, no, no!"

She began to run, blindly, into the dark. The trembling strengthened, and as it did her legs felt heavier, as if she could barely drag them through the mud and water.

Amandine tripped and fell face down. She struggled to her knees and turned around. Serand's lifeless, waterlogged corpse stared back at her, half buried in the muck.

"No! Please, no," Amandine cried.

The ground erupted and the skellix emerged. Its eyeless head turned towards her, maggot-like carapace glistening. Four huge, pinching claws rose up around it.

She screamed. Serand's bloated face turned. "Wake up, fingerling," it croaked.

Grendel bit her hand.

Amandine awoke and sat up with a gasp. Pieces of straw tumbled from her hair. Her scar was throbbing again. Grendel meowed at her from her lap, and she stroked him as she caught her breath. Fredderick was also there, his outline visible with her magical sight. The hayloft they lay in was small, but cozy, insulated by hay and warmed by the horses that lived below. It wasn't the most comfortable, or nicest-smelling, place to sleep, but it was dry and had been offered for free.

Amandine breathed deep as the nightmare fled and was replaced by actual memories. It had been a tenday since Fredderick had stumbled across her ill-fated campsite. They had passed through Ivybough and First Home. By a lucky chance they had spent an evening camping with a trade caravan around a warm fire. The rains had kept coming, but when no one else was on the road, Fredderick had used his water-controlling spell to keep them dry.

Now they were in another small hamlet that called itself Kiln, where clay was dug for pottery and bricks. The entire place smelled like wet soil, even when it wasn't raining. The Hill Folk and humans who lived here were a mixture of potters, brick makers, tilers, woodcutters and foragers with a smattering of small subsistence farms. There was no wall, no inn, not even an alehouse. People here gathered in barns and warehouses for public meals and gatherings. A kindly farrier had given them the loft for the night when the rains started, as a thank you for Amandine making the evening gathering an enormous pot of mushroom and bean soup.

Fredderick stirred. "Is it morning?" he asked sleepily.

"No, I just woke up. Go back to sleep."

"Skellix again?"

"Yes." She sometimes regretted telling Fredderick about her recurring nightmares, and he didn't know that Serand had started appearing in them, but acting like nothing was wrong would only cause him to prod her further. He yawned and rolled over.

"Maybe you could dream of some boglings to eat the colorless thing?" he muttered.

Amandine smiled at that. If only it were so simple. He drifted back to sleep. At least he didn't snore like Dena. She knew sleep wouldn't find her again so easily, so she climbed down out of the loft and walked by the stalls while Grendel followed in her wake. One of the horses whickered softly and stuck its head over the rails, perhaps looking for a treat. Amandine paused to stroke its muzzle. Sleepy contentment infused her. A bit of fresh air, and perhaps she could also return to sleep.

The night was brisk, but dry. A cloudless sky filled with colorful stars greeted her eyes. The rain must have quit while they slept. Amandine passed the farrier's cottage, where a flickering candle created an orange haze behind the drawn curtains. A dog barked somewhere in the distance. She paused, and Grendel too, but after a moment he trotted ahead of her, so she followed him. If it had been something to worry about, she was sure Grendel would have sought refuge and clued her in.

"Where are we going, Gren?" she asked.

Meow.

"Right, I'll just take your word for it then?"

His upright tail swished in a confident way. Amandine shrugged and continued to let him lead her through the hamlet. It was quiet in a peaceful way. People slept, warm in their cottages and clay-brick shacks, secure from the darkness. Breathing in the cool night air, Amandine spread her arms and felt the wind caress them. Her mind drifted as she followed Grendel, back to some of her earliest memories, in Artemis.

Among her recollections of lessons, bland meals, and sermons, she remembered a massive looming shape, like a tower made of dark-tinted glass. The memory had a hazy quality to it, as if it were something she had dreamt as a child that had inexplicably stayed with her. It sang to her. The pure, dark note it resonated with seemed to speak directly to her soul. It was something that was not of this world, and yet inextricably tied to it.

"The will of the Matron is that all souls find peace at the end of their road," the voice of Sister Corbin spoke into her mind. "Tribe matters not. Race matters not. Even those creatures unbound by time still meet the Night."

"Unbound by time," Amandine said aloud. "Like those in a dream."

She realized that they had left the hamlet behind. Her path passed through a light mist coming off the river and she could still see the outlines of the buildings in the starlight, but she and Grendel were now in the woods bordering the water. With soft steps, her feet followed Grendel, who traced his own path, and not a branch grabbed her. Nothing stuck to her clothes, nothing tripped her up. The cat wove through the underbrush and Amandine tracked him by pure instinct. The rushing sound of the river grew louder.

Overhanging branches momentarily obscured the twinkling stars above, shrouding her in darkness like a cloak. She wrapped herself in it, welcomed it. Became part of it.

As the curtain lifted, Amandine emerged from the dark embrace into a clearing. Wind passed through the surrounding trees like whispered words. In the middle was a stone. It was oddly shaped, gray and craggy. As she approached, she noticed that it was surrounded by a pale ring. A circle of mushrooms had sprouted from the loam, their small white caps standing out in stark contrast to the dark soil. Grendel paused at the edge of the circle and looked back at her.

Meow.

Amandine knelt next to him and stroked his fur as she examined the mushrooms. "Night Lady's Slipper," she said as her fingers traced the oblong caps, finding the nearly imperceptible blue veins that gave the fungus its name. They adorned the caps like ribbons on a lady's shoe.

"You can eat them, but they are quite rare," she said as she scratched his ears. "Is this why you brought me here?"

Grendel ruffled his head under her fingers and sat down, looking up at her expectantly. She smiled and plucked one from the ground and held it for him to sniff. He inspected the mushroom and then looked up at her, blinking slowly.

"No really. See?" Amandine nibbled an edge. It had a flavor like pepper and nuts, with a hint of something else. Something savory, but also slightly sweet. "They're good."

With a chirruping sound, Grendel stood back up and walked to the rock formation in the middle of the circle. She rose and followed him. As she drew close to the stone, something became apparent: it was not completely natural. It might have stood here originally, but the cracked and chipped surface showed signs of carvings. A curve chiseled here, a line there. She ran her hands over them, feeling the contours of the ancient artist's work. What had it been? A marker? Part of a building? A statue? One section of the stone did vaguely resemble a face, with lips hinted at, and the bending cusp of a nose and one eye.

The wind picked up. The hiss of it combined with the sound of water.

Shhhaaaaaa...

There was something here, she felt it. Something she needed to understand, but was just out of reach.

Shhhaaaaaa...

The wind touched her hair. It had grown out slightly since she had left Stoneman and rippled around her ears and neck.

Shhhaaaaaa...

The night, the world, the ground beneath her, seemed to bend. The night sky drew down upon her. Words entered her mind, bypassing her ears.

"*Daughter...*"

Amandine's breath caught. What? How?

"I hear you," Amandine said, still touching the stone.

"*A darkling thing exists, in the deeps.*"

"What do you mean?"

"*Bring those who carry light into the eye of the void.*"

"I—," Amandine swallowed. What was happening? "I don't understand."

"*You are the guidepost, the dreaming. Guide the child to the door.*"

"Is this magic? Who are you?"

"I AM NIGHT."

Amandine gasped. The words struck a chord in her soul. They bent the world. It twisted and was consumed by darkness. The void absorbed the stars, the ground, the trees. It subsumed her completely—swallowed her. Fear filled her mind, but her heart remained calm. This was right. The darkness was right. The fear did not control her, it was merely part of her.

"I will do as you say. I don't understand, but I will try."

As she spoke the words into the black, a sort of comprehension filled her. An acknowledgement of herself. She was the dark and the dark was her. The night was her domain. She was its child.

"Return to the dream. I watch."

Amandine opened her eyes.

Sunlight filled the glade. She was lying on the ground. The damp grass was slowly soaking into her clothes, and the chill morning air nipped at her skin. Grendel walked into her field of view. He ducked his head and touched his nose to hers like he always did when greeting her after waking.

"Gren? What happened?" her voice was a crackling whisper, and her throat felt raw. She felt a bone deep chill, like ice in her marrow. Her body began to shiver uncontrollably.

"Amandine!"

Gentle hands lifted her head. She realized she could barely move. Every muscle in her body felt wrung out, as if she had run all day, limp and useless. The cold beneath her skin clung to her like a rime of frost on her soul.

"Amandine, can you hear me?"

She managed to turn her head. Fredderick looked down at her, his face etched with concern. His dark eyes searched hers. "What happened, Amandine? Why are you out here?"

"I..." she tried to find the words through chattering teeth, to tell him about finding the stone. Walking through the woods. The enveloping darkness. But nothing came out. Even the memory of it was rapidly fading, like a dream that departed as soon as you woke up.

He helped her sit. With a frown, he reached down and picked up a mushroom with a red and yellow cap. A bite had been taken out of the side. "This is a Death Head. Even a taste can kill someone! Did you try to eat it, Amandine?"

"I don't remember," she replied weakly, finally finding her voice.

Dumpling pushed his head under one of her limp hands. He whined at her and licked her wrist. She tried to scratch him, but her fingers barely worked.

She noticed the others then. Most of the hamlet was in the clearing. Some of the people carried tools and torches. Had they all been looking for her? Why was she not in the hayloft?

The farrier that had given her and Fredderick shelter was there. "What is that on her neck, lad?"

She felt Fredderick pull at her collar. A surge of indignant emotion made her want to swat him away, but all she could manage was to twitch her wrist irritably.

"I'm not peeping, relax. Besides, I've already seen them," Fredderick muttered.

Oh, she was definitely smacking him when she could move her arms again. The heat of her embarrassment dissipated the lingering chill a tiny bit.

"There is a mark," Fredderick said. "It looks like a… flower? An orchid maybe, like what grows in swamps. Wait, it's fading. What in the hells?"

"What is its shape?" Amandine croaked.

"Sort of like a bell, but one side is longer than the other."

"That's a shadow bonnet," Amandine whispered. "Also called a darkbloom. It's Ravenex's flower."

"What in the hells?" Fredderick repeated, the worry evident in his voice now.

A woman in the crowd began to weep. Amandine realized several people had dropped to their knees. Almost everyone was making the symbol for Ravenex, with their hands curled into each other. Life and Death. The Endless Circle.

"Godsworn," someone said.

"Godsworn," another repeated.

The word became a refrain. The woman who had been crying now began to pray. Others followed her example.

"Praise the gods," the farrier said as he also made the symbol. "Your Mother honors us, and you are welcome in our hamlet and our homes. The Matron of Night protects us from the terror of darkness and sees us to our final rest. For we all close the circle."

"For we all close the circle," the crowd echoed.

"Fredderick, please help me," Amandine said.

"What can I do?"

"Get me to the bushes so that I don't throw up on you."

He lifted her and managed to help her hobble to the edge of the clearing. The hamlet folk kept their distance, but the refrain of 'godsworn' continued even as Amandine emptied her stomach into the underbrush.

What in the hells had happened to her?

A Warm Bath

"Communal bathing is common in every nation but Zulathia. Zu-lath personal space taboos are incompatible with the idea at best. Private baths tend to be an amenity reserved for the wealthy, but even then many a noble or merchant has been known to avail themselves of the public bathhouse, especially when such places offer additional services to the rich and pampered. Serentian-style houses tend to pro-vide screens and partitions. Men and women often bathe in different areas. Olgothian style baths, by contrast, are more likely to have all and sundry in one large pool, with towels provided to protect the modesty of bathers."

- A Winsome Traveler's Guide to Beregoth, Second Edition, Chapter 5, Keeping Clean

"TWO SILVER FOR both of you, please."

Amandine counted the money out. Half of it was in copper. "Are you sure you want to do this?" Fredderick asked.

"Six," Amandine replied as she handed the attendant her money.

"What?"

"That makes six times, Fredderick. You keep asking and the answer is the same. I haven't bathed in almost three tendays and neither have you. We stink. Go get towels. That stack there, the big ones."

The Brindle was a communal bathhouse in the Lowers, the community that surrounded and abutted the fortress city of Greyrock Falls. Amandine had asked about town for the best places to sleep and bathe. She and Fredderick had a room at an Inn called 'Gold Among Scree,' that was run by an Olgothian woman named Brenna of Folded Sheets. She was reasonably priced and clean, but did not offer bathing services. Hence, The Brindle.

"Sure, but we are low on coin. Unless you have a hidden reserve stashed, we'll be eating rocks."

"It will be fine. Once we find Boomer's bud, Herric, we'll ask for their hospitality and send letters back home. The ones you sent from Myron's Bend must have arrived by now, but people will be worried. And I need to tell Dena about Serand."

She pulled Fredderick by the arm down a steamy hallway to a set of shutter doors. A sign on the wall written in Olgothian and Dwarven Runes directed them to a changing area.

Fredderick sighed. "And you realize this is an Olgothian-style bath, right?"

"Yes, so?"

"Communal. It's a shared bath for everyone."

Amandine pulled a towel out of his arms and opened a side door into a changing area meant for one person. It had a small basket for clothing, which would be laundered as well. Most of their things were back at the inn, being 'guarded' by Dumpling and Grendel.

"Wear your towel if you're embarrassed," Amandine said. "You keep bringing up that you've seen me naked, I think some repayment is in order."

Fredderick turned red. Amandine grinned and shut the door in his face.

With Fredderick out of sight, Amandine took a deep breath and allowed her own embarrassment to surface while she undressed. What was she doing, flirting with him like that? He would get entirely the wrong idea. Or *was* it the wrong idea? Seeing him without his clothes on had a certain appeal, and making him squirm only seemed fair. But still...

"Goddess, Amandine, get it together," she muttered to herself. "He's in an arranged courtship. He still hasn't explained anything to you. And... and..."

Amandine threw her wrap down into the basket in frustration. Colorless man! Why did this have to be such a trial of her patience? He *had* followed her all the way to Anvilroot's doorstep. Saved her life, possibly more than once, counting that goddess-forsaken rain storm. And then there was what had happened in Kiln. They hadn't discussed it since that day. The shadow bonnet mark on her neck hadn't returned, but Amandine felt like something was different, as if something had changed in her and she couldn't figure out what that was. Being attracted to Fredderick-colorless-Stolm was only complicating things.

She tossed the rest of her dirty clothes into the basket and wrapped the large towel under her arms, tucking it at the top to hold it in place. With a deep breath, she stepped out into the hall again. A waiting attendant bowed to her and ducked inside to gather her basket. He handed her a clay token on a leather cord with a tally imprinted upon it: 23. She could use it later to claim her things. She had been in communal baths before. The orphans all shared one until they were at least ten and two, and then boys and girls were separated, but still shared. How different could this be?

The wooden shutter doors to the bathing area flapped past her as she entered the steam-filled chamber.

"Oh…" Amandine said.

She realized immediately that many of the men and women were still wearing underclothes and wraps and had saved their towels for their hair, or for drying themselves. Only a few had opted out of such propriety, and most of those were small children, who splashed playfully in the shallow end of the hot-spring fed bath. As for the rest…

An elderly Olgothian man walked by her to the shutter doors. He wore not a stitch except for a medicinal patch tied to one shoulder. It was as if a withered gojo had grown legs. And bits.

Amandine swallowed and felt her face heating up again. Perhaps she would see if there was a more private option.

"Rinse please," a woman's voice said.

She turned. A bored looking attendant in the blue shirt and pants that the employees of the house wore, pointed to her. "Yes you. Your hair is filthy, sah. If yer visibly crusty, step behind the blind there an' rinse yer arse before dippin' it."

"Oh, yes, of course," Amandine said hurriedly. As she moved to the folding screen that acted as a privacy divide for rinsing, she was secretly grateful for a way to get out of view until she could regain her composure. She passed the edge of the screen and began to undo her towel.

"Oi, just a moment."

Fredderick dumped a pail of water over his head. His towel sat nearby on a stool, where it wouldn't be splashed. He was also not wearing his underclothes.

"I… sorry," Amandine squeaked.

He turned. When he saw her he lowered the bucket to cover himself. "Well, you have now officially seen more of me than Marlette," he said in a strained voice. "May I finish?"

"Oh! Yes. Um, of course. I… yes. We're even." Amandine said quickly before darting back around the corner. There were a few more splashes interspersed by the sound of a pump lever and sloshing water.

"Ok, all yours, Amandine!"

Amandine fanned her face and tried to get her blush under control. The attendant who had told her to rinse was smirking at her.

"Oh, stop it!" she scolded her. The woman continued to smirk, but stopped staring. With a grimace, Amandine stepped behind the screen and found a bucket already filled for her. She removed the towel and doused herself. Thank the

Goddess, it was cold as well water. She shivered and did it again. After the third bucket, she felt somewhat normal again, if chilly.

She re-wrapped herself and stepped out. Fredderick had already claimed a spot against a tiled edge, near where the hot water flowed into the pool. Despite the steam, she could see he had left his towel on. She silently thanked Kayla for that. If he had decided to go full buff like the old gojo, she had no idea how she would have been able to sit next to him without being as red as a rikol root the entire time.

The water was hot, and had a mineral scent to it. This town was apparently famous for its hot spring baths, but most were at least twice over what this one cost. The Brindle seemed a popular choice for those without a lot of coin. Callused elbows rubbed with each other, and more than one person was massaging feet sore from hard work. A pair of naked children sloshed by, splashing each other and shrieking. A harried looking father, holding his towel with one hand, tried to chase after them and apologized when he nearly collided with Amandine.

She began to relax. This wasn't so bad. She would soak in her towel. Wash her hair. Scrub her nails. She would be caught dead before she arrived in Anvilroot, her long sought childhood destination, looking like she had slept in the dirt for a cycle. Even if that were true.

Fredderick had his eyes closed and leaned back against the tile as Amandine took a seat beside him. The warm water came up to her shoulders and wrapped her like a warm blanket. With a deep sigh, she settled back as well.

"So, what's the plan?" Fredderick asked, opening one eye.

"Plan?"

"Yeah, when we find this kid of Boomer's. Once they show us how to kill the rot slimes, what do we do?"

"I guess we take the knowledge back to Stoneman."

"Well of course, but... I mean, why hasn't it been shared already?"

"I don't understand."

"Dwarves never give anything for free. Like Olgothians, everything is a trade. Unlike Olgothians, there are some things they *never* trade. Like how they make pyrestone, or mirrors, or that weird slate that was in the galley. What if this is one of those things, Amandine?"

Amandine sank into the water until it was up to her nose.

"You hadn't considered that, had you?" Fredderick asked.

She shook her head.

He sighed. "Well, Chef Brutsche obviously thought there was a chance. The thing is, I maybe know a fraction about dwarves compared to what he knew. He lived with them for a while, right?"

Amandine nodded. She slowly blew bubbles into the water and sank a little further.

"How much did he teach you? You can read some runes and so can I, but what else? Um, besides that crazy meal with the live shrimp."

More bubbles.

"Hells, this is upsetting you, I'm sorry," Fredderick said, leaning back again. His long hair floated, unbound, in the water around him. "Maybe I should have brought it up earlier, but well, you always seem to take charge of stuff like this, so I took it on faith. This is going to be hard, isn't it?"

Amandine sat back up. "As if any of it has been easy so far." She ran her fingers through the water in front of her. "But I don't want to give up. I owe it to Serand, and Dena, and everyone in the Gold Hills who need to preserve what food is left. We might already be too late, for all I know, but I still have to try."

"To be clear, I wasn't suggesting that we quit."

"I know."

She swirled the water under Fredderick's floating hair. It spun into a spiral shape with the motion. "Who did you write, anyway?" Amandine asked. "When you sent your letters."

"My mother. And Kimber of course. And Sheeria."

"Oh? Not your father? And why both Kimber and Sheeria? They're married."

"My father and I don't often see eye to eye. Mother will hopefully tame his ire so long as I am accounted for. As for my cousin and her wife, I don't often get along with Kimber either, but I work for her and owed her an explanation for my absence. And Sheeria? I like her. She's been unfailingly kind since I came to the Gold Hills. Kimber is away from home often, so I felt like she deserved her own letter."

"I see." There was one name conspicuously missing from his list, but she didn't dare invoke her. Not here. Not now.

Fredderick looked at her and smiled. He took her hand, the one that was playing with his hair and kissed her fingers.

She looked into his deep brown eyes and frowned. "I wish I could tell what you were actually feeling sometimes."

"It's not obvious?"

"It's just that you are an expert at making people believe things that aren't true, Fredderick. I can just tell with most people. How they are feeling, I mean, but you baffle me."

He leaned in closer. "I could show you?"

"Don't tease, Fredderick Stolm. If you—"

He kissed her. His lips met hers, mid-word, silencing her scolding. Her eyes widened. She wanted to protest, but unlike the kiss on the docks, this one lingered. Her lips parted to take a breath, to speak, and his followed. The kiss deepened. His body pressed into hers. She began to kiss him back.

Amandine still had no idea what he was feeling, but she knew what *she* was feeling and this was *nice*. Why had he waited so long? Why had she?

Nearby, a woman giggled. A man laughed. A woman's voice spoke above them: "Oi, you two! Save it for somewhere private, sahs!"

Amandine opened her eyes and pushed Fredderick away. So many people were watching them now. She ducked down into the water, her face absolutely on fire. Fredderick peered up at the attendant who had spoken. She was crouched above them with an amused grin on her face.

"Peeper," he said with a grin of his own.

"It ain't peepin' if yer doin' it in front of all the gods and sundry!" she said with a laugh. "Better fix yer towel there, sah."

Fredderick adjusted his towel. "Two silver for the show," he said.

"Nice try, kid. You can't charge for what you've already given out for free."

Amandine felt as if she might just melt from embarrassment. She slid further down into the water until it covered her head. She needed to wash her hair anyway, right? She stayed beneath until her breath gave out and she needed to surface. Fredderick was leaning back against the tile again, his eyes shut. His hand, however, found hers beneath the water. Across from them, a woman trying to bathe an unruly child smirked at her. She pointed at Fredderick and wiggled her eyebrows.

The little boy slapped at the water and pointed at Fredderick too. "He kissed her mama! That man kissed the pretty woman with the short hair!"

"I know, Yeric! It looked like a good one too!" she said as she finally managed to get a sponge on his back. She winked at Amandine.

Pretty was she? Amandine's cheeks still burned, but the child's compliment made her feel better about it. It *was* a good kiss. It didn't replace their first, but it expanded on it, made it better. She twined her fingers through Fredderick's and leaned back to soak. Tomorrow, she was finally going to see Anvilroot. She wished Serand were with her, but at least she would not be seeing it alone.

Bed and Breakfast

"The finest quality seed oil is sourced from Zulathia. Made from the humble Split Vein Ground Nut, which is known to natives of that land as kobie. It has a mild, understated taste that brightens the flavors of food cooked in it rather than covering them up. It can be raised to a much higher temperature than other oils, making it ideal for quick frying foods that would be ruined if left soaking for too long. Although sometimes expensive outside of the steppes, it's worth every copper to have a pot in your stores."

- Seeker's Kitchen, Chapter 4, Salts, Oils, and Spices

THE INN ROOM was warm and quiet. Amandine stared up at the plank ceiling. Footsteps from another guest walking along the floor above her made the wood creak. She furrowed her brow and looked over at the sunlight peeking through the shuttered window.

Grendel lay next to her arm, rolled sideways with all four paws in the air. She rubbed his belly and he opened an eye.

"Do you think I upset him, Gren?" she whispered.

Meow.

Amandine's neck grew warm as she recalled their evening after the bath. The attendant had told them to save it, and she had taken that advice to heart. They had rushed back to the inn without even stopping to buy food for dinner.

Neither of them had bothered to light the coal warmer in the corner of the room, but it hadn't mattered. Amandine touched the parts of her he had kissed; shoulders, neck and lips. Thinking back on it made her feel a little embarrassed, she really just wanted him to come back from wherever he was so he could do it all again. Except...

"I'm a wimp, Grendel." Amandine rolled onto her stomach. Despite the heat of the moment she had found herself in, when things had started to take a more serious turn, she had quailed. "I know he wanted more, but I... I wasn't ready. I thought I was, but this is all just so weird!"

Amandine hid her face in her pillow and shrieked into it. Goddess, she was pathetic. The night had ended with her in the bed and Fredderick on the floor. She hadn't been able to sleep much, alternating between embarrassment and the desire to call him back. She imagined he hadn't slept either. They had been camping together on the road for a while now, and she could tell when he was asleep. Had he agonized over it all as much as she had? Amandine felt like a coward. The rest of it had been so good, too. She could almost feel Marlette's judging gaze and imagined her smirking mouth. *Such a fool...*

Grendel rolled to his feet, stretched, and then sauntered over to Amandine, climbed on her head and sat down.

"Ugh, really, Grendel?" Amandine said, her face turned sideways on the pillow. His tail swatted her and she spat fur out of her mouth. "Alright, alright! I get it, I'll stop being a giant puddle of self pity! Please get off my head."

Grendel didn't move. He lay down and began cleaning his paws.

"I hate you so much right now," Amandine whispered.

The door opened and Grendel bolted off the bed, making Amandine hiss in pain as his claws briefly dug in.

She rolled over and sat up as Dumpling leapt onto the mattress and charged across it to greet her. He put his paws up on her arm and tried to lick her face.

"Oi, lay off Dumpy, you're going to make me jealous," Fredderick said as he shut the door.

He sat down on the bed and Amandine realized the blanket had slipped down to her waist. She was still dressed in her shirt and underclothes, she wasn't exposed. His eyes on her made her pull it back up anyway, the heat in her cheeks only partly from embarrassment. Fredderick looked away and also turned red.

"I'm sorry, I should have knocked so you could dress."

"I didn't even know you had left, it's fine. I, um—" She opened her mouth to say something. Apologize maybe? Ask where he had been? Fredderick placed a cloth-wrapped bundle between them. Something fresh baked was inside, she could smell it. Her stomach rumbled. Loudly.

Fredderick grinned. "I guessed right," he said, unwrapping the parcel. "We... sort of skipped dinner."

"Yeah."

He handed her a roll. It wasn't like the yeasty buns Gil made with Master Hawthorne; this roll was curled on itself in a sort of twist and when she picked it up, flakes of golden crust crumbled off onto the cloth. It smelled amazing.

"Zulathian Fry Bread. There was a vendor who sold it back home in Irongate too. I haven't had any in ages," Fredderick said as he took a big bite of his own.

Amandine had a taste. It was *amazing*. Delicate and buttery, with just a hint of something sweet. "Oh Goddess," she said before taking another bite. "Maybe I'm just hungry, but this is one of the best things I have ever eaten."

"I can think of something better," Fredderick said with a sly look. He took her hand and lifted it to his face, but instead of kissing her fingers, he turned it and kissed the inside of her wrist instead.

The shiver that ran down Amandine's spine nearly made her drop her breakfast. "Fredderick, I—" she began. His lips made their way up her arm to her elbow. "Oh..."

"You were going to say something?"

"Nope." Amandine closed her eyes. "Keep going."

His lips traced their way up her arm to her shoulder, then her neck, then her lips. Amandine felt like butter that had been left in the sun. Part of her wanted so badly to resume from where they had left off, but...

His hands reached up to gently hold her head as they kissed. A thumb softly traced the scar behind her eye, and Amandine felt a twinge of shame, but then immediately squelched it. He had been there. He knew how she had gotten it and didn't care, so why should she?

"I'm sorry, Fredderick," she said as their lips finally parted. "You're not upset with me, are you?"

"Does it seem like I am?"

"Fredderick Stolm! I'm being serious."

He opened his mouth, probably to say something glib, but then his grin slipped a little and he sat up. "No, of course I am not upset with you, Amandine Who Has No Surname."

She glared at him and took a bite of her roll. Did he not know? She was officially Amandine Brutsche on the papers Serand and Dena had signed. Not that it really mattered. No one ever used it. She even sometimes forgot it was hers now.

"Hey, you keep invoking mine like my mother—it doesn't seem fair that I don't have the same advantage." His cheeky grin returned. He lay back on the bed and took another bite of his own roll while staring at the ceiling. "I think I get *why* it happened like it did. Last night, I mean. The last cycle for you has been fit for the seven hells, Amandine. I was being selfish. You didn't do anything wrong. I'm sorry."

Amandine breathed out a sigh. It was partly from relief, but the look Fredderick gave her seemed to suggest he thought she was upset still. "No, Fredderick. You did nothing wrong either. I asked you to stop and you did. Some wouldn't, you know. Thank you."

Fredderick shrugged. "I am not interested in any woman who isn't also interested. Probably the only bit of advice from my father that I completely agree with. I really like you, and I don't want to upset you, Amandine."

"You... didn't. Not really. I was flirting with you too, right? I cowered first. I don't want it to be an excuse, but you're right, the last cycle has been one of the worst of my life. What happened last night, I really liked it, but I don't want the one good thing that's happened to me recently to be clouded over by all of..." she waved her arms around vaguely. "...this. With the slimes, and Chef being released, and having to quit at the soup kitchen. Then that awful Orm woman, and the L'Eau's being nearly bankrupt, then the colorless pirates and..."

"Wait, what? Back up. The L'Eau's?" Fredderick turned his head to look at her. "Mar... Err, I heard that they were fine with money."

"You can say Marlette's name, Fredderick. I am not going to bite you if you do." She sighed again. "Well, I saw a slate with a partial ledger, and Estevan and Gia L'Eau are in deep debt. The loss of their main cash crop cost them a lot of money, and I don't think they have a good way out of it. Lord Estevan seemed very distracted when we spoke."

"Gods." Fredderick looked back to the ceiling. "The way she spends coin, you'd never know."

"Yes, well, all of that on top of the pirates and... and losing Serand. Then the rainstorm and what happened at Kiln..." her voice trailed off at the end. She wished she could remember what had really happened that night, but it was all so hazy, like a partly remembered dream.

"What *was* that, then?" Fredderick asked.

"I wish I could say, Fredderick. I can't remember most of it. But I think... I think Ravenex spoke to me."

Fredderick sat up on one elbow, his jaw hanging slightly open in disbelief. "A goddess *spoke* to you? Amandine, are you sure?"

"No, like I said, I barely remember any of it. But that much I am fairly certain of."

"Or, you were overly exhausted and went sleepwalking, ate a highly toxic mushroom and hallucinated the entire thing," Fredderick suggested.

"Or... that," Amandine admitted.

Fredderick rubbed the stubble on his chin. The wispy beard was slowly filling in. It was patchy and rough, and most of the hair was lighter than that on his head. Amandine kept picturing the older version of him with the fully grown one. It looked terrible now, but the shadow of what it would become was definitely there. She really liked it. She liked him. Colorless Marlette L'Eau!

"The godsworn thing would explain the mark, though," Fredderick said. "I wish I knew more about godsworn miracles, Amandine, but Hemm was fairly certain that it's just another form of magic."

"I can't do miracles. Unless you count my spicy stew. That seemed a little miraculous, frankly."

She was joking, but Fredderick nodded seriously. "No, that would explain a lot of things."

"I was japing."

"I know, but hear me out! You said you can tell what people around you are feeling. You talk to your colorless cat, and he *listens*. People jump up to help you who might not otherwise give you the time of day. I found you in a torrential rain storm. At *night*. Tell me truth, were you praying?"

"Fredderick, this isn't funny!"

"I'm not, for once, making a jape, Amandine! You convinced a bunch of dwarves with a blood right not to murder those captured pirates! You made stew from garbage and people drooled for it! You somehow, despite all odds, managed to kill a *skellix*! With a *knife*!"

"It's a very big knife," Amandine said in a small voice.

"Not the point! I don't think Marlette can create magic, Amandine. I think Mister Green was talking about you." Fredderick nodded and stuffed the last of his roll into his mouth.

"About me? That makes no sense."

"It makes perfect sense. He offered you an apprenticeship last year. Did you think that was an invitation to learn how to identify trees and memorize dusty history books?"

Fredderick had grown steadily more animated as he spoke, as if several ideas were all coming together in his head at the same time. It was another thing about him that she liked, actually, but the subject of his enthusiasm put a damper on it. "But how could he know?" Amandine asked.

"What color are his eyes, Amandine?"

Her blood felt like it was freezing. "Why?"

"Just tell me, when you look into that elf's eyes, what do you see?"

"Well, people say that they are green, like his name." Fredderick seemed to wilt a little. "But when I look, I see black. Dark orbs that seem to absorb light."

Fredderick sat back up. "That's it! Yes!"

"What do you mean?"

"*That's what I see also*, Amandine!" Fredderick took her hand. "Some people who can do magic are sort of, I don't know, attuned to things like fae glamours? We can see through them. Just like two tuning forks of opposing notes that when touched together stop vibrating."

"Turning fork?" Silverware that sang?

"You've never taken music lessons, right, um, like spices that cover each other up? Cancel out each other?"

"No such thing, Fredderick."

"I am trying here!"

"No, it's fine, I think I understand." Amandine squeezed his hand. "But I am not sure what to make of this."

"I am sure of it. It would explain why that crazy Night Sister followed you all the way to Stoneman, Amandine. Why Mother Jarl, of all the colorless godsworn in the area, was chosen to look out for you when Corbin left for Artemis. Even among godsworn, the ones who can create miracles are incredibly rare. If they somehow knew, I am positive they would do nearly anything to keep you in their fold."

Amandine had a revelation. "Tobe. The godsworn that was missing his tongue. If you're right, then he somehow knew."

"Tuning forks that are the same note will resonate with each other, become stronger." Fredderick nodded sagely. "I'm told that magicians with similar talents can sense each other. Even through walls and across distances."

"So you can sense Mister Green or Wizard Hemm?"

"Um, no. We're different." He looked away. "There is a lot of magic in this world."

"It feels pretty rare to me. That's why I am struggling to believe this."

"Well, to be fair, I could be wrong. I am just a hedge with an aversion to authority. I'm no expert. But it *feels* right, Amandine. It explains so much!"

Amandine ran a hand through her hair and exhaled. "Even if it's true, it doesn't feel very useful."

"What do you mean? Of course it's useful!"

"Did a miracle save Serand? Stop the slimes? Get Sister Corbin out of my life or help me when I got stranded in Stoneman?"

"No, but it helped me find you, and saved your life, and probably the rest of ours as well, when the skellix attacked. Magic doesn't always do what you want it to, Amandine. Control takes years to master. The rest of the time, it's sort of like riding an angry horse. You hold the reins tight and try not to fall off. I don't know about godsworn, but being a magus means often you have to do what the magic desires first. It's less about what you want, but rather making do with what the magic offers you."

"That sounds very similar to something Mother Jarl said to me. I bet it's the same for anyone who can use magic."

"Which includes you now!" Fredderick said, pulling her into him.

"We'll see," she pushed him gently away. "Turn around so I can get dressed."

"*Fine*," Fredderick said with a sigh. He sat up and turned away. Amandine tossed the blanket aside and quickly found her pants.

He continued to watch the wall and hummed to himself while stroking Dumpling on his lap. She supposed a peek wouldn't hurt, and thought about teasing him, but then discarded the idea as a fresh wave of embarrassment washed over her. She had never been so intimate with anyone, even if it had just been touching and kissing with clothes on. He was still courting Marlette, and that thought made her jaw clench in frustration. She needed to maintain some semblance of sense concerning Fredderick. Amandine wasn't going to label last night a mistake, but she wasn't going to allow more either.

"It's really too bad our coin is expended. I wouldn't mind another night here," Fredderick mused while she dressed.

Amandine shrugged. "Perhaps on the way back. Assuming you behave yourself."

"I *am* behaving myself. I think I behaved myself admirably last night!"

It was obvious to Amandine by his tone that he was not just talking about sparing her propriety. Her face heated again at the implication. "You are impossible! Can you not jape just to make me blush?"

"Not much chance of that."

She laughed to cover her nerves and pulled her boots on. "Gods, Fredderick, you're such an ass. Why do I like you so much?"

"My stunning good looks, witty banter, and excessive wealth?"

"You only have money to spend because you trick people out of it."

"Two of three is most of the pie."

Amandine laughed again. "Fine then, Mister Two-Thirds. I'm dressed, you can turn around. Let's go see Anvilroot!"

History and Songs

"Taxation is the mechanism by which a government funds activities that benefit the society, such as paying soldiers and building roads. In Serentia, this is accomplished through levies placed on the land-holding nobles and usage fees on roads and ports. In Olgothia, it is a tithe collected annually from all citizens. Zulathia only collects a small portion as coin, and instead accepts livestock, produce, and preserves, which are then used to feed and equip its massive army. Tren and the Kalebites possess the least restrictive taxation systems: the former collects a portion of all sales by registered merchants, landowners, ship masters and nobles. The latter requires mandated service to the nation as part of citizenship, and uses this compulsory labor to lessen the burden on individual citizens."

- Lecture Notes, Fourth Ironday, Low Summer 1202

AMANDINE AND FREDDERICK gathered their things, and with Grendel and Dumpling in tow, made their way through Lowers to the gates of Greyrock Falls. Like Myron's Bend, she found the security lax. No merchants going between Lowers and the main city were being taxed. She wondered idly if the Halifax Guild had a point with how Stoneman was run, if this was how other cities operated.

"Does no one but Everdawn collect taxes from merchants?" Amandine asked.

"What? Oh, you mean no one asking you fifty questions when you go through a colorless gate?" Fredderick scratched his head and pointed to a trio of armor-clad dwarves with wickedly curved polearms. Passing dwarves made respectful gestures, and passing humans tended to give them a wide berth. "Yeah, I have heard that folk rarely break the law in Greyrock Falls because the dwarven council is harsh on those who misbehave. Anvilroot basically subsidizes the entire area, so why tax merchants? I'll bet the market here is incredible."

He was right. Even in Artemis, she had never seen a marketplace so large and varied. The merchant's square covered an area the size of Stoneman twice over. Rows upon rows of goods from all over the world filled it, crisscrossed with paths that were absolutely packed with people. A few wagon roads were kept clear by stern-looking, armed guards, but the rest was a sea of bodies. Amandine paused to help Grendel into her satchel as the crowd became too much for him.

"I have never seen anything like it," Amandine said. "Look at all of this! Everything is here, why is there a shortage everywhere else?"

Fredderick nodded as he examined a cart full of apples. "One and three for last season's apples? They may have everything, but the prices are higher than the waterfalls. My guess would be because the large holds are buying most of it before it can get to the smaller settlements."

"That doesn't seem fair."

"It's fair, Amandine. This seems like a lot, and I am not an expert, but to feed huge cities like Irongate, Artemis, and the Maw, massive trains must pass through here on the regular to gather up the accumulated goods from the borderlands. My father is a financier of such trains to and from Irongate and, as crazy as this sounds, I don't think there's enough here."

"That does sound crazy." Amandine passed a stall packed with green vegetables and potatoes. "If the heartlands and borderlands starve, then all this dries up and there is nothing!"

"Yes, but, except in dire situations such as this, the hamlets are self-sufficient. They make as much as they need for themselves, plus a great deal extra, which is then upsold to the city-dwellers. So if you are a merchant with three thousand marks worth of beef, you can resell locally for four thousand, or take that to the nearest major hold and make triple the profit. The bigger payout always wins, Amandine. The hamlets don't have the money to compete with the buying power of a place like Irongate."

"But that's wrong!"

"That's money. Gold is the Emperor's favor."

Amandine frowned at the expression. It smacked of old imperial rule and made Fredderick sound like just another stuck up, floppy duck. "Fine, but then what I want to know next is, if your father is so wealthy, why are you always scamming people for coppers?"

Fredderick grimaced. "My family has money, that's truth, but it's my father's money. Some is my mother's too. She serves on Irongate's merchant council. Sometimes she will take pity and send funds, but my father and I... don't get along. He does not support me. I was sent to my cousin to learn how to 'support myself.' He even garnishes half my wages as a trust, contingent on my successful completion of my duties to Kimber and Lady Everdawn."

"Learning how to take care of yourself isn't a terrible thing, Fredderick. It's what I am doing."

He shrugged. "I don't mean to be a layabout, or some useless fop who spends his inheritance indulging himself, but I am not going to become my father either, no matter how badly he wants it."

"Then why go along with any of it? You don't need to do it if it makes you unhappy, Fredderick!"

"It's not that simple."

"Then make it simple and just tell me why!" Amandine rounded on him. "You keep putting me off on this. I want to be clear, I really like you, but I will not ride back-wagon to Marlette. I also don't care if you're poor, or rich, or a mage."

"Lower your voice," Fredderick hissed.

Amandine nodded, but continued to glare at him.

"Being a Stolm," he muttered. "Is like being royalty in some merchant circles. It's not just about what I want. Defying my father, hells, I'll do that just to do, but making enemies that would hurt the family? Hurt my mother? My cousins? He's not the only one who would be burned if I spilled that lantern."

With a clipped laugh, Amandine shook her head and folded her arms. "I think you really like being a Stolm, Fredderick, despite all of that. You have influence. All you had to do was mention your cousin's name to the Sheriff in Myron's Bend and Captain Craglin got almost everything he wanted."

"I was just—"

"Showing off? Trying to impress me? When will you get it? I don't care about any of that shite. The Fredderick I like is the one who makes funny jokes, who is brave in the face of hard things, who doesn't snivel about how mean his da' is! You might be more careful with your money than Marlette, but you're still obsessed with it!"

Fredderick had pressed his lips into a thin line and glowered as Amandine continued to stare him down. She sighed and threw up her hands.

"I am tired of being mad at you, Fredderick. You've helped me. A lot. I really like you and I'm so grateful for your friendship, but I will not be anyone's stone to move about the board. I left the convent in Artemis, despite all they had done for me. I left my position at Manor L'Eau, despite my love for that kitchen. If you think I am going to accept all of this just because you've helped me in the past, then you're wrong!"

"Please, sahs," a woman running a nearby cart said. "Take yer disagreement elsewhere, yer blockin' custom."

Amandine turned without another word and walked away. She heard Dumpling yip as Fredderick followed her through the market. They walked almost the entire lane before he spoke again.

"So you want me to break it off with Marlette?" Fredderick asked.

Yes! Amandine thought to herself, but instead she took a deep breath and slowed her pace, talking to him over her shoulder. "I just want you to live your life the way *you* want to. You chased me halfway across Serentia, Fredderick. I... Kayla's Heart, I lose all sense with you!"

She stopped and faced him again. "Forcing you to do anything would be just as bad as you expecting me to do something just because you want it. So, no, I'm not demanding anything. I meant what I said, though, about playing second to Marlette. I won't stand for it. So if that's your choice, then we can still be friends... but that's all. What happened last night won't happen again."

Fredderick scratched his stubble and seemed pensive. "There's more to it," he said slowly. "I... look, I also meant it when I said I don't really like Marlette. I've always liked you, since the day we met in the L'Eau's Sunrooms. That terrible livery was practically choking you, but you were still so animated and full of... I don't know. Joy? Enthusiasm?"

Amandine blushed. She hadn't found herself noticing him until later than that. That he'd been attracted to her since the start made her feel... vindicated. *Take that, Marlette.* "Ok, but then what are we going to do about it, Fredderick?"

"I am not completely sure what I can do about it from right here, right now. You have something important to do, and I still want to help in any way I can. Breaking off a courtship is not something done properly with a letter sent from half a nation away. I should speak to her directly."

With her heart thundering in her chest, Amandine forced her voice to remain steady. "Ok, that seems both fair and gentlemanly, but what about your..." she almost said 'magic' but caught herself and cleared her throat. "... apprenticeship options?"

"That's the trickier part, to be honest. Maybe Hemm will advise me further on the matter, but, I really *can't* talk about it. Not yet. This talent comes in many forms, and mine is not the same as Hemm's or Green's, or even yours."

"Still with the secrets," Amandine groused.

"Only until I can get a handle on the reins of my own life, Amandine! Surely that's something you can relate to?"

She eyed him skeptically.

"Has anyone told you that when you're being stubborn, you stick your lip out in this little pout?" Fredderick said with a grin.

Amandine rolled her eyes and began walking again. "Ugh, yes. Don't make fun!"

"Aww, come on, don't be mad!" Fredderick followed in her wake. "It's really sweet, Amandine, I can't be the only person who says so!"

"Yes, well, if you're not becoming your father, you are probably becoming Bertrand then!"

"I could do worse. At least people respect him for who he is and not how much gold he has."

Amandine couldn't really argue with that fact and it made her grumpy. She decided to let it drop, though. Fighting with him right now accomplished nothing. In a few bells, she would finally be walking into Anvilroot. She would be doing it with a friend, and that made it better.

"You're trying to change the subject, Fredderick, but I think I sort of understand." Amandine shrugged. "Thank you for being here for me. I still want your help. As for the rest..."

He strode up beside her and took her hand. She considered pushing him away, and then thought better of it. The market was crowded and it wouldn't do to get separated in a strange city. It was fine. For now. Even if the simple touch of his fingers made her heart race. Colorless man!

"I have not said my final word on this subject," she announced.

"Fair," Fredderick said with a nod.

They passed the market into the part of the city known as the Terraces. Built in rising tiers up the side of the mountain, the Terraces surrounded the enormous waterfall the city was named for. It was the source of the Wolfshenta River and fell hundreds of spans down from the side of the mountain. As they drew closer to the lowest section, the waterfall's noise increased. The view was breathtaking, but Amandine was distracted by the deafening roar of the rushing water.

"How does anyone on the highest tiers hear anything?" she half-shouted to Fredderick.

"I've never been here, but father says the nobles build into the side of the mountain using dwarven techniques. The inner chambers are muffled by feet of solid rock. Only the outer areas are noisy."

"Nobles are strange." Amandine shook her head. "I think I'd rather just have someplace quiet where I could see something amazing like that and not be deafened by it."

They followed a switchback road, staying on a side path meant for foot traffic, as they made their way up to the first terrace. The air began to fill with a light mist from the massive waterfall, and Amandine noticed many people wearing oiled cloaks. Even the wealthier citizens possessed some sort of water-proofing as part of their wardrobe, whether it was dyed leather parasols, intricate rune-emblazoned cloaks, or simply colorful drapes of fabric with a hole cut for the head to fit through. The mist created small rainbows in the air that shimmered into and out of existence. The market plaza below began to look smaller. Amandine's legs burned by the time they reached the top of the terrace and found themselves at a guarded gate.

Unlike the Lowers, the entrance to the Terraces was closely guarded. Only those in hand-carried palanquins or personal carriages were given free passage. The handful of merchants passing through to the Stone Door were being accounted for and taxed in a way that was familiar to Amandine. When she and Fredderick presented themselves for inspection, the dwarven guard only gave their meager belongings a cursory look.

"Yer knife needs a peace bond," they said to Amandine, pointing to the *Olatharr*.

"A what?" she asked.

"You need to tie it into its sheath with a cord, to make it hard to draw," Fredderick said. "Kimber has dignitaries do it inside of Everdawn's compound too."

"Aye, if ye don't have one, tha floppy hat there'll sell ya one fer a flip," the guard said jerking a thumb to a harried-looking human woman with a ledger sitting at a small folding desk.

"Thanks, sah," Amandine said. Grendel popped his head out of her satchel and meowed. The guard actually grinned, showing all of his jagged teeth, and made the flat hand motion to the cat she had seen the sailors on the Silver Mountain using, and then waved them through.

"What's a 'flip'?" Amandine whispered to Fredderick.

"A copper, I think?"

She paid the clerk and tied her blade. The Stone Door, the entrance to Anvilroot, was up one more tier, but Amandine quailed at the thought of another switchback so soon.

"Let's find something to eat before we climb again," she said.

They passed several places along the boulevards of the First Terrace that emanated wonderful smells, but the vast majority were hosted kitchens and exclusive eateries catering to those with far more money than they had.

"Surely there is a cart or something that sells to the merchants and up-bound travelers?" Fredderick groused as they passed yet another door labeled 'Locals Only.'

"Like that one?" Amandine pointed to a small, wheeled pushcart. The proprietor was a dwarf with a shaggy beard that seemed to explode from their face like a thistle gone to seed. A pair of goggles with dark lenses rested on their head. The *Ur'Mord* squinted at them as they approached.

"Humans, yah? Ye be wantin' somethin' burnt then, I suppose?" they said.

"Yes, please," Amandine replied. "Do I smell game? Is that goat or prong?"

"Goat! Only big hoary boulders eat prong. Wasteful that. Ye want it with mushrooms?"

Amandine got a skewer with chunks of cold, roasted goat and pickled mushrooms. Fredderick opted for one without fungus. He eyed Amandine's warily as she ate.

"Stop it, I'm sure these are edible—not like whatever it was I ate at Kiln."

He shrugged. "You know what they grow those in, right?"

"You know what goats eat, right?" Amandine said back.

The dwarven monger laughed in their choking, wheezy way. "Ye two are young, jus' barely what passes for a grown human, ya? Out of town too, aye? Going up a tier to the Stone Door?"

"Yes, sah," Amandine said around a mouthful of mushrooms. "It's my first time here. I have wanted to see Anvilroot for ages!"

"Well, there's a bit of a scrum. Not all the peddlers are bein' let in unless they are *Ur'mord*, or have official business. Ye might be caught in a lurch for a while."

"Why is that?" Fredderick asked. "I thought the dwarves promoted free trade at all times into Anvilroot."

"Aye, that's the usual. But things are strange righ' na. Righ' strange. Warrens goin' cold, buds vanishin' from the *nek'livol*—nursery warrens, ye all call them. Got the elders in a panic. Just two of yer days past, Hammer Jorund put out a general call fer mercenaries. The council ain't done tha' in nigh on a hundred years. I were still jus' a bud lickin' rock moss and—"

"Wait, you were a child one hundred years ago?" Amandine asked.

"One hundred and thirteen, to be exact. I remember it like yesterday. Hammer Jorund were still jus' a battlemaster then, but the Stonebound Hammer at the time, Kyrec, tha' grackle put the gold in their teeth and offered a bounty for sellswords. And by the stone they came! Seekers, mercenaries, *mord'resh*, even fae. First time I'd ever seen a court-born fae. I remember–"

"But what was the trouble?" Amandine asked, interrupting them again. She hated to be rude, but this *gyre* obviously loved their own stories, and she really needed to know if she had traveled all this way just to be shut out at the gates.

They didn't seem to mind at all. With squinted eyes, the peddler grinned savagely. "*Erestral*, dark fae. The Unnamed Court. Court-born hate 'em with a passion, and there's plenty ta hate. They got uppity and thought the *Ur'mord* were weak; tried ta have a tussle. We bloodied 'em good, but ye can't drive the spear home if ya need it to defend yer young. So we invoked the Promise in Stone, and they came. Oh, how they came. Sand-blasted fae never stood a chance. If—"

"So you think these dark fae have re-emerged? Come back to have—how did you put it?—another tussle?" Fredderick asked.

"Seems tha' way, righ'?" the dwarf said with a choking laugh. "It'll be grand ta see 'em get their pale arses thumped again!"

Amandine glanced at Fredderick. He appeared as worried as she felt. "Goddess, I really hope they let us in. We are on official business, for the town of Stoneman, but not with the council."

The dwarf blew out a large breath, making their puffy beard wobble. "Ain't no business official unless it's ta be heard by the Hammers. But they are letting some merchants in. Floppy ducks with gold to spend, and the mercenaries, o' course."

She thanked the peddler for the food, and the information. Dumpling ran ahead of them a bit as they slowly trudged up the next switchback to the Second Terrace. It was narrower, and the buildings were taller. The largest ones were built back into the cliff face like Fredderick had said, and marble and glowstone were abundant in every design. Amandine imagined how it must look at night, lit up like a cloud of stars.

It wasn't hard to find the Stone Door. The towering portal of solid rock dominated the center of the Terrace, and there was a massive queue of people waiting to get in. Amandine and Fredderick joined the back, behind a dwarf leading two prongs laden with saddle bags.

"Excuse me, sah?" Amandine asked. "How long have you been waiting?"

"Eh? Me? Only a hand of toks. Residents get moved up. The poor bastard in front of me? They say they've been here three of yer bells."

Amandine glanced ahead of them. Another merchant, a dark-skinned human woman with a cart full of barrels, stood by the draw animal. It was some sort of large lizard with a short tail that walked on its hind feet. The front arms were stubby and three-toed. It had a wide beak like a duck.

"What is that colorless thing?" Fredderick asked.

"Oh that? A kind of pack animal popular in Olgothia. Sifters, they call 'em," the dwarven merchant said.

"It's amazing," Amandine said in awe.

"It stinks," the dwarf said with a shake of their beard. "Anyone with sense won't let a sifter inta the warrens. So vile!"

"I can't smell anything," Fredderick said.

"That's 'cause yer a human, ya daft goat!" The merchant laughed.

Amandine reached into her satchel to pet Grendel. She inhaled. Yes, there was definitely a whiff of something musky from the huge lizard, but even with her senses enhanced, it was faint. She knew *Ur'mord* had excellent senses of smell, but if it was that sensitive...

"Everywhere humans are must be vile to you if that lizard stinks," she said.

The merchant laughed harder. "This *gyre* gets it! To be fair, some things you lot make smell better 'n fresh cut stone. I actually hope they do let her and the stinky lizard in. Those barrels are full of *mead*."

They said the last word with an air of longing so strong, Amandine could almost feel their desire for the beverage. All she knew was that it was a kind of wine made from fermented honey. Master Hawthorne's wife enjoyed a variety local to Stoneman. Despite the wait, she began to feel excited. They were still in line at the door and she had already seen a strange new beast and possibly discovered a new variety of honey wine.

Half a bell later, a dwarf wearing an official looking coat and colorful blindfold came down the line and began waving all of the waiting *mord* ahead of the queue.

"Oi, proper! Let in the stank lizard with the barrels, *gyre*. *Mead*." The merchant ahead of Amandine gestured to the cart with the sifter.

The dwarven official tugged their extravagantly braided black beard and shook their head. "She waits, *gyre*. Only *mord* to pass for another two city bells."

Amandine and Fredderick moved up behind the sifter-drawn cart after the dwarves departed. The woman driving the cart was Olgothian, with dark skin and golden eyes. Her hair was a pale straw color that she wore short. Amandine had only met a handful of Olgothians, mostly expats, in passing while training with the Sisters. She knew Madam Sheeria Stolm a bit better, but this woman was not the same. Everything about her was severe, from the short hair, to her sharp features, to the way she clicked her long, painted nails impatiently on the sifter's harness.

"Get comfortable, sahs," she drawled with a thick accent. "If they are even forgoing the usual bait, we stand to be waiting a very long time."

"Do you really have mead? From Olgothia?" Amandine asked.

She laughed bitterly. "Gods, child, no. This is Trenash stock. I bought it specifically to shortcut the line. I was told if you have something they want, they'll let you in more quickly. Clearly that was wrong."

"Well, if we're to be stuck together, my name is Amandine, and this is Fredderick." Amandine made a polite bow.

The woman nodded back. "Lyra of Stolen Songs."

"Your animal... may I touch it? I've never seen one."

Lyra shrugged. "They are very docile, but the kick is powerful. Approach from the front and touch the nose first."

Amandine followed her instructions and, after a moment, the large creature leaned into her hand. Lyra scratched its head and Amandine duplicated the gesture. The feeling of pleasure radiating from the sifter made her smile.

"You seem almost too young to be traveling alone. Have you been here before?" Lyra asked.

"No, sah. Our town and the area around it was hurt by a massive infestation of rot slime. We were told by a *mord* friend that one of their children might have a solution to preserve our stores for the coming shiv seasons."

"Hmm. Your story, it is much like others I have heard, from all over. Not just slimes. Unexplained rot and fungus, overly aggressive fae beasts, even one where all the eggs for two tendays were laid without yolks."

"How about skellix?" Fredderick asked.

"What do you know of Conflux creatures?" Lyra raised an eyebrow.

"One attacked us last year, and another one, massive, attacked the heartlands near Irongate."

She nodded. "I had heard of the latter but not the former. Where are you from?"

"Stoneman, sah," Amandine said.

Recognition seemed to fill Lyra's golden eyes. "I know that place. Long ago, it had a grand name. The Bulwark Eternal Among Stars and Sun Aground. It withstood countless assaults by rebels and fae. There is no song for its fall. Perhaps one still exists, undiscovered, but I have not heard it."

"You aren't a mead merchant are you?" Fredderick asked.

"No, young man, I am not. I am a historian. Here seeking old texts and lost music. Stuck in time, awaiting the colorless night."

Amandine gazed up at the sky. It would still be bells yet before dusk. "Do you really think we'll be in line until then?"

"Without a doubt, child, without a doubt."

The Stone Door

"Following the War of Shadows, the dwarven clans native to the East of Beregoth began looking hard to the future. The Eastern ranges had seen the worst fighting and suffered harrowing losses. Of the nine Ur'nyre *that had once called Olgath's Spine their home, eight remained: Magmaflow, Dark Granite, Ironheel, Diamondbeards, Coalbeards, Chainbreaker, Jaggedpoint, and Obsidian. Of these, all but the Coalbeards and Magmaflow had been decimated by the fighting. The Ironheels had only a few* nyre *left, and no buds. The missing* nyre, *the Deep Echos, had vanished when they marched in force to protect their claims on the MacDarran Highway. Rather than face a fractured decline, Galvin of Dark Granite proposed that the remaining eight* nyre *join forces under one banner, share croft and craft, and thereby survive."*

- Lecture Notes, First Starday, Low Winter 1202

THE DAYLIGHT FADED to dusk. As the sun vanished, the Terrace began to light up, just as Amandine had imagined it would. The frames of windows, the tops of garden walls, even a checked pattern in the road—all of it glowed. The illumination made people bold, and commerce continued around them even after the darkness descended.

Their place in line had advanced. Some had given up and left. Others, mainly merchants with food and drink, including the Olgothian historian, Lyra, had been allowed in. Amandine and Fredderick were near the front now, and the massive stone door was still open, but the black-bearded dwarf managing the queue hadn't returned in bells.

Dumpling snoozed in Fredderick's arms. Amandine leaned her head on his shoulder and also drifted. What a ridiculous way it would be for this trip to end, turned away at the very doors to Anvilroot. She tried not to think about Serand, but the idea that she might not be able to finish what he had started broke her heart.

The black bearded official emerged again. "Listen up! No more entries today, sahs! If you are buying or selling, you will have to wait until general trade resumes!"

Amandine awoke and stood up. "No, wait, sah, please!" She hurried to the front of the queue. The others ahead of her were dispersing with a great deal of grumbling. "Please let us in," Amandine said as she approached the dwarf. "We have a message to deliver and—"

"Nay. No one except on official business or approved commerce. Sorry, sahs, but I have my words from the Hammers themselves." They turned to go, but another voice called out.

"And what about Seekers, sah?"

Mel strode confidently up to the door, trailed by the other members of her crew, Vibrant Dawn. Her black leather scabbard was slung over one shoulder and a small backpack hung from the other.

"What do you say, blackbeard? One last entry, save the queue a space for tomorrow?" Mel grinned at the dwarf as she spoke and a gold coin danced across her fingers, then disappeared into her fist.

The dwarf eyed her and the coin, then looked at the rest of the crew. "Papers," they said finally.

Tobe stepped forward and bowed, then handed the dwarf a roll of parchment. They unrolled it and read slowly. "This is in order." They handed the roll back but left their hand out. Mel dropped the crown into their palm.

"Oh, and these two are with us," Mel added.

The dwarf raised an eyebrow. "Oh, they are Seekers?"

"Old enough to be, but no, she's our cook."

"Right, and the boy?"

Mel unslung her backpack and shoved it into Fredderick's arms, nearly making him drop Dumpling. "Porter," she said.

The dwarf's head shook, beard wagging. "Humans are mad. On yer head be it, sah." They turned and called up through the door to someone out of sight, inside and above. "Last group—Seekers—close the Door!"

Mel clapped the dwarf on the back, which earned her a glare, as she and the members of Vibrant Dawn passed through the Stone Door. Amandine was unsure if she should follow, as she didn't really work for them, and it struck her as dishonest.

"What's wrong?" Fredderick asked when he realized she wasn't coming. "They got us in."

"It feels dishonest, lying to the gate watchers," Amandine whispered. "We aren't Seekers."

"And we're still not. I'm a porter, remember? Go with it!"

Fredderick jogged to catch up, Mel's pack under one arm and Dumpling under the other. Grendel poked his head out of the satchel and meowed at Amandine.

"Better than being shut out, I suppose," Amandine said softly as she hurried to follow.

It was only as she passed the massive granite door that she realized how truly huge it was. It stretched up into the cliff at a height equal to the great trees near Artemis, and was so thick she needed three full strides to pass by its edge. It ground slowly against the packed earth below it, plowing a shallow trench where the stone had settled. She wove through the crack and into a large, vaulted hall where Vibrant Dawn and Fredderick waited for her. The door sealed behind her with a crash and grinding of stone. Tobe waved at her in a friendly way and Mel gestured for her to hurry.

Amandine caught up to Fredderick and stared, agape at the high ceilings. They stretched into the mountain above her even further than the door, and she could just make out small slit-like windows far above, where the shadows of dwarves flitted, calling out to each other in *Mord-seq*. The walls were built of cut stone, much like the bastion of Stoneman, all fitted together so tight that she could barely see the seams. A path had been lit with burning oil braziers for those that required light to see. With her enhanced sight in effect, the glare from them was almost blinding, and the enormous shadows they cast on the walls made her and the others seem like giants.

"It's so big!" Amandine exclaimed. "How? Why?"

Mel grinned. "No idea. You have a notion, Imri?"

The female elf blinked once at being addressed and looked back to Amandine.

"Giants. In ages past, in the Era of Giants, the *mord* and tusker peoples were servants of the Orrubi. Used as labor and foot soldiers, they built things for their masters to their scale. This place is ancient. Many newer *mord* cities still build at scale, however. It's what they know, and is a source of pride. In the end, they worked with my people to free themselves from the Giants, but their mighty touch is still all around."

"How do they lift the stones? Are there still giants like the ones back then? Can they—"

"Peace! I am a hunter not a scholar. The only stories I know are those told to all the members of my bloom as younglings. They focused mainly on fae contributions to the struggle, not *mord*. And yes, some Giants still linger, but they are mere shadows of the power of their ancestors. They are simple people, of simple means, who dress in hides and live in the deep wilds. I know not where any may be found."

Amandine knew. Sort of. She had learned last year that Heather had been trading with giants for aurochs meat. How many, she wondered, could stay hidden in the middle of human and elven lands like that? It couldn't be more than a few. And how simple could they be, if they had managed to tame massive aurochs herds? As silly as it was, she hoped she might meet a giant someday. The First People of Beregoth. Even if they were shadows of the ancient ones that had ruled the world for so long, they must still be amazing to see.

"Last we saw you lot was in Myron's Bend," Fredderick said. "Did you come because of the call for sellswords?"

Ragall nodded. "Yup. We spent some time on a job for the Sheriff. It paid well, but *mord* pay better. And it's been a while since we last visited."

"Was it another Skellix sighting? Did another show up outside the Conflux?"

Blueknot, shook her head and answered. "Nay, just the big bastard that tried to eat Irongate. We missed that action. Probably for the best."

"We did run into a town that had an unusually large number of lurks, though," Mel said. "We managed to scatter them and made out well, but it was very strange. Lurks are usually solitary things. They don't run in packs."

"That is odd," Fredderick said. "Where was that?"

"A small brickmaking town named Kiln. Lurks are drawn to places with a lot of death in the air. Mass graves, battlefields. We didn't find anything like that, though. Just the lurks. It was unusual to be sure, but lots of odd things have been happening of late."

Amandine and Fredderick looked at each other. She pressed her lips tight and shook her head. Fredderick shrugged and didn't say anything more.

They passed from the entry hall into a larger chamber and Amandine gasped. The hollow was so vast, she couldn't see the far edges. The ceiling was an indistinct shadow high above, speckled with glowing blue and green lights, like stars. An entire city surrounded them. It climbed the walls and clung to the edge of the bowl down lower to where an offshoot waterfall of the massive one outside drained into a small lake. Everything was stone, but in a wild array of colors, textures and patterns—swirled reds and speckled blues and massive white-gray marble slabs. Towers topped with burning pyres kept a lookout over it all, and in the distance she saw a fortress, as big as any in the world above, surrounded by a trench that smoked and steamed.

"Welcome to Anvilroot," Mel said with a flourish. "Where the meat is raw, the beer is strong, and almost everyone is shorter than you."

Blueknot cleared her throat.

"I said *almost*," Mel protested.

"You there! Seekers? Stand for inspection, sahs!" a voice boomed.

A group of armed dwarves, their wickedly sharp polearms and mail gleaming in the fire light, stepped out of a nearby dugout.

"Ah, yes, time to account for blades and such. Make sure you show them all this time, Blue," Mel said.

"Yeah, yeah," the small woman said in a grumpy tone.

Vibrant Dawn arranged themselves in a line and presented their arms to the inspecting dwarves. Tobe handed over their paperwork again. Blueknot revealed a surprising number of knives. Just when Amandine didn't think she could possibly have another secreted on her person, she would slide one out of a boot, from under a sewn leather plate, or the lining of her cloak. She even took out her hairpin, allowing her strange yellow hair to tumble free to her waist, revealing the pin to be yet another weapon. The dwarf inspecting her did not seem all that surprised at the number of them, although they did raise an eyebrow at the hairpin.

"Everything to your satisfaction, Fist Leader?" Mel asked.

Amandine noted one dwarf with a shiny steel pin in the shape of a triangle on their collar. The *gyre* in charge then. They nodded to Mel and motioned for the other guards to fall in line.

"Aye, ye can all move along. Human edibles are in the Magma Ward mostly. Keep the peace and abide by the Promise," the Fist said.

Mel nodded and waved cheerfully as the guards returned to their dugout. Her smile slipped a little when they weren't looking.

"Colorless nosy rock-rats," she muttered. It was so soft that Amandine probably wouldn't have heard it without Grendel, but Tobe also seemed to nod at the sentiment. "Alright, crew, let's go find a rowdy place with normal sized tables to have a drink!"

There was a general rumble of approval at that, although they had to wait a moment longer for Blueknot to replace all of her blades.

"Have enough?" Fredderick asked her with a smirk.

"I'm actually missin' a few. Mislaid them on the last job. Not my good ones, though. And we got paid enough that I might buy some new Mord-steel ones while we're here!"

"Cressida could use some love too," Ragall rumbled as he thumbed the blade of his axe. "Getting a bit tepid."

"Your axe has a name?" Amandine asked as they began walking again.

"Of course! All good weapons should have one. Mel's is called 'Second Winter'"

Amandine turned to Mel, "Like a Shiv Winter? Why is that?"

Mel smiled at her indulgently. "I won't break the peace bond while we're on the streets, but maybe I'll show you later."

"She'll definitely show you," Imri said as she fished inside a belt pouch. "Showing off her sword is one of her two greatest loves."

The dark haired woman gave Imri a wry grin, but didn't disagree.

"What's the other greatest love?" Fredderick asked.

"Drinking!" all the Seekers said in unison. Except for Tobe. He mimed guzzling from a mug with one hand. Mel and Blueknot laughed.

"Ah!" Imri found what she had been looking for in her pouch and held up three small clay tokens. "I still have chits for Obsidian Seat. Let us go there. I recall they had more than adequate services."

Mel nodded. "Sounds lumi. Any objections?"

No one had any and so she led them down a broad avenue lined with glowstone. Amandine tried not to gape at everything they passed. Most of the people surrounding them were *mord*, of course, but what struck Amandine was the variety. Beards of all lengths, braided, unbraided, clipped with jewelry or simply tied; they came in all colors, even a few that were decidedly unnatural by human standards. Skin as well. Many of the dwarves she saw were ruddy like Boomer or Captain Cragllin, but just as many had skin dark as charcoal, gray and slate-like, or even brown like hers.

There were also children. Young *mord* seemed to be smaller, thinner versions of the adults, without the facial hair. Kivel had been right, dwarven skin was sort of pebbly and lizard-like, but their complexions hid the strangeness of it unless one looked close.

Stone Folk were also in abundance. Amandine had only ever met or seen a handful, including Master Wizzlecog in Stoneman, and the woman who had installed the lock on Chef's pantry at Manor L'Eau, but here they were nearly as numerous as the dwarves. They were shorter, and slight of build compared to *mord*, and there were both men and women. The men often had facial hair, but unlike the dwarves' massive beards, stone folk men featured fine, thin moustaches, or neatly trimmed and pointed beards, or long sideburns that left their chins bare. Their skin tones were just as varied as their dwarven companions, but their teeth were more like a human's or Hill Folk's, excepting an additional pair of long canines that made them seem a bit feral when they smiled. Many appeared to be craftsmen, running stalls selling odd devices that whirled or smoked, and others moved in groups with tools, going to or from some task.

Some humans and Hill Folk haggled for goods, but Amandine also saw a pair of elves, both armed with bows, speaking with one of the dwarven guards. Perhaps mercenaries answering the recent call?

The odor of smoke was strong, but it didn't carry the burnt wood essence of a lit hearth. It was heavy, and pungent. There was a hint of something like rotten eggs as well, but it was faint, and Amandine supposed she only sensed it because of Grendel. No one else with her seemed bothered. There were also scents of food, mainly cooking meats. Some stalls were clearly marked in Olgothian, announcing they had fare for "Sunlit Folk," while others seemed to cater more to the locals, serving bowls filled with colorful mushrooms and strips of raw meat.

Everything was made either of stone or a strange gray wood Amandine had never seen before. The stone, for its part, was always detailed—with designs, beveled edges or even entire pictorial scenes engraved into it.

Finally, they arrived at a two-story building made of blocks of solid black stone. The gray wooden shingle over the door had no words, just an etching of an ornate throne.

"Here we are then," Mel said, gesturing to the door. "For the new kids, mind your step, the floors are polished and can be slippery."

"Yeah, like last time when we joined that brawl and Rag slid halfway across the bar?" Blueknot laughed.

"I landed on my feet." Ragall grunted as he rolled his shoulders.

"So it's a rough place?" Amandine asked.

Mel grinned in an unnerving way. "Only if you let it be. The Obsidian Seat is the best human-run tavern in Anvilroot, at least by my reckoning. Just don't pick a fight."

"Or speak to anyone," Blueknot said.

"Or look at people the wrong way," Ragall added.

Tobe held up his slate. "Or tell the tavern keeper she looks like a troll," it read.

"I never said that!" Ragall protested.

"Are we going to drink or not?" Mel asked impatiently.

Imri sighed and walked to the door without waiting for an answer. "Come with me, younglings. We will find a seat away from their ridiculous behavior."

"Hey wait, I thought you were paying, Imri?" Mel asked.

The elf pointed to herself, Amandine and Fredderick. "Three chits. Three drinks. Buy your own, please, and try not to insult the Matron when you do?"

She opened the door and strode inside, seemingly oblivious to Mel's scowling. Amandine shrugged apologetically as she and Fredderick hurried to follow her.

"The second round then!" Mel called from behind them.

The Obsidian Seat

"The Magmaflow, weary of politics, refused to join the coalition and retreated deeper into the mountains to seek its own destiny. The others formed a Council of Hammers and became the Seven Hammers Clan. Now the largest and most successful of the Ur'nyre, *the Seven Hammers is also more tolerant of outsiders than their Western cousins and does a large amount of trade with both Serentia and Olgothia from their home citadel, Anvilroot, which is located beneath the headwaters of the Wolfshenta River. Seven Hammers* mord, *because of the intermingling of smaller* nyres, *can have nearly any skin or hair color. Their Ologthian is smoother and less accented than other clans, and while tuskers are never truly welcome, all others are shown "proper* mord *hospitality" when visiting their outposts and cities."*

- Lecture Notes, Second Starday, Low Winter 1202

THE INSIDE OF the The Obsidian Seat was not what Amandine had expected. She had envisioned a place with a large open area filled with tables, but that was only half right. The middle of the room was a round counter top of polished stone with an inner half-ring of tapped beer barrels. Beside those stood an enormous bubbling pot slowly being stirred by a shirtless Hill Folk man covered in tattoos. A table next to the pot was manned by a pair of humans, one obviously Zulath, the other a dark-skinned fellow that might be Bolath or Olgath.

They skinned, boned and sliced fish into small bites that were then rolled in some kind of flour and dropped into the bubbling pot. Moments later, a large woman with braided hair and colorful arm tattoos fished the morsels out using a wire basket and dropped them into small bowls filled with a variety of grains, mushrooms, and greens.

These were then slid around the counter to patrons or carried by servers to surrounding diners. The tables that orbited the circle of activity were all screened, like Bertrand's private tables at the Stomping Golem, and the furthest tables by the walls had partitions built into them to provide privacy.

Against the back wall, on a raised dais, was an enormous chair carved from black stone. No one sat in it, and the way the servers gave it a wide berth made it seem somewhat ominous to Amandine.

Groups of *mord*, humans, and Hill Folk filled nearly every table. Imri looked about for a moment and then led Amandine and Fredderick through the crowd to a table against the back wall next to the black stone chair. A male elf was the sole occupant.

He glanced up as they approached. His hair was golden and his eyes were a clear, sky blue. He was similar to, and at the same time different than, either Mister Green or Imri, but the way he seemed to stare through all of them was very familiar.

Imri exchanged words with him briefly, and he motioned for them to sit and then went back to watching the crowd as if lost in thought.

"He says he is only waiting for a friend and will depart when they arrive. We may sit here, so long as we do not disturb his meditation," Imri explained as she ushered them onto the bench across from the elf.

"What's his name?" Amandine asked.

"I did not inquire."

"Should we whisper?" Fredderick asked as he took his seat. The elf hadn't moved since allowing them to sit, and just seemed to be staring at nothing as people passed the table and the noisy crowd milled about.

Imri smiled. "No, if he is in the Dream, he will not even notice us unless we directly address him."

"Mister Green, my *soeje*, talks about his meditations sometimes," Amandine said. "I wonder if it's the same thing?"

"You have an instructor from one of the Courts? May I ask which?" Imri seemed genuinely interested and Amandine figured it would be rude not to answer since she had brought it up.

"Starlight. He has very pale hair and skin. He's a magician, too."

"That... is interesting. It illuminates you," Imri said thoughtfully.

"How do you mean?"

"You are very mature for your age. Poised. The way you stood up to Carver in Myron's Bend was admirable."

Amandine felt slightly embarrassed by the compliment, but nodded. "Um, thank you. I just thought his terrible food needed fixing."

"The food is good here if you like fried things, but what shall you drink?" Imri asked as a server approached.

"Oh! Um, tea, I suppose. Or pressed juice maybe? If any is still left from the summer harvests."

Fredderick shook his head. "I am in Anvilroot for the first time in my life. I am trying a beer! The dwarves are famous for their brewing."

"I don't know. I understand it's a specialty here, but most places won't serve beer or spirits to you if you're not of age."

"Bah. Imri just finished telling you that you're very mature for your age." Fredderick grinned. "And you do all these crazy things despite everyone saying you're too young. Try one with me! And if you hate it, I am sure one of that lot would be happy to relieve you of it."

He jerked his thumb at the other members of Vibrant Dawn, who had managed to muscle up to the bar. Mel was engaged in an animated conversation with the tattooed woman, who eyed them all with pursed lips, especially Ragall.

"I suppose," Amandine said. She *was* curious. Part of her training with Serand had included small tastes of different spirits and beers, mainly so she would know their flavors for cooking with them, but she had never had a full mug of any that she had sampled. "But only one. You don't mind, Imri?"

"The human taboo on fermented drinks for younglings is founded on sound principles, but I am not your mother. You may order what you wish."

Amandine brimmed with questions at that. What were elven children allowed to drink? How old did they need to be to count as adults? Were there different traditions in different Courts? Before she could decide on one, however, the server reached their table.

He was middle-aged and human with a cheerful smile, although he gave a wary eye to the male elf who was still staring out into the room, unblinking.

"Er, what can I get for you, sahs?" he asked.

"*Tresbel*, if you have any still. Half-wine if not. And two beers, *mord* stock." Imri slid the clay tokens across the table.

"Oh! Haven't seen those in a while!" the server said. "Matron Gara stopped handing them out ages ago."

"My crew undertook a small task for her and she gave us some. These are the last."

"Seekers, then? Welcome back, sahs. I'll return with your drinks. Food?"

"Yes, please," Amandine chimed in.

The server nodded and took the tokens before walking away.

"Wait, don't we get to choose our food?" Fredderick asked.

"The only thing they serve is *tashi*. The fried bites of fish with grains and mushrooms. You get whatever they have that day," Imri explained.

"Oh! *That's* what *tashi* is?" Amandine asked. "I heard Serand mention it a few times. It's Zulathan, right?"

"Yes. Serand was your apprentice master?"

Amandine nodded. "He was. Pirates attacked our barge on the way North and he fell in the river."

Imri closed her eyes and laid a hand on Amandine's shoulder. "I am sorry to hear that. If he knew of *tashi* then he was well traveled. The variety they serve here uses fish caught in the underground, so it's probably quite a bit different than what he knew."

"Maybe. He lived here for a while and he could speak *Mord-seq*."

"Very well traveled, then."

"He was."

Fredderick stroked Dumpling's head as the small dog sniffed a stain on the table. "Chef Brutsche was originally from Tren, right? So he would have had to cross the entire land to end up in the middle of Serentia."

"Wait," Imri said, holding up a hand. "Your apprentice master was named Serand Brutsche?"

"Yes, sah," Amandine replied. "Blueknot said there was a Seeker once with that name as well. I think he might have actually been the one she had heard of, but it could just be a coincidence as well, right?"

"Perhaps, but a highly unlikely one. Still, to my knowledge, Seeker Brutsche died over ten years ago. Please describe him to me?"

"Oh, uh, well, he had skin like mine, but a shade darker, and his hair was graying. He slouched a bit, so he seemed shorter than he was, but when he stood up straight, he was about as tall as Ragall. And his eyes were blue. He could be very intense, but he cared about the people he lived and worked with..."

Amandine's voice trailed off. "He cared about me," she thought to herself. "When almost no one else did."

"Spring's breath," Imri said. Her expression had shifted from thoughtful to concerned. "It really was him. All these years..."

"You knew him?" Fredderick asked.

"I did. We met and even worked together on one occasion, although I was never part of his crew. Trenash people have a slanted view of fae because of the Grey Court. To think he was still alive, in the middle of Serentia of all places."

"I sort of knew he had been a Seeker once. Bertrand Kale was part of his crew I think. He and his wife own the Stomping Golem in Stoneman," Amandine said.

"Bertrand too? Telvor Aran? Hamish Peakness? Uriel of Shattered Chains? Rallindra Evos? Are any of those names familiar?"

Amandine dredged up her memory of the meeting in the Lord's Suite at the Golem. "He mentioned Peak and Uriel, but I've never met them. They're alive I think, though. Telvor is the town apothecary. Rallindra, he called her Rally, died years ago from an illness, he said."

"That colorless fool actually did it," Imri said with a smile. "He got out. Good for him."

"What I don't understand," Fredderick said, "is that if he's such a famous person, both as a chef and as a Seeker, how has he stayed hidden for so long? You lot thought he was dead, but the rest of the world knew Serand Brutsche the Chef. My family had heard of him all the way in Irongate."

"Serand is a very common male name in Tren, and Brutsche is a Serent commoner's surname," Imri said. "It's my notion that he led two separate lives for most of his career. In one, he was Lucky Salt's co-leader, and his exploits are well known, but mostly among Seekers. Many of whom, as I am sure you might have guessed, do not live very long due to our hazardous work and various personality flaws.

"In the other, he was Serand Brutsche the traveling Chef. Popping up in places near and far, throwing dinner parties for nobles of all stripes, entertaining Court Fae, and other such things. There is only limited overlap in these groups, and rumors spread like a grass fire during the Scorch. It's likely that most people never realized they were the same person. Or were purposefully led to believe they were different people."

"You said you had met him and worked with him as a Seeker? Can you—" Amandine began, but just then the server returned with their drinks and three bowls of *tashi*. Imri's drink was in a fluted glass filled with some kind of deep orange wine. The other two were tankards, enormous ones, with white-brown foam spilling down the sides. The smell of yeast and malt was strong to Amandine's Grendel-enhanced nose.

"Yes!" Fredderick said, rubbing his hands together. The server raised an eyebrow at him, but otherwise didn't comment before leaving with his tray under an arm.

"That is really a lot," Amandine said skeptically, as she eyed her own tankard.

'I know!" Fredderick said. "Isn't that lumi? Come on! A toast! To being in Anvilroot!"

He lifted his drink and gestured towards Amandine with it. She sighed and picked up her own. A little bit of foam sloshed onto her wrist. Grendel poked his head out of her satchel to sniff at it and sneezed.

"To Anvilroot!" Fredderick said, tapping her mug with his.

"To being alive, I guess," Amandine replied.

"To new acquaintances. And to old." Imri tilted her glass in to touch their mugs.

They all drank. Amandine expected the bitter flavor. It still made her tongue curl, but in the spirit of the toast she took an actual swallow of the drink instead of just sipping it. The fragrant foam reminded her of rising bread, and after the bitterness faded, something lingered. It was nutty, and savory, and there was a flavor she didn't recognize, but if she was honest with herself, she rather liked it.

"Oh my." Amandine looked at her mug with a new appreciation.

"Gods, that *is* good," Fredderick said. "I mean, I sort of half expected it to be bitter and sour, like the short ale served at the barracks in Stoneman, but..."

"There are four hundred and eighty-seven recognized variations of that drink," Imri said as she sipped hers. "They vary wildly in quality, and I am not fond of fermented grain myself, but that is one of the more exceptional ones. The tokens I exchanged were good for the house reserves, and not what is sold for coppers at the bar."

"Then thank you!" Amandine said. "This is better than I expected."

"Certainly," Imri said, tilting her head.

"You seem to know a lot about drink as well," Fredderick commented before taking another sip.

"My family were brewers and wine-makers. I took a different path in life, but the knowledge they imparted remains."

"And what is it you are drinking?" Amandine asked.

"*Tresbel*. Fae wine. It is made from fruit and spices, but humans do not generally enjoy the flavor."

"Oh! I think I understand. Chef made elven shortbreads once, and I tasted one. It... was certainly unusual, but I wouldn't say it was bad."

"He made those, did he? If I had realized he was also the famous chef, I might have tried harder to befriend him." Imri smiled. "As you said though, Seeker Brutsche could be quite intense. Rallindra even more so."

Amandine sipped and thought about that. "Blueknot said they were a couple. But he wasn't with her when I met him, he lived with an Under-Sergeant of the town militia named Dena Stonebrook. What was Rally like?"

"She was a godsworn of *Pelenastilan*, the One-Of-Many-Faces. Humans revere that god as 'Old Jack' or 'Shadow Jack'. She was one of those who could create miracles and speak to her god. I don't believe she was fully sane."

The conversation Amandine had overheard between Mother Jarl and Serand on the docks came back to her. "He didn't seem to care much for godsworn."

"You must understand, I did not know him intimately. We tracked Grimalks together for a bounty once. And met at a Seeker's Quorum another time. So I don't know what transpired between him and the other leader of Lucky Salt. Indeed, I didn't even know he had still been alive until a few moments ago. But if he had some falling out with Rallindra, that may explain his distaste for the godsworn."

"What is a Seeker's Quorum?" Fredderick asked.

"A good place to settle scores, get drunk, and brag about all of the stupid shite you've managed to survive!" a voice boomed.

Ragall approached their table, mug in hand, and when the meditating elf didn't move, he sat on the edge of the table instead. "Is he uh, you know?" he asked Imri.

She looked back at him with a long-suffering expression. "Yes. He is meditating, Ragall."

"That is so weird, right?" Ragall said to Fredderick in a lowered voice. "Like sleeping while awake!"

"The fact that humans must be unconscious to enter the Dream, we find equally disturbing," Imri said. "It's my favorite explanation for why you are all so insane, being disconnected from your conscious selves on a daily basis."

Ragall just shrugged. "Maybe. I came to check on you lot, and after all that shite about our behavior, I find you feeding the younglings beer!" He looked down at their mugs. "Is that O'Farley? Colorless night, at least you bought them the good stuff." He looked down at his own mug mournfully.

Imri's annoyed expression turned into a smile. Amandine got the impression her annoyance was some kind of play, because her next words were not sharp at all, but fond. "If you manage not to get us thrown out, perhaps I will buy you one as well."

He smiled back at her. "I'll hold you to that."

"Your arm seems better," Amandine said.

With a grin, Ragall nodded and rolled the shoulder that had been in a sling. "Yeah, that excellent food you made and a rest is what I needed, I suppose. Good thing too, what with that strange job we took after you left."

"What job was that?" Fredderick wiped foam off his cheek.

"The Sheriff sent us to look on some reports of pirates downriver. With a wumpus, if you can believe it. I thought he was making fun. Trying to bait us for fools maybe, but Mel took the job, and wouldn't you know it, we did find some folks working at piracy, and they had a wumpus. I thought the colorless things were bedtime stories."

"Rare and nearly extinct are not the same as made up, Ragall," Imri said.

Amandine had frozen in place as Ragall spoke. When he paused to drink, she said, "You found them then? Did they have any prisoners?"

Ragall gave her a confused look, but Imri saved Amandine from having to explain. "She lost her apprentice master to pirates on the way to Myron's Bend. Did the band who attacked you have a wumpus?" she asked her.

Amandine nodded.

"Oh. Oh, well," Ragall said, his bluster quenched somewhat. "No, no prisoners. A lot of soggy things they had stolen from barges—mainly food. The wumpus wasn't a threat really, Imri scared it off somehow. I'm sorry, lass."

"Slaying a rare fae beast like that would have been a crime. It was being misused and mistreated. The wumpus are gentle creatures by nature, and hide rather than fight," Imri said.

Amandine drank to hide her face. For just the briefest of moments she had nurtured a flicker of hope that maybe Serand had made it to shore. That perhaps the pirates had caught him. It was dashed so quickly that the loss of that tiny hope felt like a fresh burn.

"Woah, slow down," Ragall said. "Yer a little thing to have such a large tankard of that. It's not even watered."

"I'm fine, sah, thank you," Amandine said. She belched. The foam made her feel a bit gassy. "Excuse me," she muttered.

"That's the way!" Fredderick said with a laugh. "Now I need to catch up!"

He tilted his mug back and Dumpling jumped up on the table and chased his tail in a circle, barking. Ragall laughed as the mug thunked back down onto the table empty and Fredderick coughed.

"You well, lad?" he asked.

"Better than well! I want another!"

The Oubliette

"The Mord have no innate talent for magic. They are adept, in conjunction with their Stone Folk cousins, at creating devices and methods that counteract and confound magic in many of its forms. The Crystallians, in particular, are quite secretive about how their peculiar devices and wards work, but no one can argue with their efficacy."

- Thaumaturgical Primer, Volume 1, Chapter 8, The Mord *Exception*

AMANDINE HICCUPPED AND leaned against Fredderick. The meditating elf had been joined by another and departed, so the rest of Vibrant Dawn had abandoned the bar to crowd in around their table. She hadn't been able to finish her *tashi*, so Grendel had helped her and he now lay on his back, purring, as Imri absently rubbed his belly and listened to Mel telling a story.

"He actsh like a troll aroun' Mishter Green," Amandine said as she watched the cat. She heard the slur in her own words. Against her better judgment, she had gotten a second tankard as well. A third sat on the table in front of her, untouched. She felt so full, she was sure she would burst if she tried to drink it.

"Cats are not Fae, but they seem to know us. Curious creatures. Quite fickle. Perhaps they simply recognize kindred when they encounter them," Imri said softly.

"I've ne'er sheen any Court Fae ash fat and lazy as Gren," Amandine said. "You're all sho, bootiful."

Fredderick snorted. "Bootiful," he echoed.

"Hey are you two listening?" Mel asked, halting her story.

"Nope," Amandine said instantly. "Ish it the one about the troll with the wooden legsh again?"

"No, that was two stories ago," Blueknot said. She whittled a chunk of wood between sips of her own drink. The small object had started as a broken mug handle, but now resembled some kind of animal.

"You two are cut off," Mel said. She looked stern, but her tone indicated amusement.

"Yer not my muffer," Fredderick slurred. Dumpling barked as if in agreement.

Mel lifted her mug towards him. "You're right! Your mother would have to clean up after you once you puke all that up. I'll just let you take a nap in it."

"Eewwww." Amandine laughed. "Vomit nap!"

She started to lift her mug, but a wave of nausea rolled over her. Amandine swallowed and swayed slightly in her seat. The beer really had *not* been a luminous idea. Carefully, she set the mug back down and covered her mouth.

Tobe held up his slate. It read: "Rooms?"

"Ah, yes. Good question, sah. We've dragged you two through Anvilroot, but do you have a place to stay?

"Looking fer a bud. Friend's bud, named Herric. Tha' *gyre* is a farmer. They haf something we need." Amandine tried to collect her thoughts as her stomach roiled. The words kept attempting to slip away before she could speak them. "Was hoping to stay with them. We hab no more coinsh."

"Ah, well. How about we help you track them down in the morning," Mel said. "You can stay with Blue and I, Amandine. Tobe, will you take the boy?"

The mute man nodded and smiled a huge toothless smile.

"Thansh," Amandine said. "Yer tha besht."

"I have to know," Fredderick said, "Whatsh wif the chair?" He pointed at the black stone chair on its dais next to their table with an unsteady finger.

"Well the place is named after it, obviously," Mel said. "I think it's a relic of the First Kingdom? Before humans and the Promise In Stone? Help me out, Imri."

"That is correct," Imri said. "But as for what it is or who made it, stories vary. If it was in any way related to the Hammers or the First Council, it would not be in a tavern in the Magma Ward."

"One story I heard is that some people who touch it hear voices," Blueknot said.

"Oh! Or the one where some fellow sat it in and lit on fire," Ragall added.

"Really?" Amandine asked.

"Well, I mean, the fellow who told me was drunk, so..." Ragall admitted.

"You all are ridiculous. Everyone is spooked by the colorless chair, but it's nothing. The Matron pays a bounty to anyone willing to sit in it and raise a toast. I collected it once. It's just cold stone, you fools," Mel said.

"I'll do it," Amandine said. She stood up, wobbled a bit and steadied herself on Fredderick and then stepped over the bench. "What ish the bounty?"

"Just a few flips. Enough to cover your drinks perhaps if you entertain every-one," Mel said with a shrug.

Mel's smirk had a touch of mischief in it that reminded Amandine of the way Fredderick would get sometimes, but she didn't care. Tonight, perhaps because of the haze caused by the strong beer, she wanted to do something a little bit reckless, and sitting in a haunted chair and raising a toast with a beverage she was probably too young to have ordered sounded just right. With a nod to Mel, she picked up her drink and walked unsteadily up the steps to where the throne sat.

A few patrons noticed and cheered for her. A dwarf yelled out something in *Mord-seq* that elicited laughter. Amandine grimaced. She really needed to learn a bit of that.

"Sing a song, little bird," a woman's voice called out from the crowd.

Amandine stood in front of the chair and turned towards the room.

"Just for you, sah," Amandine called back and began to sing a jaunty tavern reel.

"I was down at the 'stead, with wool in my head
And my eyes were blind with gold mash.
And 'round from the square, with the red colored hair
Comes the haunt in the sailcloth sash.

With arms like an aurochs, and steel in her buttocks
She was a creature like no other.
So I ran like a hare, with my feet in the air
To escape your frightful mother!"

It was one of the many off-color songs Cook Kivel had taught to Gil, and while making fun of a stranger's mother with a song wasn't something Amandine would normally do, the crowd seemed to appreciate it. Tankards clapped on table tops and people laughed. No one told her to stop, so Amandine moved on to the second verse.

Apparently, Blueknot and Ragall knew the song too, and joined in from the table. By the end of the second verse, half of the room was singing along in a sort of drunken chorus. Fredderick came up the steps and stood with her, waving his mug in time with hers, and even though he didn't seem to know a single word of the tune he laughed at every lyric.

"...and that were how I 'scaped yer mo-therrrrrr," Amandine drew out the final line of the third verse. It was all she knew of the stupid song anyway. The room applauded. Someone asked for another, but Amandine needed to sit down. She took a sip from her mug and dropped into the black stone chair.

Fire.

Amandine shrieked and jumped back up. Her backside and legs felt like a hot brand had been touched to them. She dropped her mug, and it clattered down the steps, spilling foamy beer across the floor. The room had suddenly gone very quiet. She turned and looked at the chair. A red-orange glow faded from the black stone.

"What in the hellsh?" she said as she rubbed her scalded rump.

Fredderick eyed the chair warily and backed away. Dumpling started barking and he picked the dog up. There was a shout in *Mord-seq* and one of the dwarven patrons ran out the door.

"What just happened?" Amandine asked out loud. She hiccuped as her heart pounded. "It felt like it wash on fire. You said it was cold, Mel! Were you teasin' me, sah?"

Mel shook her head, her lips drawn into a line. Tobe climbed the steps and approached the chair. He ran a hand across one of the chairs arms and then jerked it back and looked at his palm, quizzically.

"Ow," Amandine whined. She sat on the stone steps to try and soothe her scald. "That colorless bounty had better be worth it!"

The front doors crashed open and a group of armed dwarves entered. They were like the ones that had inspected them at the Stone Door, but this time a mord dressed in white robes accompanied them. They held a large, rough crystal aloft as the group approached the dais.

Worried murmurs rippled through the room. Amandine made out the word "Crystallian" several times.

"This one, aye?" The white robed dwarf asked as they approached Amandine. The Matron behind the bar nodded.

Amandine stood, nervously. "All I did was sing a song, sah. I didn't mean to offend anyone!"

The dwarf stepped between her and Fredderick and the crystal suddenly flared with white light. They looked alarmed and stepped a bit closer, as if wary. With a scowl, they stared at Amandine a moment and barked something in *Mord-seq*. The armed dwarves quickly surrounded Amandine and extended their weapons, hemming her in.

"What in the hells?" Mel asked in shock. "What are you about, eh? She's a kid, sahs!"

"It's a demon. Ye've been tricked or spelled, human. Do not make trouble, the crystal is never wrong," the robed dwarf said in a gravelly voice.

"I'm not a—" Amandine began, but one of the polearms poked her in the shoulder. The cold steel pressed into her clothes and the weapon's owner yelled at her in *Mord-seq*.

Grendel dashed off the table and ran between her and the dwarf, hissing. The guard looked at the cat in confusion and backed off a step, but did not lower the weapon. Amandine picked Grendel up and hugged him close to keep him from causing trouble.

Mel began to reach for her blade. "I don't know what this is about," she said. "But I think you're wrong."

Five more armed dwarves entered the tavern. Tobe shook his head and waved her down. Mel slowly lowered her hand again. Ragall, likewise, carefully lowered his huge, heavy-bladed axe and raised one hand off the handle.

"It will be incarcerated until a magus can be summoned and you will remand yerself for questioning as to where you found it and when," the robed dwarf said. "Resist us in any way, and there will be blood."

Amandine looked to Fredderick. He was frozen in place, watching the blade threatening her, every muscle tense. He began to open his fingers.

"We'll co-operate!" Amandine blurted before Fredderick could do something stupid. "I'll go wherever you want! We don't mean harm or trouble!"

Fredderick closed his hand. "If you are going to lock her up, then you better lock me up too. I won't leave her."

Amandine's eyes widened. What in the hells was he doing? If he was free, he could try and get word to Mister Green, or Wizard Hemm. A mage that knew her and could help sort things out. She didn't want him locked up with her. "No–" she began, but the robed dwarf cut her off.

"Suit yerself. Take 'em both to the oubliettes. Bind their hands. Gag them. If they make any move to evade, try to speak, or touch anyone, kill them immediately."

One of the four dwarves produced bindings and tied their hands. Another grabbed Grendel and Dumpling and stuffed them in sacks. Grendel looked like he might put up a fight over the treatment, but Amandine touched him and he quieted and allowed himself to be taken.

"Poor thing is under its spell too," the guard said.

Four dwarves began to herd them out of the Obsidian Seat. Amandine looked back over her shoulder at Mel and the others. Mel watched them go silently, but with a concerned expression. The dwarf in the robes snapped their fingers to get Mel's attention and began speaking, but Amandine was too far away to hear what they said.

Their escort took them down a side street and into a large, fortified building. The guards muttered between themselves in *Mord-seq*. Amandine couldn't believe this was happening. This wasn't just some angry merchant looking to insult her because of her eyes; the *mord* were deadly serious. She began to sweat with nerves as they proceeded down a long, spiraling set of stairs into inky darkness. The lingering effects of the beer made it even more surreal as her eyesight swam in the darkness. One of the guards pulled out a dim chunk of glowstone so that she and Fredderick would not trip. This passage was not meant for those who needed light. There were no sconces, no braziers. The dark was as impenetrable as night. Amandine's vision allowed her to see the gray and charcoal outlines of the dwarves and Fredderick. Grendel meowed plaintively and Dumpling whined from the sacks slung over one guard's shoulder, but Amandine didn't dare make a sound to comfort them.

The air became very cold. There was little moisture to it; it was simply frigid. The group stopped in a large round chamber. There were holes dug in the floor, and some had metal grates over the top. Amandine and Fredderick were led to one. She had trouble seeing the bottom. Were they going to get a ladder or...

The butt of a polearm shoved Amandine into the hole. She shrieked through her gag in spite of herself. With a soft crack, she landed more or less on her feet, but stumbled sideways into the wall. Fredderick landed next to her. He didn't fare as well. One leg crumpled and he careened into the side of the pit and banged his head. A metal grate slid over the top above them and the dwarves' footsteps receded. Grendel's and Dumpling's plaintive cries echoed above them, though. They must have been left near the hole at the top.

Amandine pulled the gag out of her mouth with her bound hands and knelt next to Fredderick.

"Are you ok?" she whispered, unsure if a guard was still nearby. "Here, let me help you."

She pulled the gag out of his mouth and Fredderick coughed. There was a gray trickle on his forehead. Blood. The collision with the wall had injured him. Amandine dug at her wrist bindings with her teeth, but it was no use, the knot was strong. She pulled her gag up over her head and used it to dab the cut.

"I have no idea why that happened," she said, trying to fight back tears. "This is all so wrong. I'm not a demon, I swear!"

"Amandine, stop," Fredderick croaked. "Please don't cry. I know you're not a demon. It's not possible for you to be."

"Then why did that crystal say I was one?"

"Because it wasn't sensing you. The old dwarf made an assumption. Because of your eyes. You're *not* a demon Amandine."

"He said it's never wrong, though."

"It wasn't. I... I'm the demon, Amandine. It's me."

Dumpling began to howl.

A Bitter Taste

"Mages will sometimes keep familiars. These are elementals that are fabricated by the magician using advanced techniques, and then brought to life using a tiny portion of the wizard's own anima. In this way, the familiar is bound to the magician, an extension of themselves. Not every practitioner employs these artificial creatures, however. Sacrificing a piece of one's essence is not something to undertake lightly, and the destruction of a familiar can be painful to its bonded mage. Those who abstain from the creation of familiars still often have helpers. People who serve out of loyalty or fear and assist with daily chores, research, or experimentation."

- Thaumaturgical Primer, Volume 1, Chapter 5, Anima, Wards, and Elementals

"WAIT, WHAT?"

Amandine Helped Fredderick sit up against the wall of the pit and scooted away from him. He held the repurposed cloth to his forehead and took a deep breath.

"The crystal was detecting me. I'm the demon. Partly."

She shook her head and tried to clear it. The shock had sobered her a bit, but the colorless beer was still making her muzzy. "Fredderick, this isn't funny. Your eyes are dark, Serand said–"

"I know. That's the thing... ow, gods my head hurts." Fredderick held his head and leaned forward. "It happened years ago, before I came to Stoneman. I was tested for magical ability, the same as Fiona. I failed. I couldn't make the disk move.

"My parents, they shrugged it off. Maybe one in ten thousand people possess any sort of gift for magic. Perhaps even less. But I wanted it so badly. So... I did something foolish."

He groaned and shook his head. He spoke the next words slowly, as if forcing them out. "I discovered a demon. I'm not sure if I found it, or it found me, but... we made a pact. They are mostly pure anima, you see, the stuff of life and magic. Their natural forms are crude jumbles of random elements, but they can change their shape, and if they consume a living thing, they can take the form of that body."

When he paused, Amandine backed away a bit further. "So you're not the real Fredderick? He was... consumed?"

Fredderick shook his head. "No, no, I'm me. Mostly. The forms they take after consuming a creature have the tell right? The eyes. So, I gave it a sacrifice. Our old, blind, family dog."

"Dumpling," Amandine whispered.

"Yes."

Somewhere above them, Dumpling was making pitiful whining noises.

"So how does that make you a demon? I don't understand. Dumpling is the demon then."

"Its physical manifestation, yes. But as a part of the pact, I allowed it to replace a piece of my anima with a bit of its own. We're joined, Amandine. At the very core of our beings. It's the demon's anima that allows me to create magic."

His voice became faint and his head bobbed.

"Fredderick! Are you ok?"

"Tired," he mumbled. "Head hurts."

"Oh hells," Amandine hissed. She didn't know much about medicine, but the Sisters had given all of the apprentices some basic knowledge. The blow he had taken to the head was likely far worse than it seemed.

"Hello! Is anyone up there?" Amandine shouted. "Please! He needs a doctor! Hello!"

No one answered. Grendel meowed at the sound of her voice. Dumpling's whining increased.

"Fredderick! Don't sleep!" Amandine swallowed her fear and shifted closer to him. "Hey! You can't go to sleep! Try to stay awake! Fredderick!"

Amandine shook his shoulder and then lifted him back up against the wall. It was difficult to tell without light, but his eyes still seemed to be open. He muttered incoherently and his head lolled.

"Yes, that's it! Keep talking! Tell me more about demons, Fredderick! Say anything!"

"Any—thing," Fredderick slurred.

Despite her frantic worry, Amandine nearly slapped him. "If you are coherent enough to make terrible japes, then you can talk! Come on, Fredderick! *Don't sleep!*"

"Don't be mad—at me," Fredderick muttered. His eyes began to slide shut. "I'm—sorry."

Fredderick sagged. His head sank and his body went limp. Amandine checked his breath and felt for his heartbeat. He was still alive, but if he didn't get help, he might die. Or sleep and never wake up. Choking back a sob, she hugged him to her.

"Oh Goddess. Oh, Kayla. Please don't let him die," she whispered. "I don't care what he is. He's my friend! Please..."

Sadness is a bitter taste.

Amandine's breath caught. "Who said that?"

Fear is better, yes. Sharp. So sharp. Why do you fear? Why are you sharp?

She looked down. Fredderick lay unmoving in her arms, but she could feel him. Or rather, she could sense that he felt nothing. He was unconscious, dreamless. "I... I can feel him," she whispered.

Yes. We allow it.

Amandine's heart thundered in her chest. "Are you... the demon?"

These sounds used to name us, meaningless. Empty. Nothing.

"But, how?"

You taste others with yourself, taste their flavors. You know their textures. Rasping. Drawing in.

"I...are you saying you stopped me from sensing Fredderick? From knowing his emotions like I do with others?"

We would be discovered. An end to feasting. An end to taste. We hide.

"From me."

From all who touch the world.

"Mages, you mean."

More meaningless sounds. If two flavors are different sweet, they are still both sweet.

"I don't understand." The voice in her mind was silent. She felt its anticipation. "What are you waiting for?"

A question.

Amandine thought for a moment. Should she continue talking to this thing? The demon that lived inside of Fredderick? Her skin crawled at the idea. But then, maybe it could help in some way.

"Is he dying?" she asked.

Yes.

"Can you help him?"

There is too much, hmm, life. Blood, that is your sound. Too much, in the head. We cannot feel together. Bring us to us.

"To, the dog... you? But I can't, we're in a hole. With a cage on top."

You taste us. You can be a crossing. A pathway.

A chill ran through Amandine's body. The memory of another voice in her mind, like a ghost of a dream, returned to her: *You are the guidepost, the dreaming.*

"I think I can do that. I think I was meant to do that."

Accept.

Something pressed on her mind, like a jumble of tangled emotions too varied and loud to sort out. It was chaos, pure noise. Tears welled up in her eyes at the feel of it.

"So much..." she moaned.

Accept.

The pressure intensified. Amandine's breathing came in short rasps. It felt as if her head were being forced into a garlic press.

"It hurts," she whimpered.

Accept.

A second voice entered her mind.

We accept, but you are only a guest, little one. We are not for you.

Amandine gasped. The pressure lifted. She felt, she saw, she tasted. A wave of sensations, like charcoal drawings on paper, whipped by, one after another. Scents of delicious food. The loving caress of a mother. Sunlight on her skin, followed by rain. The joy of playing with a small puppy. Sadness, fear, hunger, envy, pride, happiness... calm. And then the tastes. So many, so varied. Flavors sweet and savory, sour and spicy, bitter and salty. Not just food, but other things. Emotions, memories, dreams—they all had a taste.

We feel ourselves. You are the pathway.

"Please, help him."

The second voice spoke again: *We shall aid you, little one.*

Warmth filled Amandine, as if all the joy in the world had accumulated in her heart. She wept, but not because she was sad. She had friends. Even if Serand was gone, she had Dena. She had a home. She was loved. She loved. With her heart overflowing, she gave that love away. It seemed to spiral into the quiet hollow of Fredderick's mind like water swirling out the drain in a washtub.

So sweet, the taste...

The voice of the demon faded. The swirl of sensations retreated. She was completely blind; her Grendel-vision had faded. There was no light, but she could feel Fredderick in her arms. His breathing was slow and rhythmic. He felt calm. Content. Happy. He was dreaming. The danger had passed. Slowly, the sensation of him faded as well, until she could no longer sense him. The demon had walled her off again. It didn't matter. He was going to live, and that was all she cared about. A lingering giddiness caused a small laugh to escape her lips, even as tears streamed down her face. The euphoric feeling slowly faded, leaving behind a deep weariness, as if she had been running at a full sprint in the sunlight. Amandine slumped against Fredderick and hugged him to her.

"Thank you," she said into the darkness.

A small dog's bark answered her, and then she fell asleep.

Into the Deeps

"Sorry is the lot of the mord'resh *or "clanless." In dwarven society, being part of the larger group is not just a cultural artifact, but tied to their very survival instincts. As fierce as the* Ur'mord *are, they survived in the Deeps for thousands of years, endured terrible treatment at the hands of the giants, and ultimately became the preeminent power in the Realms Beneath by virtue of this one fact: if you see a single* mord, *you can be certain there are dozens more nearby. They are pack hunters—the wolves of the underground. The clanless, for a number of reasons, have been cast out or excluded from the major* nyres. *Some form their own loose groups, but many simply live in the shadows of their betters, performing menial work and drudgery for those of higher status."*

- Lecture Notes, Third Starday, Low Winter 1202

"AMANDINE!"

With a groan, Amandine opened her eyes. Her heart raced and her breath quickened when she couldn't see anything, and then she remembered where she was. Her body ached. She had been leaning against Fredderick, who was still asleep, but the ground was hard.

"Amandine! Hey, kid! You alive?"

There was a tiny flicker of light. Amandine looked up. The voice was coming from outside the grate. "Who's there?" she croaked. Her throat felt raw.

The light grew brighter. Someone holding an oil lantern stood near the pit's edge. They leaned down closer and Amandine could see bright yellow hair.

"Blueknot?" Amandine rasped.

"Gods, it is you!" Blueknot said. "We were afraid they would just execute you out of hand, but if there's one thing a dwarf is good at, it's following rules. Give me a moment, I will get you out of there!"

"Why are you here?"

"Rescuing you of course. Seekers don't leave crewmates behind!"

"But I'm not a Seeker."

"No, but yer still crew. Mel said so and we back her decisions. Gah, colorless dwarven locks! This might take a mo'."

Amandine's sluggish brain tried to keep up with what was happening. She slowly climbed to her feet. "You are going to be in a lot of trouble with the *Ur'Mord*," she said. "You don't have to do this."

"We're Seekers, so we're always in some sort of trouble. And they'll only be mad at us if we get caught. Ah! There we go!"

There was a clank, as if a metal hasp had fallen open, followed by a loud scraping of metal on stone as the grate at the top of the pit slid away.

"Fredderick was hurt. I think he'll live, but I am not sure if he'll wake up."

A rope spilled over the edge of the pit. A long length of it landed in a pile near her feet, while the rest stretched up and out. "Tie him into that. I'll be gentle," Blueknot said.

Amandine tied the rope under Fredderick's arms and gave it a tug. He slid along the floor and then up the smooth walls. His head bobbed slightly, but he didn't wake up. He vanished over the lip and then, a few moments later, the rope dropped back down.

"Now you!"

Amandine made a makeshift harness for herself and held on as Blueknot towed her up the wall in short jerking bursts of motion. When she neared the top, the small woman held out a hand. Amandine took it in hers and Blueknot yanked her fully out of the pit in one smooth pull.

"Thank you," Amandine said.

"You're welcome!"

Blueknot smiled. She turned Amandine's wrist over in her hand. "Oh, that's pretty. I didn't notice that last night. Where did you have that done? You seem young to have such a large tattoo."

Amandine looked down. In the dim, flickering light of the lantern she could see the black marks on her wrist and forearm. It was a twining heartleaf branch, covered in lover's knots, and stretched from her elbow to the bottom of her palm. She touched it reverently. Lover's knots were Kayla's flower.

"I... don't remember," Amandine lied.

"Ah, I did that once too—well, almost. Ragall talked me out of it. I tell you, Zulathan rice-spirits are my bane," she grinned and lightly punched Amandine in the thigh. "At least yours is beautiful. These little bags are your critters, right? Let's spring 'em and get out of this colorless place."

It only took Blueknot a few more moments to open the small sacks and free Grendel and Dumpling. The cat immediately ran to Amandine and collided with her shins. She picked him up and stroked his fur, her magical sight returned as she did. Dumpling sat down next to Fredderick's prone form and cowered when she looked at him. Unlike her experience in Kiln, she remembered everything about what had happened in the pit. She knelt and put a hand on Dumpling's head.

"You're a good boy. Thank you for helping him."

The small dog licked her hand and whined. His bottom shook as he tried to wag his stubby tail. Was this tiny thing actually a demon? Amandine found it hard to believe. Perhaps she was just going mad. Hearing things. She looked down at her arm. Or maybe not.

She felt sick, remembering it. Fredderick had confessed to sacrificing a living creature to make his pact. It made her sad. Even if the original Dumpling had been elderly and lame, it seemed wrong. Every time she thought she knew Fredderick, had him figured out, he found some new way to tie a knot in her emotions.

"I don't think I can carry him," Amandine said.

"Don't worry, I'll get him." Blueknot lifted Fredderick like a sack and dumped him over her shoulder. His feet still dragged, but she didn't seem to struggle with his weight at all. "You got the dog and the kitty?"

Amandine picked up Dumpling. "Yes. Let's go."

Using Blueknot's small lantern, they made their way back up the winding stairs. The lack of railing gave Amandine vertigo. How deep down had they been? About halfway up, on a small landing that connected to more stairs, was a door. Blueknot turned towards it.

"In here. We aren't going back out the same way ya came in, they'd just catch ya again," she whispered.

Amandine nodded and opened the door for her. The passageway beyond was just as dark as the stairs.

"Do they really not need light to see?" Amandine asked. "The dwarves, I mean."

"Nope. The way I understand it, they can see things that are warm. Like living bodies. Fires. Molten rock. Even small differences in the stone around us. Some rocks are warmer than other rocks, apparently. Not enough for us to tell, but their eyes can."

"Molten rock? Like a volcano?"

"You know what a volcano is then, yeah?"

"Yes, Boomer talked about them once during a lesson."

"Boomer?"

"A dwarven engineer living in Stoneman. We would visit them some days for nature lessons. They know a lot about rocks."

Blueknot nodded. "Yeah, most dwarves do. But as I was sayin' that big hollow place we all walked into used to be the inside of a volcano. Or so the *Ur'Mord* say. Way long ago, the giants drained it somehow? Imri told the story once, but I only half-listened. Here, we go left."

They came to a split in the passageway, and Blueknot confidently strode towards the left. Amandine followed. "Where are we going?"

"I was wondering when you'd get around to asking that," Blueknot said. "Someplace safe. We've all been here before. Explored the Great Deep once for a mapping contract. I'd bet we know these tunnels better than anyone who isn't a dwarf."

The passage they were in began to slope gently downwards. Amandine was totally and completely directionless at this point. She had lost track of the number of turns they had taken, but Blueknot forged on confidently past each intersection, and so she tried not to worry. Fredderick, still senseless, bobbed on Blueknot's shoulder as she trotted quickly across the stone. His shoes dragged by the toes as she hauled him along.

"First the boat and then the rain, and now this? Maybe I'll buy him some new shoes once we're safe," Amandine mused to herself.

Dumpling yipped as if in agreement.

"What was that?" Blueknot asked.

"Oh, sorry, nothing. Thinking out loud. How much further are we going?"

"Three more crossings. If I timed it right, there will be no guards at Bright Lake. Then we borrow a boat."

"There's a lake underground?" Amandine asked in awe.

"More than one, actually. The Deeps are amazing if'n ya don't mind tight spaces on occasion. But not all of it is hospitable to folks like us."

"How so?" Amandine asked, looking for anything to keep her mind off the situation.

"Well, for instance, if you go too deep, the air gets thin. Just like if you climb a mountain too high. Dwarves are used to it, but more than one fool without a notion has simply passed out from going too far down and not paying mind. Then there are molten stone pools and the fumes they create. Those can be poisonous, even to *mord*. Dangerous mushrooms, cave beasts, dark fae—"

"Like boglings?"

"Nah, too dry for the likes of them. I'm talking folk like Hobbs, the *Iskrix,* and the *Erestral.*"

Iskrix. The word tickled Amandine's memory. She remembered where she had heard it before. "I think I've met an *Iskrix*. They served a wizard named Hemm."

"He must be quite the fellow. *Iskrix* mostly try to boss other folk about. Never do what one says, or it gives 'em a hold on ya. Even things that seem harmless."

"Yeah, that's what I was told too." Fredderick had warned her when she had met Kibble, Wizard Hemm's assistant. She felt a pang at the memory. It seemed like so long ago now, even though it had only been last year.

The closely fitted quarried blocks abruptly gave way to smooth black-gray stone that felt wet to the touch.

"Getting close," Blueknot whispered. "Keep as quiet as you can and stay near me."

The tunnel widened into a cavern with a high ceiling. Blueknot fumbled her lantern with one hand and put it out. They didn't need it, though. The chamber's craggy, stalactite-covered roof was completely aglow. Luminous moss in a variety of blues and greens shed enough light that Amandine could see clearly even without Grendel's help. An enormous lake filled the cavern. It was bigger than any lake Amandine had ever seen, even on the surface. The far end must have been at least two yarns away or more. Small boats punted around on the dark, glass-like water and *mord* fishermen tossed nets, breaking the serene surface into tiny ripples.

"It's beautiful," Amandine breathed.

"It is. I was right, the city patrol has already passed through. So we need to get to a boat. Our goal is the arm of the lake in that direction. The wide tunnel with the pointy rocks that look like teeth."

She pointed to the lake outlet, barely visible in the gloom, on the far side of the water. The stalactites really did look like downward pointed fangs.

"Won't the fishermen see us?"

Blueknot shook her head. "*Mord'resh*, most of 'em. Clanless. No love between them and the snooty-snoot Clanners. But just in case..."

She gently set Fredderick down and pulled up the hood of her cloak. She produced, from somewhere inside it, a length of braided hair that she strapped to her face with twine. A fake beard. Amandine leaned in to look. It wasn't *mord* hair. It smelled faintly of horse.

"Really?" Amandine asked. "I am pretty sure there are other things they will notice."

Blueknot might have been Hill Folk, but she was obviously female. The small woman shrugged and pulled the cloak tight around her. "I ain't hairy enough either, but so long as they don't look too close, we're fine. Rule number one of trying to blend in: always act like you belong there, even if'n ya don't!"

She picked Fredderick up again. "Alright, let's go!"

Amandine followed Blueknot across the gravelly beach to a small shack next to a makeshift dock. A line strung between two poles was draped with pale white eels. They had bright, waxy skin and horrible, circular mouths filled with tiny teeth. Amandine shuddered at their resemblance to skellix.

A lone *mord* sat on a rock, leaning forward on their knees, snoring softly. They seemed to be wearing some sort of fuzzy coat, but as she passed, Amandine realized it was fur. The dwarf wasn't wearing a shirt.

"Oh my," Amandine muttered.

"Shhhh," Blueknot hissed.

The *mord* muttered something but did not awaken.

Amandine bit her lip and remained silent as they climbed into a shallow draft rowboat. Blueknot placed Fredderick in the bottom between them and took the oars. The boat's wood was strange. Gray and almost spongy to the touch.

Once they were out in the middle of the lake, Amandine began to breathe a little easier. "You're right," she said. "You really aren't hairy enough."

"I'll take that as a compliment," Blueknot said with a huge grin over her fake beard. "Although I must confess, I had a similar reaction when I saw a half-naked dwarf for the first time."

Amandine rubbed her arms. Dumpling and Grendel huddled against her. The air was as damp and cold as a Winter morning. "I can see why having so much of it would help," she said. "The hair, I mean."

"Yeah, it's chill for certain. Hang in there. Our camp will be warm, I promise," Blueknot said as she rowed.

As they approached the lake outlet, another skiff rowed by them. Amandine held her breath as a shirtless dwarf waved at them and shouted something in *Mord-seq*.

Blueknot kept her head down and growled words back that sounded like she was clearing something spicy from her throat.

The passing dwarf laughed in their odd, choking way and did not stop.

"You speak their language?" she whispered.

"Just a smidge. Enough to order food and offer insults."

"What did you say?"

"That the fish won't bite, so I am going to use you as bait."

Amandine frowned and folded her arms.

"Hey, it worked. Dwarves are always spewing shite about non-dwarves. And they think fae have the superior attitudes. Ha!"

They passed under the looming stalactites and into a dark passage. Blueknot paused to light her lantern again. Its glow sparkled off the walls, which were laced with veins of crystal that glittered like gemstone. The current sped up slightly and the passage narrowed. At one point, it was so low and tight that Amandine could touch the ceiling. It left dusty traces on her fingers that seemed to shimmer in the lantern's light.

The watery tunnel finally widened again into another large cavern. Nothing glowed here, like at Bright Lake, and so the ceiling lay hidden beyond the lantern's reach. They approached a stony shore. At first Amandine thought it was lined with trees, but as the shapes resolved themselves, she realized they were mushrooms. Giant ones, as tall as pines, with narrow brown caps as large as wagons.

"Goddess, what an odd thing," Amandine said as she got out. It struck her that the "trunks" of the mushroom-trees were the same color as the planks on the small skiff. "Hey, they make the boats from this."

"Yup. Grows fast, sturdy, as easy to cut and shape as wood. Hells, you can even eat it in a pinch, but it tastes like boiled dirt."

"Why don't they sell it?"

"Rots within minutes in sunlight."

"Ahh..."

Amandine reached out and touched one as Blueknot collected Fredderick. Dumpling sniffed another and lifted a leg. Grendel seemed bored, but was listening intently to the sounds of the underground forest. Amandine listened too. There were chitters and creaks, a hollow thumping and other sounds of life moving in the darkness.

"Is this place safe?" she asked.

"Safer than the pit you were in. Don't worry about the noisy critters, it's the silent ones that are actually dangerous."

Amandine swallowed and followed Blueknot into the gloom.

The Cave Farmer

"Korb, called Great Caps in Olgothian, are a type of tree-sized mushroom that grows in the Deeps near water. The mord *harvest a slightly spongy gray material from it that is used like wood would be in the sunlit world. It's expensive to obtain and largely impractical due to the way it deteriorates in the sunlight; still, I own a set of bowls that I use for serving* Ur'Mord. *Even when my meals are slightly off, the touch of home they provide my dwarven guests has garnered many compliments."*

- Seeker's Kitchen, Chapter 8, Cuisine from the Deeps - Dwarven and Stone Folk Fare

THE GROUND WAS covered in a thin loam made up of whatever the tree-like mushrooms deposited. Amandine's boots squelched as she walked, and every sound they made caused her to wince. Blueknot was watchful, but seemed unconcerned, and so Amandine tried not to worry, despite every small thing that moved making her head whip around. The strange subterranean forest crawled with life—things that slithered and scuttled and even flew on shimmering wings. Most of it was tiny and looked crab or insect-like, but a few creatures moved quickly, like squirrels, except they had no hair – or eyes. She shuddered as another weird not-squirrel raced across the tops of the giant mushrooms away from their noisy feet.

A black wall of stone materialized from the gloom. Was it the cavern wall? Amandine looked up, but couldn't see the ceiling, so she wasn't sure. Blueknot shifted Fredderick's weight and turned to follow the edge of the stone, but kept her gaze out into the forest. She picked up her pace.

"We need to move quickly," she whispered. "The thumpers have gone quiet, which means a predator is near. Might just be a horker, but if it's something nasty like a night wurm or frakklin, then we want to be gone."

"I would ask what those are, but I'll just assume they are things that want to eat us," Amandine said.

"Horkers no, they are dangerous to thumpers and other small critters, but not people. Night wurms don't eat people, but one will kill anything it thinks is another predator in its territory. Frakklins are the worst. Like a ball of fur and teeth and... things. That'll definitely make a meal of ya."

"Wonderful."

"Hey, don't fret, kid. We're near the camp. This is a mostly tamed place, relatively close to the city. The *mord* frequent here to harvest building materials. It's not like we're in the Lower Reaches or the Sunless Seas. Just keep up."

Amandine rubbed her arms against the chill and walked faster, Grendel and Dumpling trailing at her heels. The ground sloped down slightly, the sound of flowing water echoing from somewhere below. Tiny glowing motes on the fins of the giant mushroom-trees created a modicum of light, enough that Amandine could see clearly, thanks to Grendel. As they drew deeper into the mushroom forest, Blueknot pulled a finger-sized chunk of glowstone from a pocket to light the way. A small stream of cold, dark water came into view, cutting through the stone in a shallow cleft, surrounded by pods of short, faintly glowing mushrooms that looked like mounds of pudding. Blueknot followed the water upstream a bit, around a bend in the blackstone wall and then seemed to vanish into a cleft in the rock.

"Hurry—in here!" her voice called from out of sight.

Using her hands, Amandine found the spot she had entered. The coloration of the stone behind created the illusion that it was a flat wall, when there was really an opening. The air immediately felt warmer when she stepped into it. A faint orange light issued from deeper down in the low-ceiling tunnel. She saw Blueknot's shadow, still hauling Fredderick, shrinking around a corner.

She followed and the cramped tunnel opened into a somewhat spherical chamber. It was toasty warm within, and thin veins of crystal in the walls glowed with a slightly pulsing, orange light. A camp had been set up inside, with bedrolls laid out, a small folding table, and a pile of backpacks and satchels. Amandine recognized three of them in particular.

"My things!" Serand's backpack sat next to hers and the shoulder satchel lay in front of them, with her *Olatharr* in its sheath resting on top.

"Yup," Blueknot said as she carefully laid Fredderick on one of the bedrolls. Dumpling ran over to him and licked his face. He mumbled something in his sleep.

Amandine checked all of the bags. Everything was in its place, except...

"Where are my letters?" She held up her satchel.

"Oh? I didn't touch your things." Blueknot took a seat on a rock. "Tobe and Mel carried those here."

"One of them was meant for the *mord* I am trying to meet!" A small well of panic was beginning to form in her gut. How would she explain anything to Herric without the letter? "I need to find out where it went!"

"It is being delivered, kid. Keep your socks on," a voice said from outside the chamber. A moment later, Mel, Tobe and a dwarf wearing a strange tabard-like shirt that bared their thick, fuzzy arms, all entered the chamber.

Mel waved to Amandine. "Sorry for going through your things, but I felt a bit responsible for your predicament and wanted to help. This, sah, is Herric McKragen. Cave farmer. He doesn't speak much Olgothian, but he insisted on coming to meet you after I gave him your letter."

Herric, whose beard was short and round-cut, nodded to Amandine. She wasn't a great judge of *mord* in general, but their dual-pupiled, green-yellow eyes were very much like Boomer's.

Mel turned to Blueknot. "Great work, Blue. You weren't seen?"

Blueknot shook her head at Mel. "No trust!"

"Just checking!" Mel put her hands up in a pacifying way.

Tobe walked over to where Fredderick was lying and crouched over him. One hand touched his forehead and then thumbed back an eyelid. Dumpling cowered away from the rotund man and tried to hide behind Fredderick's body. Mel watched him examine Fredderick and when he stood, he shook his head at her and pointed to his eyes.

"Yeah I didn't think so," Mel said. "So then, we have a mystery."

She turned back to Amandine. "I am sure you and Herric here have things to talk about, but first, I believe you owe us an explanation. Why did the chair burn you? How did you set off the Crystallian's gem? That dwarf was not boasting when he said they are never wrong. Because of their skin and eyes, *mord* have been preyed on by demons for centuries, and they take their discovery and elimination deadly serious, as you discovered.

"So, come clean. Are you a demon? I am aware that not all of them wantonly eat people, but we stuck our necks out for you, and we deserve to know."

Amandine felt sick. Mel wasn't wrong, but was Fredderick's secret hers to tell? She needed help, and they were all she had right now. But still...

"I swear, I am *not* a demon. But saying any more than that would be betraying a friend."

"Saying any less would be betraying us," Mel snapped. Her posture had changed. It was subtle, but Amandine knew what to look for when someone was ready for violence. Her hand was still not on her sword. At least not yet.

"How? You have my thanks for rescuing us, but you are all still strangers to me. We've only met twice, I know nothing about any of you!"

Mel's face darkened. Amandine wished she had put her *Olatharr* back on. It lay out of reach by the backpacks. Not that it would avail her much if Mel wanted to hurt her. The woman radiated that same aura that she had come to associate with others who were strong and had confidence in that strength. People like Serand, Dena, Telvor, and Birch. She didn't even need to touch her to sense how conflicted her emotions were.

"Melanie," Blueknot said warningly.

Mel's expression softened slightly. She closed her eyes and took a deep breath.

"Peace," Herric rumbled. Their Olgothian was thickly accented, and halting, but their tone was firm. "My sire. Knows demon signs. *Gyre*, speaks true of this one. Bud of Seeker Brutsche. Friend to my *nyre*. Demon talk is stupid. Much stupid. You say my sire is stupid?"

Herric's hands clenched into fists and their glare for Mel was intense.

Mel's posture shifted again. Amandine relaxed; the danger had passed. For now. She noticed that Tobe was also lowering his hands. Had he been ready to intervene?

"No, your sire is not stupid, sah. I meant no insult to your *nyre*." Mel made a circle over her eyes with a pair of fingers and Herric nodded. The dwarf seemed mollified by the gesture and he likewise stood down.

She turned to look at Amandine again. "It *is* strange, though, what happened. Your answer is *not* good enough. When your friend wakes, we will be asking again."

Her stare could have pinned an aurochs to the cavern wall. Amandine swallowed and nodded.

"Fair deal," she agreed.

"Ragall and Imri are scouting the area. Blue and I will go meet them. Tobe will stay here with you as protection. Have your chat, and then we need to figure out how to get you out of Anvilroot and not back into an oubliette."

Blueknot sighed and rose as Mel turned and left the cave. "No rest for small folk," she muttered. With a gentle hand, she poked Amandine as she passed. "Don't let Mel's ire deter you. She means well, honestly."

Tobe watched the women leave and then dug through a backpack and pulled out a notebook and charcoal. He sat down on the rock that Blueknot had vacated and began to write.

"Well," Amandine said, turning to Herric. "It's just us, sah. You read the letter, yes? You know what we need help with?"

Herric nodded. They uttered a growling word in *Mord-seq* and then said in Olgothian: "Rot Slimes."

Amandine sat beside her backpack, and Herric settled next to her. "They have done a huge amount of damage to the food supplies already. Our wax and our wards didn't prevent them and so we need another way. What do your people do to deal with them?"

"Soup." Herric said with a tooth-filled grin.

"Oh, uh. I thought Boomer was japing. You really eat them?"

Herric shrugged.

"Even so, that can't possibly deal with all of them. How do you manage the rest?"

With a nod, Herric reached down to their belt and untied a small clay pot. It had a spongy stopper, perforated with tiny holes, wedged into its top. They pulled the stopper out and set the pot between them. It was full of something gray and gelatinous.

"Oh my, what is *that*?" Amandine asked.

Herric rubbed two fingers over the top of the pot and made a soft cooing noise. An eye opened in the gray mass and Amandine gasped.

The dwarf continued to coo and a slimy tentacle emerged from the pot, followed by another. They were whip-like and covered with tiny pink pads on one side. Eight emerged in total and then the mass containing the eye swelled up and out of the pot and tumbled onto the cave's warm stone floor. The creature had four eyes, spaced equally around a bulbous head. It moved along the floor with its tentacles and reached three of them up to touch Herric's fingers. They smiled and retrieved a small morsel of something from a belt pouch that they dropped in front of the creature.

Its tentacles pulled the food under its body and then it flattened out onto the floor. The thing's mottled skin shifted to take on the texture and color of the stone beneath it. If Amandine hadn't been looking right at it, it would have seemed to vanish.

"How bizarre!" Amandine exclaimed. "What is it, sah?"

"Mooku."

"It's a mooku?"

"No. That is name. *Gyre* is *hrokulani*."

"Hork-a-looney?"

Herric sighed. "Not *gyre* say 'rocktopus'."

Amandine laughed in spite of it all. "I can remember that. 'Rocktopus', that's cute."

The dwarf shook his head in an annoyed way, but didn't correct her. "Eat many slime. Many many. One hand *hrokulani*, protect whole *pondo*."

"One hand? Five? This many?" Amandine asked, holding up a hand.

Herric nodded.

"How big is a *pondo*?"

Herric seemed to pause and think about the question. Amandine figured he probably didn't have the right words to convey ideas like land area.

"So, as big as this?" Amandine asked, gesturing to the cave.

"No! Much big! More big. Many this. Five hands this. More."

It still wasn't much, but if a handful of rocktopuses could keep an area that big clear of slimes, it would be a simpler thing to make sure a few were kept near the food stores.

"This is really good news, Herric. Can we buy or trade for rocktopus? Will they live in sunlight?"

He shook his head again. "No sun. Sun bad. Make dry. Dark. Wet. Is happy then."

So they wouldn't be good in the fields, but Amandine was sure someone could come up with a way to house them inside, someplace to their liking, where they could guard food. Maybe Wizzlecog.

Grendel approached the rocktopus and sniffed at it. A single tentacle lifted warily. Amandine watched, ready to pull him away if it seemed dangerous, but the cat and the tentacle merely faced off a moment longer before Grendel flopped on his side next to the creature and batted a paw at it.

"Friends," Herric said with a choking laugh. "Good with buds also. Good protector. Smart."

"They are smart, you say? You can train them?"

Herric said some words in *Mord-seq* and wiggled his fingers. The rocktopus changed to a vivid red color and unflattened itself. Herric ran two fingers along a ridge between the eyes and its entire body quivered as if in pleasure.

"I'm not sure everyone will take to them, but they are charming... in a very strange way," Amandine admitted. "May I touch?"

Herric nodded. Amandine reached out and also stroked the ridge. The animal's skin was not as slimy as she had thought, but was smooth and damp, like a frog. It continued to quiver and a tentacle reached up to touch her palm. She felt a sense of quiet contentment from it, as well as love for Herric.

"You buy *hrokulani*?" Herric asked.

"Yes, you sell?"

Herric shrugged. "Must be taught. Must care for. *Hrokulani* is *nyre*. Not thing for working only."

"I understand that. We keep animals as companions too, and they also have jobs. This one hunts vermin for us," Amandine said, stroking Grendel's belly. "But they don't hunt rot slimes. We need help."

Herric rolled their furry shoulders. "I can teach. Have buds can teach. But many *pondo* not safe. Growing *hrokulani* not possible now."

"Why, what's happened? Is it to do with the call for mercenaries that the Hammers put out?"

"Maybe," Herric said with a heavy sigh. "Nearby warrens go cold. Some *nyre* lost buds. Buds die often, even after welcome. Caves not safe. But this not same. Safe places become not safe. *Pondo* is place for food growing. Mushrooms. *Yobo*. Fish. *Kuragh*. Urm, you say horker. Large, much meat. Stupid. Good for farm."

"And these *pondo* are no longer safe? Your animals and children, your buds, are vanishing?"

Herric nodded. They looked miserable. The rocktopus extended a tentacle to wrap around a finger. Herric grinned toothily at the creature and shook their head.

"Hammers are good *gyre*. Smart. Will find the danger and kill it." They spoke the last words with an edge in their voice that made Amandine want to flinch. It struck her that the primary solution to any problem the *Ur'Mord* faced was to try and fight it. But what if it was something they couldn't fight? Something natural or magical that was beyond their ability to stab into submission? Perhaps that was why they had asked for help from outside. In that way, she and the people of the Gold Hills were the same. Asking for help outside the community to face a problem they couldn't handle alone. She felt bad for Herric, and all of the dwarves, despite how she and Fredderick had been treated.

There was a groan. Amandine looked to where Fredderick lay and saw him stir. She hurried to his side with a water skin from her backpack. He squinted in the dim orange light of the strange cave, and, with another groan, he looked away from the ceiling at Amandine.

"Had the strangest dream. Where are we?" he croaked.

Amandine helped him sit up and gave him the water skin. His hands shook slightly, but he managed to drink. Tobe had risen from whatever he'd been writing and crouched down on the other side of him. He felt Fredderick's head and then poked and prodded him in several other places in a practiced sort of way.

"He took a blow to the head in the pit, sah. Will he be well?" Amandine asked.

Tobe shrugged. He turned Fredderick's head toward him with a meaty hand and looked into his eyes.

"Hello to you too," Fredderick mumbled.

The large man released him and returned to his rock. Amandine shook her head while watching him. "Vibrant Dawn rescued us," she explained. "But you were hurt. I thought—" Her voice caught before she could say anything else.

Fredderick's arms embraced her from behind. She brought her hands up to hold his for a moment, but Herric and Tobe were watching them, so she gently pushed him away. "I'm fine," she said. "I'm just glad it wasn't worse for you."

As she pulled her arms away, he grasped her wrist and turned it over. "What's this? Oh..." Fredderick said when he saw the heart-leaf markings. "It happened again?"

Amandine glared at him and shook her head, giving a sharp jerk of her chin towards Tobe. He had looked up from his writing again, eyes fastened on her arm. He seemed thoughtful.

"Sorry," Fredderick whispered.

With a sigh, Amandine tried to pull her sleeve down, but it wasn't long enough to cover it all.

"So, what did I miss?" Fredderick asked. Dumpling had curled up next to his hip and Fredderick's fingers absentmindedly scratched his head.

"A cold pit, an even colder lake, a bunch of half-naked dwarves and a forest of giant mushrooms."

"Wow, all of that? That will teach me to stay up past my bedtime."

Amandine smiled. "Your dumb mouth is fully healed at least. This *gyre* here is Herric. The bud of Boomer's we were to meet."

"Excellent! Did you learn what we needed?"

"Well yes, but there is a problem."

"Of course there is." Fredderick groaned. He rubbed his temples. "Ok, hit me. Metaphorically, I mean."

"Well, the *pondo*, their cave farms I think, are unsafe right now. Whatever has put Anvilroot on edge is out there."

"It's not just Anvilroot," Mel's voice said. She entered the cave, followed by Blueknot and Imri. A fourth person walked beside her, but it wasn't Ragall.

The newcomer was an elf, with ears that were long and thin, like Mister Green or Imri's. He—she was assuming it was a he—was tall, and lithe, with pale, blue-white skin and long, black hair. Amandine realized with a shock that his skin was translucent. She could see muscle, tendons, and veins. His eyes were pale white. The dark pinpricks of his pupils contrasted sharply within them.

Herric stood upright as if the floor were hot. They began shouting angrily in Mord-seq. Mel tried to speak to them, but the dwarf radiated so much rage and fear, Amandine could sense it from clear across the chamber.

"Foolish humans! You bring death here! Unnamed Court! Dark fae! We are all dead stone!"

Unnamed Court

"For reasons I will not go into until later lectures, Court Fae, as you know us, do not have godsworn in our midst. We acknowledge the existence of the gods and have names for them, but they are not, in large part, for us and we are not for them. The exception to this is the Unnamed Court. The Erestral. They follow Ravenex with unfailing devotion. Some writings dating back to before their exodus from the sunlit world claim that the goddess was actually born to them, somewhere in the Deeps. Hubris perhaps, but as the origin and purpose of the gods in this world are still unknown, who is to say? I, for one, harbor the opinion that lack of grace and sunlight has made the Erestral quite mad. What few writings we have from them are so contrary and disjointed that a coherent picture of their culture and beliefs is, for now, as big a mystery as the gods themselves."

- Lecture Notes, Second Windday, High Winter 1202

IT WAS SEVERAL chaotic moments before Mel and Tobe managed to restore order. Herric sat huddled in a corner of the chamber, staring wide-eyed at the translucent fae. The blue-skinned elf seemed unfazed by Herric's outburst, although Amandine thought she detected a tiny bit of smug satisfaction from him at the dwarf's discomfort.

Ragall had come inside from where he had been standing watch. He leaned against the wall near the entrance, slowly dragging a whetstone along the blade of his axe. His eyes never left the fae.

Everyone else was arranged in more or less a semi-circle around him, seated on the floor or leaning against the wall where it wasn't hot. Mel shot Herric one last look and then folded her arms.

"Alright sah, one more time for all present," she prompted.

"You may call me Ko," he said. His Olgothian rang with a shrill, dissonant accent. It made Amandine twitch. Like fingernails scratching a slate. His clothing was sparse, thin wraps of wispy cloth that barely covered his waist and legs, and left his chest and arms bare. Amandine wondered what it was made from.

"Very well, Ko," Mel said slowly. "Our forbearance is not unlimited. You know why we are here."

"To kill my people. Because the *mord* paid you to. I am completely aware of your purpose here, human."

"Tough luck getting caught then, eh?" Blueknot said.

The fae laughed. It was oddly musical, given how dissonant his speech was. "Caught? You found me because I wished to be found, you foolish, small creature."

"Say it again, you freak!" Blueknot leapt to her feet.

"Blue! Your turn! Sit down!" Mel barked.

Blueknot glared at Mel, but nodded and took her seat again.

"Your leader is wise." Ko's smile was eerie and skeletal. Amandine could see his teeth and jaw muscles through his cheeks.

"No, I just don't fancy killing anyone who surrenders to me. Even if I have been paid to. Makes the beer taste stale later on," Mel said. "Now, if you don't mind, Ko, get to the colorless point."

Ko rolled his shoulders. "Blood is already being spilled. Your foolish Seekers and the rest who came, lured by coin, are being killed by my people when they encroach on our dominions. They have killed some of us too, but this fighting is pointless. You are hunting the wrong prey."

"Lies! Dark fae speak not truth!" Herric yelled. "Stealing buds, kill for fun. Scree! Sand! Brittle words! Brittle stone!"

"Ah, yes. We sometimes do those things. You are right to fear. Vermin should always fear the larger predator."

Herric stood and bared his teeth. Tobe had to physically restrain him from attacking the elf.

"Sah! Enough!" Mel said to Ko. "Hear me. I am willing to let you have your say, but if you continue to taunt the *mord*, I will ask Tobe to let him go."

"Then he would die."

"And I'll help him," Mel continued. She drew her sword from its black sheath in a smooth motion and grounded the point. Where the metal touched the stone, wisps of steam rose. The bright silver blade seemed to warp in Amandine's vision, as if she were trying to look at it beneath clear water.

The fae eyed the blade warily. It was the first emotion other than smug calm he had displayed so far and Mel seemed to notice.

"So you know what this is, then, yeah?" she asked.

He nodded.

"Right then. Get. To. The. Point."

"The humans, *mord*, and surface fae. You are hunting us, but the current losses the *mord* are suffering are not our doing. At least, the vast majority are not."

"What is it then?" Imri asked. "What sort of threat would cause the *mord* so much distress? They dealt with the dragon without seeking aid. What could possibly—"

"Dragon?" Mel and Amandine asked at the same time.

Imri sighed. "Before you all were born. Not important, merely a basis for comparison. If they could deal with such a creature without seeking aid, what would have them so out of sorts at this time?"

Ko rolled his shoulders again. Amandine got the impression it was something like a shrug.

"A thing has been birthed in the deeps. A being of darkness made flesh," he said.

"A darkling thing..." Amandine whispered.

The fae turned to face her. "The child knows of what I speak?"

"Me? No, I just—"

"You bear god-marks. Those Without have spoken to you?" Ko gestured to Amandine's arm.

"Wait, you are godsworn? A *Speaker*?" Mel broke in.

"I... I am not sure. There was this thing in the woods and... oh Goddess, this is insane," Amandine said.

Tobe clapped his hands. Mel looked at him. He pointed to his mouth and then at Mel.

"Yes, I know you told me your suspicions," Mel said. "But if that's true, she really can't be a demon, can she?"

"I told you I am not!" Amandine's hands clenched into fists. "You won't listen!"

"Heart-leaf. She's Cult of Kayla," Blueknot said.

Amandine threw up her hands. "I'm not Cult of Anything! I ran away from the Ravenex convent in Artemis because I wanted nothing to do with that shite! I have no idea what any of this means!"

"How interesting," Ko said. "Humans really don't understand anything. How you took over this world is a grand mystery."

"Manners," Mel hissed, tapping her sword's tip on the stone.

Ko grimaced, but refrained from a response.

"Look, kid, I owe you an apology," Mel said. "I've got nothing but respect for the godsworn, honestly. But if you really have no idea what it means to bear those marks, then you need to find someone who does, immediately, before it causes you harm."

Tobe nodded emphatically.

"Can we focus?" Fredderick asked weakly.

He still couldn't stand without being dizzy, but looked like he might try for Amandine's sake. She appreciated his support, but also didn't want him to strain himself.

"I... I heard a voice... on my way here." Amandine said. "I think it might have been Ravenex. It spoke of a darkling thing in the Deeps. That I was to bring those who bear light to it."

Just speaking the words made her feel like she was losing her mind. That had been a dream, right? But then, the marks on her neck. The ones on her arm. Had Kayla spoken to her as well? Was that the voice which had filled her with so much love? The thought scared her to her core, but at the same time, she hoped to hear it again. To feel that way again. And that also frightened her.

"What else did you see?" Ko asked softly.

"I... saw a tower. It was as if it were made of dark glass. Rising into an endless sky."

Ko took a deep breath and spoke a few words in his discordant elvish. He closed his eyes and opened his arms, as if for an embrace. Mel shifted, but Ko made no other move.

"I welcome the presence of Those Without among us. Great Mistress, I ask for your blessing to guide this one to the places below."

Amandine's breath caught. She felt it. That sensation in her mind. It was just like when—

"*This one speaks with my voice,*" Amandine said. She heard the words coming from her own mouth—could feel herself thinking them before she said them—but the compulsion to speak was so strong it was almost painful.

"*Bring her to the crystal womb. A bridge is needed. Do not delay. Go in darkness.*"

The sensation left Amandine in a rush. Her body felt like she had been sprinting for a mile. She gasped in short, rasping breaths, doubled over, then collapsed to her knees. Her skin felt like it was covered in icy water and she began to shiver uncontrollably. After a moment, she managed to compose herself and looked up. Everyone was staring at her. Blueknot's expression was horrified. Tobe's brow furrowed, eyes assessing. Imri and Ragall exchanged darting glances.

"What in the colorless world..." Mel began.

"I... don't know what just happened," Amandine said as she fought to control her chattering teeth. "I don't know why I said that."

"Godsworn," Ragall rumbled. He made the sign of Ravenex with his hands.

Amandine's chest tightened so she could barely breathe. She looked down at her arm. The heart-leaf was gone. With searching fingers, she felt her neck. A glance at Fredderick confirmed it. He nodded to her.

"The shadow bonnet. It's back, Amandine," he said.

"The Mistress has spoken. I will guide you below, to serve her will," Ko said.

"You're not taking her anywhere," Fredderick growled.

Amandine stood and touched his shoulder. "If I go with you, Ko. To this place. Will it stop whatever is hurting the *mord*? Will it stop the killing?"

"There will always be killing. The darkness demands it. Only those who kill faster and then feed survive here, child. But it will stop the *needless* killing. Death without purpose is waste."

"I will do it." Amandine's heart thundered in her chest. It was the only way. To help her people, she needed to help Ko's people—and Herric's, first. "Take me to this place."

"Amandine, no," Fredderick said. Dumpling whined.

"Fredderick, I have to. If I walked away from this now, I don't think it would go well for me. At least, not until I can learn how to control... whatever is happening to me."

"Then I am going with you." Fredderick wobbled to his feet.

"You can barely walk..." One of Amandine's legs wobbled as the chill slowly faded.

"You're one to talk!" One of Fredderick's legs nearly gave out as well, but he winced and straightened his spine.

"We're coming too," Mel said.

Amandine started to protest by reflex, then caught herself. Vibrant Dawn had gathered around Mel. All of them seemed resolute. Blueknot nodded to her. They were battle-hardened. They knew the terrain. What kind of fool would she be to say no to that? Instead, she nodded back.

"The Mistress made no mention," Ko began, but Amandine cut him off.

"They come with me." She moved closer until she was within a finger of the eerie fae and glared up at him, her arms folded stubbornly in front of her.

After a moment, Ko cocked his head slightly. An acknowledgement? Agreement?

"Follow me then, sunlit fools. There is no denying the Mistress of Night."

Apples and a Tin of Fish

"Trail rations are best fer two things: breaking teeth, and ballast."

- Serand Brutsche

THEY PASSED THROUGH the tree-shrooms in a loose group with Amandine, Herric and Fredderick in the middle. Mel and Ragall walked at the flanks, Imri and Blueknot behind. To Amandine's surprise, Tobe took the lead position with Ko. Despite the fact he didn't appear to be armed, the Seekers all looked to him every time there was a noise that might mean trouble.

The only thing of note they encountered, however, was a horker. They were ugly things that looked like a weird cross between a toad and a boar. It made a strange burbling noise as they passed, but fled into the murk when Imri loosed an arrow at it.

"You eat those?" Amandine asked Herric.

The dwarf nodded, their eyes never leaving the dark fae leading them. "Meat, eggs. Skin is good for... um, good for make things. Things to wear." They pointed to their sleeveless tunic. Amandine looked more closely and realized the pebbly texture matched the horker's mottling. It didn't look like leather, though. It was thin and light as linen.

"That's actually sort of neat. I wouldn't mind clothing made from that. It looks comfortable."

Fredderick made a disgusted face, but Herric nodded.

"We live through this, my *Ur'gyre* make for you. That *gyre* is skilled with skin and bone. Good things. Solid stone."

"Oh? Is that your..." Amandine searched for the right word. The usual male and female words a human would use were irrelevant to the *mord*. Then she remembered what Boomer had called Dena. "...mate? That *gyre*?"

"Aye. Solid stone. Our buds are strong. Only three have died. One will soon be a sire. Orvil. That *gyre* makes me proud. Stone Guard. Very strong."

Ko turned his head and frowned at the mention of Stone Guard. Amandine didn't know who they were, but it sounded martial. Like the Stoneman Militia. Perhaps part of the city guard of Anvilroot?

"Your family — I mean your *nyre*, must be huge," she said.

"Nah. Small. Strong. Like *hrokulani*. We are part of Seven Hammers. Largest grackle. Many small, strong *nyre* make larger, stronger *nyre*."

"The *Ur'nyre*," Fredderick said.

Herric nodded.

"Humans do it too. We just don't often have such clarity about it," Fredderick said. He panted slightly as he limped alongside Amandine. "We make towns and cities and nations, but even when we are a group, we act selfishly. Like lone grimalks."

"Oh, don't get too poetic," Mel said as she scanned the forest. "There are plenty of *mord* in every *nyre* who don't give a lick about the next dwarf over. The Seven Hammers are a hegemony based on money and power just like everywhere else."

"Stupid things you say," Herric growled.

"Maybe, but tell me, sah, when was the last time you have even spoken to one of the *mord'resh*? Or perhaps one of your cousins in the Magmaflow clan?" Mel asked placidly.

Herric glared at her, but didn't answer.

"I thought not." Mel shrugged. "How much further, Ko?"

"We will not make it without rest. There is a place we can stop soon to regain our strength."

"Grand," Fredderick muttered as he wheezed slightly.

Amandine tried to prop him up but he waved her away. She worried that even though his head had been healed, that some sort of wound lingered. He was exhausted, limping, and not breathing easily.

The group passed from the mushroom forest into a series of bubble-like pockets of stone, connected by what Herric said were old magma tubes. The smooth black walls glistened like polished glass and reflected their torches and lamps. Ghostly lights crawled along the stone that almost looked like wisps. Ko led them deep into the honeycomb of tunnels, through passages that grew increasingly narrow, to a point where they all had to crawl to navigate them.

Amandine shuffled through on her knees and stood up. The chamber they had entered was massive, nearly the equal of the one that contained Bright Lake. Like that place, there was also a large body of dark water, still and glass-like in the flickering fire light. The water lapped gently at the smooth black stone ledge they stood upon, and stretched off out of sight into the gloom.

Blueknot pulled a canteen off her backpack and knelt to fill it. Ko made a slashing arm gesture and stepped in front of her.

"Do not! You will find this water to be unclean. It would make you ill, or even kill. The layers of rock beneath it contain things that make it toxic."

"Colorless night! It's going to be a long hike back with nothin' ta drink!"

"Will there be someplace where we can refresh water later?" Mel asked.

Ko nodded.

"I'll share, Blue," Mel said. "I have extra."

Ragall and Tobe had already begun assembling a small campsite: laying out bedrolls, setting up an oil-fueled warmer, and unfolding a small camp table. Tobe carefully unwrapped a pair of glass flasks filled with an orange, oily substance and placed them under the camp table. It was amazing to Amandine how much gear the two men managed to carry, especially given Ragall's enormous weapon.

"I will scout the perimeter," Imri announced.

"I will accompany you, cousin," Ko said.

Imri bristled. "You do not get to be familiar with me, traitor," Imri hissed at him. Her sudden anger at the other fae reminded Amandine of the one time she had seen Mister Green angry. Imri seemed to bristle like a cat, her eyes narrowed to slits. "I abide you because I trust Mel, and because it appears we have the will of a goddess to contend with, but if it were up to me, I would have slit your throat and left you for the colorless horkers. Am I understood?"

Ko said something in what sounded like elvish, but the pattern of it was wrong, like a lurin played off-key. It made Amandine wince slightly, listening to him. Imri did not reply, but merely turned and walked calmly into the darkness. A moment later, Ko followed.

"I will shadow them," Blueknot murmured.

Mel nodded and the small woman crept into the darkness after their footsteps had fallen out of hearing.

Amandine laid out her bedroll a little bit away from the others and guided Fredderick to it. He stretched out on it with a groan and quickly fell asleep with Dumpling tucked under one arm. Grendel slid out of Amandine's satchel and stretched as well, then climbed up on Fredderick's stomach and curled up.

"Hey, kid," Ragall said, motioning her over.

"What is it, sah?" Amandine asked as she approached.

"Well, I know Mel just said you were our cook to help you out, but your food at Carver's dump was lumi, and I don't even like spicy things. Think you could turn some dry rations into something less awful? We don't have a fire, just the warmer..." his voice trailed off as Mel glared at him.

"Don't be an ass, Rag," Mel scolded.

Amandine shook her head. "No, it's fine, sahs. I'll try. It's really the least I can do considering how much you all have helped Fredderick and I."

Ragall grinned and upended a small sack. Several oilskin wrapped parcels tumbled out, as well as three apples and a wide metal tin. "We should only use about a third of this if you can manage. We'll need food for the return trip. Hunting here is not great. Even if you cook it, horker tastes like feet."

Herric grumbled something in *Mord-seq* from where they sat. The rocktopus sprawled on his lap while they stroked it like a cat.

"Really, sah?" Mel asked, looking over at them. "I've heard that humans actually taste more like pork."

The dwarf gaped at her for a moment. Mel said something in *Mord-seq* and Herric looked away.

"Please don't be mean to them," Amandine said as she sorted through the rations. "They farm horkers. I'd be insulted too."

"Wasn't mean." Mel dug through her pack. "Just reminding him that not all humans are deaf, dull stones. You'll find, I think, that dwarves have more respect for you if you show some teeth. Here, add this to the pot."

Amandine didn't care for the way Mel talked about others. Blueknot claimed she meant well, but her casual pettiness set Amandine's teeth on edge. Dwarves weren't 'he' or 'him' and deaf people weren't 'dull.'

Mel noticed her scowl. "Come on, don't be a grumpus. Here, catch." She tossed a small cloth parcel. When it landed in Amandine's hands, she knew instantly from the smell what it was.

"Mist cheese! This is really expensive. You use it for trail rations?"

"Not usually, but a little fancy nibble might raise some spirits. What do you think you can make?"

Amandine knew immediately. "The tin has meat?"

"Fish in seed oil," Ragall said.

"Perfect!"

Her annoyance with Mel forgotten, Amandine set the cheese on the table and carefully unwrapped it. Mist cheese was slightly moist and soft, just right for melting. It had a sharp flavor since it was made partly from goat's milk. She retrieved one of her small knives from her pack and broke the block into crumbles.

Next, she opened one of the parcels Ragall had dumped and found that it contained hard biscuits, dried gojo, and sticks of *meela*, the elven oat and honey concoction Gil had been so keen to make.

"Are all of these the same?" she asked. Ragall nodded. Amandine opened a second parcel and portioned out the items.

She pried open the lid of the tin next. It had about twenty or so sardines with the heads, but gutted and steeped in a thick yellow oil. With the knife, she removed a third of the fish and replaced the lid, then wiped them down and removed the heads.

Finally, she took one of the three apples. Carefully setting it on the table, she unsheathed the *Olatharr* and began slicing it. An apple was the first thing she had ever cut with the knife, shortly after it had cut her, and it still proved just as keen. Its razor sharp curved edge made thin slices, almost translucent, into a small stack that beaded with juice from the fruit.

"I can't say I have ever seen a war-knife used like that," Ragall commented as he watched. Mel and Tobe had stopped working and started watching as well.

"You changed the handle," Mel said.

Amandine nodded. "Yes. Dena, the woman who adopted me, she taught me how to use a knife to fight, but I am bad at that. This is how I use knives. To have the right grip, I needed a different handle."

She finished the apple and then used the knife again to split the fish, and separated the hard biscuits. Crumbled mist cheese went on the biscuit halves, followed by fish, followed by more cheese. Then she carefully set the half-stacks on the flat lid of the oil warmer. It wasn't a proper cooking fire, but she hoped the brass top would be warm enough to melt the cheese.

"Now we wait a moment," Amandine said.

"You thought of doing this all just now?" Mel asked.

"Um, no? Yes? Sort of?" Amandine fumbled. "Hot nibbles were Sunflower's specialty, but I watched her make pate toasts and cheese soups so many times, it just sort of came to me."

"Huh." Mel watched the cheese slowly begin to melt across the hardtack. "That's fairly clever."

"Not done yet!" Amandine said. Despite their unusual location and harrowing circumstances, she found herself lost in the project. Time seemed to slow as she watched the cheese and fish meld. She forgot about dwarves and fae. Goddesses and Seekers. It was just her and the food.

As the cheese began to finish, she took the *meela* and wrapped it in one of the oilskins and handed it to Ragall. "Give that a smash with something heavy, please? Break it up?"

Ragall shrugged and took the oilskin, then set it on the ground and smacked it hard with the broad side of his axe. He carefully picked it up and handed the flattened parcel back. Amandine took a handful of the crumbled honey and oats and sprinkled it into the melting cheese. Then she removed each half-stack from the lid, using a cloth so she wouldn't burn herself.

With steady fingers, she plucked slices of apple from the pile she had cut and folded them into loops before tucking them in fans across the top of each stack.

"Well, I'll be a troll-arsed tusker. That is the first time a pack of trail rations has ever looked that good," Ragall said in amazement.

"I hope they taste as good as they look." Amandine wiped her brow. The concentration she had been exerting to get it right had made her sweat, despite the chill air.

"Should we wait for the others?" Ragall asked.

"Hells with that." Mel reached out and took one of the nibbles. The hot cheese scalded her fingers and she blew on them before having a bite. "Oh, gods," she said.

Ragall took one as well. His face lit up as he tried it. "It's still salty rations, but somehow... better. Like everything is just — wow."

Amandine noticed that Tobe was not eating. He smiled and nodded at her.

"Do you not like fish, sah?" she asked.

"He doesn't have teeth," Mel said around a mouthful.

"Oh! I completely forgot! I'm so sorry."

Tobe shook his head and pulled out a waterskin with an especially large nozzle. He popped off the cap and sucked something out of it. Then handed it to Amandine.

She took it and sniffed. It was some kind of half-fermented milk. Like the kind Miss Jacinda would sometimes use to create whey for yogurt. There was something else mixed into it. It was pungent, but not foul. "What is this?" she asked, handing it back.

"Olgothians call it *shebula*," Mel said. "It's a mixture of curdled milk, mashed boiled tubers and some spices that stave off rot. It tastes like death, but doesn't require chewing. They feed it to their slaves. It's got all the things in it to keep you going, if you don't have a tongue to taste it."

Tobe nodded, took another pull, and then wiped his mouth.

"You were a slave?" Amandine asked.

Tobe nodded again.

"And they took your–" she couldn't even bring herself to finish the sentence.

"Yeah, and his teeth," Mel said. "Bastards. But they got theirs in the end. You don't mess with Berindor." She held out a fist to Tobe and he grinned and pressed his own fist into hers.

"Since he can't have it, I'll take his!" Ragall rubbed his hands together.

"You'd better share with Imri, or she might kick you out of bed, Rag." Mel laughed.

"What she doesn't know..." he said as he reached for the food.

"Where are they? Shouldn't they be back by now?" Amandine asked.

Mel paused mid-bite and frowned. "Well it *is* a really large cavern. You can tell by the way it echoes, and how the light doesn't reach the far side. But yeah, Blueknot probably should have checked back in by now."

Herric said a few words in *Mord-seq*. Mel shook her head. "No, sah, I don't think Ko did anything. I don't trust him, but I don't think he was lying to us either."

"Why do you think that?" Amandine asked.

"Two reasons. The first is that his people do not take reckless chances. They already got trounced once, so badly it almost ended them. Court fae do not have as many children as humans. They mature slowly and live longer than us. Far, far longer. If it was a ploy to kill us, we'd have been ambushed by now. I doubt they would risk another open war against all of the sunlit world in their weakened state. Second, he's desperate. The Unseen Court do not make contact with anyone. Not even the other Courts. The fact he approached us at all reeks of desperate action. Whatever is harrowing them, he needs someone strong to see it gone, and who better than a bunch of sunlit warriors and godsworn? The same strength that nearly hunted his people to extinction.

"No, he is scared to death of us, but wants to use us for his own ends. Killing us before he gets what he needs is not what he has planned, I think. If we find and defeat whatever it is he wants us to kill, then all bets are off."

Mel pushed the last bit of her food into her mouth and chewed thoughtfully as she watched the warmer's light.

"Plenty of things could have happened," Ragall said softly, his food forgotten. "What's your call, Mel?"

"I'll go and find out. Just me. If I am not back in two bells, abandon camp. Get out of here and don't look back."

Mel stood and slung her sword over her shoulder. She clapped Tobe on the back as she walked past and he nodded and pressed a hand to his heart.

"I should go too," Ragall said, standing as well.

"No. The greenies need looking after. If something happened to them because of sentiment, you know what Imri would think," Mel said.

Ragall sighed, but sat back down.

Amandine watched Mel walk off into the shadows. She barely made a sound as she moved.

"You and Imri are close?" she asked Ragall while watching where Mel had vanished.

"Ah, yeah. You gathered that pretty easily, I'm sure." He rubbed his beard with a calloused hand and looked over at Tobe. The large man pressed his palms together and then opened them to Ragall like a book.

"Her full name is Imrithallianthia, of the Court of Breaking Dawn, and I love her more than my own life. But if there is one thing you should know about fae, little one, it's that vows are more than words to them. Breaking a vow you have made to a fae—that they have accepted—is painful to them, and possibly deadly to us. I have made many to her. But the one Mel is talking about... I vowed I would never put my love for her over my sworn duty to protect others in need. Mel's right. You need me here, so I stay."

"I'm sorry, sah," Amandine said. "I don't want to hold you back."

"You don't." His expression broke into an easy smile. He picked up his axe and stood. "My own words, my own promises, bind me. There's a difference. Thank you for the meal, by the way. It's possibly our last. I am really happy that it was so delicious."

He turned to watch the darkness with Amandine.

"You're welcome," Amandine said softly.

Strength

"The Brothers, Berindor and Akradath, eldest of the gods, have alternately led the Pantheon over the ages, with Akradath being ascendant currently. Akradath is the god of Knowledge, and because of his marriage to Milintanth, he also has some sway over Light. His followers fill his temples with huge libraries and, like their god, hold the discovery and preservation of knowledge to be the greatest form of devotion. Akradath is reason before emotion, knowledge over intuition, and curiosity for all things. His brother, Berindor, is the god of Strength, War, and to some extent, the earth itself. The Dedicated use his temples as places to forge tools and weapons, plan battles, and train warriors. He is not married, but has alternately been the lover of Delinkhal, Ravenex, and Kayla. Berindor is action over parlay, emotion over reason, and above all, strength–both mental and physical. He respects order, like his brother, but does not share the same moral compass. With Berindor, the ends justify the means."

- Lecture Notes, Second Windday, High Winter 1202

FREDDERICK CONTINUED TO sleep as Amandine checked on him. She sat on her knees and leaned over to part his hair, then lifted his shirt to check for blood or bruising. He had no visible wounds, but his color was wrong. His breathing came in short, labored gasps.

Dumpling sat next to his elbow and watched her work. She scowled at him.

"I thought you healed him?" she whispered. "He's sick and getting worse. Why?"

The small dog lay down and looked up at her with large watery eyes and whined.

"Oh, fine. *Now* you're just a dog. When I actually need answers!"

Grendel rubbed up against her and she stroked him absently. Even with his gift of night vision, it was difficult to see in the cavern. The darkness swallowed everything it touched. She rubbed her eyes in tired frustration. It had been a bell already and Mel had not returned with news.

Tobe made a sound and she looked up. He sat with his back against the cavern wall, holding the book he'd been writing in. With a beckoning gesture to her, he patted the ground next to him.

Amandine left Fredderick and took a seat beside him. Tobe opened his book, and using a loose sheet of paper, covered most of the page–except one line at the top: "I wanted to speak with you. Will you sit with me a bit?"

Amandine read the line slowly. His writing was clean, but she still struggled with written words sometimes.

"Um, sure, sah. What did you wish to discuss?"

His hand slid the paper to uncover a different line: "You are godsworn, and a Speaker. How long have you known?"

At first, Amandine thought he was talking about the fact that she could speak. Then she realized that "Speaker" was some sort of title. "I haven't known, um, I mean... I don't know, sah. Nothing like this has ever happened to me. I had a strange dream, that maybe wasn't a dream, where Ravenex spoke to me at the standing stone near Kiln? But that was recently. Before that, I was normal."

Tobe pointed at her neck. She couldn't see it without a mirror, but she knew he was pointing at the darkbloom mark. He set down his book and made the joined, cupped hand symbol for Ravenex. Then he crossed his palms beneath his sternum, the symbol for Kayla, and pointed to her arm. The gesture had the feeling of a question.

"I'm not really sure. We were in the pit. Fredderick was hurt. I heard a voice. It was different from the first vision. Peaceful. Kind. I felt... happy. It helped me to keep him alive, but he's still not well."

She left out mention of Fredderick's demon and hoped the omission—the lie, didn't show on her face.

Tobe nodded and held up two fingers, his eyebrows raised. He made the symbols for Ravennex and Kayla again.

"Do you mean have both spoken to me? I... suppose so, sah? I think they did both speak to me. It sounds insane to say it out loud."

He shook his head and picked up his book. With a surprisingly light touch, his large hand flicked through the pages. The loose paper was once again placed against a page to show only one line: "You are not crazy."

"How did you know I would say that? Is your book magic?"

Tobe smiled and shook his head. He pointed to his temple and then the page.

"You thought you were crazy too? Are you also godsworn, sah? You and Mel have both mentioned Berindor. Is that the god who speaks to you?"

He nodded.

"Do you also get marks when... you know."

Tobe took one hand and rolled up the other sleeve of his simple robe. Winding vines, thick with thorns and small, arrow-shaped leaves covered it, from the middle of his forearm up. They seemed inked on his skin, like Amandine's, but many of the thorns were tipped red and she could swear, from the corner of her eye, that some of the vines *moved*.

He picked up the book again and turned more pages, and then pointed to a passage that took up half the page: "Those marked by commune with a god change. The marks become bolder, more detailed, and more permanent as your bond grows. Mine have not faded in twelve years. Eventually, if you survive, yours will remain as well. They will become a part of you on the outside as your god becomes part of you on the inside."

"If I survive?" The note of fear in her own voice frustrated her. She couldn't seem to get a grasp on the reins of her own life anymore.

Tobe nodded solemnly.

"How? How do I survive it? Every time it's happened, I feel afterwards as if I have been dragged by a horse. Is there a secret you can tell me?"

With another shake of his head, Tobe reached out and patted her knee.

Amandine felt tears welling up in her eyes, but forced them back. "I didn't ask for any of this. I don't want it. But I don't know how to stop it either."

She sniffed and wiped her nose. "Thank you, Tobe. For your help. And your honesty."

He smiled and nodded. Amandine gripped the side of his massive palm and squeezed.

ANGER. PAIN. RAGE.

With a sharp intake of breath, Amandine retracted her hand as if she had been burned. Tobe looked down at her with a concerned expression. She knew that she had taken in his emotions, what he was feeling. It had been violence, barely contained. A knife balanced on the edge of another knife. So much hurt filled Tobe that even remembering it made Amandine shudder.

"You... you're hurting, sah. So badly," Amandine whispered. The tears she had fought back began to leave trails down her cheeks in spite of her wishes. How did one person contain so much raw, unfiltered anguish?

"How do you endure it?"

Tobe sighed. He took the loose sheet of paper out of his book and gently set it on the ground next to her. With a grunt, he regained his feet and walked over to where Ragall stood watch. Amandine took the paper sheet and looked at it.

There was something written, in Tobe's precise hand, on the side that had been facing down.

"Berindor is Strength."

Amandine carefully folded the paper and tucked it into her coat. "What does that make me, then?" she said to herself. Two goddesses had spoken to her. Had marked her. They couldn't be more different. Was she trapped between them? Was there a choice for her? Or would she have to walk the path Mother Jarl had spoken of, the one set before her? Was this what she had been speaking about? Had the sisters known this would happen to her? Fredderick seemed to think so.

She put her head in her hands and curled up her knees. The tears continued to fall, but it was mostly frustration that drove them now.

Meow.

Grendel rubbed up against her legs. He wove around and underneath them and then pushed his head under her arm to find her downturned face. He purred as his nose touched hers.

Amandine laughed in spite of it all. "You found me," she said with a sniffle. "I can't hide from you, can I?"

Meow.

With a deep breath, Amandine sat up and wiped her eyes with her palms. She was filthy again. That wonderful bath seemed so distant now. The kiss she had shared with Fredderick felt like it had been part of a different world entirely. She looked over to where he lay, pale and silent.

"I wish I knew how to help."

Broken Ice

Deep stone. Shroud of Darkness./
Always touching. The path of Heat guides our steps./
Echos of things distant. Warnings. Callings./
The Hunt moves in silence. It seeks the scent of Prey./
Silence broken. Black arms grab and pull./
Teeth tear. Spears break. Shattered stone./
Abandon stealth. Gyre flee./
The Hunt has become Prey./

- The Frakklin, Mord *epic, eighth stanza, transliterated by Lyra of*
Stolen Songs

TOBE SAW MEL first. Amandine was startled by his sudden movement and peered past him into the shadows. With a wordless cry, he dashed away from the camp as Mel emerged from the gloom. She was supporting Ko with one arm. Deep gashes in his translucent skin bled purple and blue. His left arm was limp; the wrist and forearm seemed unnaturally turned. It must have been disconnected or broken at the elbow.

Mel was in a similar state. An eye was caked shut with blood that plastered the hair on one side of her head. She used Second Winter as a walking stick to propel her across the stone and its point trailed smoke on the rock where the blade touched. Her right pant leg was missing, torn and cut short. Strips of it now bound a wound on her thigh, the dark cloth soaked through with more clotted blood. Amandine could tell she was in pain, and the way she leaned made her think she might have cracked or broken ribs.

Ragall ran to join Tobe. They took Ko from her arms and brought him back to the camp while she limped behind them. The fae's head lolled as he mumbled something, his eyes unfocused.

"What happened, Mel?" Ragall asked, his voice strained.

"Ambush," Mel said. "His own people, some other fae I didn't recognize. *Iskrix*, maybe. They were being helped by—"

A high pitched shriek reverberated off the cavern walls. Mel turned, her one good eye wide with fear.

"No..." she breathed. "No! I killed it!"

A black, rope-like tentacle whipped out of the darkness and coiled around Mel's head. She was yanked off her feet and dragged across the stone towards the shadows. Her sword clattered to the ground and created small wisps of smoke where the blade touched the stone's surface. Ragall dropped Ko against Tobe and charged towards her, grabbing the haft of his axe where it lay propped up against the camp table as he passed it. He leapt over Mel's struggling form and swung the heavy blade downwards. It sliced through the slimy appendage in a single stroke, sparking as it hit the stone beneath.

"Tobe! Fire!" he yelled.

Tobe grabbed the glass flask from under the table and tossed it in an arcing, underhand throw. Ragall caught it one-handed, turned and threw it into the darkness in a smooth motion. When it struck the stone, somewhere out of sight, fire bloomed into an orange ball. Amandine could feel the heat of it all the way over where she was against the wall.

The flames backlit a hideous form. Its body was massive and round, covered in coarse fur. Segmented legs, like a crab's, sprouted from its underside and framed an enormous, sucking maw. File-like rows of teeth gnashed as dozens of black tentacles whipped around the creature in a frenzy.

"Gods, is that a frakklin?" Ragall hefted his axe. "It's *huge*!"

Mel coughed as she unwound the tentacle from her face. The oil-fueled flames were beginning to die. She scooted away from the beast and retrieved her sword. The giant frakklin's tentacles beat at the flames as it hissed in fury.

"I *killed* it!" Mel repeated, unsteadily regaining her feet. "I don't understand!"

"Where are the others?" Ragall asked. Amandine could sense the fear in his voice.

Mel shook her head.

"Oh no," Amandine said. "Imri... Blueknot..."

Ragall threw back his head and screamed in anger. As the frakklin began to move again, he charged.

Tentacles lashed. Ragall sheared through one, and slapped aside a second. Mel rolled to avoid another. One crashed through the camp, knocking Tobe off his feet. Amandine ducked as another sailed mere fingers above her and slapped the wall with a meaty sound. She drew her *Olatharr*. The wave-like patterns in its blade reflected the dying embers of the oil fire beneath the monster.

She dashed on all fours to Fredderick and shook him. "Fredderick, wake up! Please! We can't stay here! We have to run!"

Dumpling whined and nudged her hand. She pushed him away.

"Stop being a dog and be useful instead!" she yelled. Fredderick moaned and stirred, but did not awaken.

Mel cried out. Amandine looked up to see her coiled once again in the creature's tentacles. Ragall hacked at the beast's body, harried by pointed, chitinous legs and tentacles from all sides. Amandine looked down at her knife. Was it sharp enough to help? Did she dare try? She couldn't imagine how she might attack something so large with such a small weapon, but they needed help.

There was a roar from behind her. Tobe dashed past her, flinging his robes to the side. Amandine had thought the man was stocky and perhaps a bit fat, but free of his bulky shroud, Tobe was a massive wall of flesh. She could see every tendon as he flexed, every muscle. It was like one of the Sister's anatomy diagrams with the skin still on. The thorny vines, his god-mark, climbed all the way up the arm he had shown her, across his back and down the opposite arm.

As he ran, his body almost seemed to expand. The vines writhed on his skin. His guttural howl became deeper, more feral. Just before Mel was shoved into the maw of the beast, his massive hands grasped the tentacles and pulled. With an awful snapping sound, they tore free from the thing's body in a gout of black ichor. It howled, but instead of retreating from the man that had wounded it, the frakklin turned to face Tobe. Every remaining tentacle lashed out at him.

"Please, wake up Fredderick!" Amandine shook him again. He mumbled something, and his eyes fluttered, but he still didn't stir from the bedroll. Out of pure desperation and fear, Amandine slapped him. "Wake! Up!"

Herric appeared at her elbow. "We must run! Frakklin feel no pain, only hunger! Come! Hurry!"

Amandine spun and faced him, standing so that she towered over the stocky dwarf. "I am *not* running! Not without my friends! Flee if you want—I'm staying!" She gripped the handle of her knife so tightly that her knuckles popped. Shoving down her fear, Amandine turned back to the fight.

Ragall lay senseless against a wall, his axe on the ground. Mel raised her blade and swung, deflecting a lashing tentacle away from her fallen comrade. Tobe was wrapped in several of the slimy appendages. He howled like an animal in rage and pain.

Amandine stepped forward. Herric caught her arm, halting her.

"No! No!"

"Let go of me!" She shook Herric free and turned once more.

With a scream, Tobe's eyes bulged. A crazed expression like nothing Amandine had ever seen had taken over his face. There was a squelching and snapping noise and then the tentacles encircling his body tore. Tobe's arms ripped free of the fleshy bonds, and the severed halves of the creature's tentacles dropped like coils of loose rope around his feet. He grabbed the stubs before they could retract and heaved. The frakklin's crab-like legs sought purchase on the stone, but skittered uselessly as its body was swung in an arc, hand-spans above the ground. Tobe circled it around him once and then released it. The massive furry body landed in the dark pool of the cistern with a terrible screech that cut off as it sank beneath the surface of the poisoned water, leaving small dark ripples in its wake.

Silence descended. The only sounds were labored breathing and lapping water. Tobe turned to Mel and howled into the silence. She dropped her sword and made the symbol of Berindor, fists pressed together, with her hands.

"Berindor... is strength," she said between gasping breaths.

Tobe groaned and sank to his knees. His body almost seemed to deflate as his rage subsided. He sagged to the ground like a doll dropped by a careless hand. The silence returned.

Mel knelt and picked up her sword. "We need to leave," she said softly between breaths.

"Yes! Leave!" Herric hopped from foot to foot.

"But the others!" Amandine protested. "Ragall, Tobe, Fredderick, even Ko. We can't–"

Mel turned to her. She opened her mouth to speak–and then Herric screamed.

Amandine spun. A tentacle had emerged from the dark lake and coiled around Herric. It dragged him towards the water, which was beginning to bubble and churn. She didn't even think. With a cry, Amandine ran to him, slipping on the smooth stone. As she fell, she gripped the knife with both hands and struck the tentacle. It passed through the disgusting flesh as easily as the apple. A jet of black ichor spattered her. It stank like rot.

"Look out, kid!" Mel called.

Another tentacle wrapped itself around Fredderick's leg. The frakklin began to rise from the water. Amandine made a low dive across the stone and hacked at the tentacle holding Fredderick, but her angle was bad and the knife bounced off the rubbery skin. She grabbed the slimy arm like a bundle of greenstalk and chopped again with the *Olatharr*. A strange feeling of peace filled her as the grotesque flesh parted for the blade. It was disorienting. It was like the sense she received when touching a dead person. Quiet. Peaceful. In the middle of that, however, was something else. Something not right–.

Ah. There you are. I see you now.

Amandine gasped at the voice in her mind and dropped the severed appendage.

Dumpling yelped. Yet another tentacle had grabbed the tiny dog. Amandine scrambled in a panic to try and reach him. She dove again, but the scruff of his neck slipped from her fingers. With a pitiful yelp, Dumpling slid away from her as the monster's gaping maw emerged.

"NO!" Amandine screamed.

A blast of cold air enveloped her. It was as if all of the heat had been instantly sucked from her body. Her breath caught in her throat as the wave of cold moved past and over her. The tentacle holding Dumpling became covered in rime. The water crackled as ice crystals formed across its glassy surface, locking ripples in place like frosting on a cake. The frakklin's half-submerged body sprouted spikes of ice. Its fur became encased in frost. Icicles draped down from its teeth.

The cold air relented and Amandine's breath returned. She rolled over and looked up. Fredderick stood above her, his hand outstretched. Wisps of vapor trailed from his extended fingers. He was white as death, and his eyes — they were pale blue, like ice on the surface of a lake. WIth a grimace, he whispered one word as his breath passed his lips in a cloud of mist.

"Break."

There was a sharp cracking noise. Fredderick clenched his fist and lowered it. Amandine glanced back over her shoulder. The frakklin, completely frozen and entombed in ice, began to shatter. Pieces of it fell and cascaded with glass-like tinkling sounds. A moment later, all that remained was a pile of ice and unrecognizable bits on the surface of the frozen pond.

Dumpling dashed past Amandine, and Fredderick knelt to pick him up. As the small dog licked his face, he regarded her with a distant, cold expression. "Are you alright, Fredderick?" she asked. "Your eyes, sah..."

"You're a mage," Mel said in awe as she limped up to them.

Fredderick looked at her, his gaze seemed to pass right through Mel, as if she wasn't even there. He nodded and turned his face back to Amandine. Holding Dumpling in one arm, he reached down and offered her a hand. It was cold against her palm as he helped her up.

"Is that why — no, there's no time. We have to try and revive the others and escape." Mel shook her head.

Amandine shivered and tried to put Fredderick's odd behavior out of her mind as she brushed frost from her clothes with numb fingers. "What about Imri and Blueknot?"

"The fae that attacked us has them. Blue was down. Maybe dead. Imri told me to escape, and I listened." Mel returned to where Ragall lay and felt his neck for a pulse. "What I don't understand is how that thing followed me back to camp. It had Ko. I stabbed it through the center from behind, where its vital organs are. I have killed frakklin before. It was *dead*."

Amandine gripped the hand that had touched the monster's tentacle. "Yes. It was dead, sah. I... could tell. But something was... I... I don't know how to describe it. Inside it. Making it move, like a puppet."

I see you now. The memory of the voice she had heard when touching the monster made Amandine shudder.

"How–" Mel began, but then she took a deep breath. "Godsworn. Ravenex. Makes sense. But answer true, was it you?"

"Me?" Amandine asked incredulously. "I have no idea how to do anything with... this!" She gestured emphatically at her neck. "Even if I *could* make dead things move, I wouldn't. That's *wrong*. Ravenex is peaceful transition. Not... whatever that was!"

"It never tried to grab you. Not once," Mel said.

Fredderick spoke. His voice was cold, emotionless. "You are a foolish bitch."

Mel's expression became angry and she opened her mouth, but her one eye grew wide as Fredderick slowly raised his hand and extended his fingers.

"Stop it!" Amandine shrieked. She slapped his hand down and pushed him away. "What is wrong with you, Fredderick!"

He turned from them without another word, stroking Dumpling.

Mel slowly knelt and picked up her sword from where she had dropped it. Her eyes never left Fredderick. "Peace, magus... or whatever you are. I am no threat to her." She turned to Amandine. "So, what do we do now, little godsworn?"

Amandine blinked in surprise. Mel was asking *her*. "I... I have no idea." A tired feeling came over her. This was all too much. Too much for just her to deal with. And now Mel, the veteran Seeker, was asking her what *she* thought they should do? All Amandine wanted was a nap. And a bath. And maybe a hot cup of tea. She wanted to feel safe, and surrounded by people who trusted her. As she glanced between them all, she found none of that. Mel's suspicion. Fredderick's strange, icy indifference. Herric's bald fear.

Meow.

Grendel emerged from her satchel, where he had apparently been hiding, the little coward. He headbutted her legs and she picked him up. His furry, warm body lessened the chill she was feeling from Fredderick's magic. She buried her nose in his fur and he began to purr.

"Then, we have to leave. Possibly without these two if they can't be roused. None of us can carry them. Staying here is not an option," Mel said.

"You would just abandon them?" Amandine asked.

"Not by choice. By necessity of survival. Whatever is brewing down here is beyond us. The *Ur'Mord* and the Seeker's Guild need to be warned."

There was a cough. Amandine saw Ko sit up from where he had been laid out.

"Sunlit warriors, please," he wheezed. "Do not abandon my people. It must be stopped before it can grow. You, child who can touch Those Outside. We need you. The Night Mother spoke through you. It cannot be chance that I was set on my course. It is not chance that you are here now." He coughed again and clutched his side with his twisted arm. "Please."

Amandine considered for a moment and walked over to him.

"Careful," Mel said.

"If you mistrust him so much, Mel, why did you save him?" Amandine asked. "Ko, give me your hand."

He reached up with his free hand and clasped hers. As she pulled him to his feet, she felt his emotions wash over her. Anxiety, fear, sadness, loss... hope. Tiny and flickering, like a candle at the end of its wick.

"Do you really trust me?" Amandine asked, still holding his hand.

"Yes."

It was the truth. She could feel it. There was no guile in him. He was exactly what and who he had always professed to be. He *was* afraid. Mel had been right about that. Not of them, but that they would betray his trust. His hope. Snuff out that tiny flame in his heart.

"Take me there," Amandine said.

"Wait, what?" Mel said, aghast.

"I am not as mercenary as you. I won't abandon hope because of fear. At least for a little while, I *must* walk the path before me. The walls are stone, and making my own path would take more strength than I have."

Ko nodded. Despite his pain, he smiled. She sensed his relief and felt the spark of hope grow stronger.

"*I'm* the foolish bitch?" Mel spat, making a rude gesture. "Mage, your little bird has me beat by a yarn!"

Fredderick turned to look at her, but said nothing, his face expressionless.

"I belong to no one, and I resent the implication." Amandine released Ko's hand. "If you need to run, Mel, then do so. I won't. But please, don't leave them behind. They're your friends. They need you. Ko, can you walk?"

He nodded, his strange skeletal expression twisted in pain, but Amandine didn't doubt his resolve.

"And what if you run into something else like that?" Mel pointed to the slowly melting pile of frost-covered tentacles, flesh, and the sheet of ice it all sat on.

"It will not touch her," Fredderick said over his shoulder.

Amandine hated the lack of warmth in his voice. What had happened to him?

Mel threw her hands up in the air, but offered no further retort.

"Go with her, Herric. Warn your people," Amandine said.

Herric nodded as he shot nervous glances toward Fredderick.

"Lead the way, Ko," Amandine said. She picked up her satchel and backpack. Once Grendel was safely stowed, she and Fredderick followed the fae into the darkness. She looked back as they walked. Mel was still watching them, framed by the dim, flickering light of the warmer. She shrank behind them until all Amandine could make out was the glow of the smoldering oil. Soon, even that was swallowed by the shadows.

You and We

"The MacDarren Highway is the Olgothian name for the network of deep tunnels, old lava tubes, mines and other passages that once stretched from the Great Deep beneath Anvilroot to the Vault of Adriss in the Sky Barrier Peaks; the mountain range on Olgothia's Western border with Zulathia. No longer safe as a trade route, the Highway was overrun after the War of Shadows and while all of the major Ur'nyre *still make attempts at reclaiming parts of it, the vast majority remains unnavigable and perilous."*

- Lecture Notes, First Starday, Low Winter 1202

AMANDINE DIDN'T KNOW how long they had been walking. She hadn't slept during their brief encampment and the lack was wearing her down. At first she had tried to track time by silently humming a song to herself in her head. It was a love song that Kivel used to sing, but it didn't take long for the repetition of it to start giving her a headache. She didn't know any of the words anyhow.

She blinked sleepily and stumbled. Fredderick caught her by the shoulders and kept her from falling.

"Be careful. The floor here is uneven."

His voice was still oddly monotone, but he wasn't wrong. The relatively smooth walls and floors of the old volcanic cysts and tunnels had been replaced by fractured rock that was cracked and broken along the lines of its strata. Thick veins of white crystal striped the walls. They seemed to soak in the blue tinted light from Fredderick's spell so that they glowed and shimmered as the trio walked past.

Amandine's mind drifted. She tried to remember what the sun looked like, but it felt far away, even in her imagination. Dumpling trotted ahead of them, sniffing at the bits of crystal and stone. She tried to guess what he was thinking. That he acted so much like a dog, when he really wasn't, continued to baffle her. Why? She still had so many questions, and Fredderick's behavior since waking up worried her.

His hands caught her again before she stumbled into a stalagmite. "You're going to hurt yourself."

With a deep breath, Amandine shook her head to try and clear it. Goddess, she was *so tired*. She didn't think she'd ever been this exhausted in her life. Even after the fight with the skellix, there had been a pause, a respite. When was the last time she had actually slept? In the oubliette? How long had she been asleep? What day was it, even?

"I need to stop a moment." Amandine put her hand on the wall. "Please."

Ko halted and looked back at them. "How long do you need? Time is against us. If so many of the Kin are under its control, then it may already be too late."

"Kin? You mean the *Iskrix* and other fae as well?"

Ko nodded.

"Your haste will injure her," Fredderick said.

"I'm fine, Fredderick," Amandine said, pushing him away. "I am just tired."

"Forgive me. My anxious behavior is personal in nature," Ko said. "We can let you rest. Briefly."

"Personal how?" Amandine asked.

"My child. My son. Sabo. He was chosen, like you, like his mother before him, to speak for Those Without. It is a great honor. But the melding was flawed. What inhabits him is not, completely, the Dark Lady. The minds of those he touches... they become lost."

"That's awful," Amandine whispered, turning away. "I'm sorry, sah."

"I am hopeful that the goddess may act through you to rescue him. Rescue us."

Show the child to the door.

Amandine shook the voice from her mind and slumped against the wall. "I will still help, sah, if I can. My feelings tell me this is the right thing to do, but if there is another creature like that frakklin, I don't know if I'll be able to do anything." She leaned her head back against the rough stone and closed her eyes. She felt Grendel stick his head out of the satchel and nudge her hand, so she stroked him while she rested her eyes. A warm contentment radiated from the cat, even though he was hungry. Amandine was too. She hadn't even tasted the nibbles she had made...

Meow.

A cold nose. A rasping tongue. Amandine opened a bleary eye. It was dark. She was lying on her side. But how? She had been against the wall, just closed her eyes for—

Amandine sat up with a start. "I fell asleep? How long..." Her voice trailed off. Fredderick was seated against the wall across from her, Dumpling on his lap. He had attached his blue-white mage light to a rock near his feet. Ko was nowhere to be seen.

"Fredderick, where's Ko?" A feeling of dread began to creep up her spine.

"He left," Fredderick said without looking up at her.

"Why? When?" Amandine stood and peered down the dim tunnel. "How long ago?"

"Hard to tell time here. A few bells, maybe?"

"A few bells? By the Night Mother's Hair!" Amandine quickly checked to make sure she still had all of her things and stood up. "Why didn't you wake me!"

"I tried, you wouldn't wake up."

"And you let him just leave? Did he say why he was leaving?"

"No."

Her head spun. Despite the rest, she was still exhausted. "This is really bad, Fredderick, we need to find him!" She bent down to lift Grendel into the satchel. Fredderick didn't move.

"What are you doing?" she asked.

"You shouldn't go further," Fredderick said. "I can feel it now. Waiting. It knows you're here. It's hungry."

"Feel it? I have no idea what you're talking about. You've been acting strange since you were hurt, Fredderick. What is wrong with you? You're scaring me!"

Fredderick and Dumpling looked up at her. They moved their heads together in unison. Their eyes locked with hers and the creeping chill Amandine had been feeling spread up her neck and into her chest.

"What have you done to him?" she whispered.

"I protect him. We are one. His death would wound me. Wound us. I wish him no harm. I wish myself no harm."

"Then let him have his own body."

"We cannot. He is weak. Hurt. He was close to death and his mind suffers. I was asked to do this, I did not take."

"How do I know you're not lying to me?" Amandine slowly backed away.

"We do not lie to you, She Who Makes Wonderful Tastes. He wishes you to be his mate. Your death would harm us. I protect you from harm. I protect us from harm."

His mate? Amandine's insides recoiled at the thought of the demon watching through Fredderick's eyes when he had kissed her. When he had touched her. "That danger has passed. Even though he asked—please, let him go."

"He did not ask. You did. He agreed."

"I—what?"

"You asked that I not be a dog. That I be useful. I am not a dog. I am useful."

Amandine felt sick. She had done this? "I didn't mean—"

"We agreed. This was the best way. You are sad. That is not a good taste."

With a deep breath, Amandine closed her eyes and ran her hands through her hair. This was a nightmare. What was she going to do?

"You should not go further," Fredderick said again.

"And going back solves what?" Amandine asked, opening her eyes. "No. You would just be executed."

"We would hide."

"Would you? They found you pretty fast last time. No. I am going. Even... even if it kills me. This is the path before me. The way out of this mess. One way or another."

Fredderick and Dumpling continued to just stare at her. Amandine couldn't take it anymore. She turned and walked away.

No one followed.

Dragon's Egg

"Who are the Unnamed Court, you ask? Thousands of years ago, shortly after Emergence and the loss of the Summer Home, all of my people lived as one group. This Court went by different names, depending on whom you asked, but in the North, we referred to it as Itlethlial, the Ingathering. Alas, as with all peoples, our differences in philosophy caused this group to splinter. It was informal at first, but as the centuries wore on, the informal cliques became more stratified, more distinct. Fae in my lineage adapt to the environments they dwell in, so physical changes had also been occurring—skin, hair, eyes, and senses all adapted to our chosen homes. When Queen Sil passed on nearly five thousand years ago, the last vestiges of the Ingathering disintegrated and the Courts as they exist today formed. The Court of Breaking Dawn in the forests of Serentia. The Court of Evergreen, in the Sky Barrier Mountains. The Court of Azure Waves, keepers of the four seas. The Court of Blades, who humans call the Grey Elves, in the lands adjacent to old Bolathvia and the Conflux. The Court of Verdant Titans in the dense jungles to the South, wild and free. Which brings us back to your question: this was also when the Erestral estranged themselves from the greater collective and retreated into the depths. They chose the darkness of their goddess instead of Light and Grace, and we all mourn for them."

- Lecture Notes, Second Fireday, High Winter 1202

"SO THIS MUST be a *pondo*," Amandine said to herself.

Glowing moss dimly illuminated the long cavern. Her Grendel-vision allowed Amandine to make out the details. There were wide shallow pools of water covered in a thin film of algae. Dozens of varieties of mushrooms covered the walls and grew in strips of humus along the floor. They had gone wild with neglect, but still seemed to grow in somewhat orderly rows and circles. A home, carved out of the living stone, was inset into a wall. It had a single round window. The gray mushroom-wood door had mostly rotted away, and a peek inside revealed more decaying furniture and stone fixtures. The entire farm had the feeling of something old. No one had tended this place in a very long time.

From where she had lost Ko, there had been only one viable path to where she was now. There had been a handful of offshoots that led to precipitous drops, dead ends, or looped back to the main tunnel. More than once, she had narrowly avoided falling to her death down one of the steep sinks, primarily thanks to Grendel's enchantment.

"He had to have come through here, Gren. Do you think you can tell where he went?"

Grendel's ears twitched as he walked along in front of her. His ambling route through the underground farm seemed aimless, but his tail and ears told her he was looking for something. Maybe food, maybe Ko, as she had asked. She continued to follow and let him work. Four exits led from the cavern, including the one through which she had arrived. Eventually she would have to pick a direction, but she needed some clue, some way to narrow down the search.

A patch of mushrooms climbing the wall caught her eye.

"Forest buttons? Down here?" she asked herself. Carefully, she plucked one. The shape was right, and the smell. She pried the bulb open to examine the fins—brown fins were safe, black meant it was a ghost button and inedible. The faint light of the moss let her see that they were brown.

"Thank you, Serand," Amandine said as she wiped the button free of the sludge it had been growing in and popped it in her mouth. It was just a button mushroom. Not even cooked. But right then it tasted like a sweet—like the most succulent morsel. She swallowed and picked a dozen more, cramming them in her pockets, then ate four more off the wall.

Grendel walked up to her. She hadn't even noticed him leave after discovering the food. He had a small animal in his mouth. It looked sort of like a giant cricket, but had fur. It emanated a faint sulfurous smell.

"Ewww. Well, I mean, ok. If that suits you."

Meow.

"I get it, mice are better, but we both have to make do, right?"

She stroked him to renew her sight, then let him eat his prize while she explored the *pondo* further. There were signs of an animal pen against one wall, but like the door and the furniture, the gray planks had all but disintegrated and now served as beds for even more mushrooms. She scanned the ground for footprints, for anything that might indicate where Ko had gone.

As she searched, Amandine began to hum to herself. The tune had no words, only melody. It just seemed to come to her as she moved through the notes, as if she was following along with–

She heard it. Music so faint, so soft, that if not for her enhanced hearing, she would have missed it. The tune she was humming wasn't just coming to her, she was following along! Amandine stood perfectly still, closed her eyes and tried to focus.

"There…"

Amandine stepped in the direction of the song, listening as she went.

"Definitely there!"

The passage leading to the music was an open cleft. It would be too narrow for her backpack. With a pang of regret, Amandine unslung it and dropped it on the floor. "If I get killed doing this, I won't need it anyway, right?"

Grendel ran through her feet and into the passage ahead of her. Amandine turned sideways and began squeezing through. It was a tight fit in places. She tucked her knife up under her arm to keep it from catching. A button on her coat was clipped off and she couldn't bend over to fetch it. She was incredibly glad for the wrap under her shirt. Dena had been absolutely right. Thinking of Dena brought on a pang of sadness. Amandine missed her terribly. Her bad jokes, her kind advice, her cheerful smile. Even those painful, tiring training sessions. If she lived through this, Amandine vowed she would never complain about one again.

Sucking in her breath to make herself as thin as possible, Amandine pushed through the last few spans of the cleft. She gasped in relief when the walls parted into a wider crevasse. Water trickled from somewhere above. The darkness over her head stretched past where even her eyes could see. Grendel sat a short distance away. Amandine took a moment to catch her breath. When she started to approach him, Grendel turned and continued to lead. The walls of the split were craggy and uneven, as if the hands of a giant had torn the very bedrock asunder. The floor angled down in the middle, creating a shallow runnel that collected the dripping water. It flowed in the direction she was walking. The music was clearer now. It echoed, haunting and mournful, off the stone surrounding her.

"So beautiful, but so sad," Amandine whispered. Even speaking low, her words seemed to reverberate.

Meow.

Grendel's voice rang out like a gong. It bounced along the ridges and clefts like a feline chorus. The music stopped.

"Gren!" Amandine hissed. "I am trying to foll—wait. If they stopped it means whoever is singing can hear you, doesn't it? We're close."

Amandine pressed herself against a wall and continued cautiously down the cleft. Slowly, the singing began again. She was close now. A light flickered in her vision in the distance. A torch or lantern? No, it was the wrong color. It reminded her of the ball of light Fredderick could make. Thinking of him, of how she had left him behind, brought another pang—of guilt this time, but what else could she have done? The demon was obviously more interested in what it needed for itself than her, or Fredderick, or anything else. She couldn't help him, had no idea how to even begin helping him. Amandine sighed. She would be lucky if she could help herself, as things stood. She felt an urge to continue on, despite her melancholy. The mark on her neck seemed to throb in time with her breathing, in time with the song.

The floor began to slope up. Water pooled and seeped away down a thin crack to one side. The illumination spilled from an opening at the top of the rise. It was blue-white and pulsed faintly, like a heartbeat. The rise was steep, but Amandine gritted her teeth and began to climb.

Her arms and legs burned as she approached the top. The source of the light was a crack in the ceiling above her. Small sparkling lights reflected on the stone around her. The singing was loud now, as if it were just in another room, many voices joined together in a haunting chorus that tugged at her heart. Amandine pressed herself flat against the stone to rest her arms. Just a little bit further. Grendel lay down next to her, his tail swishing. His eyes focused, like hers, on the light ahead.

"Ok, Gren," she whispered. "Quietly. Let's see who it is."

She crawled slowly on her belly up the last few spans, trying not to dislodge any stones that might give her away. Amandine peeked up through the crack into the chamber beyond, and had to suppress a gasp.

Once, on a trip through the markets in Artemis, she and the other Bone Guardian apprentices had passed a cart selling "dragon's eggs." They weren't actually eggs, but oblong rocks made of boring gray and black mottled stone. But when carefully split with a hammer and chisel, the insides revealed a hollow filled with crystals. Blue, green, red, purple, yellow. Every color one could imagine, sometimes blended like a rainbow. She hadn't been able to stop looking. It took the Sister in charge three tries to finally get her attention and haul her away by the arm.

The chamber above her was like those eggs, but the size of a townie house. Jagged crystals gleamed in the light cast by half a dozen glowing spheres, identical to Fredderick's, affixed to various outcroppings. The lower half, past where she was peeking, was bowl-shaped. All of the floor crystals had been demolished and ground smooth, making the surface gleam like polished glass. A wide gash in the far wall led into darkness. Two hulking creatures, with long sinuous bodies, guarded the far opening. Their narrow, fanged, black-scaled faces were turned away from her into the dark, watchful and silent as death.

The rest of the chamber was filled with people. Most were pale, blue-skinned fae like Ko. Their hands were raised, along with their voices, as the song she had been hearing filled the air. There were others as well, *mord* dressed in tattered rags, black skinned *Iskrix* in intricate robes of silk and scales. Even more that she did not recognize. Long necked creatures with humanoid bodies and scales like lizards. Small winged people that floated like butterflies...

Imri. She stood near the center, her hands raised. Her voice joined with the others. Blueknot was there as well. Her face was battered. Blood soaked her bright yellow hair, but, like Imri, she sang with her arms outstretched. And then there was Ko. He stood directly behind the figure seated in the middle of the chorus.

It was a child. A fae child. His blue, translucent skin was stretched tight over an emaciated frame. His hair was merely wisps of white that barely covered his scalp. Amandine could see his internal organs. Blood pumping through him, air filling his lungs. The musculature and bones were familiar, almost human, but not quite. It hadn't occurred to her before now that fae might look different on the inside than humans. At least a little bit. He sat cross-legged, facing towards her, his eyes closed.

The boy said a few words in elvish. Although they seemed a whisper, it filled the room. The singing stopped. Ko stepped aside from the child, and faced the crack where Amandine hid. He spoke, but the voice that emanated from him was not his. The grating, discordant quality of the fae's speech was amplified. The crystals around the chamber seemed to quiver, as if every syllable shook them.

"God-child. Speaker for the Night Mother. I see you. I have felt you since the Mother spoke through your flesh."

The child opened his eyes. They were pale blue-white, nearly colorless.

"Come to me, Amandine."

A Darkling Thing

"I will not honey-coat it: being a Speaker is perilous, daughter. While the status seems to confer long life and good health to those blessed with it, you are nevertheless mortal and can die, whatever the voices of the gods might seem to be telling you. It's not only the gods that should concern you, however. Speakers serve as focal points for the faithful. Many will rely on you, ask you for answers that are sometimes hard to give. Those outside the Church often view powerful Speakers as threats, and more than one Speaker has met their end by an assassin's knife. For now, you will continue as you are in secret, my heart: Dedicated and no more. But eventually your blessing will need to be revealed to the wider faith, and it will demand much of you."

- Letter from Mother Greymist Jarl to her daughter and former student, excerpt

AMANDINE CLIMBED OUT of the crack and stood. The air in the chamber was oddly warm, but despite that, she felt cold. Those eyes. Was this a demon? Was this what they actually were like?

"Who are you?" Amandine asked. She spoke the words in a steady voice, even though she was shaking on the inside.

"Names are irrelevant," the voice coming from Ko intoned. "But this one was called Sabo. You have courage. It is a trait the Mother favors."

"If I come to you, will you release these people? Will you let them go?"

The boy's head cocked slightly sideways as if in confusion. "Would you remove your fingers if someone asked you? Your hand? You are not here to trade."

"They have done nothing to you."

"Correct. Some tried. They are not strong enough. They could and can do nothing against me. Come."

"What if I don't?"

"You will. This is the path before you."

Amandine took a step forward and stopped. "What is it you want from me?"

In unison, every person in the room turned from Sabo to face Amandine. Their feet struck the floor together like a drum.

"You will come to me, or be brought to me. It is the same."

"Answer my question!"

"You," Ko hissed in the discordant voice. "I want you."

Amandine took another step forward. "For what reason? What is it I can give you?"

"I grow, as all things do, in all that is. This form can not reach the sunlit world. It is weak. You will replace it."

Her hands began to shake. He—it—wanted her? To become her so it could leave this place?

"I refuse," Amandine whispered.

"You can not. This is your path."

She took another step towards the child. The compulsion to draw near was so strong, she couldn't control it. Amandine tried to reach for her knife, but her fingers wouldn't grip the handle. They slid uselessly off of it as if it were greased. Her feet continued to move, as if she were sleepwalking.

"Yes. Good," the voice crooned.

You are the guidepost.

The thought came unbidden to her mind. Her vague memories of the night that Ravenex had spoken to her snapped into focus.

"If this is my path," she said as she approached, "it's yours as well."

"Truth. Our paths shall join. Become one."

"No. There is always more than one path."

"Amandine!"

Fredderick's voice cut through the dream-like haze clouding her mind. She heard steel striking stone and then a clap like thunder. Voices shouted. The snake-like creatures guarding the entry moved in a frenzy. They snapped and bit at something she couldn't see behind the crowd of people in the crystal chamber. A feral roar shook the air.

"They mean nothing."

The voice pulled at Amandine's mind. She felt herself sliding back into the haze like a person drowning in quicksand. "No..."

You are the dreaming.

Ravenex's words once again rang in her thoughts. How did one become a dream? What were dreams? She was close to Sabo now. His wide, pale eyes stared up into hers. He looked so small, but there was something large within him, something too big to comprehend, and yet...

"You are a child," Amandine whispered.

Bring the child to the door.

She had a vague sense of motion around her. The people in the chamber were moving. Away from her, towards something.

Sabo stood. He was nearly Amandine's height but so thin. His arms were bones, covered in skin. He raised one and touched a soft, cold palm to her forehead.

A connection began to form, like she had done in the oubliette with Dumpling. There was no asking permission this time, though. Sabo's—the demon's—mind crept through hers like oil soaking through a dishrag. Amandine tried to resist it, but it was like trying to will fire not to be hot—water not to be wet. She was powerless to stop it.

Another deafening roar shook the fog that had overtaken Amandine's mind. A huge form crashed through the gathered people, straight towards her. With an effort, Amandine managed to focus her eyes. It was Tobe.

His arms swung, knocking aside fae and *mord* that tried to stop him. Ko stepped between Sabo and the huge man, only to be struck by one of his giant fists and knocked to the floor, senseless.

Sabo turned and spoke in elvish. Amandine didn't understand, but at the same time, heard the voice, once spoken by Ko, now echoing in her mind.

"You will not interfere, That Which Is Strength."

Amandine knew what was going to happen instantly, felt the demon's intentions as clearly as if they were her own. "No! Tobe, don't! Get away! Away!"

Tobe loomed over Sabo, his eyes bulging, his breathing like a blacksmith's bellows. The vine markings writhed and twisted across his skin. Massive hands reached for the fae child.

Sabo extended a frail arm and placed his palm against the godsworn's chest. Tobe gasped as Amandine felt him die. Like a candle being blown out. His eyes became vacant, glass-like. His arms sagged and the vines stopped moving and began to vanish from his skin. With a rattling exhalation, he dropped to his knees, and then fell sideways to the floor.

"No!" Amandine screamed.

She could see Mel now, and Ragall, charging across the room to her. Fredderick was with them. No, they needed to stay away! She knew what the child was and they didn't. She and the demon were linked now, nearly one.

"Please," she cried. "By the Goddess, stay back. Don't touch him!"

It was an effort to make her arms do what she wished, but Amandine raised them to either side of Sabo, palms out as if to push them away. Mel stopped. The others did as well. Amandine felt the fog returning to her mind. She knew it was useless to fight it.

"Goddess," she prayed. "I don't know what to do…"

Sabo turned back to her, ignoring the Seekers. He didn't need to fear them. He was Death, and the living could not defeat that. Struggling against it only made it seek you faster.

Show him the door.

The small cold palm pressed against her head again. Translucent, frail fingers touched both of her temples. Her scar began to throb. She could feel it—the demon who had once been Sabo. It was cold. Hungry. Alone.

"I'm sorry for you," Amandine said. "To be abandoned like this. I'm an orphan too."

There was no reply. She felt a chill infusing her body, her feet and legs began to go numb.

Show him the door.

It was not a memory. The voice was faint, but it was not hers. "Where? Where is the door?" Amandine thought desperately.

You have passed through it once before. When we last spoke. The key is in your pocket…

"No," Sabo's voice said in her mind. "You are mine, not hers any longer. I have claimed you."

Amandine reached into her pocket. It was full of mushrooms. The chill had crept up to her knees and was spreading to her back. Her head was pounding now, blurring her vision. Willing her fingers to work, she grasped a handful of the forest buttons and pulled them from her jacket.

In her palm sat a collection of small red and yellow capped mushrooms. They were not forest buttons. How? And then Amandine remembered Kiln. The stone in the forest by the river. The mushroom that in her dream had been a Lady's Slipper. It had become a poisonous Death Head. She understood now. Slowly, painfully, she raised a mushroom to her lips. The others tumbled to the floor from her numb fingers.

"What are you doing?" Sabo's voice demanded.

Amandine took a bite. "Showing you the door," she thought back to him.

Her arm jerked, dropping the mushroom, as something took control of it. She felt her jaw clench, she couldn't chew. Holding her breath, Amandine swallowed the bite.

She felt him withdrawing, pulling away from her mind, but Amandine stubbornly held on. Like a rope-tug game between her will and his.

"No, no!" Sabo shouted into her thoughts while the child's body shook his head and repeated the words in discordant Elvish.

Amandine felt a burning in her stomach, in her throat. The bile began to rise, but she forced it down. Sabo's partial retreat enabled her arms again. She reached out and pulled the child into a gentle embrace.

An emptiness began to fill her mind, her vision darkened at the edges, and the pulsing, dull pain from her scar began to fade. The world became fractured, like a pane of glass shattered on the floor. Her knees buckled and she slumped to the ground, pulling Sabo with her.

"It's all well," she whispered as the demon flailed within their joined souls. "I will take you. You will not be alone. We will go together."

Weeping filled her thoughts. Tears ran down her cheeks. The burning spread to her chest. Amandine gasped for breath and felt her heart begin to slow. Voices shouted. But they were far away. In another place. She was darkness. Darkness was her.

"Thank you."

The voice was not the demon's. It was not the goddess' either. It was tiny and faint. Barely a whisper in her mind. And then it too faded, and passed into the dark.

Green Dress

"People used to ask me what being godsworn is like. I would often use these moments to play the dumb mute, to my shame. But I ask, how can one fully describe it? When I am Berindor, I am fury incarnate. I am rage. I am violence. And when I am not, I contain it all. It's like holding the lid on a pot down as it tries to boil over, burning your flesh all the while. But Berindor is Strength, and so I endure it. To not, to simply give up, is not Strength. Further, it is not me. So many of those touched by the gods succumb to doubt, fear, and eventual madness. I believe it's because they are unwilling to accept the aspects of themselves that reflect the god that has chosen them. I met someone recently. A young girl who is still struggling to find that acceptance of herself. I want to help, but there is none to be given. Two different gods have touched her. A thing so rare, I am at a loss to say I have ever heard of it before now. I hope she succeeds. I hope she survives. I will do my best to see that she does both."

- The journal of Tobenick Freeman, final entry

PURRRRRRRRRR.

Amandine was someplace warm. A waft of heated air flowed over her, reminiscent of Manor L'Eau's cellar. She left her eyes closed. The darkness was nice. There was a weight on her chest that rumbled like Grendel purring. That was nice too, but she wasn't ready to face the afterlife yet. Soon enough. She would be here for the rest of time, right? That's how it worked, wasn't it? A few moments more wouldn't hurt either way.

Something creaked, like a chair with loose joinery. Curiosity made her open one eye. She was in a bed, with heavy blankets tucked up to her chin. Serand sat in a chair next to her, reading a book.

"I'm glad you're here too," she whispered to him. "The afterlife would be lonely without a friend."

Serand looked up from his book. He appeared older than she remembered, more worn around the edges. Was that extra gray in his hair? That seemed unfair. You should be able to look however you liked when you were dead.

He dropped his book. It fell to the floor with a leathery slap. Amandine frowned. Serand was always very careful with his books. That seemed completely out of character for him. He leaned over and stroked her forehead. His face broke, and tears fell from his cheek onto hers. Was he weeping?

"Don't cry. It's well. I'm here now. Are my parents here too? I really want to meet them," she said in a scratchy voice as she reached a hand out of the heavy blankets to wipe his face.

Serand laughed through his tears. "No. No, fingerling, they ain't here. Yer not dead, is why."

The weight on Amandine's chest shifted. Grendel's face appeared over the lip of the covers and he touched his nose to hers.

"I'm... not dead?" But she had felt it so clearly. Her life fading, her heart slowing. The cold and dark and...

"Oh, Goddess!" she tried to sit up, but had barely moved before Serand gently pushed on her shoulder, pressing her back down. She felt so weak that it took him almost no effort.

"You *are* naked under all that wrap, though," he said, drying his eyes. "Please jus' lay there a bit longer. Until the doctors say it's safe fer ya ta get up."

Amandine lifted her blankets a finger's width and peeked. Her face turned red and she dropped them. It was true. Not a stitch.

"How? How am I not dead?" she asked, if only to distract herself from her embarrassment.

Serand shook his head. "That's between you an' Ravenex, little godsworn. I have no colorless idea. But I'm certainly glad she left ya here fer a time yet."

"How... do you know?" Amandine asked softly.

Serand pointed to his neck. "Darkbloom lily. Like a fresh tattoo, from about here ta halfway down yer back. It's still there. That old creature must have had her claws deep in ya ta leave it so long."

Amandine wiped her face with a hand, trying to process everything she was hearing. Grendel began licking her fingers. "So long, you say? How long have I been lying here?"

"Two tendays, more or less." Serand sat back in his chair again. He seemed to move stiffly, as if he was in pain. "That's just here, mind. It took a few days fer them Seekers what hauled ye out o' the Deeps ta make it back ta Anvilroot."

Amandine stroked Grendel as she stared up at the ceiling. It was solid stone. There was only one place she could think of that featured a ceiling like that. "We're still in Anvilroot, aren't we?"

"Yup."

It was then that she finally believed him. This wasn't some pre-death fever dream. She was alive. She had survived. How?

"And how are you here?" Amandine asked, "I saw you take that wound, and then fall into the river. You... never came up."

"Ah, well, I guess I'm a bit rusty af'er all these years. Careless ta let such an amateur stick a blade in me. I got free o' that colorless tusker and surfaced, but I were half a yarn downriver by then. Ta think that lot had a tamed wumpus. I've seen some strange shite, lass, but that was up there."

"We moved so slow. How did you not get to Myron's Bend to meet us?" Grendel began to purr again and lay down so that his tail kept flicking Amandine in the face.

"Can't run on a bleeding leg. Hells, I could barely walk. Bastard got me good, but not in the big vein. Jack's own luck fer sure." He sucked at his teeth for a moment before continuing. "I eventually bumped into some travelers on the Obsidian Highway, and they got me ta Myron's Bend, but you and Fred were long gone by then. I took ill with a fever. Too much strain, wound weren't properly cleaned. Near cost me the colorless leg. I stayed at some refuse bin called The Watery Crossroads while I recovered. The food was awful. I made the snivelin' weasel who ran the place let me cook my own meals."

Amandine laughed weakly. "Yes, I've been there. The food really was disgusting. Fredderick won a bet on me against that fellow's stew."

"Heard about that!" Serand said, chortling to himself. "Folk were still gossipin' 'bout it when I arrived. One fellow even claimed it cured his back aches for over a tenday."

"Well, given recent events, that might have been true," Amandine said after spitting Grendel's tail out of her mouth. He draped it across her nose instead.

"Yeah, well... hmm... yup, it might have been hadn't it?" Serand sounded thoughtful.

"Um... where's Fredderick?" Amandine asked. She flicked Grendel's tail. "Would you please, sah!" she scolded.

"I was wonderin' when ye might ask about him. He's stayin' in Greyrock Falls fer the moment. Anvilroot made the lad downright jumpy. We can go visit once yer up an' about."

Amandine nodded. She didn't know if she wanted to visit him yet or not, but she was glad that he'd made it out of the Crystallians' reach.

"I'll go tell the doctors that yer awake. They'll be in a knot fer sure. No one has ever woken up after eating a Death Head. Not that they know of."

"I've done it twice now. I think."

"Best not make a habit of it, all the same." Serand stood, then bent and retrieved his dropped book. He was definitely hurting.

Amandine watched him leave silently, limping on the leg he'd been stabbed in. Moments later, two *mord* doctors entered the room and began poking and prodding her. They asked her to sit up and remove her blankets, which was embarrassing at first, but Tilly had been right. Dwarves didn't care at all about human bits, unless it was for some obscure academic reason, like: "Why didn't this one die from Death Head toxin?"

They finished their examination and the one that spoke Olgothian told her in a heavily accented voice that she was fit to walk, slowly, and should not eat solid foods for another tenday. Amandine waited until they were gone and then carefully hauled herself out of bed and wobbled around the room for a moment. Her legs were unsteady at first from disuse, but seemed to gain strength quickly. She wouldn't be running anytime soon, but she felt confident she could maintain her balance. A few moments later, she found clothing tucked into a footlocker. Her boots were there, and socks, and underclothes and...

"Colorless bastards," she breathed.

With unsteady hands, she lifted the green dress out of the locker and held it in front of her like something dirty. She checked again; there were no other clothes.

She sighed. There was no way she was going to walk out of the room naked. Even if the *mord* were indifferent, Serand might die of shock. Then again, if this was his colorless idea, he might deserve it.

Amandine put on the dress. She hated it. The way it was cut, she couldn't wear a wrap, and the low hemmed neckline exposed far too much of her bust. It bared her shoulders, and her legs were chilly, even with the socks. The fabric hugged her in a way that was wholly unfamiliar and uncomfortable, but it was better than nothing. Something in the pocket poked at her thigh. She dipped her hand inside and fished about. Whatever it was, it was cold metal and had some kind of hasp. Amandine opened her hand after removing it and revealed a small, black-lacquered pin. It was a darkbloom, the symbol of Ravenex. She knew the pin well. Sister Corbin wore one exactly like it.

"Sacred night," Amandine said under her breath. Did that mean Sister Corbin was here? There was no way she would countenance a garment like the one she was wearing, though. Who had pu/t it there? What did it mean?

She tried to put the pin out of her mind, opened the door and stepped out of the room. The beginning of a harsh scolding started to form on her lips. What was Serand thinking, allowing the godsforsaken dress?

"Amy!" Gil cried. The words Amandine had prepared fled her mind. His concerned expression melted into joy as he dashed across the small sitting room and gathered her up in an enormous hug. Tilly sat in a padded chair near the door. She broke into a grin and walked over to add herself to the embrace.

Serand stood by the door with his arms folded. "Hey now. Let her breathe, you two! She's been next ta dead fer over half a cycle!"

"No, don't stop!" Amandine hugged them both tighter. "What in the Goddess' names are you two doing here?"

Gil stepped back and wiped his eyes. "When Fredderick's letters reached Stoneman, it caused a bit of a panic. Half the colorless town wanted to race up here and find you two, it felt like, but Dena talked sense into most of them. I wasn't going to be left behind, though. No way!"

"It's truth!" Tilly added, bouncing on her toes. "Uncle Aran and Master Kale gave me leave to go with him. As if they could have stopped me! I've been of age for years. It was quite tha' trip! I've never slept outdoors before!"

"Who else—" Amandine began.

"When did you get that done?" Gil asked. He pointed to his neck. "It looks like it must have hurt!"

Amandine touched her neck where the godmark was. "Um, yeah, it did, actually. Quite a bit."

Tilly grinned and gestured with her hands as she spoke. "In Zulathia, folks get tattoos to show their life's stories. I recently got a couple too! Don' have nearly sa many as my ma', though, and definitely not sa many as Uncle Aran. Mine 're stupid things, actually. I just got 'em because I was allowed to finally, an' I thought they was pretty."

"They *are* pretty," Gil said. "Whatever your mother thinks."

"Oh? Can I see them?" Amandine asked.

"Oh! Um, well. They ain't someplace I should probably be exposin' in public." Tilly blushed.

Amandine looked at Gil and raised an eyebrow. He suddenly turned red as well and glanced away.

Serand chuckled. "You lot..." he said, shaking his head.

"Don't tease!" Amandine scolded.

"Nah, it's a fine thing, 'specially after so much trouble. You know what else is grand? Herric agreed ta help us. He and his buds will be training those strange critters..."

"Rocktopus," Amandine corrected.

"Aye, those. They'll be trainin' a batch and Wizard Hemm will come collect 'em when it's time. Also arranged fer Stoneman ta get some relief supplies, when the weather allows."

"Oh that's fantastic!"

"Best part is, they won't even charge us a coin. Hammers agreed ta pay fer all of it. Whatever those Seekers did while ya were down there stopped the attacks, and some of the folk gone missin' were even rescued. That crew is gettin' the hero treatment right now. There's rumors that the *Erestral* have retreated from the caves that marked the line between them and the *mord*. Centuries old borders, simply abandoned. Strange winds. What *did* happen down there anyway, 'prentice? I got part of the story from those Seekers, but I'd like ta hear yer account."

Amandine shook her head. She wasn't ready to relive that. Not yet. "I'll tell you later, Serand. I promise."

"Us too?" Gil asked.

His grin made Amandine a bit sad. Gil probably thought it was some grand adventure. Had he already forgotten the skellix? How awful that was? And this had been worse.

"I... I will, but not for a while. Please."

Gil's smile slipped as he seemed to catch her mood. "Ok, Amy. There's no rush."

"Thanks, Gilly."

The door to the sitting room opened and two more people entered. Gil and Tilly both straightened and bowed respectfully. Serand stopped slouching a bit, even if he didn't bow.

"Ah, the doctors told me you had awakened," Mother Jarl said. "Excellent."

Amandine almost didn't recognize her, outfitted as she was in a plain woolen dress and riding boots. The only indication that she was a high ranking priestess was the golden sunrise pendant hanging from a chain around her neck. Her hair was tied up in a simple, pale silver-white bun that reminded Amandine uncomfortably of Sister Corbin. With a serene gaze she surveyed the room, and fractionally inclined her head to Serand. He nodded back.

"Hi, Amandine," Fiona L'Eau said. She was standing next to Greymist wearing a silver and blue dress. Her family's colors. She rocked on her heels and fidgeted with her fingers.

"Mother Jarl! Fiona! You both came as well?" Amandine asked.

"I financed the trip," Mother Jarl said. "You look well, Amandine, all things considered. A bit thin, but well."

"I..." Amandine looked down at her feet. "I should have told you I was leaving. I'm sorry."

Greymist's smile never faltered. "I bear no grudge, Apprentice. I trust the experience was educational?"

Amandine glanced up at her but didn't answer.

"I left you something in the pocket, but I don't see you wearing it," Mother Jarl said.

Reflexively, Amandine's fingers touched the pocket that held the pin. "I... why?" she asked.

"She has marked you. And you have spoken for her. More than once, by the look of it."

Gil and Tilly glanced back and forth at them in confusion. Amandine cleared her throat and gestured to her clothes. "I don't think it goes well with this."

With a smirk, Mother Jarl simply nodded. "No, I suppose it doesn't. Please keep it then."

Amandine bit back any further response. She didn't want the colorless thing, but saying "no" right now seemed out of the question. Her eyes drifted to Fiona. She was bobbing on her toes, looking anxiously at Mother Jarl. The barely contained emotion was such a Fiona-like thing that it made Amandine smile. Greymist stepped back and motioned for Fiona to go ahead.

Fiona bounced forward as Gil and Tilly stepped away. Tilly even bowed slightly. Amandine sometimes forgot, because of their friendship, that Fiona was nobility.

"You do look well," she said. "I am so glad. We feared the worst."

"I'm happy you came all this way, but shouldn't you be in lessons? Because, you know." Amandine wasn't sure if Fiona's recently discovered gifts were common knowledge.

She smiled, extended a finger and scrunched up her face. A moment later, a small ball of light appeared over the tip. It was the size of a coin and glowed with a golden-orange hue. Fiona released her held breath, looking pleased with herself.

"*Soeje* came with us. I've been practicing the entire trip!"

"Mister Green is here too? How many others? Where is he?"

"Oh, that's all of us. Unless Master Kale snuck onto a barge like he was threatening to," Greymist said with a laugh. "I left *Soeje A*—I mean Mister Green, at the Academy with the other scholars. They are discussing that... *thing*." Her mouth twisted into a grimace, the first sign of displeasure Amandine had seen.

"Oh, and what do the learned folk think?" Serand asked.

"What thing?" Amandine added. Fiona, who had been playing with the tiny ball of light, making it bounce from finger to finger, turned to listen as well.

Greymist sighed. "Upon arrival here, and after inquiring after you, we heard a story about how a young human girl had sat in an infamous stone chair in the Magma Ward. That it burned her as she touched it and that when the Crystallians were summoned, she was determined to be a demon and then thrown in prison.

"I had an opportunity to examine this chair, along with, err, Mister Green, and we believe it is a relic of the Reconstruction Era in dwarven history. Predating the

Arrival by at least three centuries. It was intended to reveal demons, or people infested with them. The trouble is, such devices also react to godsworn Speakers. Hence the terrible misunderstanding."

"What?" Gil and Tillandra said in unison. "They threw you in prison, Amy?" Gil added, aghast.

Fiona looked so surprised it almost made Amandine laugh. The tiny ball of light vanished into a wisp of golden vapor. "You're a *godsworn Speaker*? I mean, like *actual* godsworn? Not just the folks who wear the robes?"

Greymist cleared her throat.

With her face flushed red, Fiona turned back to Mother Jarl and bowed. "I'm so sorry!" she squeaked.

"Yes, yes, please, it's all well. Just remember that the ability to create miracles is not a requirement for pious service. Anyone with a love for the gods can do it."

Serand snorted in derision. Greymist frowned at him but did not comment. Instead she said: "I intend to petition the Academy for the chair's removal into the hands of the Divine Conclave. Akradath's scholars can study it, and then see to its destruction, the vile thing. I don't abide demons, but the device is outmoded and cruel compared to the Crystallians' more modern methods."

"Which still marked her wrong," Serand said.

Mother Jarl exchanged glances with him once again. This time Serand relented. "Apologies, sah."

"You can create godsworn miracles, Amy?" Gil asked. He looked like someone had slapped him.

Tillandra stared at Amandine as if she had sprouted horns. "So, um, should we bow or somethin'?"

"Oh Goddess, please don't," Amandine pleaded, her voice almost a whine. "It's all too much as it is. I barely know what I am doing. Just tell people it's a tattoo, yes?"

Tilly looked unsure for a moment, and then she smiled and nodded. "Ok."

Gil also nodded. "Whatever you want, Amy! I won't say a word!"

"Can you walk, apprentice?" Greymist asked. "I have arranged for apartments here for you and Master Brutsche, as well as the rest of us. Young master Stolm has similar accommodations in the fortress town, as was his preference."

"We're staying?" Amandine asked as Serand opened the door and began ushering them outside.

"No help for it, fingerling," Serand said. "The pre-shiv rains have been torrential. Part o' the Obsidian Highway washed out. It's unnavigable past Last Tree. River is flooding and unsafe. The *Ur'Mord* have halted all barges in either direction. We either wait out the storms and hope the roads 're seen ta before Winter, or risk a human crewed barge in the inclement weather."

"An excellent summary, Master Brutsche," Mother Jarl said. "We couldn't move you while you were ailing Amandine, and you will still need time to recover. We may be here for quite a while."

"What about Dena, Serand?" Amandine asked.

"Gettin' word ta her was difficult fer sure, and I miss her," Serand said. "But Green did me a favor and got a message ta her through Wizard Hemm. It'll have ta do for now."

"It cost you a promise of shortbreads didn't it?" Amandine grinned. Serand grunted, but didn't disagree.

As the others filed out the door, Amandine lingered near Serand. "I'm really glad you're alive, sah."

A rare grin crossed Serand's face from ear to ear. "I would say the same for you, Amandine. I really thought—"

She cut him off by throwing her arms around him in a fierce hug, her face pressed into his shoulder. Amandine felt like her heart might burst, but didn't shed a tear, didn't speak. Her tears had been used up when she believed he was dead, gone forever. All she wanted was to hold him a moment and feel him breathing, and how miraculous that felt.

Strong arms and gnarled hands returned the embrace. Serand's breath stirred the top of her hair as he hugged her back, just as tightly. "Yeah, fingerling, me too. Me too."

They departed the hospitaler's grounds and strolled along a broad, paved road near the center of the city. The keep, the one surrounded by the steaming volcanic pool, was close to the campus, and Amandine could see the details in the stonework from here. Grendel ran along ahead of them, as if he were a guide, looking back occasionally to make sure they were all there. As they passed a small park with stone statues of important-looking *mord*, an orange blur dashed out of the shadows and tackled Grendel to the paving stones. Spice loomed over Grendel, swatted him twice more and dashed off again. Grendel gave chase and the two cats vanished back into the stonework.

Amandine laughed and clapped her hands. "Oh! I'm glad he's okay too!"

"Aye, it'll take more than a dunking to put that creature down," Serand said fondly.

"Oh! Amy! I almost forgot!" Gil exclaimed. "I have some news from town. About Heather Mince, the Stockyard Matron!"

"Ohhhh!" Tilly squealed as she bounced in excitement.

"Fine, you tell her," Gil said with a grin.

"Well, the thing is," Tilly began, her face beaming, "Master Birch the animal handler? You know, the one she hired last year? She asked him ta marry her! In fron' of an entire auction crowd. People thought it was a jape, but he agreed!

Kissed her right there in front of about fifty ranchers and merchants. Word got 'round pretty quick. Some folk 're bein' cruel. On account of him bein' Hill Folk and her bein', um... big. But they look *so* happy! I think it's romantic!"

"It really is very sweet," Fiona agreed. "Mother even offered to help pay for a dress fitting, seeing as Matron Mince is an upstanding citizen and finding a tailor to do lace in her sizes will be, ah... challenging."

"Kayla's Heart! Chef!" Amandine's mind rushed back to what seemed another life, when she had last spoken to Heather.

Serand seemed surprised to be addressed by his title so suddenly, and looked over his shoulder at her from where he had been walking ahead with Mother Jarl. "Aye?"

"I need you to teach me how to make a cake."

"You know how to make..."

"No! A very specific one. You made it for a Shiv's End feast. With strawberries and cream and some kind of cheese."

Serand's eyebrows rose to his hairline. "Oh? And how in the hells did ye hear 'bout that thing? I haven't made one o' them in years, not since that Shiv, actually."

"It's Heather's favorite. I made a promise!"

"Is it now," he said with a wry grin. "Well, if'n we can find the ingredients, we can try. It's a trick ta be sure, but we'll have plenty o' time fer trainin', I think."

"A cake made from *cheese*?" Gil wrinkled his nose. "That sounds completely mad."

Gil and Tilly began a good natured argument over what a cake made of cheese might taste like, and Amandine let her mind drift as they walked. This moment felt like waking up from a nightmare. The last several cycles, with all that had happened, were as far away as the sun had been while she was in the Deeps.

"Speaking of dresses," Fiona said softly. "You look very pretty in that one."

"I hate dresses," Amandine said airily.

"Oh... oh." Fiona's face fell. "I... I wanted to bring you a gift, but I didn't know what to buy. I ran into Sunflower when I went to the Gold Hills hamlet one afternoon on a ride and she said that you'd look nice in a green dress..."

Amandine winced. "I knew it!" she hissed. "Of course it was her! Well you got your colorless wish, Sunflower! You'd better not be smirking, wherever you are!"

"I'm sorry," Fiona said.

Guilt settled in Amandine's stomach like a stone. Glancing over at her friend, Amandine realized that the cut of Fiona's dress, with the low shoulders and neckline, was identical to hers. Only the colors differed. "No. No, I'm sorry Fiona. It's lovely. She fooled you, and I'll have a prank or two for her when we get home, but... I really like that you got this specifically for me. Thank you."

Fiona's expression lifted back up. "I meant it. You look wonderful, whether you like wearing it or not. And this too." She brushed her fingers along the night bloom mark to where it vanished into the back of the dress. "I like it, and not just because of what it means. It... suits you."

"Does it?" Amandine mused. "I suppose a dress once in a while would be fine."

The pleased look on Fiona's face made Amandine smile as well. How had she ended up with so many fine friends? She leaned over and whispered to Fiona. "I am not supposed to eat solid food for another tenday, but to hells with that! I haven't had anything but whatever gruel they were forcing down my throat for *two* tendays and I'm *starving*. I intend to sneak out later and stuff myself silly. Are you interested?"

A mischievous grin snuck across Fiona's face.

"Very."

Eternally Yours

"Those who have split their anima with a demon, sometimes known as 'half-demons' or 'changelings' are a rarity amongst Practitioners. Not because they do not lack power. As it happened, a few of those responsible for both the razing of Eastern Olgothia (which created the Sea of Glass) and the creation of the Conflux were changelings. Rather, it is because many changelings do not gain magical ability as part of their pacts. This requires a greater sacrifice on the part of the demon, and such lopsided arrangements are uncommon amongst creatures noted for their lack of empathy. Indeed, many changelings often complete their transformation into full demons within a scant few cycles or years of their pacts. That said, because a demon's true form is pure anima, the stuff of magic itself, the abilities of these unorthodox magi often outstrip those of peers with tens of years more experience in their naturally occurring abilities."

- A Treatise on the Nature of Demons, Changelings, and Elemental Constructs, Of Those Combined, Arentilinanthian of Starlight

AMANDINE LAY UNDER her covers and stared at the stone ceiling. The bed beneath her was made of *korb* and horker hide, the mattress stuffed with fiber also drawn from the giant mushroom-trees. Her wool blankets were sunlit-made, however, and warm.

"Grendel," she called softly.

With a chirrup, Grendel's weight landed on her stomach. She stroked him and the room became visible around her. Simple furnishings of gray wood and a rack of her clothes surrounded the bed. A stone-bead curtain led into the rest of the warren. It had been nearly a cycle since she had woken up in the hospital. She and Chef had accepted rooms in the warren belonging to Norrel, the dwarven sailor from the Silver Mountain whose life she had saved. Mother Jarl had offered them accommodations, of course, but Amandine didn't want to be any more attached to her, or to the Church of Time, than she already was. Furthermore, as Serand had pointed out, refusing such an offer would have been deeply insulting to Norrel and their mate.

Grendel began to purr as she sat up and continued to stroke him. She could have asked for a lantern or candle, but given her shared enchantment with Grendel, she had declined out of respect for her hosts. Dwarves never lit their warrens except on certain occasions. Thin veins of luminescent crystal in the stone walls provided enough illumination to get about even when she didn't have Grendel to hand.

A glance at a small Stone Folk clock on the washstand told her that it was 'third anvil bell,' or 'sixth city bell' by the time reckoning of sunlit peoples.

"We're breakfasting at the Stone Bowl today, Gren," she whispered as she stood up. "Everyone is going to be there, so mind your manners."

Meow.

Amandine and Chef had been using the kitchen at the Stone Bowl, a dining room run by an Olgothian Chef and acquaintance of Serand's, as a place to continue her training. Normally, she would have been there with him already, but today was special. She and the members of Vibrant Dawn were going to be debriefed and honored by the Hammers. It wouldn't do for a noted guest to work in the kitchen at such an event. Amandine was actually grateful for the extra sleep. She was still recovering from her incapacitation and tired easily, but she was also incredibly curious what Chef Brutsche and Chef Polina of Flashing Knives would be serving the varied array of people slated to be present.

She quickly dressed in a clean Apprentice's outfit, slung her *Olatharr* across her chest, and gave herself a once over in the mirror above the basin on the washstand. Her hair was properly trimmed and short again, so it only took her fingers to set it right. She scrubbed her face and hands and then hurried out.

Lekrim, Norrel's mate, called out to her in *Mord-seq* as she passed through the tunnels between chambers.

"*Lok zag na,*" Amandine called back. *I see you.* It was a common *mord* greeting and acknowledgement, and pretty much the only thing she could say in their language without tripping over the syllables.

With a friendly wave, Lekrim emerged from a nearby room and said something else. They were taller than Norrel and kept a longer beard that was intricately braided and decorated with colored beads and small glittering gems. Lekrim said a few words that she didn't comprehend, but it sounded like a question. Amandine also felt a faint twinge of curiosity from Lekrim and managed to guess what it meant.

"I am going to the Stone Bowl for the meeting with the Hammers," Amandine said slowly. She had been trying to teach Norrel and Lekrim the Ologothian language as well, with limited success. Lekrim nodded, smiled, and waved her on. The message had been understood.

Amandine stepped carefully through the warren's central room. Something lay in wait for her there. She could sense the intent. A small form launched itself at her from the shadows. Amandine laughed and dodged, spinning in a circle. One of Lekrim and Norrel's buds, newly arrived from the nursery warrens and yet to earn a name, tumbled past her and quickly sat up, snarling.

"You almost got me that time, sah!" Amandine said as she thumped her chest in a form of dwarven salute.

"*Nog?*" the bud asked as it watched her quizzically. It bared its rows of needle-like teeth.

"Food? Maybe later. You like *sek*, right?"

"*Sek! Nog!*"

Grendel hissed and the tiny *mord* child scurried for cover behind a chair.

"Spoil them," Norrel said in Olgothian as they entered the room.

"No! A reward for a well executed ambush, sah!" Amandine said.

Norrel laughed in the choking wheezy way of dwarves and nodded as his short, bushy beard wobbled with mirth. "Yes. Good."

"I'll be back after eighth city bell!" Amandine called as she departed the warren.

The huge bowl shaped depression that contained Anvilroot spread out before her as Amandine passed the bead curtain that served as the front door. Norrel and Lekrim's home was high on a sloping wall in the Coalbeard district. Steam rose from the volcanic cleft surrounding the Hammer's Citadel, far below in the center of the city. The Stone Bowl was near there, halfway across the depression from where Amandine stood. The view still left her in awe. Anvilroot was easily as large as Artemis, where she had grown up. In some ways she preferred it. Dwarves, by and large, were rough spoken and direct. If you were a friend, they made it known. If you were an enemy... well she had learned the hard way what that was like. It was better, she had decided, to know where one stood.

She took her time walking the streets toward the dining room. The Shiv had begun in earnest and the weather outside had rapidly turned frigid. More than one dwarf or Stone Folk she passed bore the remnants of ice slowly melting from their boots, clothes, or beards. The First Winter was upon the world and wouldn't break for at least three cycles. Then would come the Scorch, where the weather would swing the other way like a heavy bell. Dry heat, persistent sun, and shorter nights would bake the land for another cycle, sometimes two, and then rapidly descend back into Second Winter, the Shiv Winter, before True Spring arrived again.

Her path took her onto a broad avenue that the *mord* had named 'Honor's Trail.' Most non-*mord*, even some of the Stone Folk, called it 'Hammer Street.' Massive, finely chiseled stone statues of past dwarven leaders made ranks along its path. It followed a slightly arcing route from the markets, directly to the central keep and its vaporous moat. The crowds were sparse, this early in the day, but there were still a good number of people using the broad lane as a throughway to the various districts surrounding it. Amandine even passed a curtained palanquin borne by clay and metal automatons. They reminded her of the Stoneman, but smaller, and more ornate. Whoever rode behind the curtain was both wealthy and important.

The Stone Bowl was a single story masonry building off of a side street that lay in the keep's shadow. Coal braziers lit the cobbles, and beneath the dining room's shingle, a second, smaller sign had been hung that read "Private Dine-in, no open tables" in both Olgothian and Dwarven runes.

As Amandine approached the door, Gil and Tilly emerged from a side alley. Both of them were blushing and holding hands. Between Gil's rumpled hair and Tilly leaning in to whisper in his ear, it didn't take much imagination to guess what they had been up to.

"Luminous day, sahs!" Amandine called. She grinned when Gil jumped as if someone had goosed him.

"Amandine!" Tilly only looked surprised for a moment and then wriggled her fingers in greeting. She dropped Gil's hand and gathered her up in a hug. Grendel wove between both of them, purring loudly. "Almost everyone else is already inside! Ne'er see so many fancy lookin' dwarves in ma' life! And I don't know wha' yer Chef and his friend are cookin' but it smells so good!'

Gil crushed them both in his arms. "It's good to see you! It's been almost a tenday!"

"When I'm not training with Chef, I am taking lessons with Mister Green and Mother Jarl on alternating days. The doctors that nursed me have been demanding that I keep visiting them as well. I think my not dying has given them a mystery they want to solve," Amandine said with a laugh.

"Yeah? Well, I am glad you lived, and I don't need to know why!" Tilly said. "Have you met Herric's, um, bud? Orvil?"

"Oh! They're the one who's in the Stone Guard. Yes, Herric mentioned them several times, but we haven't met."

"He's here today in place of his... da'? Mum? What do you call a dwarven parent?" Gil asked as he fumbled for the words.

"It's Sire, at least in Olgothian. I can't pronounce it in *Mord-seq*." Grendel pawed at Amandine's leg and she picked him up. "So Herric didn't come?"

"No. He's busy on his farm, so he sent his kid," Tilly said.

Amandine nodded. "I'd like to meet that *gyre*." She didn't correct Tilly's pronouns. Many humans struggled with *mord* only having a single gender. Amandine had referred to Boomer as 'he' nearly the entire time she had lived in Stoneman before she had learned more.

"He's going to give us jobs, um, of a sort," Gil said.

"Doing what?"

Tilly cut in before Gil could explain. "Well, Gil is strong, and I know how ta fight and he offered to train us like they train recruits for tha Stone Guard!" Tilly bounced on her toes. "We can't get back ta Stoneman and our old jobs 'cause of the colorless Shiv righ' now, and it sounds more fun than sittin' around starin' at all the rocks, yeah?"

"Do the Stone Guard often train non-*mord*?"

"No, he's doing it as a favor to Mother Jarl. And because I think Tilly impressed him." Gil smirked.

"It was jus' a simple staff pattern. It wasn' even the hardest one I know!" Tilly looked away, cheeks turning rosy.

Amandine laughed. "Then I know that *gyre* was impressed. I've seen you training with your uncle too. You're amazing!"

"Thanks, Amandine. I ain't the one that helped save the entire colorless city, though. Wha' you did was truly heroic!"

With a sigh, Amandine felt her mirth squelched a bit. "Yeah, well, someone told me once that most heroics are just accidents you manage to survive somehow. I kind of understand what he meant now. I don't feel all that heroic."

Tilly gave her a look and started to say something, but was interrupted as the palanquin that Amandine had passed rounded the corner. The golems stomped in time as they moved, their feet clanged like gongs on the street's smooth paving stones.

"What in the hells is that?" Gil exclaimed.

The automatons came to a slow stop in front of the Stone Bowl and steadily lowered their burden in a single smooth motion. The curtains parted and the oldest dwarf Amandine had ever seen stepped out. Their hair and beard were shockingly white and the visible skin of their face and hands was gnarled, like old, wrinkled leather. A large silvery hammer with a beveled head, a blacksmith's tool, hung from an ornate gold and gem encrusted belt. The rest of the old dwarf's clothing was made of a pale, gossamer fiber that Amandine recognized as silk from *iknans*, or cave spinners—grub-like creatures that spun webbing like spiders to capture small prey in the tunnels and caverns of the Deeps. It was mainly used as threading due to its strength. To have an entire outfit made from it was more than just extravagant.

With a curious glance at the three of them, the ancient *mord* walked by with a measured pace. They disappeared past the open doors to the dining hall and Tilly leaned over to whisper to Amandine. "Who was *that*?"

"I have no idea." Amandine shook her head.

"That was Firnak Grandhammer, High Seat of the Seven Hammers, *Ur'svok* of the Dark Granite *nyre*."

Amandine turned as Mister Green approached them from the alley. "*Soeje!* I didn't see you there!"

"I did not wish to be seen. You three should be inside already. Firnak was the last to arrive."

"Oh! Let's go, Tilly!" Gil said.

"A moment, Amandine, if you please," Mister Green said. He watched the others vanish inside before speaking again. "Fredderick Stolm will not be attending this morning."

Amandine felt a lump in her throat and nodded.

"You understand why, of course?"

"Yes, *soeje.*"

Mister Green lowered his voice. "This place is perilous for him. Even being so close as Greyrock Falls—where he's currently residing—is a risk. The Seekers may not be a threat, but if any of the *mord* within this building knew of his actual condition, his life would be forfeit. Whatever they may ask you to do or say this morning, please keep that in mind."

"I haven't told anyone, *soeje*," Amandine said carefully. "But, how long have you known?"

"I have suspected for a very long time. Since he first arrived in Stoneman, in fact. Demonic presence is not something you miss, once you have become accustomed to the feel of it."

Amandine considered that. How *had* Mister Green become 'accustomed' to recognizing demons? She wasn't sure she wanted an answer. His dark eyes seemed to swirl thoughtfully.

"You wish to ask something of me. What is it?" Mister Green folded his arms behind him.

"You won't hurt him?"

"Only if required to, for my own defense. No, child, I wish to help the boy. I always have. His path to magic is one especially fraught with danger. Practitioners who gain their power from pacts with demons often end up wholly subsumed by those creatures. That he has made it this long without guidance is both intriguing and unusual. I will not reveal him to anyone except Highrobe Hemm, although I suspect he already knows. Possibly another old acquaintance of mine as well. This knowledge is not truly safe with anyone. Even your godsworn matron, Mother Jarl, would be compelled to seek his death if she knew the truth."

"If everyone is so afraid of demons, then why would you help him at all?"

A thin, feral grin spread across Mister Green's features. "I do not follow pre-scribed paths or established doctrine. If he has caused no harm, then no harm will be caused to him. This is the way of true balance, whatever others may think."

"Thank you," Amandine said.

"You have not yet been to visit him. He asks about you."

Amandine looked down at her feet. She still didn't know what to do about Fredderick. His behavior after Dumpling had taken over his body had been un-settling. There were many things about his entire situation that were unsettling.

"He sought his power, you did not, but you both have abilities that will put others off their ease. He requires a friend, and still considers you one." Mister Green handed Amandine a small folded letter sealed with wax. "I will not counsel you on what you should do—this is a decision for you alone. But it is my learned opinion that you both may have something to gain by continued association."

The imprint on the seal was a circle within a square, a simplified version of House Stolm's sigil. Amandine took it from Mister Green and silently considered the seal as she rubbed a thumb over it.

"I will go inside and make excuses for you. Don't tarry over-long, student," Mister Green said. He turned and walked away.

With a sigh, Amandine broke the seal with her thumb and opened the letter:

> *"Amandine,*
>
> *I heard you had recovered from what happened in the Deeps. I understand if what occurred there, both to you and between us, has created a wall that you don't wish to climb. I am well. Dumpling is well. We are both, separately, well, and I hope that you might come and visit. I have included the location of the boarding house I am staying at below this missive. Regardless of your choice, I want you to know it brings me joy that my efforts were not wasted, that you still breathe, that you will continue to cook amazing food, that you will bring happiness to so many with who and what you are. If I have any regrets, the things I have done to help you are not among them. Please give my best to Tillandra and that rock-headed baker boy.*
>
> *Eternally yours,*
> *Fredderick Stolm"*

Amandine read the letter three times. Had Fredderick and Dumpling gone back to their original bodies? His words seemed to imply that. She considered visiting him. Maybe that wall wasn't as high as he thought. Dumpling might be a demon, but—she touched her neck where the darkbloom peeked above her collar. What was that compared to actually speaking to a *Goddess*? Perhaps Mister Green had a valid point.

She carefully folded the letter and placed it in her pocket. "I lose all sense," Amandine muttered, her neck growing hot. "Every last scrap." Her fingers wiped at her eyes as she took a breath to compose herself, and then entered the Stone Bowl.

Speaker

"The Seven Hammers are led differently than other Ur'Nyre. *The clans of the West have Primes, a sort of King if one ignores the gender implications in the title. The Magmaflow have a High Stone. This alpha-led organization is actually the traditional model, not only for* mord *government, but for dwarven homes and families as well. It's instinctual to them to follow the most capable individual. The Seven Hammers, by contrast, are made up of many smaller* nyre, *brought together after the War of Shadows for the common good and survival of all. Each clan within the collective has a traditional, alpha-leader, but those leaders confer in council with each other, and the human nations and fae Courts they treat with, in order to make decisions for the collective."*

- Dwarven Society and Governance, Insights into the Minds of the mord, *Chapter 2*

A LONG TABLE had been placed within the Stone Bowl's main dining hall. Half of it was set with ornate metal plates and *korb* bowls for the dwarven delegation. Firnak Grandhammer sat at the head, their silver hammer hanging from its loop off of the back of the chair they sat in. Another richly dressed *mord* was leaning in to speak quietly while Firnak nodded along. The other Hammers conferred in low voices. All of them were richly appointed and important looking, but one dwarf in particular stood out of the pack. They wore black-dyed boiled leather armor with the silver triangle pin indicating a military rank of Fist Leader. The hair on their head had been shaved so that only one thin strip remained. It was greased and stood straight up like a snapjaw's crest. Their beard, by comparison, was short and neat, save for two long braids down the sides.

Amandine approached. "Are you Orvil, sah?"

"Aye. Ye be Amandine, yes? Yer a skinny thing! I imagined an *Erestral* slayer ta be more muscles and shoulder!" The words were spoken with a playful glint in his strange orange eyes and Amandine felt his amusement.

"I'm her, sah. Your sire was a great help to my family and township, and I wanted to thank that *gyre* properly."

"Then ye've told that *gyre*. My bond on it, I'll pass your words!"

"Excellent, thank you."

"Aye. And if ye get the chance, tell my grand-sire, Boomer, that I am naming my mate's second bud after that *gyre*. Tell that grackle a visit to the clan is in order or I'll come and drag that arse back to the warren fer a proper hunt!"

Amandine laughed. "I would like to see that! I'll tell Master McKragen, my bond on it also."

"Grand," Orvil said with a toothy grin.

With a nod, Amandine took her seat between Orvil and Mel. The other half of the table was set with clay plates and fine ceramic bowls for the humans, Hill Folk, and fae present. Gil and Tilly sat next to Fiona and Mother Jarl. Mister Green was speaking to a scholarly-looking dwarf on the mord-half of the table. The human ambassador to the Seven Hammers, Milo Longshore, sat to the other side of Mister Green, and seemed absorbed in a document he was reading. Amandine hadn't ever spoken with him, but Serand had told her that he had been at the hospital several times to check in after she and Vibrant Dawn had emerged from the Deeps.

The Seeker crew sat in a row next to Amandine's plate. Mel was closest and smiled at her as she took her seat. Imri and Blueknot were next, and then Ragall, who sat next to an empty plate. Tobe's seat.

Amandine let her mind wander as the conversations ebbed and flowed around her. Grendel wove around her ankles and eventually settled between her feet. Mel leaned towards her. "You look well. Any idea what they will be serving?" she whispered.

"No. Chef Brutsche refused to tell me. But I imagine I will get a lesson on how it was made later on."

As if summoned, Chef appeared in the doorway to the kitchens and scanned the room. His hard blue eyes stopped at every seat. When they passed Amandine, he nodded to her.

"It's strange," Mel said as she hooked an arm over the back of her chair, "seeing Seeker Brutsche. He is different than I imagined he'd be. I always had a picture in my mind of someone more like Ragall, but he sort of reminds me of my mum."

"Your mother? How?"

"Hard. Watchful. Careful with words, but quick to act. He moves like a cat. He teachin' you anything other than cooking?"

"Like what?"

"I don't know. Seeker stuff. Trail craft, fighting, that sort of thing."

"No, sah, he doesn't. The woman he lives with, my adoptive mother. She's an Under Sergeant in the Stoneman Militia. I have gotten some instruction from her, but... I don't really like fighting."

Mel shrugged. "Probably for the best. It's a dirty business." Her tone took on a soft, cold edge.

Amandine noted how her eyes drifted to Tobe's empty seat. She began to say something, but then Chef Polina entered the room with a rolling cart covered in bowls of food.

"First Course!" Chef Brutsche announced in a carrying voice. "Ceremonial *palik'sag*. The Flavor of Darkness and Life!"

He said a few more words in *Mord-seq*, and the assembled dwarves growled, then pounded the table in approval. Chef Polina bowed and also said a few words in the dwarven tongue, followed by more pounding. She was Olgath and of an age with Chef, with dark brown skin and light brown hair partly hidden under a colorful headwrap. Her eyes were a sharp orange-yellow color that stood out against her serious features. With precise motions, she swept up a bowl of what looked like raw cubes of meat and began carefully placing one in the very center of each bowl, starting with Firnak. The cubes were red and glistening uncooked flesh, coated lightly in oil.

As Chef Polina passed Amandine and deposited her cube, she whispered. "Sunlit folk have beef, not horker. No one will be sick for participating in the rite."

Amandine nodded and examined the morsel on her plate. It was rich and marbled, from a fine cut—perhaps the loin. The faint scent of rindcuff drifting from it was only detectable because Grendel was touching her. It was probably used to preserve the meat's color, rather than add flavor.

"I must decline," Imri said as Polina passed her.

The Olgath Chef merely nodded and placed a leaf-wrapped parcel on her plate instead. "No one will be left out. I have accounted for varied palates."

Imri nodded gratefully and smiled at Polina. The ambassador also declined the meat and took a leaf-wrapped bite instead. Amandine noted that Mister Green accepted the meat, however. He raised an amused eyebrow at the other fae, but Amandine got the impression that Imri was explicitly ignoring her teacher.

Once everyone was served, Firnak Grandhammer began to speak. His speech was entirely in *Mord-seq* and Amandine maybe understood one word in ten.

"What are they saying?" she whispered to Mel.

"I am not sure," she replied.

"It's a passage from an old *mord* epic," Orvil cut in softly. "Lots o' fancy words, but the part that matters is 'and so the hunters took their prey and tasted darkness, tasted life.' That *gyre* is talkin' bout this nibble here. It's raw, see, it has the flavor of the life that was taken for it, gathered from the darkness it grew in."

Amandine nodded. She saw the ambassador also whispering to her friends and Mother Jarl, probably for the same explanation.

Firnak finished his recitation and the dwarves responded with more table slapping. Then, without further ceremony, they all picked up their bites and ate them.

Cautiously, Amandine took hers and watched the others. She had never eaten raw meat before. She wasn't sure what it would be like. Mister Green, for his part, seemed to be savoring the morsel. Fiona took a cautious bite and, after a surprised expression, finished it.

That settled it for Amandine. She popped the bite into her mouth and chewed. It was extremely tender. More so than any cooked beef she had eaten. The faint hint of rindcuff oil did not cover the flavor of the meat, but it wasn't terrible either. It was rather delicious, in fact. There was a slightly gamey taste, with something else she couldn't quite put her finger on. It was fresh, and savory. She wondered if this was the flavor of darkness and life that Orvil had been talking about.

"Vault raised cattle," Mel said thoughtfully. "Better than horker for certain." Ragall chuckled and grunted his agreement.

Multiple courses were served after that: spicy *sek* with mushrooms, soup with fish, smelly cheeses made from prong milk, and more. The dwarves took turns standing to speak, some in Olgothian and others in *Mord-seq*. They gave eulogy to those who had fallen fighting the *Erestral*, or spoke of brave deeds performed by the Stone Guard and others who had tried to explore the Deeps in search of those that had been enslaved by Sabo.

Amandine had not been fully aware of the scope of Anvilroot's distress until now. The numbers of people who had died or gone missing was staggering. The people rescued from the crystal chamber had only represented a tiny portion of those Sabo had enslaved. She shuddered to think of what would have happened if he had been allowed to take her form and travel to the sunlit world.

"Seeker Hartlock. Would you please tell us your tale now?" Firnak said.

Amandine turned in her seat to watch as Mel nodded, then stood. She started with her crew's arrival in Myron's Bend, and went on to tell the story of Amandine's foolish bet with Carver and then her crew's foray into the Millbreak woods to confront the pirates.

Next she spoke about the lurks near Kiln. "Most of them were gathered around an old standing stone outside of the village." Her hands moved to illustrate the shape of the ancient plinth. "They seemed drawn to it. In hindsight, I believe we might know why. This young lady right here."

The godmark on her neck tingled and Amandine tried not to melt into her seat as the various dwarves, Seekers, and her friends all turned to stare.

"She was later revealed to be a Speaker for Ravenex, just as our crew's leader, Tobenick, was a Speaker for Berindor."

This caused some muttering from the *mord* at the table, but Mel continued on as if they didn't exist. She told them of the scene in the Obsidian Seat, but did not mention how Blueknot had freed Amandine and Fredderick from prison.

"Godsworn Speakers have the power of their gods to command, sahs," Mel said with a shrug when the question of their release was raised. "Dig a deeper hole next time?"

The muttering increased, but Mel continued with her story, unperturbed. "You have Herric's account to confirm most of this, but now I will tell you what happened after we were separated from the Speaker and the young mage. We thought at first, weakened as we were, to return to Anvilroot with a warning, and to seek reinforcements. But Tobe insisted we press on after them, despite how wide the stones had been arrayed before us. We found the mage alone with his dog. It was his familiar, perhaps. They were in the tunnels almost another day's walk deeper into the caverns from the poison lake. Amandine had left him, it seems, after some disagreement, to continue on with Ko, the Erestral who surrendered to us.

"We followed their trail further. It was slow and treacherous, and before long we came to an abandoned farm. There were several exits, and we had no idea which way to go from there. Ragall found Amandine's backpack near a thin vent in the cavern wall. Torches revealed a button on the floor within it. None of us could follow that way, and so we were at a loss, but the magus came through in the end. He bade his familiar to sniff out the 'darkling thing' that had so distressed the *Erestral*. The little runt didn't look like much, but led us true through the caverns and fungal forests, along a wider route that brought us to the hollow full of crystals described in my report."

Mel paused for a moment and took a sip from a mug of tea before continuing. One of the well-dressed dwarves in attendance spoke up in Olgothian: "And you saw the changeling? The demon that your report named 'Sabo'?"

"Not at first. There were a pair of nightwurms blocking our access to the chamber, as well as many dark fae, enthralled *mord*, and others under the sway of the demon."

"The demon was controlling nightwurms?"

Mel nodded. Amandine saw Mister Green raise an eyebrow, and the muttering from the dwarven end of the table increased again.

"How did you overcome them?" the ambassador asked.

"Again, the magus. He produced a thunderclap that stunned the beasts. Ragall and I used the opportunity to overpower one, and then the other, although we both took wounds. The young wizard continued to employ magic to fling shards of crystal, toss possessed persons into one another, and generally cause havoc while we cleared a path. Tobenick called upon Berindor," Mel paused and took a deep breath, visibly overcome, "for the final time. He cleared a path to the demon, but we did not recognize it for what it was fast enough. It slew him, and Amandine managed to break its hold long enough to warn us."

Amandine reached up and grasped Mel's wrist. Mel's hand was shaking, even though her voice remained steady. "Something happened then, something I can't explain. Amandine and the demon drew close, and it spoke in Elvish. It... whimpered, and then both of them collapsed in a heap. All at once, the room full of people also collapsed. Like puppets with cut strings. I wasted no time, and took the demon's head. I salted the eyes. I believe now that it had already perished. Godsworn Speakers can not be taken by demons. It made a mistake, but I was allowing no chances then."

Mother Jarl nodded in approval and then spoke. "Did the Goddess speak again?"

"No, sah. We thought Amandine had died as well. But she was still breathing. The captive *Erestral* and other fae began to recover. Ko wept over the corpse of his child, who the demon had stolen the body of. When mourning was finished, and the dead were tended to, and those who had regained their minds had been accounted for, we quit that colorless place. The rest you know, from the many accounts of the survivors."

Mel sat back down. She gave Amandine's hand a squeeze under the table but did not look at her.

"Speaker Amandine." Firnak Grandhammer rose from their seat. "What say you?"

Amandine swallowed and stood. Being addressed by that title, even if it were true, twisted her stomach into a knot worse than being called a Cook had. "I believe it to be true, sah. Ravenex has spoken to me. I did encounter a demon. As for the rest... I thought I was dead too. I'm glad that I'm not, but..."

The ancient dwarf nodded slowly. "Aye, so it shall be carved in runes, then. Bring in the, ah, *guest*, Fist Leader."

Orvil slid their chair back and ambled into a side room off the dining hall. A moment later they returned, and with them was...

"Ko?" Amandine's eyes widened.

The eerie fae was dressed in a ceremonial robe that better covered his translucent skin. He gave Amandine a wry smile and bobbed his head in acknowledgement. Chef Butsche and Chef Polina emerged from the kitchens as well and stood watching by the hearth.

"What in the colorless pit is that... *thing* doing here?" Blueknot shrieked as she shot to her feet.

"I came to offer terms for peace," Ko said, spreading his arms wide. "I was told my intent would be judged. What was the verdict, *rek'nilahsal*?"

"You all can't be serious!" Blueknot continued. She looked at Mel and then to the Hammers. The *mord* looked unhappy, but none of them spoke. "Gods, has this entire colorless world gone mad? He *ambushed* us, Mel!"

"His mind-slaved kin did, yes," Mel agreed. "I understand it was hard, Blue–"

"Hard? *Hard*?" She slammed her fist on the table, causing plates on the other side to jump. "It's wasn't hard, it was the hells made real, Melanie! Tell her, Imri!"

Imri looked at Blueknot and then looked down, and then away. "It was all of that. But one of the Traitor Court has offered peace. For the first time in over a thousand years of no contact with my kin. I will hear what he has to say."

Blueknot just stared, aghast, at her crew. "I can't believe this. Mel? You too?"

Mel shook her head. "I don't trust him, not really. But look around, Blue. There's something wrong with the world. Strange shite is afoot and there's nothing to gain by fighting if there can be a peace, even a small one, instead."

"To the pit with that! Here's your peace, Melanie Hartlock!" Blueknot made a rude hand gesture. "Consider this my forfeiture. I won't crew with anyone who gets in bed with a creature like that!"

"Watch your tone!" Ragall jumped to his feet. Imri placed a hand on his arm and he slowly sat back down.

Amandine *felt* everyone. The anger, the frustration, the hurt. It was nearly overwhelming. "Please! This is so pointless! Stop fighting!"

Blueknot looked past Mel to her. "Nothing good ever came of Ravenex or any of her followers," she snarled. "We should have left you in that hole!"

"That's *enough*, Blueknot!" Mel rounded on her. "This girl saved the lives of this entire colorless city! Spew your bile elsewhere!"

"Gladly," Blueknot hissed. She whirled about and stormed out of the dining hall. Amandine flinched when the front doors slammed.

An uneasy silence descended over the room. It was Ko who finally broke it. "She will not be alone in her opinions. But what I bring to you is true. The *Erestral* will sue for peace. Hunting of *mord* will end. We will share maps of the MacDarren highway so that old claims may be restored to the clans that once owned them. In return, we will be allowed access to the sunlit world through Anvilroot and have an established embassy here by which we may treat with other nations and courts. The time of our seclusion has ended."

"Centuries of bad blood will not simply rinse, even for a chance to reclaim lost mines and homes." Firnak shot a skeptical glance at the dark fae. "But we will talk. Do you speak for all of your Court?"

"I do."

"Why now?" Mister Green asked, interjecting. "As my cousin says, it has been over one thousand years. One thousand, three hundred and thirty-seven, to be precise, since the Unnamed Court vanished into the Deeps."

Amandine's godmark twinged again. She flinched slightly as a stinging pain pinched at her neck. Ko turned to look at her.

"Because the Goddess of Shadows said it was time." His eyes locked onto Amandine's. "A new Speaker has been chosen. We bow to Her will."

Be the guidepost.

The voice was faint, barely a whisper. Amandine wanted to ignore it, but it felt like that would be ignoring herself. "I will help in any way I can," she said.

"As will the Church," Mother Jarl chimed in. "Milintanth's interests lie in peaceful accord. We would mediate, if the Hammers will allow." She eyed Amandine sideways and gave her a barely imperceptible shake of her head.

"We shall adjourn for now, then," Firnak said with a dismissive wave. "Fist Leader, show *ambassador* Ko to quarters suitable to that station. Bright Light Jarl, Ambassador Longshore, Seekers, please retire with the council to convene further."

Amandine felt frustrated. Ko had looked at *her*. Ravenex wanted her to do... *something*, but what? It was obvious that she would not be included in whatever was going to occur between the *mord* and the dark fae.

As most of the room filed out into an adjoining parlor, Chef Brutsche approached and laid a hand on Amandine's shoulder. His eyes followed hers to where Firnak and the others exited.

"So they kicked ye off the grown-up's table, eh?" he said softly. "Don't fret it. If that old bird, Ravenex, has something more ta say to ye, they won't be able ta stop her. In the meantime, why don't you come join Chef Polina and I in the kitchens? We made some sweet things that need proper approval."

Spice poked his head out of the kitchen doorway and meowed. Grendel dashed off after him. Amandine took a deep breath and let the frustration melt away. Chef was right. What did she know about treaties anyway? All Amandine wanted was to cook delicious food and make people happy.

"I may need my council to confer on the matter," she said as she glanced up at Chef.

"Who–"

"Tilly! Gil! Fiona! Chefs Brutsche and Polina need expert opinions on desserts! Let's convene!"

"Alright! Now we're talkin'!" Gil exclaimed as he and Tilly made for the door. Fiona squealed joyfully and ran ahead of them with her arms outstretched like a bird.

Mister Green also made his way in that direction. "You owe me a treat as well, Brutsche," he said in passing.

Amandine trailed behind the elf and smiled as Chef's raucous laughter followed her to the kitchens.

Acknowledgements

I'd like to thank all of the people who have continued to support making the Seeker's Kitchen what it is. My talented editors, RoAnna Sylver and Rebecca Scharpf; their efforts have made this a stronger story from start to finish. Readers L. Drane, C. Castille, M. Ellsworth, and my lovely wife, Alex, who helped alpha and beta read and provided encouragement and suggestions. To my amazing artists Natalie Bernard (cover), and Gianne Rabena (character art), for bringing these characters and their world to life visually. Fellow author A. Parise, who has an eagle eye for formatting errors and who is familiar with and commiserates in the independent author's journey. Finally, a big thank you to all of the amazing authors and editors at Midnight Tide Publishing. The camaraderie and support of fellow authors means so much in this industry. You are all incredible.

You can find more of Natalie's amazing paintings here:
  https://www.nataliebernard.com/

Gianna Rabena's art can be purchased via ko-fi when commissions are open:
  https://ko-fi.com/ggravenworks

About the author

Jason grew up (mostly) in central California, surrounded by rolling hills, wheat fields, and grapevines. He has been creating worlds for himself and his friends for decades, and is a gigantic nerd for everything sci-fi and fantasy related. Role-playing games, board games, video games and cooking are just a few of his many hobbies. He currently lives near Portland, OR, in a muli-generational home with his wife, two kids, two in-laws, and a neurotic bernadoodle.